IN LOVE
AND WAR

Lily Baxter lives in Dorset. She is the author of *Poppy's War*, *We'll Meet Again*, *Spitfire Girl*, *The Girls in Blue* and *The Shopkeeper's Daughter*. She also writes under the name of Dilly Court.

D0832351

Lily Baxter
IN LOVE AND WAR

arrow books

Published by Arrow Books 2014

2 4 6 8 10 9 7 5 3 1

First published in Great Britain in 2014 by
Century
Random House, 20 Vauxhall Bridge Road,
London SW1V 2SA

www.randomhouse.co.uk

Addresses for companies within The Random House Group Limited can be found at:
www.randomhouse.co.uk/offices.htm

The Random House Group Limited Reg. No. 954009

A CIP catalogue record for this book
is available from the British Library

Penguin Random House is committed to a sustainable future for
our business, our readers and our planet. This book is made from
Forest Stewardship Council® certified paper.

Printed and bound in Great Britain by Clays Ltd, Elcograf S.p.A.

Typeset in Palatino by Palimpsest Book Production Limited,
Falkirk, Stirlingshire

For Ann and Bill Spivey

Chapter One

Sutton Darcy, Dorset, August 1914

The sound of marching feet had brought the whole village out onto the main street to see the newly formed Pals battalion go off to war. Elsie Mead had been on her way home to Tan Cottage, having just left Colonel Mason's house on the edge of the village where she had been dressing Mrs Mason's hair. Cora Mason was many years younger than her husband and considered herself to be a leader of fashion, even though she had to make do with the minimum of servants to manage her household. Without the benefit of a personal maid she often called upon Elsie to put her hair up in the elaborate Pompadour style, made famous by the Gibson Girls at the end of Queen Victoria's reign, and Elsie had not the heart to tell Cora that this was no longer the height of fashion. Today of all days Cora said she wanted to stand at the colonel's side and make him proud, and Elsie had done her best to execute the complicated coiffure while listening politely to Cora's incessant chatter. She had answered in monosyllables and nods of her head where appropriate, but her thoughts were with the young men who were leaving home to fight for their country. She had known all of them since they attended the village school together, and now they were going off to face the horrors of war.

She stopped to wave to the Dodd brothers, Luke, Frank and Jim, whose father was a fisherman and would now have to find another crew. Mickey Fowler winked at her and tipped his cap and his brother Joe blew her a kiss. She could not help thinking that the game birds on the Winter family's estate would be safer in the absence of the Fowler boys. They were a wild pair, but they were not bad at heart. She had danced with both of them at the last harvest supper, but this year the celebrations would be shadowed by worry and even loss. It did not bear thinking about. It was a ragtag band that set off on the great adventure and their young faces glowed with excitement. She made an effort to send them away with a cheerful smile, but she had a feeling of foreboding as she made her way home, stopping first at the doctor's surgery to collect a bottle of laudanum for her sick mother.

It was a hot day and the sun beat down on her bare head as she walked along the lane between hedgerows heavy with dusty green foliage and busy with the wildlife that lived and foraged in the knotted roots and branches. Hedge sparrows popped up like tiny automatons and disappeared just as quickly. Field mice rustled the leaves and hedgehogs curled up amongst the dead leaves and slept until dusk when they came out to look for food. It was all so familiar, and yet the cloudless sky and summer sun were overshadowed by world events that had reached out to touch a sleepy English village.

Elsie stopped and looked round as someone called her name.

'Elsie, wait.' Phyllis Piper, one of the housemaids who worked at Darcy Hall, came running towards her. 'Wait a minute,' she said breathlessly. 'I've been sent to see if your ma is well enough to return to work. We're short-handed because two of the housemaids have left to find jobs in the town, and some of the other girls are threatening to do the same. There are plenty of jobs vacant with so many men enlisting, and they're taking on women.'

'Ma is confined to bed, Phyllis. I don't know when she'll be well enough to work again.'

'Mrs Tranter will skin me alive if I go back without someone to give us a hand. Miss Marianne is arriving today and there's a big dinner party planned for tomorrow. We're going to need all the help we can get.'

Elsie eyed her thoughtfully. 'I suppose I could help out for a couple of days. I've applied for several jobs as a lady's maid but most of them want someone to live in, and I can't leave Ma while she's so ill.'

Phyllis took off her straw hat and fanned herself vigorously. 'You was unlucky that old Mrs Tonbridge popped off so sudden. I've heard that Rose Hill is up for sale.'

'I'd been with the old lady since I left school. I did everything for her and she was good to me. Positions like that don't come up very often.'

'It won't be the sort of work you're used to, Elsie, but if you don't mind doing the cleaning it will be a big help.' Phyllis moved a little closer, glancing over her shoulder as if expecting to find eavesdroppers lurking behind the hedge. 'They say in the kitchen that Miss Marianne's aunt wants to see her married off as soon as possible and out of the way.'

Elsie was in a hurry to get home but she could not resist a bit of gossip that might cheer her mother up. 'Surely it's up to Miss Marianne's parents to look to her future.'

'Ah, yes, but they're still in India and will be for some time. Miss Marianne's twenty-first birthday is tomorrow.'

'And they're planning a party for her. That's as it should be, Phyllis.'

'It's more than that, Elsie. Miss Marianne will come into her majority tomorrow, and she won't need her aunt and uncle to look after her. Not that she ever paid much attention to anything they said, but now she's coming home from that posh finishing school in Switzerland we're expecting fireworks.' Phyllis grabbed Elsie's arm, her eyes brimming with excitement. 'We think she might tell Mr and Mrs Winter to pack up and leave. They won't like that because they've got used to treating Darcy Hall as if it was theirs, and we all know that they're as poor as church mice.'

Elsie threw back her head and laughed. 'You're a terrible gossip, Phyllis.'

Offended, Phyllis shrugged her shoulders. 'It's God's honest truth. But what shall I tell Mrs Tranter?'

'I should be looking for war work, but I suppose another few days at home won't hurt, and I don't really want to go away while Ma's sick.'

'Does that mean you'll help out? I'm desperate, Elsie, or I wouldn't ask.'

'I need the money, so I'll do it.'

Phyllis slapped her on the back. 'Thank God for that. I'll go back and give Mrs Tranter the good news. Can you come this afternoon?'

'I'll try.'

'That's the spirit.' Phyllis rammed her hat on her head and hurried off in the direction of Darcy Hall, leaving Elsie to go on her way.

The small bedroom in Tan Cottage was shrouded in darkness and stuffy with the sickly sweet smell of chronic illness. Flies trapped behind closed curtains buzzed and battered the windowpanes in their attempts to escape into the sunlight, and the bedsprings creaked with the invalid's smallest movement.

Monique Mead lay propped up on pillows, her face as white as the cotton sheet that was drawn up to her neck. Dark smudges underlined her eyes and her thin hand plucked at the counterpane as she controlled her breathing with difficulty, but she managed a smile for her daughter. 'Did it go well?'

'Mrs Mason was satisfied with the result, Ma. More important, how are you?' Elsie perched on the edge of the bed. 'Are you hungry?'

Monique shook her head. 'Not really, but I am thirsty.' She began to cough and reached for a hanky. Elsie's heart sank when she saw the telltale flecks of blood. 'I'll get you some fresh water and you must take your medicine. I asked Dr Hancock to call.'

Monique shook her head, lapsing into her native French as she did when overcome with emotion. 'Non, chérie. Non.' She drew a faltering breath. 'We can't afford it.'

Elsie laid her hand on her mother's brow, and felt the heat of fever. 'Yes, we can. I've got some work at Darcy Hall, and Mrs Mason gave me a tip. She likes to be generous with her husband's money.' She stood up. 'Don't worry, Ma. Everything will be all right, you'll see.' She spoke with more conviction than she was feeling. Her mother's condition had deteriorated and Dr Hancock was not optimistic. 'Your mother ought to be admitted to a sanatorium,' he had said on his last visit. But of course that was out of the question. There was no money for private treatment and the public wards were overcrowded. Monique had a morbid fear of hospitals and with good reason, having watched her husband's slow and painful death. Elsie's father had served under Colonel James Winter in the Boer War, and had been invalided home but had succumbed to his wounds in a military hospital. Memories of sitting at his bedside were still fresh in Elsie's mind even though she had only been eight years old when he died, and her mother murmured his name during recurrent bouts of fever. Elsie was painfully aware that the disease of the lungs was slowly consuming her mother's frail body, but she tried to push such thoughts to the back of her mind as she hurried outside to the communal pump and drew a bucket of water.

Elsie was in the scullery at Darcy Hall washing the dishes after luncheon had been served above stairs when bells started jangling and a buzz of excitement was followed by the sound of pattering feet. Phyllis poked her head round the door. 'Come on. We've got to go outside and welcome Miss Marianne home.'

Elsie dried her hands on a tea towel and followed the rest of the servants outside into the stable yard. They scurried across the cobbles, chattering excitedly as they made their way to the front of the Jacobean manor house where they stood in line waiting for the motor car to come to a halt.

'New-fangled contraption,' Cook muttered under her breath. 'Give me a carriage and pair any day.'

Mrs Tranter, the housekeeper, shot her a withering look. 'Shh.'

Cook's lips tightened into a thin pencil line but she knew better than to argue.

Elsie was almost exactly the same age as Miss

Marianne Winter, and she was mildly curious to see how she had turned out after her two years in the posh finishing school. She had seen her in the distance on the rare occasions when she had been permitted to accompany her mother to work, but she had not been allowed to stray into parts of the house or garden frequented by the family. Marianne Winter had spoken to her once when Elsie had been helping to groom one of the horses, and then it had only been to challenge her right to be there in the first place. Elsie had told her to mind her own business and had received a stern lecture on manners from the head groom, but Marianne had merely laughed and led her pony to the mounting block.

Elsie craned her neck to look at the fashionably dressed young woman who alighted from the chauffeur-driven motor car. As a child she had heard the servants mutter about a passing resemblance between them, but now, despite the difference in their clothes and the way they wore their blonde hair, looking at Marianne Winter was like seeing a mirror image of herself. She was aware of sideways glances from the kitchen maids as they bobbed curtseys. Elsie remained stiffly upright. Such a show of subservience seemed very feudal and outdated, and she was not dependent on the Winter family for her living. If anything her brief experience of labouring in the kitchen made her even more determined to find herself a well-paid job so that her mother need never return to menial work.

Marianne smiled graciously and had a few words with Mrs Tranter and Cook, briefly acknowledging the underlings before entering the house to be greeted by her aunt and uncle. Soames, the butler, closed the double doors and Mrs Tranter ordered everyone to return to their work.

Phyllis fell into step beside Elsie. 'Did you see the outfit she was wearing? I daresay it was straight from Paris. It must have cost a fortune.'

'I expect it did.'

'Aren't you envious, Elsie? I know I am.'

'Not really. I don't think she's happy.'

Phyllis stared at her open-mouthed. 'How can you say that? How could she be miserable when she's got looks and money?'

'I don't know. It's just a feeling.'

'You and your feelings,' Phyllis said, giggling. 'I remember when we was in Miss Murray's class at school, you was always making excuses for the old bat, when the rest of us hated her.'

'She had a miserable home life. Her father was a drunkard and a bully. He went to prison for beating a man half to death.'

'Stop dawdling, you two.' Mrs Tranter's voice echoed round the stable yard. 'There's work to be done.'

Later that afternoon, Elsie arrived home to find Dr Hancock just about to leave Tan Cottage. He greeted her with a serious look on his lined face. 'Monique tells me that you've been doing her job at Darcy Hall.'

'I'm just filling in, doctor. I hope to find war work so that I can make life easier for my mother.'

He shook his head. 'She is a very sick woman, my dear. You will need to be very strong for her, but you must prepare yourself for the inevitable.'

'I know.' Despite her determination not to cry, Elsie's eyes welled with tears and she swallowed hard. 'I've seen her slipping away from me, day by day.'

He laid his hand on her arm. 'Have you anyone you can call on to be with you?'

Elsie shook her head. 'No, sir. Ma's family disowned her when she married an Englishman. I've never met them.'

'What about your father's family?'

'He was brought up in an orphanage and enlisted when he was just a boy. There is no one.'

'Call me day or night if her condition worsens.' He gave her a tired smile and went to untether his horse. He climbed onto the trap and at a flick of the reins the animal ambled off down the lane.

Elsie hurried into the house and went upstairs to tell her mother about Miss Marianne's return home, and to pass on messages from the kitchen maids wishing her a speedy recovery. A smile hovered on Monique's lips as she drifted off into a laudanum-induced sleep, and Elsie went downstairs to eat her supper of bread and cheese. Miss Marianne would be dining on trout caught in the river that ran through the estate, followed by grouse which only the day before had been roaming in the heather. Sent by train from Scotland, the birds would be roasted and served with a red wine sauce. Cook had been preparing the crowning glory of the welcome home meal that afternoon, and the sight and scent of the strawberry parfait had made Elsie's mouth water.

She finished her meal and made herself a cup of tea, which she took into the small garden at the back of the cottage. She had not had much time to weed the vegetable patch, coming home late every evening from Rose Hill. Convolvulus had all but strangled the white roses that her mother loved so dearly, and nettles grew where once she had tended potatoes, carrots, parsnips and onions. In winter there had been cabbages to pick and the root vegetables they had managed to store, but this year there was nothing other than weeds and wild poppies.

The sun was plummeting in a fireball and the sky was streaked with scarlet and orange. Purple shadows lengthened and a cool breeze ruffled Elsie's hair, but the smell of the kitchens still lingered on her clothes and her hands were red and sore from the use of washing soda and strong soap. The feeling of fatigue was overwhelming, and when Elsie finished her tea she went indoors to get ready for bed. She had shared her mother's room until her illness but now she slept on a flock-filled mattress in the corner of the kitchen. She checked on Monique before lying down to sleep, but even at rest she slept lightly, waking at the slightest sound, ready to answer the faintest call from the sick room.

When she arrived at work next morning she expected to find the usual bustle of activity as the family breakfasts were prepared. In winter the housemaids would be rushing around clearing grates and lighting fires before the family had awakened. The parlour maids would be poised ready to take the silver dishes filled with fried eggs and crisp bacon, devilled kidneys and buttered eggs to the dining room, ready for Mr Winter and Miss Marianne to select whatever took their fancy. Mrs Winter always had her breakfast brought to her room, and never rose from her bed before mid-morning. Elsie had learned all this from her mother and she found it hard to imagine living in such idleness and luxury.

She sniffed appreciatively at the delicious aromas that tantalised her taste buds as she walked through the scullery. In the kitchen Mrs Tranter and Cook had their heads bent over a sheet of paper, and they were clearly unhappy.

'How does she expect us to sort this out at such short notice?' Cook complained.

'You're the expert, Mrs Coker. Surely you learned the French names for all these dishes when you were training as a cook.'

'No,' Mrs Coker said flatly. 'It never came up. We're in England and we don't do fancy French stuff.'

'But Mrs Winter wants to impress the guests.'

'I started working in the kitchen at Belvedere Castle when I was ten, and they didn't have menus written in French, English or any other language. It would have been considered very vulgar and not done.'

'Well, Mrs Winter wants it like this and who are we to argue?'

Mrs Coker lowered her voice. 'She's not top drawer. Her father was in trade, we all know that, and it shows.'

'Shh.' Mrs Tranter glanced round anxiously, but the kitchen maids within earshot were either too busy to listen or feigning deafness. 'Not so loud.' Her gaze fell on Elsie and she beckoned to her. 'I want a word with you.'

Elsie hurried over to them. 'I'm sorry if I was a bit late, but I had to make Ma comfortable.'

'This would have been something that came easily to your mother, Elsie. Did Monique teach you to speak French?'

'Yes, Mrs Tranter. I spoke French before I learned English.'

'But you were born in Sutton Darcy, weren't you?' Mrs Coker fixed her with a penetrating stare.

'Yes, Mrs Coker.'

'Never mind that,' Mrs Tranter said impatiently. She thrust the menu into Elsie's hand. 'Can you translate this into French and write out twelve copies in a neat hand? Mrs Winter wants one put at each place setting this evening.'

'Yes, I can.'

'You may go to my office and Phyllis will take your place for as long as it takes you to complete the task.'

Phyllis muttered something beneath her breath as she headed for the scullery.

'If you've anything to say then speak up, Phyllis Piper.'

'It was nothing, Mrs Tranter,' Phyllis called from the depths of the scullery.

'There's a lot to do today,' Mrs Tranter said firmly. 'We must do our best to make Miss Marianne's twenty-first birthday dinner a truly memorable event. All the guests are important but there is a family from Paris amongst them.' She turned to Elsie with a thoughtful look. 'Are you fluent in French?'

'A little out of practice, but yes, I think so.'

Mrs Tranter's stern expression melted into a beaming smile. 'A French-speaking maidservant would be certain to impress the guests. Come with me, Elsie. I'll see if we have a black dress that will fit you. There are plenty of caps and aprons in the linen cupboard. You can go to my office when we're done.' She marched off, leaving Elsie little option but to follow her.

'I have a black dress at home, Mrs Tranter. Until recently I worked for Mrs Tonbridge at Rose Hill.'

'You are a trained lady's maid?' Mrs Tranter said, glancing over her shoulder.

'I am.'

'Well don't get ideas above your station. This is only a temporary position. Tomorrow you will go back to washing dishes and scouring pans, and then only until your mother is sufficiently recovered to return to work.'

Elsie spent all morning in the housekeeper's office translating the menu into French and copying it out twelve times in her best copperplate. Mrs Tranter inspected each one, even though she had admitted she did not understand a word of French. 'Excellent,' she said with a smug smile. 'I'll show these to Mrs Winter. By the way, she wants you to take Nancy's place when the guests arrive this evening. Mr Soames will tell you what to do.'

'I'll do my best, Mrs Tranter.'

'In the normal course of events you wouldn't speak to the guests, but Mrs Winter wants you to pay particular attention to the rich French banker and his wife. Mr and Mrs Bellaire are coming with their unmarried son, Henri. Do you understand what I'm saying, Elsie?'

'Yes, Mrs Tranter.'

'And you are to assist Mr Soames in the dining room. Nancy will be there too and you will do as she does. Now, you may go home and get your dress.' She glanced down at Elsie's scuffed shoes. 'I hope you have a better pair than that.'

*

Monique was thrilled to learn that Elsie had been promoted, even if it was a temporary measure. 'They have seen that you are special, chérie,' she said breathlessly. 'You've been chosen to impress the guests.'

Elsie plumped up the pillows. 'It's only because I speak French. Who are these people that Mrs Winter wants to impress?'

'Madame Bellaire and Miss Marianne's mother met at finishing school in Paris. When the colonel was posted to Delhi, Miss Marianne was sent to boarding school in Buckinghamshire, and she spent every summer with the Bellaires in the south of France.'

Elsie nodded her head. 'I remember now, although I wasn't very interested at the time. What went on at Darcy Hall was like something I read about in books.'

'Mr Bellaire owns a bank in Paris and he's very rich. His son would be quite a catch and all the servants know that Mrs Winter is keen to see her niece married and out of the way. Miss Marianne is and always has been a bit of a handful, as you know. She turned the whole house upside down when she was younger.' Monique covered her mouth with her hanky as a bout of coughing overcame her.

'You mustn't overtire yourself, Ma,' Elsie said anxiously. 'I'll get home as soon as I can and tell you all about it.'

Monique lay back against the pillows, pale and

exhausted, but her eyes were shining. 'Perhaps Mrs Winter will offer you a permanent position.'

'Maybe, Ma. We'll see.' Elsie measured out the prescribed dose of laudanum and dropped it into a glass of water. 'I wish I didn't have to work tonight. You will be all right, won't you?'

'Of course I will. You must remember every little detail to tell me.'

Elsie waited while her mother drank the medicine. She refilled the glass with water and set it on the small table at her bedside. 'I'll get my dress and shoes and then I'm off. Wish me luck, Ma. I've never waited on table for a posh party.'

'You'll be fine. You're a clever girl; you can do anything if you put your mind to it.'

Wearing her black dress with a starched white head-band and freshly ironed apron, Elsie waited nervously in the oak-panelled entrance hall, standing just behind Soames as he opened the doors to admit the guests. Mr and Mrs Winter waited in the drawing room to greet them but Marianne had not yet put in an appearance. It was a warm evening and one by one the chauffeur-driven limousines pulled up outside the manor house, depositing the affluent owners in style. There were no coats to take but the gentlemen sported white silk scarves, gloves and top hats, which they handed to Elsie without so much as a second glance. The ladies glittered in their beaded silk-chiffon gowns with diamond earrings and necklaces adding an extra fiery sparkle. Soames wafted them to the drawing room and Elsie was left alone, but at that moment the last guests arrived and Monsieur and Madame Bellaire were admitted by Fred, who was a gardener by day but had been compelled to put on an ill-fitting footman's livery for the occasion and was sweating profusely.

Monsieur Bellaire handed his hat, gloves and silver-headed cane to Elsie. His elegant wife eyed her curiously, but before she could speak a young man strode into the hall, coming to a sudden halt when he saw Elsie. 'Marianne?' he said, laughing. 'Is this one of your pranks?' His dark eyes flashed with amusement.

Elsie bobbed a curtsey. 'I'm afraid you are mistaken, sir,' she murmured in French. 'I am Elsie.'

'No!' He twirled her round. 'You are joking, of course.' His English was perfect but with a slight accent that made him even more attractive. 'You are a little devil, Marianne Winter.'

Chapter Two

Elsie felt herself blushing furiously. 'I am sorry, sir. But I am not who you think I am.'

'I should say not.' Marianne's voice rang out behind them. 'What is going on? Have I stepped into a French farce?'

Henri stared from one to the other. 'Marianne?'

'How could you mistake a maidservant for me, Henri?' She smiled, but Elsie was not fooled for a moment. It was obvious to her that Miss Marianne was both hurt and angry.

'I beg your pardon, ladies,' Henri murmured in French.

'She speaks English,' Marianne said sharply. Her lips curved into a smile but her eyes flashed. 'She's a girl from the village.'

Elsie bobbed a curtsey. 'I'm sorry, Miss Marianne.'

Marianne opened her mouth to speak but Henri forestalled her. 'The mistake was mine, mademoiselle.' He took Elsie's hand and raised it to his lips.

For a fleeting second he held her gaze with a sympathetic smile and her skin tingled at the touch of his lips. She stood transfixed, unable to speak or move.

'How extraordinary,' Madame Bellaire murmured. 'There is a likeness, I suppose.'

'I can't see it myself.' Monsieur Bellaire kissed Marianne on both cheeks. 'You look beautiful. It is too long since we last met.'

Marianne gave him a beaming smile. 'Thank you, monsieur. I missed my summer visit to your beautiful chateau at Le Lavandou.'

'I don't know when we will enjoy such luxury again,' Henri said with a heavy sigh. 'The German army is advancing all the time, but we will fight them to the last man. They won't capture Paris.' He proffered his arm to Marianne. 'I'm going to enlist when we return home.'

Madame Bellaire sent him a warning glance. 'There is to be no talk of war this evening, Henri. We are here to celebrate Marianne's coming of age.'

'And it was so good of you to come all this way just for me.' Marianne laid her hand on Henri's sleeve. 'Come and meet my aunt and uncle.' They walked off in the direction of the drawing room followed by Henri's parents, leaving Elsie standing in the hall, not knowing quite what to do.

She was relieved to see Soames hobbling towards her, but his expression was not encouraging. 'Why are you standing there doing nothing?' He glanced anxiously at the pile of top hats, scarves and gloves that she had placed on an ornately carved side table. 'The guests' belongings should be put in the cupboard, taking care to ensure that they are paired together. It would be a disaster if you mixed them up.'

Elsie stared at the panelled wall. 'I don't know where it is, Mr Soames.'

He tut-tutted. 'You should have been given instructions earlier. I can't do everything.' He pressed one of the oak panels and as if by magic a door opened to reveal a deep cupboard. 'Sort that mess out and then come to the dining room. Observe Nancy; follow her lead and try not to spill anything.'

In the dining room Elsie stood back, watching carefully while Soames and Nancy moved round the table like dancers in a beautifully choreographed ballet. The soup was served, followed by the fish course and then the entrée. Sorbets were brought to clear the guests' palates in preparation for the grand entrance of the main course. Graham Winter drank heavily, leaving his wife, Josephine, to preside over the meal which she did nervously at first, trilling with laughter at everything Colonel Mason said while Cora looked on with pursed lips. Marianne sat between Henri and the local magistrate, Sir John Galbraith, and she slipped naturally into the role of hostess, putting her aunt firmly in her place.

Elsie could not help being impressed by the seemingly effortless way in which Marianne engaged everyone in conversation, diverting attention from her uncle's clumsy attempts to act as head of the household and her aunt's lack of social graces. Sir

21

John's mousy little wife spoke only when spoken to, even though Madame Bellaire did her best to make sure she was not completely ignored, while Monsieur Bellaire chatted to the vicar's wife, who was unlucky enough to sit next to Graham Winter. She blushed rosily every time he made an inappropriate remark, which Marianne attempted to cover up by changing the subject. Eventually he fell asleep over the dessert and had to be helped from the room by Fred and Soames. Marianne waved aside her aunt's feeble attempts to apologise. She rose to her feet and breaking from tradition suggested that they might all like to adjourn to the drawing room for coffee. Elsie could only admire her coolness and the aplomb with which she treated a situation that had threatened to spoil the evening. She felt quite sorry for Josephine Winter, whose plans had gone sadly awry, leaving her the object of pity instead of being hailed as a successful hostess.

Elsie stood aside as the guests rose from their seats, somewhat bemused by the odd turn of events, and trooped out of the dining room. Henri paused for a moment as he was about to walk past her. 'This has been quite an evening, mademoiselle. I apologise again for my mistake earlier on.'

Lost for words she managed a shy smile and bobbed a curtsey. Marianne gave her an appraising look as she took Henri's arm and swept out of the room.

Nancy nudged Elsie in the ribs, grinning. 'You're

for it now. Fred saw what the French chap did. He thought you was Miss Marianne. What a laugh.'

'It was embarrassing. No wonder she was annoyed.'

'Well, you're only helping out, so she can't sack you,' Nancy said cheerfully. Her smile faded and she put her head on one side. 'But if you was done up like her you could pass for sisters.'

'Get on with clearing the table,' Soames said impatiently. 'There's work to be done.'

Nancy began stacking the crockery onto a galleried tray. 'They say the colonel, Miss Marianne's father, was quite a one when he was young.' She winked and grinned. 'You know what I mean?'

'No,' Elsie said flatly. 'And I don't want to know either. There's always someone ready to gossip and spread rumours.'

'Not me, I promise you.' Nancy picked up the tray. 'I'm just taking this lot down to the scullery, Mr Soames. I'll be back in two shakes of a lamb's tail.'

Soames glanced round the room, shaking his head. 'It wasn't like this in the old days when Colonel and Mrs Winter presided over dinner parties. The world is changing and not for the better. Finish clearing up, Elsie, and check with Cook before you go home. She might need help in the kitchen.'

'Yes, Mr Soames.'

He left the dining room and Elsie worked methodically until the table was clear and everything ready to take down to the kitchen. Fred had been sent to help and he took the heaviest tray. 'This isn't the sort of work for a man,' he grumbled. 'I'm going to the recruiting office tomorrow.'

Elsie managed a smile. 'Good luck, Fred. I think you're very brave.'

His ruddy cheeks flushed to a deeper shade of red. 'Thanks, Elsie. I wish everyone thought like you. My old mum is going to kill me when she finds out.' He lumbered out of the dining room, his heavy footsteps clumping on the polished floorboards as he made his way to the kitchens. Elsie picked up a tray of glasses and was about to follow him when the door opened and Henri Bellaire strolled into the room. He came to a halt with an apologetic smile. 'I'm sorry, I didn't mean to startle you, but my mother thinks she left her lorgnette on the table.'

Elsie put the tray down again. 'I haven't seen it, but I'll have a look.' She knew she was blushing but she went in search of the missing eyeglass and found it on the floor beneath Madame Bellaire's chair. She handed it to him. 'It's lucky no one trod on it.'

'Thank you, Elsie. It is Elsie, isn't it?'

She kept her eyes averted. 'Yes, sir.'

'Are you angry with me, Elsie?'

She looked up and realised that he was serious. 'No, sir. Of course not. It was a mistake.'

'You are very alike,' he said thoughtfully. 'At least in looks, but not, I think, in temperament.'

'I wouldn't know, sir.'

'You don't have to treat me like the enemy,' he said with a rueful smile. 'All this will change, you know. The feudal system imposed by the rich on the poor will be consigned to history.'

'If you say so, sir.'

He looked her in the eye. 'The words tumble from your lips, but I don't believe it's what you think or feel.'

'It doesn't matter what I think or feel, sir.' She held his gaze.

'You don't believe that and neither do I.'

'All right, then. Since you want to know what I think – you might equally say that the oppressive system imposed on women by men should be consigned to the history books. Women should have the vote and be able to do jobs that have only been done by men. That's already begun to happen.'

'I knew it.' He threw back his head and laughed. 'You have the face of an angel and the soul of a suffragette.' He clicked his heels together. 'I salute you, Elsie.' He turned at the sound of footsteps.

Soames stood behind him with a stony expression on his face. 'May I be of assistance, sir?'

Henri waved the lorgnette at him. 'No, thank you, Soames. I came looking for this. Thank you for your help, Elsie.' He strolled out of the room, and Elsie snatched up the tray.

'I hope you weren't forgetting your place, Elsie.'

'Of course not, Mr Soames.'

'You're needed in the kitchen. Take that tray down and Fred will bring the rest. Below stairs is where you belong, my girl.'

Elsie bit back a sharp retort. She could not afford to lose her job, even if it was only temporary, but she had no intention of remaining in service for the rest of her life. She had tried hard to hide her true feelings, but Henri Bellaire had seen through the thin veneer of humility she wore at work, and he had sensed the rebellious spirit that was her real self. She went back to washing dishes with a renewed sense of optimism. What happened next was up to her, but her first priority must be to nurse her mother back to health. The doctor's prognosis might be wrong. Miracles could sometimes happen.

Elsie was peeling potatoes next morning when Nancy stuck her head round the scullery door. 'You're wanted in Miss Marianne's room. You're for it if you ask me. She was giving you black looks last night.'

Elsie wiped her hands on her apron. 'It wasn't my fault that her boyfriend needs glasses.'

'That's a good one,' Nancy said, giggling. 'Tell her that, I dare you.'

'I will if she gives me a hard time.' Elsie paused in the doorway. 'You'd better point me in the right direction. I don't know where her room is.'

'Come on, I'll show you. This old house is a maze of corridors and we don't want you to get lost. You

26

might never be found again until you're a skeleton with bleached bones.'

'You do talk a lot of rot, Nancy.'

'Come.' Marianne's bored voice acknowledged Elsie's tap on the door. She opened it, mouthing a word of thanks to Nancy.

'Tell us what she says,' she whispered.

Elsie entered the room, closing the door behind her. 'You wanted to see me, Miss Winter?'

Marianne was sitting at her elegant rosewood dressing table. She turned her head to give Elsie an appraising look. 'Cora Mason tells me that you're a good hairdresser.'

'I'm a trained lady's maid.'

'So I heard.' Marianne turned away to gaze at her reflection in the mirror. 'I want my hair bobbed. Can you do it?'

'I've seen a picture of Irene Castle and her bob, but I've never cut hair like that.'

Marianne shook out her long flaxen curls. 'I want a change. I'm taking charge of my own life from now on.' She took a pair of scissors from a drawer. 'Do it. I want a bob just like Irene Castle.'

Elsie hesitated. 'Are you sure?'

'Cut.' Marianne thrust the scissors into her hand. 'Do it, please.'

'Well, since you ask so nicely,' Elsie said, chuckling. 'But don't blame me if you don't like the result. I can't glue it back on once it's cut.'

Marianne turned to her, frowning. 'You have a lot to say for yourself.'

'I'm not here on a permanent basis, Miss Winter. I'm only filling in for my sick mother.'

'Why did you leave your previous employer?'

'Mrs Tonbridge died.'

'I see.' Marianne eyed her thoughtfully. 'Are you going to look for another position?'

'People like me can't afford to be idle.'

'You sound militant. Are you one of those women who chain themselves to railings outside public buildings?'

'No, but I wish I was. I think they're very brave.'

'Are you going to stand there and lecture me on women's suffrage, or are you going to cut my hair?'

'I can do either or both at the same time,' Elsie said calmly. 'Which would you prefer?'

For a brief moment Marianne looked taken aback and then she laughed. 'You have spirit, I like that. I'll opt for the cut without the sermon.'

Elsie wielded the scissors. 'How short do you want it?'

'Daringly short. Do you know how to finger wave? It's all the rage in London.'

'I've seen it in magazines. Mrs Tonbridge might have been an elderly lady but she liked to keep up with fashion.'

'That's how I intend to grow old, absolutely disgracefully.' Marianne gurgled with laughter. 'You'll find a towel in the airing cupboard and there's water in the jug on the washstand, if you want to work on damp hair.'

'Yes, of course.' Elsie made her preparations and began to cut, working quickly and methodically. She was aware that Marianne watched every snip of the scissors, but she did not allow her concentration to waver for a second. Once started her only concern was to create a style that was flattering to the face and a work of art in itself. Marianne, unlike Cora Mason, was silent throughout, reserving her comments until the last strand of hair was in place.

She stared at her reflection and a delighted smile lit her face. 'That's wonderful. Just what I wanted.' She met Elsie's anxious gaze with a nod of her head. 'You are an excellent coiffeuse. Pass me my handbag; I must give you something for your trouble.'

Elsie shook her head. 'I'm being paid to work here, miss. I'd rather be cutting hair than washing dishes.'

'Is that what you do? I thought you'd been taken on as a parlour maid.'

'I do whatever I'm asked to do.'

'Nevertheless, I insist on giving you something extra. Buy some flowers or chocolates for your mother.' Marianne rose from the stool in front of the dressing table and shook out her skirts. She reached for her handbag and took out a purse. 'Thank you, Elsie.' She pressed a florin and a silver sixpence into Elsie's hand. 'I can't wait to see Henri's face when he sees my new hairdo.'

'You look like a film star, and I'm not just saying that to flatter you.'

'Maybe you ought to cut your own hair,' Marianne said with a wry smile. 'I confess I was a bit miffed when Henri mistook you for me, but I think it might be amusing to change places on the odd occasion.'

'I don't think you'd enjoy washing pots and pans in the scullery, Miss Marianne.'

'Nor would I, but if you were to take to my bed with a headache, or some minor affliction, I could go out with Henri unchaperoned. It would be such a lark.'

'And Mrs Tranter would sack me on the spot. That wouldn't be much fun for me.'

'I suppose you're right. But you're wasting your talents slaving away in the scullery. You can do better than that.'

'I intend to, miss. There's no question about that.'

Marianne's new hairstyle created a sensation in the household. Mrs Winter was horrified, or so Nancy said when she returned to the kitchen after serving lunch in the dining room. 'I thought she was going to faint or have one of them apple-eptic fits you hear about. She said that Miss Marianne's mother would be furious if she saw her looking like a shorn sheep.'

Mrs Coker nodded her head. 'A very elegant lady is Mrs Winter. It's a pity she left Miss Marianne to go wild the way she has. I thought that posh finishing school would sort her out, but it seems I was wrong.'

'Well I think she looks nice,' Phyllis said boldly.

'And when did you see her?' Mrs Coker rounded on her. 'You should have had everything done and finished before the family are about.'

'I'd just cleaned the lavatory for the second time this morning, Cook. Mr Winter had left it in a terrible state.'

'We don't want to know that, Phyllis. Get on with your work.'

Elsie emerged from the scullery, wiping her hands on a tea towel. She had heard the conversation but it was not her place to defend or criticise Miss Marianne. 'I've finished the dishes, Cook. Is it all right if I go home to check on Ma? I'll only be an hour or so.'

'I suppose you'll be too grand to wash dishes now that you're Miss Marianne's hairdresser,' Mrs Coker said with a grim smile.

Elsie shrugged and laughed, but she was conscious of the sideways looks given her by the kitchen maids, neither of whom had ever been particularly friendly towards her. 'It was just the once, Mrs Coker. I doubt if I'll be called upon again.'

She left the kitchen, well aware of the rumblings of jealousy amongst some of the servants, but she set off for home with the coins jingling in her pocket and she stopped at the village shop to buy some of her mother's favourite biscuits and a jar of Bovril, which would make nourishing beef tea.

'How is Monique?' Mrs Rogers, the genial woman who ran the village store, asked the same question every time Elsie walked through the door.

'About the same,' Elsie said briefly. She knew that whatever she told Mrs Rogers in confidence would be common knowledge within minutes.

'How are you getting on at Darcy Hall?' Mrs Rogers scooped digestive biscuits from the cardboard box and weighed them on the big brass scales. 'And how is Miss Marianne? I daresay she'll find it very quiet now that she's back at home.'

'I expect she will.'

'She'll probably go out to India to find a husband. There isn't much choice for a young lady of her class round here, especially now the eligible young men are queuing up to enlist.'

'I really don't know, Mrs Rogers. I just wash dishes. The family don't confide in me.'

Mrs Rogers tipped the biscuits into a paper bag and swung it expertly so that the corners made neat twists. She placed it on the counter. 'I'll just have to wait for Nancy or Phyllis to come into the shop. They're treated like part of the family, so they say.'

'I'm sure they are. Now I really must hurry as I've only an hour off.' Elsie paid for her purchases and hurried from the shop before the curious Mrs Rogers could ask any more questions.

The sun was shining from a sky so blue that it

hurt her eyes, and heat rose from the dusty pavements burning through the thin soles of her boots as she walked homeward. Several women stopped her to enquire about her mother's progress and Elsie could not bring herself to tell them that there was little hope. If she kept up the pretence that her mother would regain her health perhaps it would come true. She quickened her pace, thinking how pleased Ma would be to have some sweet biscuits to go with her cup of tea. She would tell her about Miss Marianne's new hairstyle and the sensation it had caused, and how finger waving was not as difficult as she might have supposed. As she rounded the bend in the lane she saw Miss Peabody, the district nurse, wheeling her bicycle through the front gate of Tan Cottage. She waved and called her name. 'Wait, please.'

Miss Peabody stood very still. 'You've saved me a ride to Darcy Hall, Elsie.'

'What's wrong?' The words tasted bitter in her mouth and the look on Miss Peabody's face confirmed her worst fears.

'Dr Hancock has taken her to the hospital, Elsie. I'm afraid she took a turn for the worse.'

Elsie clutched the gatepost for support as her knees threatened to give way beneath her. 'How serious is it, Miss Peabody?'

'I can't say, but you'd better go to the hospital.'

'I'll go right away. You wouldn't know what time the next bus is, I suppose?'

'There are only two a day and I think the first one has gone.'

'Then I'll walk.'

'It's eight miles to the hospital, Elsie. I'd lend you my bicycle, but I need it to do my rounds.'

'Thank you, but I've walked to town before. It's not that far and at least it's not raining.'

Miss Peabody managed a tight little smile. 'That's right, my dear. It's a fine day, we must be grateful for small mercies. You might get a lift if you're lucky.'

With the paper bag containing her purchases still clutched in her hand, Elsie set off in the direction of the hospital. It was early afternoon and there was very little traffic about, apart from the odd farm wagon. The Roman road stretched before her like an endless grey ribbon, the farmland on either side bounded by low hedgerows that afforded little shade. Somewhere high above a field of ripe corn a skylark hovered, warbling its melodious song, but the only other sound was the crunching of her feet on the hard ground.

She stopped for a moment to catch her breath and spotted a cloud of dust in the distance which seemed to be coming nearer. The sound of a motor car engine grew louder and an open tourer travelling at some speed came into view. She moved closer to the hedge as it approached, but it was only when the vehicle slowed down and came to a halt beside her that she recognised the driver.

Henri raised the goggles to the top of his helmet.

'Good afternoon, Elsie. I have it right this time, have I not?'

His expression was comical and yet apologetic and quite irresistible. She smiled. 'Yes, you do, sir.'

'Where are you going on such a hot day? There's nothing for miles.'

'To the hospital.' Her voice broke on a suppressed sob. 'My mother was rushed in and I must see her.'

His smile faded. 'I'm sorry to hear that. I hope it's not serious.'

'It is, I'm afraid.'

'Is there anything I can do?'

'If you're going to Darcy Hall would you be kind enough to tell Mr Soames why I haven't returned to work?'

He leaned over to open the door. 'Get in. I'll drive you to the hospital if you can give me directions.'

She shook her head. 'Thank you, but it's not necessary.'

'I can't allow a young lady to walk all that way in such heat. I will drive you there in no time.'

'But it's in the other direction, and it's miles out of your way.'

'I would feel bad if I abandoned you here. I can see that you're upset and I'm sure Marianne will not mind waiting for a little while longer.'

'You really don't have to do this. I'm used to walking.'

'And I'm used to people doing what I ask.' He

laughed and his eyes crinkled at the corners. 'Please do not disappoint me.'

She was hot and tired and extremely anxious and it was easier to accept than to resist. She climbed in beside him. 'Thank you.'

'It's my pleasure. I like to show off my prowess as a driver.' He repositioned his goggles, engaged gear and spun the car round with a squeal of tyres. 'Unfortunately this motor car is only mine while I am here in England, but I have a similar model at home in Paris.' He gunned the engine and drove off.

It was the first time she had ever travelled in a horseless carriage and the speed was both exhilarating and frightening. She held on tight, closing her eyes at first and then opening them to marvel at the effect of scenery flashing by faster than she could have imagined. Henri glanced at her and grinned. 'You are not scared?'

'No,' she said firmly. 'Of course not.'

'Marianne also likes to go fast.'

The excitement and thrill of the experience was suddenly dimmed by the mention of Marianne's name. For a short while Elsie had been able to forget her troubles and enjoy the novelty of being treated as an equal by a man like Henri, but the moment had passed. 'Turn left here,' she said abruptly. 'The hospital is at the end of the road. You can't miss it.'

He turned the wheel and swung the vehicle round. The motor drew to a halt outside the front entrance, and Henri climbed out onto the gravel. He took off his helmet and goggles and moved swiftly to open the door for Elsie. 'That was better than walking, was it not?'

She allowed him to help her out of the car, enjoying the sensation of being treated like a lady. 'Thank you so much, Monsieur Bellaire. It was very kind of you to go out of your way like this.'

'I will wait for you.'

'Oh, no, really I couldn't expect you to do that.'

'How will you get home?'

'I don't know. I expect there'll be a bus.'

He frowned. 'You will be returning to Darcy Hall?'

'Yes, of course.'

'Then I will wait for you.'

She could see that to argue was useless, and her desire to see her mother overrode all other considerations. She hurried into the hospital, leaving Henri to follow or not as he pleased.

A nurse showed her to the side ward and asked her to wait in the corridor. Elsie caught a glimpse of the bed and the movement of nurses fluttering about the room like grey and white doves, but the door closed again, shutting her out. She was tempted to barge in and demand to see her mother, but just as she felt she could bear it no longer the door opened and Dr Hancock emerged.

'Elsie, my dear, I am so sorry.'

Chapter Three

Henri had waited for her and he offered to drive her back to Darcy Hall. 'You should not be alone at a time like this, chérie,' he said gently.

Dazed and too shocked even to cry, Elsie shook her head. 'I don't belong there. I should go home.'

'I'm sure they will look after you,' Henri insisted. 'Unless you have someone close who could be with you tonight.'

'I've no family in England.'

He shot her a curious glance. 'Does that mean you have relations in France? I only assume that because your French is flawless.'

'My mother's family are French, but they cut her off when she married Pa.'

'I'm sorry. That must have been a matter of great sorrow for her, but if you will allow me to take you to Darcy Hall I'm certain that Marianne will see that you are looked after.'

'No. Thank you, Monsieur Bellaire, but I want to go home.'

'It's Henri,' he said softly. 'I am your friend, Elsie. I think you should not be alone tonight.'

'I grew up in Tan Cottage. It's where I live,' she said simply. 'Please take me home.'

He left her at the door and she did not invite him in. She was not ashamed of the tiny one up, one down cottage, but she wanted to be alone. Her mother's sudden death from a haemorrhage had come as a body blow. Even though she had been warned that the end might be imminent, deep down Elsie had clung to the hope that it might not be so. Now it was final. She had seen her mother's dead body and kissed her marble-like cheek as if she were saying goodnight, but it was a long and never-ending darkness that had taken her mother from her.

She slumped down on a wooden chair at the kitchen table and it was only then that she realised she was still clutching the bag of biscuits and the jar of Bovril. She put them down and sat staring at them as if they were the last tangible link with the mother she had just lost. The sun went down and shadows gathered around her until she was in almost complete darkness, and at last tears came. She buried her head in her arms and sobbed.

She awakened to sunshine and birdsong, and for a moment she could not think why she was slumped over the kitchen table and not in her bed. She raised her head and the realisation that she was completely alone hit her with such force that it took her breath away. She rose unsteadily to her feet and moved stiffly to the back door. Outside the air was redolent with the scents of late summer. The fragrance of honeysuckle and the white roses that her mother had loved mingled with the scent of warm grass, and there was the unmistakeable tang of salt from the sea only half a mile away across the chalk downs. It was a new dawn and a new day. Nothing could take away the pain of loss, but the feeling of grief was tempered by the knowledge that her mother's suffering was over. Ma might be gone, but Elsie could still feel her love enveloping her like a warm blanket, and no matter what the future held, nothing could take that away: Ma would live in her heart forever, and she must do her best to make her proud. She caught a sudden waft of her mother's favourite cologne and she felt her presence even though she could not see her.

She walked slowly to the pump and worked the handle; water spurted out, creating a rainbow, and she stuck her head beneath the ice-cold stream. She straightened up, shaking the droplets from her long hair. Acting on a sudden impulse she hurried back into the house and searched the dresser drawer until she found a pair of scissors. If this was to be a new beginning then she would be one of the emancipated women who were going to help run the country in time of war.

She took one tress at a time and snipped through her wet locks until she had created a semblance of the bob she had styled for Marianne. She seized a towel and roughly dried her hair, feeling suddenly light-headed and free, but there was something else she still had to face.

She went slowly up the stairs to her mother's room. It remained just as it must have been when Ma had left it, frozen in time like a still life. The bed was unmade and the medicine bottle, glass and jug of water were on the table. The sickly scent of illness pervaded the atmosphere and Elsie moved swiftly to open the window. Her mother's brush and comb lay on the pine chest together with the faded photograph of Elsie's father, standing proud in his army uniform. She ran the comb through her rapidly drying hair which had already begun to curl wildly, and she stared critically at the result in the fly-spotted mirror. With several snips of the scissors she evened off the ragged ends, and nodded to herself, acknowledging her work. 'I'll make you proud of me, Ma, and that's a promise I intend to keep.'

When Elsie walked into the kitchen at Darcy Hall there was an awkward silence. Mrs Coker offered her condolences in a brusque, slightly embarrassed manner. 'Monique will be missed,' she murmured, casting a critical eye over Elsie's new hairstyle. 'Put your cap on. This is no time for frivolity.' She returned to kneading the bread dough with renewed vigour. Phyllis and Nancy were over-effusive and hugged Elsie, but if they had any opinions as to her short hair they kept them to themselves. The rest of the servants muttered words of sympathy and then hurried off to go about their duties as if nothing had happened.

Later that morning, after luncheon had been served and cleared away, Mrs Tranter made a special point of taking Elsie aside and telling her that the job was hers for as long as she needed it. It did not seem appropriate to mention the fact that she would be leaving as soon as she was able to find work elsewhere. In the meantime there were funeral arrangements to be made, although Elsie had no idea how she would raise the money to pay for such a solemn event. She went about her duties in a haze, finding it increasingly difficult to concentrate her thoughts.

When the last dish was washed, dried and put away Mrs Coker waited until everyone, with the exception of Elsie, had hurried off to enjoy their brief period of free time. 'Mrs Tranter agrees with me that you should have the rest of the day off. There must be arrangements to be made and that sort of thing.' She hesitated, staring at a point somewhere above Elsie's head. 'It's a difficult time for you, I know.' She cleared her throat noisily and patted Elsie on the shoulder. 'I'll see you in the morning, first thing, and don't be late.'

'Thank you, Mrs Coker.'

Elsie found herself alone in the vast echoing kitchen. The silence was worse than the general hubbub of voices and the clattering of pots and pans. It was hot and stuffy and she took her cap off, wiping the perspiration from her brow. She had finished mopping the floor and was about take the bucket outside and empty its contents down the drain when she heard quick footsteps on the stairs. She turned and was surprised to see that it was Marianne who entered the room. She paused, a picture of elegance in a cream shantung outfit with the fashionable peg top silhouette, which made her look as though she had stepped from the pages of *Weldon's Ladies' Journal*. She stopped, staring at Elsie in amazement. 'You did it. You cut your hair.'

'I wanted a change.'

'Good for you,' Marianne said, smiling. 'It suits you.'

'Did you want something, miss?'

'Yes, I was looking for you as it happens.' The hobble skirt forced Marianne to take tiny steps as she made her way carefully across the wet floor. 'I was so sorry to hear about your mother. I would have come down earlier but Henri had to leave for London and his parents are returning to Paris, so I drove them to the station.'

Elsie shivered even though the heat in the kitchen was stifling. She had hoped to see Henri again, if only to thank him for his kindness, but now he had gone she felt as though she had lost more than a friend. 'Of course,' she murmured. 'I understand.'

Marianne hesitated, biting her lip. 'It's rough luck, old thing. I know what it's like to be without your mother, even though mine is still in the land of the living.' She threw up her hands. 'I'm saying all the wrong things, but I just wanted you to know that you have our sympathy, and if there's anything I can do to help . . .' Her voice tailed off. 'You're not crying, are you?'

Elsie dashed her hand across her eyes. 'No, Miss Marianne. I'm just a bit tired, that's all.'

'Of course you are. I doubt if you slept much last night.'

'I'm fine, really I am, and I must get on.'

'Yes, I understand.' Marianne began to retrace her steps, but stopped, turning to Elsie with an embarrassed smile. 'Look, I realise things must be difficult for you – financially, I mean. I wouldn't have thought of it myself, but Henri said you were probably a bit hard up and, well, to be blunt, Elsie, what I'm trying to say is I want you to send the account for the funeral expenses to me.'

'To you?' Elsie stared at her in astonishment. 'Why would you want to pay for my mother's funeral?'

'I've just come into the money left to me by my grandfather, and it seems the right thing to do. You must allow me to help, if only to prove to Henri that I'm not a spoilt army brat, I'm quite the reverse, in fact.'

'He asked you to do this for me?'

'Not exactly, but he's very generous and does all sorts of things for his employees when they're in difficulties. Besides which he's as rich as Croesus, which explains my family's clumsy attempts at matchmaking.' Marianne gurgled with laughter. 'Don't look so shocked; it's still the done thing in my set, but I'm not playing their game. Henri and I are like brother and sister. I'll pick the man I want to marry. Anyway, I'm digressing. Will you allow me to do this for you?'

'I – I don't know what to say.'

Marianne put her head on one side, frowning. 'I'm free this afternoon, as it happens, and I'm at a loose end. Why don't I come with you to see the vicar? It's clear that you could use a friend.'

'I'm not a charity case,' Elsie said sharply. 'I'm sure you can find something to do that's more amusing than helping me to arrange my mother's funeral.' She knew she was being unreasonable, but she felt as if the last vestige of pride had been stripped away from her. She snatched up the bucket and marched out into the yard.

Marianne had gone when Elsie returned to the kitchen and she felt ashamed of her outburst. It had been kind of Marianne to offer financial help, but they were not friends and never could be: the social divide was too great to allow that to happen, and she did not want to feel obligated to the Winter family. A life in service was not for her. Marianne's careless words had made her realise how foolish she had been to imagine that Henri Bellaire was interested in her as a person. He must have seen her as another opportunity to help someone less fortunate than himself, and she herself had been dazzled by his charm and good looks. 'You're an idiot, Elsie Mead,' she said out loud. 'And talking to yourself is the first sign of madness.'

*

Elsie was on her way home when she heard the roar of a motor car engine and the parp-parp of its horn. She jumped aside, almost tumbling into the ditch as the car screeched to a halt at her side.

'I thought you could do with a lift?' With the engine still running Marianne leaned across and opened the passenger door. 'Hop in.'

Elsie hesitated. She should refuse and keep her pride, but curiosity overcame caution and she climbed in beside her. 'This is Henri's car.'

'It's mine for the time being. He decided to travel by train and left it in my safe keeping until he returns at the weekend.' Marianne accelerated and the vehicle leapt forward in a series of bunny hops. 'I haven't quite got the hang of the thing yet,' she said, laughing. She shot a sideways glance at Elsie. 'Do relax; I'm perfectly capable behind the wheel. I had a few lessons in Switzerland from a divine man who was the brother of one of my best friends. Unfortunately he turned out to have a wife and child in Hampstead, but I didn't find that out for quite a while, and I didn't let on for a long time after that.' She chortled with laughter. 'Are you shocked, Elsie?'

'No, I don't think so.' Elsie held on to her straw hat.

'You're full of surprises. I had you down as being an innocent and maybe a bit of a prude.'

'I grew up in Sutton Darcy. You'd be shocked if you knew half of what goes on.'

'You must enlighten me some time, but first things first. Where would you like me to drop you?'

'I was on my way to the vicarage.'

'I thought as much. I'm sorry I upset you earlier. I'm not noted for my tact, Elsie. Am I forgiven?'

'Actually I'm the one who should apologise,' Elsie said with a reluctant smile. 'You were trying to help, but you must understand why I couldn't accept such a generous offer.'

'Apology accepted. I did think you were a bit hard on me, although I still don't see why you won't allow me to pay for the funeral.' Marianne swerved in order to avoid a pothole. 'Your mother was kind to me when I was a child. I used to sneak down to the kitchen when the servants had their afternoon break. Monique was always there, mopping the floor or scrubbing that huge pine table, and she used to look the other way when I raided the pantry for jam tarts or biscuits. She always had time for me and we had long conversations in French, which helped no end when I spent my summers in Provence with Henri's family.'

'I didn't know that, but it's typical of Ma. She was the nicest, kindest person I've ever known.'

'So you understand why I want to make sure she has a proper send-off? I'm sure my father would agree with me, if he were here now. He always took an interest in the servants' welfare, and I know for a fact that he thought highly of your mother.'

'Ma cried when your parents left for India. She was very loyal.'

'Which is all the more reason for the Winters to honour her memory. What do you say to that, Elsie?'

Monique's funeral took place a week later. The younger men from the village were notable by their absence as the congregation filed into the church, but those who were left behind had come to mourn for a woman who, in life, had been considered an outsider, even though she had come to Sutton Darcy as a bride more than twenty-three years ago. Marianne had seen to it that everyone from Darcy Hall attended the service, including her aunt and uncle, and to Elsie's astonishment Henri had travelled from London for the occasion, although she suspected that the real motive for his visit was to collect his motor car.

The service was short but moving and Elsie found it almost impossible to control her emotions, but when she saw the coffin lowered into the ground it was so final that she could not contain her tears. Despite the fact that people surrounded the grave she had never felt so lost and alone. Marianne slipped her arm around her shoulders and gave her a gentle hug. 'We'll take you home, Elsie.' She turned to Henri. 'I've invited everyone back to the Hall for light refreshments. Will you drive, or shall I?'

Tables and chairs had been set out on the lawns in front of Darcy Hall and trestles set up to hold barrels of beer and cider. Lemonade and ginger beer were provided for those who did not drink alcohol and the kitchen staff bustled to and fro with plates of sandwiches, meat pies, cakes and biscuits, all prepared under the strict eye of Mrs Coker.

Despite the sadness of the occasion a party atmosphere began to emerge, especially when the barrels were tapped and Soames produced a bowl of fruit cup, to which he was seen to add half a bottle of brandy. People began to relax and soon they were laughing and chattering. The sun beat down from a cloudless sky but its heat was tempered by a cool breeze off the sea, and for a while it seemed that everyone was able to forget the war that overshadowed their daily lives.

Elsie stood back for a moment, watching the mourners shake off the mantle of sobriety as they began to enjoy themselves, even if some of them looked a bit shifty as they sipped their drinks and munched on the sandwiches and pies. She had been surprised and touched by the condolences she had received. Monique Mead might have been known as the Frenchwoman, but it seemed that in death she had, at last, been accepted by the villagers as one of their own.

Elsie turned with a start as Marianne tapped her on the arm. 'It's going well, isn't it? We've done Monique proud.'

'It's all down to you,' Elsie said earnestly. 'I can't thank you enough for taking all this trouble. Ma was a very modest woman. She wouldn't understand why there was all this fuss over someone like her.'

'We're all important. I'm only just beginning to

realise that.' Marianne gazed round at the crowd of women wearing black. 'I'm afraid this is a sign of things to come. All these families have sent someone close to them to war, and who knows how many will come home? You've made me think about something other than myself, Elsie.'

'Me? How? I don't understand.'

'I know you want to leave here and do something for the war effort. I thought at first that you were crazy, but while I was organising all this I've spent time in the village, talking to people. The war in Europe is going to affect all of us, and we can't pretend it's not happening.'

'But you don't need to work. I have to earn my own living.'

'I can't rusticate here for the rest of my life. I'm driving back to London with Henri in the morning.'

'You're leaving home?'

'I'm considering my options. I've been invited to stay with an old school friend whose aunt has a flat in London. She's Felicia Wilby – you must have heard of her.'

'Felicia Wilby the actress?' Elsie was impressed.

'That's right. It's going to be fun, and I can't wait to get away.' Marianne looked round and waved. 'There's Henri. I must go and rescue the poor fellow. Cora Mason has got her claws into him and she'll bore him to death.' She hurried off across the crushed grass.

Elsie stood for a moment, watching the people

she had grown up amongst as they made the most of the free food and drink. It was hard not to feel bitter, and yet Ma had never held a grudge against the people whose prejudices had kept them from welcoming her into their midst.

'Elsie.' Henri strode across the lawn, coming to a halt at her side. 'Are you all right?'

'Yes, thank you.'

He smiled but there was a question in his dark eyes. 'You are so polite, chérie. Would you tell me any different, I wonder?'

'I am sad, of course, but I am grateful to Miss Marianne for doing all this.'

'It is too much, yes?'

She nodded. 'It is a bit too much.'

'Marianne means well, I think.'

'You're going back to London tomorrow.'

'We leave in the morning. I wanted to say au revoir.'

'You mean goodbye.'

He raised her hand to his lips. 'No, that's not what I meant. We will meet again, Elsie.' His dark eyes held her gaze and he smiled. 'Your new hairstyle suits you very well. I like it.'

He strolled off, returning to Marianne's side as she chatted to the vicar and his wife. Elsie could still feel the soft imprint of his warm lips on the back of her hand and she raised it to her cheek, holding it there and printing it indelibly in her memory. Even a scullery maid was allowed to dream. She came back to earth as Mrs Coker lumbered towards her.

'We could do with a hand clearing away,' she said breathlessly. 'Emily's been at the fruit cup and Nancy's had to put her to bed.'

'I'll come now.'

Mrs Coker hesitated. 'Take a tip from me, Elsie. Don't get involved with them upstairs. It can only lead to heartbreak.'

Tan Cottage echoed with memories, but the over-riding feeling was one of sadness and loss. Elsie could not bring herself to sleep in her mother's bed. Even though she had changed the sheets and had hung the counterpane outside in the sunshine, the smell of the sick room still lingered in the folds of the material. Sometimes she awakened in the middle of the night thinking she could hear her mother coughing, and would rise from her bed on the kitchen floor, but then she remembered that Ma was no longer with her. The sounds persisted and she realised they came from the pasture where the cows made noises that sounded oddly human in the still of the night.

Elsie continued to work in the kitchens at Darcy Hall, doing what was required of her without complaint, but as the days went by and she read about the atrocities in Europe, she became even more determined to do something that would contribute to the war effort. Young men were dying in their hundreds of thousands, and the plight of the Belgian refugees, displaced by the advancing German army, struck a chord deep within her. The newspapers were filled with stories of families torn apart and women and children arriving in England with little more than the clothes on their backs. She knew she must do something, but it was difficult to know where to start.

In the privacy of her own home she studied the situations vacant columns in the newspapers discarded by Mr Winter, but she had had to wait until no one was looking before she had taken the relevant page and slipped it into her apron pocket. If it became common knowledge that she was seeking employment elsewhere she might lose the job she had, and that would be a disaster. It was difficult to save enough to pay the rent on Tan Cottage as it was, let alone find money for necessities. It was late September and there was a hint of autumn in the air. The leaves on the trees were heavy with dust and beginning to turn subtle shades of russet and gold. Skeins of wild geese flew overhead morning and evening, honking and calling to each other as they headed for the fields where they would feed on the ears of corn left after the crop had been harvested, building themselves up to face the winter. The cold weather was coming and there would be the additional expense of paying for coal and candles or lamp oil. Mrs Tranter had offered Elsie a bed in the attic rooms with the junior kitchen maids, Emily and Jane, but if she accepted a live-in position she feared she might condemn herself to a life in service. She had glimpsed another way of life and been treated as an equal by Marianne and Henri, and nothing would be the same again. Cook and Mrs Tranter had tried to warn her against becoming too friendly with her employers, and Elsie was beginning to realise that they were right.

Marianne had been in London for almost a month and no one knew when she might return. It was obvious to Elsie that both Marianne and Henri had moved on within their own circle and that she had been forgotten. For all she knew Henri might have returned to France and might even have been one of the casualties of the battle of Le Cateau that had claimed so many lives. She had applied for several positions locally without success. A cordite factory had been set up at Holton Heath, but it would cost her more to travel there each day than she could earn, and although she did apply she received a negative response by return of post.

On her day off she caught a bus to the nearest town and made enquiries at the railway station to see if they needed porters or someone to work in the tearoom, again without success. She tried the bus depot but they needed drivers and she had to admit that she had never been behind the wheel. She went into shops and offered her services but the shopkeepers seemed to favour young boys or older men, and she was turned away. She spent a few pennies on a cup of tea and a sticky bun, and caught the bus back to Sutton Darcy feeling frustrated and angry. She boiled an egg and buttered a slice of bread, and was just about to sit down to eat her frugal meal when someone rapped on the front door. She went to open it and to her surprise it was the rent collector. He doffed his cap. 'Good evening, Miss Mead.'

'You're a day early, Mr Thompson.' She reached into her pocket and took out her purse.

'Only a day, Miss Mead. Is it a problem?'

She counted out the coins. 'No. I made sure I have enough.'

He took the money and dropped it into a leather pouch. He hesitated, eyeing her warily.

'Was there something else, Mr Thompson?'

'I'm afraid so, Miss Mead. I have to give you a week's notice to quit Tan Cottage.' He took an envelope from his breast pocket and pressed it into her hand. 'I'm sorry, but it's the landlord's orders.'

'I have to leave my home? Why?'

'I'm sorry, Miss Mead. The landlord is terminating the agreement, which was with Mrs Monique Mead. It's only just come to his attention that the lady is deceased.'

'But you can't turn me out. I've been paying the rent regular as clockwork.'

'I know, but it's not my decision. The owner has another tenant in mind who can afford to pay almost double the amount your mother was paying.'

'You can't do this to me.'

'I'm afraid I can, miss. You have a week to pack up and leave Tan Cottage, and that's final.'

Chapter Four

Elsie sat in the corner of the third class railway compartment, staring out of the window as the train chugged into Waterloo station. It came to a halt with a screech of iron wheels on iron rails and a huge burst of steam from the massive engine. There was a moment of chaos as the other passengers gathered their possessions and reached up to heave their luggage from the racks. She sat very still, waiting while they jostled each other in their efforts to climb down to the platform, even though Waterloo was the terminus and the train would be there for some time before it began its return journey.

A couple with two noisy children were the first to alight, followed by a burly man wearing a mustard yellow suit which made him look like a bookie or a barker at a fairground. He tipped his bowler hat and apologised as he trod on Elsie's toe and had to turn sideways to get his bulk through the door. He was followed by two prim ladies dressed from head to foot in black, who had sat side by side with their knitting needles clicking all the way from Southampton. They had cast darkling looks at the badly behaved children, tut-tutting but not daring to speak out. Elsie was the last to leave the compartment and she stepped down onto the platform, standing very still while people rushed past her to the barrier. London had a strange smoky smell combined with the hot metallic odour emanating from the hissing steam engine. The air felt heavy and warm compared to the fresh sea breezes on the coast, and everywhere there was noise and bustle.

She made her way to the barrier and handed in her ticket, but the feeling of excitement and anticipation evaporated as she emerged from the station concourse and stepped into the busy London street. Nothing could have prepared her for the sheer volume of horse-drawn traffic interspersed with motor vehicles, and the pavements were crowded with people who all seemed to be in a tearing hurry. The noise and the confusion made her head spin, and worse still she had no idea how to get to her destination. Mr Soames, who had worked in London as a young man, had advised her to take a cab to the address she had been given by the charity that had offered her work. She had read an article about the Women's Emergency Corps in *The Times*, and had written off to the address in Baker Street, citing her fluency in French as her most useful asset. The reply had been swift and positive, offering her a job as interpreter. There had been no mention of a wage, but she assumed that they would not expect her to work for nothing, and had written back accepting the post.

It was only now that she realised how little she knew of life in the big city and hailing a cab was easier said than done. She waved hopefully at a likely-looking vehicle but it sped past her, and she was just beginning to wonder if she was invisible when a hansom cab drew up at the kerb and a man leapt out, tossed a coin to the cabby and strode into the station. Elsie ran up to the cab, waving frantically. 'I want to go to Baker Street, please, sir.'

'Hop in, miss.'

She heaved her suitcase into the vehicle and climbed in after it, falling onto the seat as it lurched forward into the seething mass of traffic. Elsie did not know which way to look. There seemed to be places of interest on both sides of the road and then they were crossing Waterloo Bridge and she had her first sight of the River Thames, wending its majestic course through the city in sinuous serpentine curves, its coffee-coloured tidal waters gliding onwards to join the North Sea. Her knowledge of London had been gleaned from reading newspapers and looking through magazines discarded by Josephine Winter, but nothing had prepared her for the reality or the cost of the cab ride to Baker Street. She paid the cabby what he asked and then she remembered that Mr Soames had warned her that tipping was expected, and she gave him threepence, which seemed to satisfy him, but left her with an extremely light purse. She picked up her suitcase and walked into the office of the Women's Emergency Committee.

The woman who interviewed her wore a business-like shirt and tie and a tight hobble skirt. She placed a cigarette in a long holder and clenched it between her teeth, eyeing Elsie through a plume of smoke. 'So why do you want to do charity work, Miss Mead?'

Taken aback, Elsie struggled to find an answer. 'I need a job, miss, and I'm fluent in French.'

'My name is Charlotte Greenway. You may address me as Charlotte or Miss Greenway.'

'Yes, m— I mean, Miss Greenway.'

Charlotte leaned her elbows on the desk, fixing Elsie with a hard stare. 'You do realise that this is unpaid work, don't you?'

'Unpaid?' Elsie gulped and swallowed as her throat constricted in panic. 'But – but I thought it was a proper job. I've come all the way from Dorset and I gave my notice in at Darcy Hall.'

Charlotte's stern expression softened and she took the cigarette holder from her mouth, flicking ash into an overflowing ashtray on her desk. 'I see.' She stood up and paced the room, replacing the holder between her teeth. 'This is unfortunate.' She came to a halt beside Elsie. 'We do have an amenity fund. I might be able to organise a small remuneration for you, but I'm afraid it won't be enough to live on, unless you have somewhere to stay that costs next to nothing.'

Elsie rose to her feet. 'I've nowhere to stay. I'm afraid I've wasted your time.' She was about to leave the room but Charlotte barred her way.

'Sit down before you fall down. You're as white as a sheet.' She opened the office door. 'Rosemary, bring us two cups of tea, there's a good chap.' She guided Elsie to the nearest chair. 'When did you last eat?'

'Breakfast, I think. Yes, it was breakfast.'

'And it's now five o'clock. How do you expect to look after refugees if you can't take care of yourself?' Charlotte perched on the edge of her desk, swinging a booted foot and puffing on her cigarette. 'How old are you, Elsie?'

'I'm twenty-one, Miss Greenway.'

'That's something. I thought for a moment you might still be a minor. You look very young, and you're newly arrived from the country. Do you have any friends in London?'

Elsie thought of Marianne but abandoned the idea. She shook her head. 'No.'

'And you have nowhere to stay?'

'No. I was hoping to find a hostel somewhere. Mr Soames said there were such places for working girls.'

'And who is Mr Soames?'

'He's the butler at Darcy Hall, where I was employed in the kitchens, although I'm a trained lady's maid.'

Charlotte looked up as the door opened and Rosemary walked in carrying two tin mugs of tea. She placed them on the desk. 'Is there anything else, Charlie?'

'Not unless you've got any biscuits out there. I think Miss Mead is in need of a little sustenance.'

Rosemary shot a curious glance at Elsie. 'I think there are a couple of ginger nuts in the tin. Will they do?'

'Capital. Bring them in, old thing, and then you'd better pack up for the day. You were here before I was this morning.'

'Thanks, Charlie.' Rosemary winked at Elsie as she left the room, returning seconds later with three ginger nuts on a chipped saucer. 'You can see that we don't waste money on fine china, Miss Mead.'

Elsie managed a weary smile as she took a biscuit. 'Thank you.'

'You look done in, if you don't mind me saying so,' Rosemary said, frowning. 'Have you come far?'

Charlotte took the saucer from her and laid it on her desk. 'Miss Mead has nowhere to stay. Have we got any addresses she might try? Most of the lodging houses will be full but she might be lucky.'

'It's all right,' Elsie said hastily. 'I don't want to put you to any trouble.'

'Have you got enough money to pay for a bed and a hot meal?'

'I don't know why, but I thought it would be provided. I realise I was wrong, but I thought a charity would look after its staff.'

Rosemary chortled with laughter. 'You are fresh from the country, aren't you, Elsie? This is London, my love. Everything costs and most of the ladies who work here are bored rich women who normally wouldn't get out of bed until midday. I'm the exception but I'm an out of work actress and they do pay me a measly few bob for the privilege of being involved in a good cause.'

'Rosemary is paid from the amenities fund, as you will be should you decide to stay. We're very short of helpers who are fluent in any language but their own, and I can't afford to send you back to Dorset.' Charlotte stubbed out her cigarette. 'Come on, Rosie. Surely you must know of a place nearby where Elsie could get a bed for the night?'

'You can come home with me,' Rosemary said with a cheerful grin. 'I rent an attic room in Crawford Street. It's not exactly Buckingham Palace but it's clean and dry. Breakfast and supper are included in the rent. Mrs Crabtree isn't the world's best cook but I've a good supply of milk of magnesia.'

Elsie looked from one to the other, receiving a nod and a smile from Charlotte. 'Rosie has an impish sense of humour, but she'll look after you. Go with her now, Elsie, we'll have another chat in the morning.' She reached for another cigarette. 'I'll see you both at eight o'clock sharp. There's another trainload of refugees to meet at Victoria station at nine and we need to be there early.'

It was raining outside and Rosemary had a brief struggle to unfurl her umbrella, half of which hung limply like a broken arm. She set off along Baker

Street at the quick pace which Elsie had come to recognise as the London walk. Everyone here seemed to be in a tearing hurry to be somewhere else. Their legs worked like pistons as they marched, heads down, towards the tube stations, while others came to a sudden halt at bus stops, tagging on to the end of long queues.

'We'll walk,' Rosemary said firmly. 'It's not far and most of the buses have been commandeered to transport the troops, so the ones that are left are infrequent and overcrowded.'

Elsie was too tired to comment and it took all her concentration to keep up with Rosemary's long strides. The rain trickled off the idly flapping part of the umbrella, soaking the woollen hat that her mother had knitted before the disease consumed her fragile body. Rosemary ploughed on, crossing roads and weaving her way between the traffic with blatant disregard for the danger. Elsie was at once impressed and terrified as the horns of the motor cars blasted in her ears and the shouts of the carters and cabbies merged into an irate chorus.

'Clay Street,' Rosemary said breathlessly. 'We're almost there.'

Elsie's spirits rose as they hurried along Crawford Street. The terraced Georgian houses were well kept and prosperous-looking with an air of quiet respectability, but Rosemary took a turning on the left and they were in a different world. Clay Street was a narrow thoroughfare lined with a mixture of mews cottages, workshops and four-storey buildings of indeterminate age and no particular architectural style. There was a gas lamp at each end of the road, but in between was a pool of damp darkness. Rosemary seemed undeterred and she marched up to one of the taller buildings and knocked on the door. 'Mrs Crabtree doesn't allow us to have a house key,' she said cheerfully. 'But there's always someone who will let me in.' She let down her umbrella and gave it a vigorous shake. 'Someone's coming.'

The door creaked as it opened and they were admitted by a small woman wearing an old-fashioned black bombazine dress. Her grey hair was scraped back into an uncompromising bun, skewered with what looked like a pair of knitting needles. Elsie did not like to stare. 'Who's this, Miss Brown?'

'A friend, Mrs Crabtree. She needs a bed for the night.'

'I got no spare rooms, Miss Brown. You know that as well as the next person.' She stared pointedly at Elsie's suitcase. 'Can't take in no one. Full up.'

'She can sleep on the sofa in my room, Mrs Crabtree. Just for tonight. Miss Mead is new to London and has nowhere else to go.'

'It'll cost you two shillings and that includes supper and breakfast. I can't say fairer than that.'

Elsie was about to protest that Mr Soames had told her she could get a week's lodging for three and six, but Rosemary sent her a warning glance. 'Thank you, Mrs Crabtree. I'm sure that's agreeable, isn't it, Elsie?'

The front door was still open and she could hear the rain beating down on the pavement, and somewhere along the street a gutter was overflowing. Elsie shivered and nodded her head. 'Yes, that's fine, thank you.'

'Well shut the front door then,' Mrs Crabtree said irritably. 'You're letting the damp in and the heat out.' She stomped off along a narrow passageway, disappearing into the dark.

Elsie closed the door. 'It seems a bit expensive to me, Rosemary.'

'This is London, love. You can't afford to be too fussy and there's a war on. Accommodation is hard to find, as you'll discover when you have to help the Belgian refugees. I'd say that's the hardest part of the job, but we do our best. Follow me. It's a bit of a climb but we're young and healthy.' She headed for the stairs and Elsie followed her.

The top landing was narrow and uncarpeted. Their footsteps echoed off the sloping ceiling and they were in almost complete darkness. A small roof window was encrusted with soot and bird droppings and it leaked, but Rosemary did not seem to notice and she walked to the end door, unlocked it and went inside, beckoning to Elsie. 'This is it. Home sweet home.' She lit a gas mantle and it fizzed and popped, sending out a dull yellow light and leaving a distinct odour hanging like mist in the stuffy atmosphere. Propping her wet umbrella up against the wall, she took off her outer garments, tossing them over the back of a chair. 'Make yourself at home, Elsie.' She went down on her hands and knees in front of a small cast-iron fireplace and struck a match, setting light to the twists of paper and kindling. 'It's not too cold, but I do love a fire in the evening. It's extravagant, I know, and it's hard work carting coal up from the cellar, but it's my one bit of comfort and I refuse to do without it, even though old Crabtree charges me twice what it costs her to buy the coal. She's a tight-fisted old skinflint.' She sat back on her haunches watching the flames lick up the chimney. 'Supper is at six sharp, so we have to be downstairs a bit earlier or we won't get a seat at the main table. If we have to sit by the window we get the leftovers, and they're always cold.'

Elsie took off her wet garments and copied Rosemary by hanging them over the back of the second of the two kitchen chairs set around the small pine table. She glanced around the room, which appeared to have been furnished from second-hand shops and auction sales. Nothing matched, and the single bed had one leg propped up on a brick. Rosemary's clothes hung on what looked like a washing line strung between two beams and the only other furniture was a chest of drawers and a sofa that sagged in the middle, and was draped with an old patchwork quilt. 'It's very kind of you to put me up like this,' she murmured, wondering how Rosemary could bear to live in such a dingy, colourless room.

'I'm glad of the company.' Rosemary leaned forward to pick lumps of coal from the scuttle with a pair of tongs. 'And to tell the truth I was a bit like you when I first came to London.'

'Where did you live before you came here?' Elsie moved to the sofa and sat down.

'I grew up in Essex. We had a nice place in Leytonstone, but then my father was painting a house and the scaffolding broke. He died a week later in hospital.'

'I'm so sorry. That's dreadful.'

Rosemary nodded. 'It was such a blow, and then a year later my mother remarried. I tried to like Albert but we just didn't get along, and then one day when Mum was out he . . .' Rosemary broke off, taking a deep breath. 'Well, he behaved towards me in a way that wasn't how a stepfather should treat his daughter.'

'What did you do then?'

'I slapped his face and I told Mum, but she didn't believe me, and he was a good liar. I packed a bag that night and went to stay with my gran in Walthamstow. She paid for me to learn shorthand and typing, but then last year she died and I was all alone. I applied for a job in a law office in Lincoln's Inn and that's where I met Charlie. She's a qualified solicitor, but she gave it up at the outbreak of war and joined the Women's Emergency Corps.'

'She gave up a well-paid job?'

'She has independent means. Her father is a High Court judge and her mother is a member of the

Women's Social and Political Union. Charlie talks about the Pankhursts as though they were part of her family, but she's a brick and I'd do anything for her.' Rosemary piled more coal on the fire and stood up, shaking out her skirts. She glanced at the clock on the mantelpiece. 'Look at the time. I'd better show you where the bathroom is. I hope you brought a towel with you; Mrs C doesn't supply linen. Then we should get down to the dining room before the travelling salesmen get there. You'd think they hadn't eaten for days the way they shove food into their mouths, and then there are the permanent lodgers, they're even worse. You have to be quick here – it's boarding house reach, as my mum used to say.' She hurried to the door and held it open. 'Come on, Elsie. This will be an experience you won't forget in a hurry.'

The bathroom was on the first floor and there was a separate lavatory next door. 'Mrs C is proud of her bathroom,' Rosemary said, chuckling. 'The enamel's worn off inside the bath and it scrapes your bottom when you sit down, so be careful. Oh, and there's only hot water first thing in the morning and early in the evening, so you've got to be quick if you want a warm bath. There's always a queue, so you have to judge your timing as this is the one and only bathroom. There's another lavatory in the back yard if you're desperate.'

'We had a zinc tub in front of the fire at home,' Elsie said, smiling. 'And the privy was in a little shed built over a stream. You can imagine the rest.'

'C'mon,' Rosemary said, tugging at her hand. 'Let's get to the dining room before the men. It's stew with sinkers.'

'Sinkers? What are they?'

'Dumplings, but when Mrs C makes them they really are sinkers. They're heavy and floury but they're filling, so eat as many as you can because there's precious little meat in the stew and not too many vegetables either.'

The sinkers lay heavily in Elsie's stomach, but she managed to get some sleep on the lumpy sofa, even though the springs stuck into her each time she moved. She awakened to find Rosemary up and dressed. 'If you hurry you might get to the bathroom before the others,' she said cheerfully. 'They're a lazy lot and lie in bed until the last moment.'

Wearing a borrowed bathrobe, Elsie raced downstairs to the first floor and just managed to slip into the bathroom before a sleepy-looking middle-aged man who complained loudly as he stood outside the door. She gave him an apologetic smile when she emerged, having had a strip wash in tepid water. He muttered something under his breath and slammed the door. 'I'll get up earlier tomorrow,' she murmured as she went upstairs. She paused when she reached the top landing, wondering if she could start work and find alternative accommodation at the same time.

Back in the room she found Rosemary waiting for

her. 'Hurry up and get dressed, Elsie. It's the same at breakfast as it is in the evening.'

'I hope it's not toasted sinkers,' Elsie said, pulling a face.

'Well, tonight it's mince followed by spotted dick and custard, and tomorrow it'll be fish cakes and bread and butter pudding.'

'I can't wait.' Elsie hopped on one leg as she pulled on her stocking. 'Does that mean you want me to stay?'

'It's rather nice to have company, and maybe Mrs C will do a deal with the rent as we're sharing. That is if you don't mind sleeping on that awful sofa.'

'I don't want to put you out, Rosemary.'

'Nonsense. There's a war on; we've got to help each other.'

Elsie started work that morning. She and a group of French-speaking volunteers were sent to Victoria station to meet the exhausted and overwrought refugees, most of whom were women and children, and some frail and elderly men. Their needs were as varied as their stories, and they were touchingly pleased to find someone who could speak their own language. Elsie was very much the new girl and for the first few days she worked alongside a more experienced charity worker. Being unfamiliar with London it took her some time to find her way around, but she was quick to learn and eager to help the people displaced through no fault of their own.

After a fortnight, her mentor decided to let Elsie deal with a mother and her six children who had been travelling for days and wore the dazed look she had seen on so many faces. Armed with a list of cheap lodging houses and families who were willing to give homes to the displaced victims of war, Elsie did her best to get the family settled in their new accommodation. It was rewarding but exhausting work and she returned to the lodging house each evening too tired even to eat, although it was not too much of a hardship to forgo Mrs Crabtree's culinary efforts. She existed on tea and toast, which she made in front of the fire in the attic room, supplemented by bowls of broth from the soup kitchens set up to feed the hungry refugees. At night she slept as best she could on the uncomfortable sofa and awakened each morning with backache and a stiff neck, but she could not afford to rent a room of her own and she was grateful to Rosemary for allowing her to stay.

It was not easy sharing such a small space, and as there were no laundry facilities in Mrs Crabtree's establishment the girls were forced to wash their undies and stockings in the bath and hang them over a rickety old clothes horse that Rosemary had bought in a second-hand shop. Condensation dripped off the walls and by the middle of December Elsie had developed a chesty cough that refused to go away, despite copious doses of Owbridge's Lung Tonic.

'You should see a doctor,' Rosemary said one morning as she pulled on her clothes. The temperature in the attic had dropped dramatically during the night and ice frosted the inside of the dormer window. 'You don't want to be ill at Christmas.'

Elsie sneezed into a handkerchief. 'I'm all right. It's just a cold.'

'You'd better watch out you don't go down with lung fever like your poor ma,' Rosemary said gloomily. She sat down to put on her stockings. 'I'm going to my cousin's house for the festivities. You won't be staying here, will you?'

'I expect so, but I'll probably catch up on my sleep. I can't think of anything I'd like more than a day in bed with nothing to do.'

Rosemary eyed her with a worried frown. 'It won't be much fun here. I'd ask you to join us, but Jessie has a large family and a small house in Barkingside.'

'Don't worry about me. I'll be fine, really.' Elsie's teeth were chattering so loudly that it was almost impossible to talk and she finished dressing in silence.

'Tell you what,' Rosemary said eagerly. 'I'm going to Oxford Street at midday. I love Selfridge's and I could die happy in the perfume department just breathing in all those glorious scents. Anyway, I'm going to buy a small present for Jessie, and I'd value your advice.'

Elsie knew that she would not get out of it easily and she nodded. 'All right. As it happens I'm just

72

doing house calls this morning to make sure my families have got everything they need. I'll meet you there.'

'One o'clock,' Rosemary said, smiling. 'We might not be able to afford to buy anything much but we can pretend.'

Business as usual. The sign in the window of Selfridge's made Elsie smile, despite her sore throat and runny eyes. She had only ventured a few times to the busy thoroughfare of Oxford Street with its large department stores and bustling crowds, and it gave her a thrill to see the lavish window displays. She had found London overwhelming at first but she was becoming accustomed to the fast pace of life, and even though she had no money to spend on luxuries she took pleasure in simply looking at the items that only the wealthy could afford. She saw Elsie and waved as she hurried to meet her.

It was warm inside the store and they were almost overwhelmed by a heady mixture of expensive perfumes and toiletries. A neatly dressed shop assistant held up an atomiser filled with golden liquid and puffed a little of it in Elsie's direction. 'Would Madam care to try our latest acquisition from Paris?'

Elsie shook her head. 'No, thank you.' She took a step backward, although she would have loved to try the perfume, but she had only a few pennies in her purse.

'I will,' Rosemary said, peeling off her glove and exposing her slim wrist.

The shop assistant beamed at her and squeezed the silk-covered bulb, spraying Rosemary with expensive French perfume. 'Madam has good taste. A bottle of this would make a wonderful Christmas present, and with the war in France who knows when we will get fresh supplies.'

Rosemary sniffed her wrist with closed eyes and a beatific expression on her plain features. 'I'll have to find a rich gentleman friend to buy it for me. Ta, love.' She walked on, taking Elsie by the arm.

'The only blokes I meet wouldn't know a French perfume from a bottle of brown ale,' she said, giggling. 'One day I'll find a man who'll treat me like a princess.' She stopped suddenly, squeezing Elsie's wrist. 'Like him over there. I bet he's buying that big bottle of scent for his lady friend.'

Elsie looked round and her heart lurched against her ribs. 'Henri,' she murmured.

'Do you know him?' Rosemary stared at her in amazement. 'Surely not. Look at the cut of his coat. I bet it's cashmere, and those cufflinks he's wearing must be solid gold.'

'I don't know him well.' Elsie experienced a feeling of panic. She must look a fright in her shabby overcoat and woollen hat, and a runny nose and red eyes would not improve her appearance. She did not want Henri Bellaire to see her in this state and she put her head down as she attempted to hurry past, giving him a wary sideways glance. But for some reason best known to him, he looked up and saw her. His smile dazzled her, and judging by Rosemary's reaction she felt exactly the same. 'Cor,' she whispered. 'He's the best-looking toff in the store.'

'Elsie.' Henri walked towards them, holding out his hand. 'How nice to see you again. I didn't know you were in London.'

'I'm working here now,' Elsie said shyly.

'No, really? I didn't realise you had left Darcy Hall.' Henri turned to Rosemary with a charming smile. 'Henri Bellaire, mademoiselle.'

'Ooer,' Rosemary said, blushing. 'How do, sir. I'm Rosemary Brown.'

'Enchanté,' Henri said gallantly.

Rosemary shot Elsie a mischievous smile. 'I'd better look for that present, Elsie. I'll see you later.'

'No, don't go,' Elsie said hastily, but Rosemary was already weaving her way through the crowds. She glanced up at Henri and was about to speak when a bout of coughing made it difficult to catch her breath.

'You are unwell.' Henri's brow puckered in a worried frown. 'You should not be out on such a day as this.' He glanced out of the window at the rain bouncing off the pavements into the overflowing gutters. 'Where do you live?'

'Not too far from here, but I'm quite all right, thank you. It's just a cold.'

He looked at her more closely. 'I don't think so,

Elsie. I am not a doctor but I'd say you have a fever. You must allow me to see you home.'

The mere thought of Henri visiting the cramped attic room she shared with Rosemary made her feel ten times worse. Her head ached and her throat was sore, and her limbs felt leaden, but she had no intention of allowing him to take her to Clay Street. 'It's very nice to see you, Henri. But I couldn't take you out of your way.'

He took her by the elbow, propelling her towards the glass doors. 'At least allow me to hail a cab.'

'I'll take the omnibus to Baker Street. I have to work this afternoon.'

'You're in no condition to travel on public transport or to return to work.' He opened the door and escorted her out into the blustery street, where he hailed a cab. 'Where do you live?'

'Clay Street, Marylebone.'

He repeated the address to the cabby and helped her into the cab, climbing in to sit beside her. 'I would never forgive myself if I allowed you to make your own way home on such a day, when you are obviously unwell.'

She had thought he would drop her outside the lodging house but he insisted on seeing her to her room, and she could tell by his tight-lipped silence that he was shocked. She unlocked the door but she did not invite him in. 'Thank you for bringing me home. I'll be all right now.'

He glanced over her shoulder and his frown deepened. 'This is not good, chérie. Why do you live like this?'

She met his horrified look with a steady gaze. 'This is all I can afford, but it's fine. Rosemary and I share the room and we keep each other company.'

'Two of you share this dreadful place?'

'It's clean and it's cheap. I don't want to sound ungrateful, but perhaps you should go now.'

'Marianne would be shocked if she could see how you are forced to live.'

'With respect, it's nothing to do with you or Miss Marianne, and this is luxury compared to how some of the Belgian refugees have to exist. Thank you again, Henri. Goodbye.' She slipped into the room and closed the door before he had a chance to argue, sliding the bolt across in case he tried the handle. She waited, listening with her ear to the wide crack in one of the panels, and after a few moments she heard his footsteps retreating down the stairs. Breathing a sigh of relief, she made her way to the sofa. She did not want charity from anyone, nor their pity. She had made a life for herself in London and she was doing a worthwhile job. She just needed to shake off the cough and cold and then she would be fine.

She was awakened from a deep sleep by someone hammering on the door. At first she thought it was part of her dream, in which she had been running away from a nameless person who had chased her through a dark forest and along a muddy riverbed where her feet kept getting stuck in the thick black silt. Someone was calling her name and she recognised the voice.

'Elsie, open the door, please. I know you're in there and I only want to make sure that you're all right.'

Chapter Five

Drunk with sleep and a large dose of cough linctus, Elsie moved groggily to the door and drew back the bolt. She stepped aside as Marianne swooped into the room, stopping with a dramatic wave of her hands as she took in her surroundings. 'My God, what a hole! Henri was right.'

'What are you doing here, Miss Marianne?'

'I came to see you, of course. Henri told me you were sick and that you were living in a hovel but I thought he was exaggerating. You know how the French are.' She looked with distaste at Rosemary's unmade bed and the rumpled coverlet on the sofa. 'Why didn't you come to me, Elsie? I would have helped you find better accommodation than this rat's nest.'

'I didn't know where to find you, and anyway, why would you care what happens to me? I'm not your responsibility. I can look after myself.'

'You're ill. It's quite obvious and no wonder, living in a slum like this.' Marianne fingered a damp stocking as it hung limply on the clothes horse. 'The war is changing everything, and if women can do the same work as men for the same pay then all this inequality will disappear. You might not believe this, but I myself have a job.'

Elsie sank down on the sofa, staring at Marian wide-eyed. 'You go out to work?'

'Yes, I'm a secretary at the War Office. Of course I had to bluff my way in as I can't type and I've no idea how to write shorthand, but I'm managing very well.' She hesitated, staring hard at Elsie. 'I'm assuming you must have found employment of some kind too.'

'I'm an interpreter, helping the Belgian refugees.'

'Good for you. But it obviously doesn't pay very well.'

Silenced by a bout of coughing, Elsie shook her head.

Marianne sat down beside her. 'Look, Elsie. I don't want to patronise you or to interfere in your life, but you and I grew up in the same village. You might say that we're sisters under the skin, and I don't like leaving you in a place like this when you're obviously unwell.'

'I'll be all right,' Elsie murmured, sneezing into a hanky. 'I've got the rest of the day off.'

'It's less than a week until Christmas. Have you anywhere to go other than here?'

'I'm working every day and I'm helping to organise a party for the refugees in the East End on Christmas Eve.'

'I'm staying in a lovely large flat in Cromwell Road. Anthea's aunt is a darling and very public-spirited – she's gone to France to entertain the troops.' Marianne rose to her feet with a determined look on her pretty face. 'I can't leave you here like this. You must come with me now and spend Christmas with us.'

Elsie was momentarily lost for words. 'I – I have to go to work.'

'Nonsense, you're sick. I'd be happy to telephone your boss and explain.'

'It's very kind of you, but I can't impose. Besides which, your friend might object.'

'Anthea will be off somewhere with her boyfriend, Tubby McAvoy, and Henri is returning to France in the morning, so I'll be left all alone.' Marianne held out her hand. 'Come on, Elsie. Leave a note for your friend and pack a few things in a bag. I'm not leaving you here, and that's that.'

Felicia Wilby's flat was situated on the third floor of a five-storey terrace built in the last quarter of the nineteenth century, or so the caretaker informed Elsie at length when they arrived at the house in Cromwell Road. He encompassed the echoing marble-tiled entrance hall with a wave of his hand. 'This establishment has electricity and internal plumbing,' he said proudly. 'Leave your luggage and I'll send the boy up with it when he returns from his errand.'

'Thank you, Bailey,' Marianne said, meeting his curious gaze with a smile as she dropped Elsie's cardboard suitcase at his feet. 'Come along, Elsie. There are quite a lot of stairs to climb to the third floor.'

Elsie followed her to the foot of the wide marble staircase. Looking up, she could see a seemingly endless set of landings framed by iron banisters and polished mahogany balustrades. As they made their way upwards Elsie could only be glad that Miss Wilby's flat was on the third floor and not at the top of the building. Marianne was ahead of her but moving slowly, hampered by her hobble skirt and muttering about the impracticability of such a stupid fashion. 'Why can't we wear trousers like men?' She rang the doorbell. 'I must get Felicia to give me a key.'

A maidservant ushered them in. 'Miss Wilby is in the drawing room, Miss Winter.'

Elsie looked round in awe. The main entrance hall might be on a grand scale, but this much smaller version was decorated and furnished in a style that she recognised as art nouveau. In quiet moments, when there was no danger of being caught idling by Mrs Tranter, she had leafed through Josephine Winter's magazines and had admired such glamorous interiors.

The manor house was grand in its own way, but Felicia Wilby's home spoke of taste, refinement and above all, money. The walls were painted off-white, and the parquet floor was stained and varnished to a glassy sheen. Crystal chandeliers had been replaced by rainbow-coloured Tiffany lampshades, and rather odd-shaped chairs, with high backs shining with black lacquer, stood sentinel either side of the double doors which led into the drawing room.

Anthea Wilby was sitting in a chintz-covered armchair, reading a book. She looked up and smiled. 'Marianne. I was beginning to wonder where you'd got to, and I see you've brought a friend with you.'

'Anthea, this is Elsie Mead. She's the brilliant person who bobbed my hair.'

Anthea rose to her feet and shook Elsie's hand. 'How do you do, Elsie? You might like to have a go at mine sometime. I'm sick of having hair down to my waist.'

'Leave her alone, Anthea. The poor thing has the most ghastly cough and cold. I just hope it isn't flu. Anyway, she needs looking after and I thought she could have the spare room for a few days.'

'Absolutely fine by me, darling. I'll be out most of the time anyway. Tubby's making noises about joining the Royal Flying Corps and I'm trying to dissuade him. I'd rather have a live boyfriend than a dead hero.'

'Wouldn't we all?' Marianne said, chuckling. She turned to Elsie with a bright smile. 'I'll show you your room. Bailey should have sent your luggage up by now. He's a pet but don't get him talking or he'll never stop.' She opened the door and led Elsie to a room at the end of a wide corridor. 'This is yours,' she said, ushering her inside. 'The bathroom is opposite, and I'm next door, so if you need anything you only have to call out.'

'Thank you, Miss Marianne.'

'It's just Marianne. We're both working girls now, so we're equal.' Marianne patted her on the shoulder. 'A couple of days' rest and a comfy bed will do wonders for you, old thing. Dinner's at seven thirty, but do join us in the drawing room when you feel up to it.'

'Thank you, Marianne. I really am grateful.' Elsie stepped over the threshold with an involuntary gasp of surprise and pleasure. Somehow she had expected to be consigned to a box room at best, and it was hard to believe that this light, airy space was for her alone. The stylised rose pattern of the wallpaper was repeated in the curtains and the upholstery of the chaise longue placed beneath the tall window. Down below she could hear the traffic in the busy Cromwell Road, and found it oddly comforting. She turned to examine the burr-walnut dressing table, which boasted a triple mirror, and, as if that was not luxury enough, there was also a tall cheval glass. She tested the bed, perching on the edge of the mattress. It was soft and yet springy, and the sheets were the finest Egyptian cotton, and the coverlet quilted pink satin. She had to pinch her arm to realise she was not dreaming, but to have a double bed to herself seemed almost sinful. Not so long ago she had slept on straw-filled sacks on the dirt floor of Tan Cottage.

After several days in bed, Elsie woke up one morning feeling much better, and after a luxurious bath in an elegant modern bathroom with a seemingly endless supply of hot water, she dried herself on soft fluffy towels. She dressed, brushed her hair and made her way to the dining room. Marianne and Anthea were just finishing their breakfasts.

'You're up,' Marianne said, buttering a slice of toast. 'You look more like your old self.'

'I feel a million times better,' Elsie said, smiling. 'I've never felt so pampered in my whole life.'

Anthea glanced at the clock on the mantelpiece. 'Golly, is it that time already?' She jumped up from the table and brushed crumbs from her uniform jacket. 'It's time I wasn't here.' She gave Elsie a friendly smile. 'You're looking well. Quite different from the poor bedraggled creature you were when you arrived.'

'I feel so much better; thanks to you both.'

'It's good to see you up and about. Sit down and have some breakfast.' Marianne raised a teacup to her lips, sipped, and put it down with a clatter. 'I'm off in a minute as well, but I hope we're finishing early as it's Christmas Eve.'

'Toodle-pip, old thing,' Anthea said, making for the door. 'I've got to dash because I'm on duty in fifteen minutes. I'll see you at Frascati's this evening.' She rushed out of the room.

'What does she do?' Elsie asked curiously.

'She's a despatch rider. Tubby has a motorcycle and he taught her how to ride, so she applied for the job and got it.' Marianne put her cup back on its saucer. 'We're all doing war work of one kind or another.'

'And you're a secretary at the War Office?'

'I am indeed. Anyway, about this evening, you'll come with us, won't you, Elsie?'

Elsie took her seat at the table. In front of her a boiled egg sat beneath an embroidered cosy. She looked up, startled. 'I'm sorry. I don't know what you're talking about.'

'I thought I told you about it, but maybe I forgot. Anyway, it's a Christmas party at Frascati's. Do you know it?'

Elsie took the cover off her egg and tapped the top with a spoon. 'The only places I know in London are the Lyons teashops.'

'Then this will be an experience. It's a very nice restaurant.'

'You're not serious, are you?'

Marianne raised an eyebrow. 'Why wouldn't I be?'

'It's awfully kind of you and Anthea to have me here, but I don't expect to be included in your social life.'

'Surely you don't want to stay in the flat with Cook? Even Violet is going out on Christmas Eve.'

Elsie sliced the top off her egg. 'I don't know any of your friends and I haven't got anything to wear.'

'You know Anthea, and you'll meet Tubby, he's a hoot. Then there's Algy, my date for this evening, and there'll probably be one or two others.'

'It's very nice of you to invite me, but . . .'

'No buts. You're coming with us, Elsie. I've got a wardrobe full of evening dresses and you can borrow one if you like. We're much the same size and height.' Marianne's determined expression melted into a persuasive smile. 'Come on, Elsie. Say you'll come. Anyway, you'll be doing me a favour because one of the girls at work has dropped out, and you'll even up the numbers.'

Elsie paused with the spoon halfway to her lips. 'Put like that, how can I refuse?'

'Good girl. You might even enjoy it.' Marianne stood up and reached for her handbag. Despite what Marianne had said about her lack of training, Elsie thought that she looked every inch the efficient secretary in a high-necked cream blouse worn beneath a smart and doubtless very expensive navy-blue two-piece. Marianne's bobbed blonde hair shone like silk, and a touch of rouge on her cheeks and a hint of lipstick emphasised the delicate bloom of youth and good health. 'I'm a complete fraud,' she said, smiling. 'I can only type with two fingers and I write in longhand, telling my boss off if he dictates too fast, but somehow I muddle along.' She looked round as the door opened and Violet sidled into the room. 'We're not ready to clear the table yet, Violet.'

'It's not that, miss. I wanted to catch you before you left for work.'

'Can't it wait? I'll be late if I don't hurry.'

'It's just that I want to give a week's notice, miss.'

Violet eyed her warily. 'I've got a job in munitions at Woolwich Arsenal.'

'Good heavens, why?'

'The pay is good, and I can live at home. I'll be doing my duty for king and country too.'

Marianne shrugged her shoulders. 'Oh, well. Jolly good for you. I'm sure we'll manage. Now I really must fly.' She hesitated in the doorway. 'Miss Mead will be borrowing one of my evening dresses, Violet. Could you show her where they are?'

'Yes, miss. Of course.' Violet waited until Marianne had left the room. She picked up the coffee pot. 'Would you like some fresh coffee, miss?'

'Yes, please.' Elsie plucked a slice of toast from the silver rack. 'Where do your family live, Violet?'

'In Woolwich, miss. That's why I want to work nearer home. Mum hasn't been too well and I could help with the nippers.'

'I expect you'd like to be with them today, wouldn't you?'

'I have to work, miss.'

'I think you should go home and be with your family. I'll do whatever it is you usually do.'

Violet stared at her wide-eyed. 'You're joking, miss.'

'I'm deadly serious. I've nothing to do today and you can't teach me anything about cleaning and housework. Go home, Violet. Enjoy your family Christmas.'

'What will Miss Winter say?'

'Leave Miss Winter to me.'

'It's really kind of you, miss. I dunno if I ought to, but if you're sure . . .'

'I'm quite sure.'

'I'll show you Miss Winter's wardrobe first, and then I'll introduce you to Cook. She's a nice old soul, and easy to get on with as long as you don't get in her way.'

'I'm sure I'll manage.'

That evening the hackney carriage dropped Marianne and Elsie off outside Frascati's restaurant in Oxford Street, and the doorman rushed forward to shield them from the rain with his umbrella. The weather might be cold and wet but warmth and light enveloped them as they entered the magnificent vestibule. Columns sculpted with caryatids supported the arched ceiling, and crystal chandeliers spread pools of shimmering light on the thick red carpet. The air was redolent with the fragrance of expensive perfume and pomade. Their outer garments were spirited off by a cloakroom attendant and they were escorted into the Winter Garden where Marianne's friend Algy waited to greet them. He kissed Marianne on the cheek but when he saw Elsie he looked from one to the other in amazement. 'You didn't tell me you had a sister, Marianne.'

'It's a common mistake,' she said airily. 'This is my childhood friend, Elsie Mead.' She turned to Elsie with an encouraging smile. 'And this of course is Algernon Fortescue-Brown, known to his friends as Algy.'

He took Elsie's hand with a courtly bow. 'How do you do, Miss Mead? I'm so sorry to stare, but the likeness is quite astonishing. You might well be twins.'

'How do you do?' Elsie wondered vaguely if she was supposed to curtsey, but Algy's friendly manner was disarming and she smiled. 'A lot of people have said so but we can't see it ourselves.'

'I'm dying for a drink, darling,' Marianne said sweetly. 'You promised me nothing but champagne this evening. Remember?'

'Of course. Nothing but the best for you, Marianne, my dear.' He proffered an arm to each of them. 'What a lucky chap I am to have the company of two beautiful young ladies.'

'You're a dreadful flatterer,' Marianne said, smiling. 'But it's only the truth, after all.' She shot a sideways glance at Elsie when they reached their table on the edge of the dance floor. 'I hate to admit it, but you look far better in that gown than I ever did.'

'I don't believe that for a second,' Elsie said, chuckling. 'But thank you, Marianne. I really appreciate all this.'

'What are you two talking about?' Algy demanded, handing them each a glass of champagne.

'Nothing important,' Marianne said, raising her glass. 'Happy Christmas, darling.'

Elsie echoed the toast and took a seat, watching the couples gyrating on the dance floor. Music and laughter filled the air and clouds of cigarette and cigar smoke wafted upwards into the glass dome. She looked round at the well-dressed people who were out to enjoy themselves, seemingly oblivious to the fact that war was raging on the other side of the English Channel, and that the rain beating down on London might also be drenching the troops in the trenches. Everyone, it seemed, including Marianne and Algy, was laughing and chatting as if nothing in the world would ever change. She looked up with a start as Anthea arrived at their table with Tubby in tow. 'Merry Christmas, everyone,' she said, smiling. 'This is lovely, Algy. How kind of you to invite us to your party.'

He rose to his feet, holding out a chair for her. 'Thank you for coming, Anthea. I see you've brought old Tubby with you.'

'Less of the old,' Tubby said, grinning.

'We're an odd number, Algy,' Marianne said, looking round. 'I thought you'd invited one of your eligible bachelor friends?'

'I did and he's just arrived.' Algy waved to a man who was threading his way through the crowd. 'I invited Guy Gifford. He's a good chap, but he keeps himself to himself. I thought this might bring him out of his shell. He doesn't seem to have much of a social life.' He moved towards him holding out his hand. 'Guy, old chap. Glad you could make it.'

'I didn't realise it was such a formal party, Algy.' Guy cast an anxious eye over the men's evening dress. 'I came straight from the office and didn't have time to change.'

Elsie sensed his discomfort, even though he hid it well. Marianne's friends had been charm itself, but she still felt like the odd one out.

'Never mind, old chap. It's my fault; I should have put you straight.' Algy slapped him on the back. 'I think you know everyone, except this lovely young lady, who's a friend of Marianne's. Elsie Mead, Guy Gifford.'

'How do you do?' Elsie was not sure whether etiquette required her to shake hands with a strange man, but she held hers out.

'How do you do?' Guy shook her hand and his features were transformed by a charming smile. Elsie warmed to him instantly. No one could call him handsome, but he had nice eyes. She could not decide whether they were brown or hazel, and his softly waving hair was a shade between dark blond and warm chestnut. He was the sort of man it would be easy to walk past in the street, but his smile would be hard to forget.

'There's an empty chair beside Elsie.' Algy patted Guy on the shoulder. 'Sit down and have a glass of bubbly.'

'It's nice to see you again, Guy.' Marianne turned to Algy, holding up her empty glass. 'Top-up, please, darling. It is Christmas and we have to enjoy ourselves. It's compulsory, especially in wartime.'

'You do talk a lot of rot, Marianne,' Anthea said, chuckling. 'I'd like to dance. How about it, Tubby?'

'Of course, my dear. Only too happy to oblige.'

He rose to his feet and led her onto the dance floor.

Guy sat down beside Elsie. 'This isn't really my sort of thing, as you might have guessed.'

'It's not mine either.'

He seemed to relax and the tension lines on his forehead smoothed out. 'That makes me feel much better. Would you like to dance, Miss Mead?'

'It's Elsie, and you might be sorry you asked if I tried to do this one. I used to go to dances in the village hall, but it wasn't anything like this. It's a foxtrot, isn't it?'

'Actually I think it's a one-step.' He stood up, holding out his hand. 'Let's try, shall we? To tell the truth I'm not very good on the dance floor either.'

Surprisingly, and probably because there was not much space in which the couples could perform, Elsie managed to follow Guy's movements without treading on his toes and she began to enjoy herself. She was about to walk back to their table when the music finished, but the orchestra struck up again almost immediately, and Guy tightened his hold on her hand.

'This is one I can do without fear of harming anyone. Shall we show them how it's done?'

'Why not?' This time she found herself clasped to his chest as they twirled round to the strains of a Viennese waltz.

'You're a very good dancer, Elsie.'

'I'm just following whatever you do.'

'That's what makes you a good dancer. You make me feel that I'm good at it too.'

She looked into his eyes and smiled. 'I was dreading this evening, but I'm glad I came now.'

'Me too.'

She was suddenly serious. 'But I had promised to attend a party in the East End for the Belgian refugees. I feel very bad about letting them down, although I don't suppose they'll miss me.'

'It's a worthy cause. How did you get involved?'

'I'm an interpreter.'

'I'm impressed. Do you speak French and Flemish?'

'My mother was French and it was my first language, but I don't speak Flemish.'

'And you obviously enjoy your work.'

'Yes, I do, and I admire the people we try to help. They're wonderfully resilient and brave, especially when you think that they've lost everything and had to leave loved ones behind.'

'Would you like to go to the party for your Belgian friends?'

'I would, awfully.'

He stopped in the middle of the dance. 'Then that's what we'll do. This overt hedonism doesn't seem right in the face of what others are suffering at the moment.'

'You want to come with me?'

'I wouldn't dream of letting you venture into the East End on your own at this time of night. Shall we go?'

Chapter Six

The church hall was situated in a grimy East End back street. Elsie felt distinctly overdressed for the occasion as she stepped down from the hackney carriage. The rain had ceased but the wet cobblestones were slicked with faint pools of oily light from the gas lamps. The door opened and a woman emerged carrying a sleeping child in her arms. Elsie recognised her at once and stepped forward. 'You're leaving the party early, Jeanne,' she said in French.

The woman nodded and gave her a weary smile. 'The little one is tired. I'm taking him back to the lodging house.'

'Is everything all right? Have you all you need?' Elsie studied the woman's face. She looked pale and drawn and there were dark shadows underlining her eyes. 'Have you eaten today?'

'Yes. I have no complaints.'

'You look exhausted.'

'It's hard with young children, but we will manage. God permitting we will be able to return home before too long.'

'Amen to that.' Elsie patted her on the shoulder. 'Get the little one home, and I'll call on you soon.

You must let me know if there is anything I can do to help.'

'Thank you.' Jeanne cast a sideways glance at Guy and walked away.

'You're doing a difficult job,' he said, holding the door open for her. 'But I suppose it has its rewards.'

'At least I'm doing something worthwhile, although I wish I could do more.' Elsie entered the building and her nostrils were assailed by cigarette smoke, the hoppy aroma of beer and a curious mixture of hard-boiled eggs and pickled onions. One look at the table laid out with the food was enough to convince her that the volunteers had done their best, but it was hardly up to Frascati's standards. They had not stopped to dine, although she had seen people eating delicious-looking food, which in itself seemed wrong when others were starving. She was hungry, but she did not want to take food from the mouths of people whose need was far greater than her own. The fare might be plain but it seemed to be going down well with the partygoers. The children in particular were digging into the rather stodgy-looking cake, and the sausage rolls were disappearing fast. The vicar came forward to welcome them. He eyed Guy curiously. 'I see you've brought a friend, Elsie.'

'Mr Gifford was kind enough to escort me, Joe.' She pulled her coat round her to hide Marianne's expensive evening gown, even though it was hot and stuffy in the crowded hall. 'We were at another Christmas party.'

'I understand, my dear. There's no need to feel awkward. I'm sure our Belgian guests wouldn't begrudge their good friend an evening of relaxation. Why don't you take your coat off and have a glass of punch? There's not much alcohol in it but it's quite palatable.' He turned to Guy. 'May I get you a glass of beer, Mr Gifford?'

'Thank you,' Guy said affably. 'A beer would be most welcome, and it's Guy.'

'John Johnson.' The vicar seized Guy's hand and shook it. 'But everyone calls me Joe.' He strolled off in the direction of the makeshift bar.

Elsie waited until he was out of earshot. 'I'm sure you didn't mean that.'

'Actually I prefer beer to champagne, and even if I didn't I would not want to offend the good vicar. He's obviously doing his best to look after his adopted flock, and it can't be easy.'

'He's a good man,' Elsie said, nodding. 'And his wife is an excellent woman. She works tirelessly for the poor and needy and this is not a rich parish. I admire them both tremendously.'

'One thing puzzles me, Elsie,' he said slowly. 'Don't take this the wrong way, but I don't understand your relationship with Marianne. You two may have a passing physical resemblance but you are complete opposites.'

'Marianne is a good friend,' Elsie said defensively. 'She's been kind to me since my mother died last summer.'

'I didn't know. I'm sorry.'

'Thank you. I'm coming to terms with it now, but it was a terrible shock.' She glanced down at the expensive dress in pale pink chiffon embroidered all over with glass bugle beads, created no doubt by a fashionable designer. 'This isn't the real me, Guy. I borrowed this gown from Marianne. I was a lady's maid and then I took over my mother's job, charring at Darcy Hall. That's how I know Marianne. I'm not one of her set.'

He threw back his head and laughed. 'Neither am I, come to that. I have a fairly menial position in the War Office, and I was a grammar school boy. Tubby and Algy are old Etonians.'

Elsie was about to answer but a group of children had spotted her and they abandoned the food table to cluster round her. She laughed, urging them to speak one at a time and returning hugs from the younger ones while paying due attention to their older siblings. Guy sipped his beer, and even though she sensed that he was watching her she felt comfortable in his presence. She looked up and smiled at him over the children's heads, but before she had a chance to say anything her attention was claimed by several of the mothers who wanted to talk to her.

In the end it was the vicar's wife who came to her rescue. She spoke in rapid French to the group who had gathered around Elsie, and somewhat unwillingly they dispersed. 'Miss Mead will be back after Christmas,' Mrs Johnson said firmly. 'Enjoy the party, ladies. And children, you must leave some cake for everyone else. We don't want you being sick all night or crying with tummy ache.'

Joe returned, having separated two boys who were fighting and made them shake hands. He embraced Elsie warmly. 'Thank you for coming to join us tonight, my dear. These poor souls must gain comfort from the fact that someone cares enough for their welfare to abandon their own Christmas party in order to spend time with them.'

Elsie realised that she had allowed her coat to fall open, revealing the evening gown. 'I'm sorry. I didn't want to show off, and it's not mine, Joe. It's borrowed.'

He smiled. 'Don't apologise, Elsie. You're young and you have every right to enjoy yourself. Don't you agree, Guy?'

'I do indeed, but I'm not really part of this. I feel that I ought to go, but I don't want to leave Elsie without someone to escort her home.'

'Of course you must go if you want to, but I'm staying,' Elsie said firmly.

'It's a rough area,' he said in a low voice.

'Don't worry, Guy. We'll make sure that Elsie gets a cab back to Cromwell Road.' Joe turned to his wife. 'I think you should take your place at the piano, my dear. The older children will hopefully wear off some of their energy by dancing.'

'Of course.' Mrs Johnson smiled and patted Guy on the arm. 'Don't worry about Elsie. She'll be quite safe with us.' She made her way to a rather battered-looking upright piano at the far end of the hall, next to which stood a spindly Christmas tree decorated with paper streamers and tinsel.

'I think I'd like to stay if that's all right with you, Joe.' Guy proffered his arm to Elsie. 'Perhaps we should start the dancing. At worst it will provide entertainment for everyone else.'

'Splendid idea.' Joe moved towards the centre of the floor, dispersing a group of children who looked as though they were about to start a wrestling match. 'Take your partners, please, ladies and gentlemen.'

'And children,' a small voice piped up.

Joe looked down at the small girl and smiled. 'Yes, Claudette, and children, but there will be no fighting or hair pulling. I will deal strictly with any wrongdoers.'

At a signal from her husband Mrs Johnson began an energetic rendition of the Maple Leaf Rag. 'We'll do the one-step,' Guy whispered. 'We're pretty good at that.'

Elsie abandoned her coat and allowed him to lead her into the centre of the floor. She could feel the blood rushing to her face as all eyes were upon them. 'They seem to think we know what we're doing,' she murmured.

'Let's show them then.' Guy gave her an encouraging smile and waited for the beat. 'Here we go.'

Encouraged by a round of applause they started to dance and suddenly the floor was crowded with couples, but there were not enough men to go round and the remaining women partnered each other, which caused a great deal of mirth. The children joined in with boundless energy and the rafters rang with Scott Joplin's lively music and the sound of laughter. The dance ended and everyone clapped their hands, calling for more.

Joe rushed up to them, grinning broadly. 'This is fantastic. To see everyone forgetting their plight even for a few minutes is utterly wonderful.' He waved to his wife. 'Encore, my dear. Encore.'

Obediently Mrs Johnson launched into a polka and by the time it ended everyone was breathless and in need of refreshment, including the pianist herself. Elsie took her a glass of punch. 'You are a very talented musician.'

Mrs Johnson drank thirstily. 'Thank you, but I'm very out of practice.'

'No one would ever know it, and they're all having a wonderful time, thanks to you and your husband.'

'You should take a lot of the credit, Elsie. Your ability to converse with them in their own tongue has made all the difference. The Flemish speakers seem to understand French almost as well as their own language, which is a great help.'

'Don't overtire yourself, Mrs Johnson, but I'm sure everyone would appreciate a few more dances.'

'I could go on all night. I rarely see my husband looking so happy. He is the one who works tirelessly for all his parishioners. I'm merely his helpmate.'

'And I know he couldn't manage without you.'

'Your young man is coming to ask you to dance again,' Mrs Johnson said, smiling. 'He's very nice, Elsie. Quite a gentleman.'

Elsie looked round and saw Guy walking towards them. 'He's not my young man,' she said hastily. 'We only met this evening. I hardly know him.'

'Well he likes you, dear, and he doesn't look the sort of man who is normally at ease with young ladies.'

'How can you tell?'

'Many years of listening to the woes of young curates and parishioners have made me sympathetic to the emotional problems of others. Life is very difficult for people who are shy.' Mrs Johnson struck a chord on the piano and started playing a waltz. She looked up and gave Guy an encouraging smile. 'Everyone can waltz, Mr Gifford. Even my husband, and he most definitely has two left feet.'

Guy bowed politely. 'May I have the pleasure of this dance, Elsie?'

She took his hand. 'I'd be delighted, Guy.'

'I'm glad I stayed,' he said as he whirled her round in time to the music. 'To tell you the truth I wasn't looking forward to this evening, but it's turned out much better than I expected.'

She met his candid gaze and realised that it cost him a lot to make such an admission. 'Why was that?'

'I don't go to many parties,' he said slowly. 'I usually find it hard to socialise.'

She smiled. 'You're doing very well tonight.'

'Thanks to you, Elsie. I usually find it quite difficult to get on with young ladies.'

'So how do you know Marianne?'

'We work in the same department at the War Office. Algy is my boss, and we get on tolerably well, but I wouldn't say we're bosom friends. I'm not even sure why he invited me to Frascati's.'

'I'm very glad he did, or I would have had a miserable time.'

'Shall we sit the rest of this one out? I hate shouting above the music.' He guided her to a row of empty chairs set against the wall.

'What did you want to talk about, Guy? Or are you simply tired and need to rest?'

His eyes twinkled and he laughed. 'Are you saying I'm an old man, Elsie?'

'I don't know how old you are.'

'I'm twenty-seven. I suppose that is old to someone like you.'

'I'm twenty-one, and age doesn't come into it. I like you, Guy. You're easy to talk to and you don't make me feel inferior.'

He stared at her in genuine surprise. 'Why would you feel like that?'

'As I said before, I was in service. My father died when I was very young and Ma and I were poor. We had a struggle just to survive.'

'It doesn't change who you are as a person.' Guy leaned back in his chair. 'I don't agree with unthinking acceptance of the class system. In my opinion people should be judged for their own qualities and capabilities and not because of some accident of birth. This war is a terrible thing, but if it brings about social change, then some good might come out of it.'

'Why should that be? There have been wars before.'

'But not on this scale. The whole world is being drawn into the conflict and I don't think anything will be the same when it comes to an end.'

She looked up realising that someone was trying to attract their attention. 'It's the vicar. I think he's trying to tell us that this is the last waltz.'

Guy leapt to his feet. 'We mustn't miss this opportunity. May I have this dance, Miss Mead?'

'Certainly, Mr Gifford.' She stood up and stepped into the circle of his arms. 'It's been a lovely evening, Guy. I've really enjoyed myself, and everyone here seems to have absorbed a little of the Christmas spirit despite their personal problems.'

'May I see you again, Elsie?'

She had been comfortable in his company, but her heart and her head were filled with romantic thoughts of Henri and it would be unfair to lead Guy on. 'Yes – perhaps – but I'll be back at work on Saturday. I've already had too much time off.'

'But it's Boxing Day. I was hoping we might go for a walk in the park.'

The disappointment in his voice was echoed in

his eyes, and she felt a sudden sense of panic. He might be looking for a romantic attachment, but she was not. Henri was definitely beyond her reach, but she had fallen in love with him the first moment they had met, and she was certain that no one could take his place. 'I'm sorry, Guy. Another day, maybe. Now I really should be getting home, but thank you for coming here with me. It's been lovely.'

'At least allow me to see you home.'

She could not refuse and somehow she did not want to. 'Thank you,' she said simply.

'What on earth will we do without Violet?' Anthea demanded, waving a slice of toast and marmalade in the air before taking a bite.

'I'll put an advertisement in *The Lady*,' Marianne said with a careless shrug. 'At least Cook is staying on. We can manage for a few days without a maid, but I'd be lost in the kitchen.'

Anthea swallowed and licked her lips. 'Me too. I can't even boil an egg. I suppose we could get food sent in from Fortnum's.'

Marianne turned to Elsie. 'Can you cook?'

'Yes, a bit.'

'That's all right then. You can make breakfast and we'll eat out for the rest of the day.'

'But Cook isn't the one who's leaving,' Elsie pointed out. 'I'm going back to my lodgings after work tomorrow, so I won't be able to help. How are you both at cleaning and lighting fires?'

Anthea pushed her plate away and stood up. 'It can't be that difficult, but I've no intention of putting myself to the test. Anyway, Tubby will be arriving soon and then we're going to his family seat for the grisly get-together for all his ghastly relations. I'll be staying the night, heaven help me. Their house is ancient, cold and draughty and I'll probably catch pneumonia, but hey ho, one has to do one's duty.' She grabbed another slice of toast and left the room, munching it as she went.

'That leaves us and the turkey, darling,' Marianne said, filling her cup with coffee. 'Algy invited me to stay with his family in Buckinghamshire, but I couldn't face it.'

'He seems keen on you,' Elsie said cautiously. 'Don't you like him?'

'Oh, he's fun and good-looking, but it's never been serious. Not on my part. Now if Henri had asked me to spend Christmas in Paris I'd have swum the Channel to get there, but I haven't heard from him since he left.'

'You're very fond of Henri, aren't you?'

'Of course I am. I told you, Elsie, we're like brother and sister. I adore his parents but there's nothing serious between Henri and me.'

Elsie was not sure she believed her. She rose to her feet. 'Violet has the day off, so perhaps I'd better clear the table.'

'You're a guest here, but since you've offered, thanks.' Marianne reached for her handbag and took out a silver cigarette case. 'With Felicia away it's all right to smoke in the dining room. She says it puts her off her food.' She selected a cigarette and lit it with a match, inhaling with a satisfied smile. 'I'm afraid I haven't got a present for you, Elsie, because I had no idea we'd be spending Christmas marooned in this flat like pirates on an atoll.'

'That's all right, Marianne. I haven't got one for you because I'm a bit short of the rent money this week.'

Marianne stared at her through a haze of smoke. 'Really? I don't know how the landlady has the gall to charge rent for that dreadful attic. How much do you need?'

'No, really. Thank you, but I'll manage somehow.' Elsie began stacking the plates.

'Nonsense. Call it a loan, or perhaps it can be the Christmas present I neglected to buy. How much?'

'Five shillings,' Elsie whispered. 'I had to buy some stockings and have my boots repaired. I'm not normally so extravagant.'

Marianne took out her purse. 'Good God, I don't call that being extravagant. You must be working for next to nothing.'

'I'm doing something for other people. It's a charity and I'm lucky to get anything at all.'

'You're being exploited,' Marianne said, taking another puff on her cigarette. 'It's slave labour, if you ask me.'

'I'm not complaining and I enjoy helping the

refugees. I'm glad to do something to help win the war, even if it's only in a small way.'

Marianne leaned back in her chair, staring at Elsie as if seeing her for the first time. 'I'm not sure if you're heading for sainthood or if you're a gullible fool.'

This made Elsie laugh and she tossed a table napkin at Marianne. 'I'm neither, and it wouldn't hurt you to help out. Poor Mrs Beale is slaving away in the kitchen just so that you and I can gorge ourselves on turkey and the trimmings. I think she needs a break as much as anyone.'

'Oh my God,' Marianne said, rolling her eyes. 'You're not going to make me give my Christmas lunch to the poor like Marmee in *Little Women*, are you?'

'Don't tell me you actually read the book?'

'My governess adored it and insisted on reading it to me.' Marianne stubbed her cigarette out on a saucer. 'I'll make sure the next maid puts an ashtray on the table, just until Felicia returns, of course.' She took two half-crowns from her purse and laid them on the table. 'Merry Christmas, Elsie.'

Elsie smiled and pocketed the coins. 'Thanks. I promise I'll pay you back as soon as I can.'

Despite her initial refusal to help in any way, Marianne relented when the festive meal was served and insisted that Mrs Beale should join them in the dining room. She plied her with sherry and wine and when the pudding had been flamed, served and eaten, she told her to take the rest of the day off.

'You're not going to leave me with the washing-up, are you?' Elsie demanded.

'Actually, I'm not such a heartless bitch,' Marianne said, laughing. She rose to her feet and rolled up her sleeves. 'I'll wash, you can wipe.' She leaned over Mrs Beale who was suspiciously red in the face and seemed to be having difficulty in keeping her eyes open. 'Mrs Beale, I think a nap would be beneficial, and don't worry about preparing supper. We'll help ourselves. There's plenty left.'

Mrs Beale staggered to her feet. 'Thank you, Miss Marianne. It's been very enjoyable.' She teetered towards the door and Elsie rushed over to open it for her.

'Can you manage?'

'Thank you, miss. I'm perfectly capable of getting to my room unaided. Merry Christmas.' Mrs Beale marched out of the room, swaying a little, but keeping her head held high. 'I can manage perfectly well.'

'Come on then,' Marianne said, pulling a face. 'Let's get this over and then we can sit down and relax, although I don't know what we'll do for the rest of the day. I'm beginning to wish that I'd joined Algy in Bedfordshire, no offence meant, Elsie. But I was never one for purely female company, as you might have guessed.'

'We could always go for a walk,' Elsie suggested

eagerly. 'Maybe we could go to Hyde Park or Kensington Gardens.'

'Walk?' Marianne glanced down at her high-heeled shoes. 'In this weather? Are you completely mad?'

They spent the next half hour in the kitchen, tackling the washing up. Marianne did her best, although Elsie had to slip the occasional piece of crockery back into the hot water to make sure that it was clean, but when it came to the roasting tin and saucepans Marianne gave up. 'My hands are raw,' she complained. 'I can't imagine how anyone could do this day in and day out. I need a sit down, a cup of coffee and a cigarette. Leave the rest, Elsie. Violet can do it tomorrow.'

'You've done your bit. Go and sit down and I'll make the coffee.'

'You are multi-talented, darling. I love you.' Marianne breezed out of the kitchen, leaving Elsie to finish cleaning the pots and pans. She could not simply walk away and leave the detritus for Violet to find in the morning, and her conscience would not allow her to leave the kitchen in anything but a pristine state. She made coffee and took a tray into the drawing room.

Marianne looked up and smiled. 'You took your time. I suppose you stayed like a good little slavey and left the kitchen spotless.'

Elsie put the tray down and poured the coffee. 'Of course.' She grinned. 'I wish that Phyllis and

Nancy could have seen you washing dishes. They wouldn't have believed their eyes.'

'Well it won't happen again, Elsie. I'm not the domesticated kind. When I decide to marry it will be a man who can keep me in the way to which I am accustomed, as the saying goes. I don't believe in love in a garret. No sugar, darling, and just a dash of milk.'

Elsie placed the cup of coffee on an occasional table beside Marianne's chair. 'I'm very grateful for everything, but I'm going back to my lodgings tomorrow. I have to work.'

'You did say that, but surely they won't expect you to work on Boxing Day?'

'I volunteered a week or so ago. I didn't know I'd be spending Christmas with you, and anyway, I don't want to outstay my welcome. You and Anthea have been marvellous, but it's time for me to go.'

Marianne leaned forward in her chair. 'You could stay here, you know.'

'Me? Stay here?'

'That's what I said. To be honest, Elsie, with Violet leaving us in the lurch like this, Anthea and I are going to find it very hard to manage.'

'But you're going to advertise in *The Lady*.'

'I rang an employment agency and they told me that young women no longer want to work in service.'

Elsie sat down, holding her cup of coffee with both hands. 'Are you offering me a job?'

'No, of course not.' Marianne shook her head vehemently. 'We'll all have to do our bit, I know that. While this beastly war goes on we'll all have to pull our weight, but Anthea and I haven't a clue how to do the simplest things. We've been utterly spoilt all our lives, I acknowledge that freely, and the fact is that we need you to show us the way. Besides which, I enjoy your company. Do say you will, Elsie. Please.'

Chapter Seven

He was the last person she was expecting to see. Elsie had just returned from the East End after a long day sorting out the problems of some of the refugee families, and it was a shock to walk into the drawing room in Cromwell Road to find Guy Gifford standing with his back to the fireplace, even though no one had thought to light the fire and the temperature in the room was only a few degrees above that outside. 'Elsie. It's good to see you again.' He took a step towards her with his arm outstretched and then hesitated, dropping his hand to his side. 'I would have come sooner, but we had a bit of a crisis at work.'

'I've been busy too.' Elsie glanced at Marianne who was huddled in a chair, shivering. 'Why didn't anyone light the fire?'

Marianne wrapped her cardigan around her slender body. 'Thank goodness you're home, darling. I can't get the beastly thing to light. I've used up a whole box of matches but it just belches smoke at me and goes out again.'

'I offered to have a go,' Guy said hastily. 'But Marianne seems to think I'm fairly useless at anything practical.'

'And you are.' Marianne tossed her head. 'You can't even sharpen a pencil at work without breaking the lead.' She turned to Elsie with a persuasive smile. 'When you've had time to take your coat and hat off, would you light the fire? I'd have asked Mrs Beale but I gave her a couple of days off to visit her daughter in Croydon. Anthea is out with Tubby and I was going to make Guy a cup of tea but the milk's off, so we had to make do with gin and tonic.'

'I could go down to the cellar and fetch some more coal,' Guy volunteered as Elsie peeled off her gloves.

'It's all right, Guy,' Marianne said firmly. 'Bailey does that sort of thing, or he sends his son to do it for him.' She reached for her glass. 'We were thinking about going out for lunch, Elsie, but now you're here perhaps you could rustle something up in the kitchen. I'm sure Mrs Beale must have left the larder packed with food.'

'I suggested we grab a sandwich,' Guy said with a hint of a smile. 'But Marianne said she hasn't quite mastered the art of making one, and she has the nerve to criticise me.'

'I'll see what I can do.' Suddenly everything was back to normal. Elsie knelt down in front of the grate and began clearing the mess that Marianne had created. In minutes she had flames licking up the chimney, igniting the soot on the fireback so that it sparkled like tiny glow worms before dying away. She added the coal piece by piece, and when she was certain that it would not go out she scrambled to her feet. 'There, it's not so difficult.'

'For you, maybe,' Marianne said, sighing. 'Heaven knows, I've tried to follow your example, but I don't seem to have any talent for domesticity.' She glanced at Guy and shook her head. 'Don't give me that look. I know you think I'm useless, but I have my good points and both Anthea and I love having Elsie here with us. We don't take advantage of her good nature.'

'Of course you don't,' Elsie said without giving Guy a chance to defend himself. 'I had to move out of Clay Street anyway because Rosemary's sister was ill, and she felt she ought to move to Woodford to help look after her little ones. Anyway, Mrs Crabtree had somebody lined up to take the room.'

'A good thing too,' Marianne said firmly. 'You should have seen it, Guy. I don't know how the landlady had the nerve to charge anyone to live in such squalor.' She stretched out her hands to the fire. 'You're a wonder, Elsie. I thought we'd go out and eat later, but I'd kill for a sandwich or something to keep me going.'

Elsie exchanged amused glances with Guy. 'Can I get you something? It's no trouble.'

'Thanks, but you must allow me to help you.'

'No, Guy,' Marianne said firmly. 'You can't leave me in suspense. Please take a seat and tell me more about this work that I'm to train for.' She looked up at Elsie and grinned. 'I'm one of the chosen ones, Elsie. What do you think about that?'

'Chosen for what?'

'I'm going to be a spy. Isn't that exciting?'

'A spy? You're joking.'

Guy moved to the sofa and sat down. 'It's hush-hush. You won't breathe a word of this to anyone, Elsie.'

'Of course not, but it sounds really dangerous. What must she do?'

'I won't know until I've done my training,' Marianne said, sipping her drink. 'But I expect I'll be sent behind German lines. I rather fancy myself as a femme fatale.'

'The work of the Secret Service Bureau really is top secret,' Guy said with a wry smile. 'Marianne has been picked because of her excellent command of French, but I can't tell you anything more than that because that isn't my job.'

'Isn't it thrilling?' Marianne held her empty glass out to Guy. 'A refill would be nice, and I rather fancy a chicken sandwich. Mrs Beale cooked one before she left for the suburbs. You'd better examine it carefully though, Elsie. It might have gone off.'

Elsie left the room, mulling over the prospect of Marianne risking her life by joining the secret service, of which she knew virtually nothing. She had read books about spies, but they had all been men and she could not imagine how a woman, especially one like Marianne, would fit into such a role. She went to the kitchen and examined the chicken. 'It's definitely off,' she said when she returned to the drawing room moments later. 'The bread is stale, the milk is sour and the cheese is wearing a blue fur coat.'

Guy stood up, brushing the creases down in his pin-stripe suit. 'Then may I suggest we go out now? It would be my pleasure to treat you both.'

Marianne began her job in the New Year. She was sent to the Admiralty in Whitehall where she was to work in the department of cryptanalysis, known as Room 40. 'It's all top secret, Elsie,' she said cheerfully at the end of the first week in her new position. 'But I'm working with several other girls and we're situated in the same corridor as the boardroom and the First Sea Lord's office. I can't tell you details, of course, but it's all to do with decoding messages sent by the German navy. It's much more interesting than working as a secretary in the War Office. Anyway, I was a lousy typist and couldn't always decipher my own writing. I think they were glad to get rid of me.'

Elsie found herself wishing that she could do something more exciting than her new job, which entailed teaching French to young soldiers, most of whom were more interested in asking her out to dinner or inviting her to a dance on a Saturday night than in learning the language. She was still involved with the Belgian refugees who were already settled in London, but the number of arrivals had slowed down dramatically as it became almost impossible for them to escape from their motherland, although a small number still managed to travel through neutral Holland. She spent as much of her free time as she could in Hackney, helping Joe Johnson and his wife to make the lives of those who were settled in London more bearable, and she was conscious of the fact that simply listening to what the displaced Belgians had to say was perhaps her most vital function.

As the weeks went by she saw more and more of Guy. He was the one person in whom she could confide when she found her work too onerous, or when she became too involved with a refugee family and needed to remain detached and professional. He was never judgemental and invariably came up with a solution that she might have missed. Their friendship deepened but she was uncomfortably aware that his feelings were much more involved than her own. She knew that he had fallen in love with her and she wished that she could respond, but Henri was never far from her thoughts and always in her heart. She knew she might never see him again, and when Marianne received a letter from Madame Bellaire telling her that he had enlisted, Elsie struggled to keep her emotions in check.

She tried to let Guy down gently, telling him that she did not want to get involved with anyone in such uncertain times, when any one of them might be killed even though they were not directly involved in the war. Zeppelin attacks on the east coast had begun in

January. Innocent civilians had been killed and injured. It was only a matter of time before the deadly airships made their silent way to London and caused even more damage and destruction. She explained at length, but Guy insisted that he was a patient man who was more than willing to remain her friend; living in hope but never pressing her for more than she was prepared to give. It was humbling and also rather frightening, but she had come to rely on him. He knew almost everything about her, apart from the secret love she kept locked away in her heart.

The misery of a wet winter gradually ended and a long-awaited spring arrived in London, heralded by the golden trumpets of daffodils in Kensington Gardens. Anthea was at home more often at the end of the working day as Tubby had enlisted in the Royal Flying Corps and was training at the School of Military Aeronautics near Reading. She was proud of him, of course, but also fearful for his safety as he had completed the necessary dual instruction time and was about to go solo. She joked about it, but Elsie noted the twin furrows of worry on Anthea's previously smooth forehead, and the way her fingers shook as she lit yet another cigarette, and tried to make light of her worries. It was on such evenings when they gathered together to give mutual comfort and support while listening to the gramophone and enjoying the latest patriotic songs like 'Keep the home fires burning', and 'Goodbye Dolly Gray'.

One evening when Anthea had been particularly depressed, having not heard from Tubby for almost a week, they were sitting in the drawing room after supper, which Marianne and Anthea had managed to cook with a limited amount of success.

'Don't grumble about the food,' Marianne said severely. 'There are shortages. I defy a French chef to produce a wonderful meal from the ingredients we had to hand.'

'It was very nice,' Elsie said tactfully. 'A few weeks ago neither of you could cook and now you can make a decent meal. You should be proud of yourselves.'

'Absolutely,' Anthea said with a satisfied smile. 'Tubby will be amazed to learn how domesticated I am these days.' She shot a wary glance at Marianne. 'You're not your usual self this evening. Have you got man trouble again?'

Marianne opened the onyx cigarette box on the table and found it empty. 'Where is Felicia when you need her?' she groaned. 'I wish she'd stop flitting around the battlefields entertaining the troops. She's needed here.' She fished in her handbag and brought out a battered cigarette packet. Taking one, she lit it and inhaled deeply. 'Felicia gets to see all the action and we're stuck here in London.'

'It is man trouble,' Elsie said, winking at Anthea. 'Who is it this time, Marianne?'

'I've done with men altogether. The last chap I went out with was a pain in the neck, and he absolutely refused to join up even though I tried to show him that it was his duty.'

'Perhaps he's a conscientious objector,' Elsie said reasonably. 'Maybe he doesn't believe in war.'

'He insisted that he was doing valuable war work, and I told him that all able-bodied men should enlist in one of the services and I didn't want anything to do with a coward.'

'That was a bit hard, wasn't it?' Elsie took the record off the gramophone and replaced it in its cover. 'Maybe he was telling the truth. You're always saying how lives are being saved by all the intelligence you and your colleagues gather.'

'I think Marianne is right,' Anthea said firmly. 'Men should fight for their country, although I wish Tubby hadn't enlisted in the Flying Corps. It's so dangerous and there are terrible accidents even in training.'

'Life is a risk,' Marianne said airily. 'I've put in for a transfer and hope they'll send me abroad. I'm getting bored with sitting on the sidelines in London. I want to do something more active.'

'You are doing something useful,' Elsie said stoutly. 'Why do you want to expose yourself to danger when you're doing a good job here?'

'Because I want excitement,' Marianne said, taking a last drag on her cigarette and tossing the butt into the empty grate. 'I don't want to be one of the privileged few living in comparative luxury. I want to do something worthwhile for a change.'

'We're just lucky not to have been killed in one of those dreadful bombing raids,' Elsie said sharply. 'The people in the East End and in coastal towns have suffered dreadfully.'

Anthea yawned and stretched. 'I'm going to have a nice warm bath and then early to bed.' She stood up, and as she opened the door the telephone shrilled, making them all jump,

'Oh, God,' Anthea said, clasping her hand to her chest. 'Who's ringing at this time of night? It must be bad news.'

Marianne settled further down in her chair. 'If it's him, tell him I'm out.'

'I'm not answering it.' Anthea sent a pleading look to Elsie. 'Would you be a dear and get it? I just can't.'

Elsie jumped up and hurried into the hall. She was still slightly nervous of speaking into a machine. One had been installed at Darcy Hall, but Soames was the only servant who was allowed to answer it. She picked up the handset and unhooked the receiver. 'Hello,' she murmured. 'Who calls?'

'Elsie, is that you?'

'Guy? Is something wrong?'

'I – I'm sorry to call so late in the evening, but I need to see you.'

'There is something wrong, I can tell by your voice.'

'It's nothing really. Could you meet me at Lyons teashop in Piccadilly tomorrow afternoon at two? I need to talk to you.'

'Can't you tell me now, Guy?'

'Not really. Sorry, Elsie, but some things are difficult to talk about on one of these contraptions. Will you be able to get away tomorrow?'

'Of course I will.'

'Goodbye, I'll see you at two.'

Guy rose from the table in the teashop window and pulled out a chair for her. Elsie gave him a searching look and was worried. 'Are you all right? You sounded upset on the telephone.'

He waited until she was seated and took the chair opposite her. 'A woman in the office gave me an envelope at lunchtime yesterday.' He avoided meeting her anxious gaze by pouring the tea. 'You can probably guess what it contained.'

'No! Surely not.'

'A white feather.' He passed a brimming cup to her. 'I must confess it shook me. I thought I was doing a worthwhile job, and I never thought of myself as a coward.'

'You're not,' Elsie said angrily. 'It was a beastly thing to do. Who was she?'

'Someone I hardly know. Anyway, it doesn't matter.' He looked up, meeting her gaze with a steady look. 'I've enlisted.'

Elsie reached out to cover his hand with hers. 'Oh, Guy, I'm so sorry. You shouldn't have taken any notice of the spiteful bitch. You are doing something worthwhile.'

A faint smile curved his lips. 'The trouble is I have to agree with her. I'd convinced myself that I was doing the right thing because I hate violence of any kind, but now I realise that this is something I have to do.'

She nodded, understanding his motives but anxious for him. 'I suppose it's the army for you?'

'I'm no sailor, and I think I'm too old for the Flying Corps. They want bold young chaps who aren't afraid of anything, like Tubby McAvoy and Algy Fortescue-Brown.'

'Has he joined up too? Marianne didn't mention it.'

'Yes, he's dead keen. It seems the fashionable thing to do, and Marianne's too busy lobbying her new boss for promotion to bother much about poor Algy. He's a has-been as far as she's concerned.'

'It's not like you to be catty, Guy.'

He shrugged his shoulders. 'I know and I'm sorry, but Marianne has quite a reputation for being fickle.'

'She just hasn't met the right chap yet. I bet you wouldn't say that if she was a man. He'd be a bit of a lad with the girls and that would be all right.'

'Don't let's argue. I'm sorry if I said anything to upset you.'

'I can understand if you're feeling on edge, but don't take it out on poor Marianne. She's just eager to get on in her job. There's nothing wrong with that.'

'She's got her sights set on military intelligence,' Guy said in a low voice. 'I'm only telling you this because you're so close to her. You ought to know what she's up to.'

'I've heard her mention it, but I didn't realise she was actually serious.' Elsie pushed her plate away. Suddenly the toasted teacake did not look so appetising. 'I'll have it out with her this evening.'

He frowned. 'I didn't mean to cause trouble between you, but I know how close you two are, and she might tumble headlong into something she can't handle.'

'Marianne likes to get her own way,' Elsie said with a reluctant smile. 'And she always wants to be noticed. I suppose it's because her parents have never shown much interest in her. Colonel Winter is too busy with his army career and Marianne's mother enjoys being a colonel's lady.' She squeezed his fingers. 'Anyway, you're more important at the moment, Guy. Let's talk about you. Do you have to go away for training? How does it work?'

'I expect there's some basic training, but with the huge numbers of casualties they're experiencing every day I don't think it will be long before Private Gifford is sent off to fight in the trenches.'

She stared at him, nonplussed. 'But I thought someone like you would be eligible for a commission, Guy.'

'As I told you, I was a scholarship boy at the local grammar school. My father was a bank clerk and he couldn't have afforded to pay for my fees had I failed the entrance examination.'

'There's nothing wrong with that,' Elsie said stoutly.

'My parents still live in a terraced house in Ilford and Dad gets the train to work every day. Mum stays at home and keeps house and my younger brother works in the accounts department at Selfridge's. We're a very ordinary family and what I'm trying to say is that I'm not top drawer like Felicia and Marianne.' He grinned and shook his head. 'Well, perhaps they're more middle drawer than top drawer but they're further up in society than I am. I've worked hard to get where I am in the War Office, but I'll never get any further. It's very much an old boys' club.'

'I think you should be proud of what you've achieved, and I think you're terribly brave to enlist.'

'Joining up scares me stiff, Elsie. I'm just an ordinary chap, not the heroic kind at all.'

She shook her head. 'You've got real courage and I admire you for it.'

'Thank you. You'll never know how much that means to me.' He looked away, blinking hard and clearing his throat. 'I'll carry that memory with me from now on, and every time I want to give up I'll think of you and remember what we're all fighting for.'

She averted her eyes, giving him time to compose himself. Damn war, she thought angrily. The battle-fields were soaked in the blood of young men who did not deserve to die. She could only hope and pray that Guy would come home safely.

When they parted outside the teashop, Elsie watched him walk away with a feeling of deep sadness. He had only hinted at the depth of his feelings for her, and for that she was grateful. In such circumstances she knew that others in his position might have declared their undying love, extracting a promise to marry when the war was over. Whatever Guy said about his humble beginnings, he was too much of a gentleman to put her in such a position, and that made it harder for her to send him away with a peck on the cheek. His quiet devotion touched her deeply and she knew that he would make a kind and loving husband who would do everything in his power to make her happy. The fact that he had told her a little about his family made him even more special in her eyes, but only as a dear friend. She ought to be able to love him, but her stubborn heart would not obey her head. She admitted as much to Marianne that evening when they were alone in the drawing room after dinner.

'You were right not to make promises you couldn't keep,' Marianne said airily. 'Wartime romances seldom work out, or so I've been told. Guy is a splendid fellow and all that, but he's not for you.'

'I just wish I felt differently. He's a good man and he deserves more.'

'I agree, but I'm afraid you would be bored to

death with him after a week, and ready to commit murder after a month.'

'You do exaggerate,' Elsie said, smiling. 'You're being ridiculous and you know it.'

'You've got a more important destiny, my dear.'

Elsie placed her empty coffee cup on the table. 'Really?'

'I'm serious for once,' Marianne said, leaning towards her. 'I'm fed up with being one of Blinker's Beauty Chorus.'

'What on earth is that?' Elsie demanded, giggling.

'The head of Room 40 is called William Hall and his nickname, for some odd reason, is Blinker. Anyway, I've been working hard to get myself seconded to military intelligence in Paris. It's all absolutely top secret so don't breathe a word to anyone, not even Anthea.'

'I knew you were up to something, but how does it concern me?'

Marianne lit a cigarette. 'Because I know you're worth more than the job you're doing.' She held up her hand as Elsie opened her mouth to protest. 'You've done sterling work, I know that, but you're a clever girl and you speak French like a native. Can't you see that all that talent is being wasted?'

'I thought I was doing something extremely useful.'

'And you are, of course, but isn't there a tiny part of you that would like to do something more exciting? Don't you feel a bit frustrated by having to allow the men to risk their lives while we sit at home and knit balaclava helmets?'

'You know I can't knit.'

'This isn't a joke, Elsie. I've applied for a transfer to Paris and I want you to come with me.'

'That's mad. I'm not employed by the secret service, for a start, and I wouldn't know what to do. I'm no spy, and neither are you if it comes to that.'

'Who knows what we can do?' Marianne took a drag on her cigarette and exhaled through her nostrils. 'I'm not certain I'll get on with their odd-smelling tobacco, but that's the least of my problems.'

Elsie stared at her, shaking her head. 'Why do you have to be so flippant, Marianne? Is it so hard to admit that you want to serve your country?'

'I've had such an easy life. I know I've never wanted for anything, other perhaps than my parents' attention, but I'm never likely to get that. The only really happy times I remember are when I was with the Bellaire family in Provence. I adored le Lavandou and their villa overlooking the sea. Henri and I used to roam the countryside like young gypsies and we were free. I doubt if I'll ever feel that again.'

'But wartime France won't be the same, Marianne. How would you feel if the Germans take Paris? They're not far away, according to the newspapers.'

Marianne stubbed out her cigarette, fixing Elsie with an intense stare. 'I want to help in some small way, and I'd give my life if necessary, but I can't do it alone. I need you with me, Elsie. You know how useless I am at looking after myself. You wouldn't want me to starve because if you're not there to see that I get proper meals I'll waste away or turn to drugs like cocaine or opium to get me through the day. What do you say? Will you come with me? '

Chapter Eight

For a moment Elsie thought Marianne was joking. 'You're talking utter nonsense.'

'I'm not. I desperately want you to come with me, Elsie. Together we can bring the whole German army down, but separately we're just two ordinary girls.'

Elsie stared at her with a mixture of amusement and exasperation. 'I love my work for the Women's Emergency Corps, and anyway, I can't just bowl up to the War Office and demand to be sent to Paris as a spy.'

'No, of course not, but you're half French – don't you want to help your compatriots?'

'That's not fair. Of course I'd like to do more, but I'm useful here.'

Marianne's eyes shone with enthusiasm. 'But you could do so much more and so could I. If you agree, I'll put in a good word for you and who knows what they'll say. It's worth a try and I can be very persuasive.'

Elsie sighed. She knew when she was beaten, and in a funny way she felt responsible for Marianne, who might have been born to wealth and privilege, but beneath the confident façade she had caught glimpses of a lonely spirit desperate for affection. 'All right, but I still think you're mad. Maybe they won't give you the job, and I'm almost certain they won't take me on.'

'They will, if I've got anything to do with it.'

But change did not happen overnight and life went on much as usual for Elsie. Guy had been sent to an army camp near Dover to undergo his brief period of initial training before being posted to northern France. It came as a surprise when he sent her a telegram saying that he had a 24-hour pass and would she meet him outside Lyons teashop in Piccadilly?

She was oddly nervous as she waited in the busy thoroughfare, and she hardly recognised him when he came striding towards her. She had grown used to seeing him in his formal black pin-stripe suit with his immaculate white shirts and Gladstone collars, but this tall man dressed like a soldier looked so unlike the Guy she knew that he seemed like a stranger. It was only when they were seated at their table, drinking tea and nibbling toasted teacakes, that she began to see glimpses of the old Guy as he began to relax.

His witty account of happenings in the training camp, and his impression of the sergeant major who dominated the lives of the new recruits, made her laugh until she cried. She had almost forgotten how much she enjoyed his company, and then he produced a small box from his inside pocket. Her smile faded and her mouth went dry. He laid his hand on hers. 'I love you, Elsie. I wanted to tell you when we met here before I left for camp, but my courage failed me. I had this ring in my pocket then but it didn't seem like the right time.' He took a deep breath and flicked the box open. 'Don't say anything yet. I've been rehearsing this for days. I know it's a lot to ask, and I shouldn't try to tie you down when there's a good chance that I might not return, but I'd die a happier man if I knew you felt a fraction of what I feel for you.'

She stared down at the small solitaire diamond, winking at her in the late spring sunshine that filtered through the window. 'I don't know what to say, Guy.'

'But you do have some feelings for me?'

'Of course I do. You're a wonderful person and good friend, but . . .'

'But you don't love me enough to want to marry me.'

'No. At least, I don't know. This isn't fair, Guy. It's so unexpected that I don't know what to say.'

He snapped the box shut and returned it to his breast pocket. 'I'm sorry, Elsie. My timing is all wrong.'

She pushed her chair back and stood up. 'I'm so sorry, Guy.'

'Don't go. Stay for a while longer.'

She fought back the tears that threatened to

overwhelm her. 'We'll do this some other time. When this is all over . . .'

He rose to his feet. 'Will you give me your answer then?'

'That's a promise I can keep.' She moved swiftly round the table and gave him a hug. 'Take care of yourself and come home safely.'

He held her in his arms and then released her. 'That's a promise I might not be able to keep.'

Bailey was in his cubbyhole when she arrived home and he greeted her with a cheerful grin which faded quickly and was replaced by a look of concern. 'Are you all right, miss?'

'Yes, thank you, Bailey.'

'Things are always more difficult at times like these,' he said philosophically.

'Yes, they are.' She made her way towards the staircase.

'You'll find a surprise waiting for you,' he called after her. 'She gave me a shock, I can tell you.'

With his words barely registering, Elsie climbed the stairs. She longed for the privacy of her bedroom where she could have a good cry and release all the pent-up emotions of the last few hours, but she knew that was unlikely to happen. She tried to compose herself, knowing that Marianne would spot that there was something wrong the moment she saw her.

She let herself into the flat and her nostrils were

assailed by the pungent smell of French cigarettes. Marianne was in the entrance hall waiting for her. 'She's home,' she said, pointing to the drawing room. 'Felicia breezed into the flat this afternoon dressed in khaki with her things packed in a kitbag. She looked like Vesta Tilley dressed up as a Tommy. I quite expected her to give us a rendition of "Jolly Good Luck to a Girl Who Loves a Soldier". Anyway, come in and meet her. She's been asking about you.'

Speechless, Elsie followed her into the drawing room and saw her hostess languishing on the sofa with a glass of gin and tonic in one hand and a cigarette in the other. Elsie had seen the photographs of Felicia in her prime which were dotted about the flat and she had been a picture of elegance, but this woman was thin to the point of emaciation. The skin was taut over her high cheekbones and her patrician nose gave her profile a dignity that was lacking in the posed studio portraits. Her blonde hair was scraped into a tight chignon at the back of her head, and even without make-up she was stunningly handsome. She put her glass down and rose to her feet, holding out her arms. 'Elsie, my dear, it's lovely to meet you. Marianne has told me all about you.'

Elsie was startled by this unexpected welcome, and she felt her cheeks redden. 'It's very kind of you to allow me to stay in your flat, Miss Wilby.'

'It's Felicia, darling. Miss Wilby sounds like an eighty-year-old Sunday school teacher.' She sank back onto the sofa, and launched into an account of her experiences on the Western Front with lurid descriptions of the privations she had suffered along with the troops, and the sights she had witnessed in the field hospitals where she went to visit the injured men. Elsie felt physically sick at the thought of Guy, who was so fastidious in all things, being catapulted into such horrendous conditions. She found it hard to imagine him covered in mud from head to foot, like the men Felicia described, their flesh tormented by fleas and lice and their sufferings unimaginable.

Elsie waited for Felicia to refresh herself with a mouthful of gin and tonic, and she stood up. 'It's my turn to cook supper,' she said apologetically. 'I'd better get on with it or we won't be eating until midnight.'

'You girls have done wonders without staff.' Felicia held her glass out to Marianne. 'A top-up would be wonderful, darling.'

Elsie made her escape to the kitchen.

'One gets so tired of bully beef,' Felicia said, attacking the lamb stew with relish. 'This is delicious, Elsie.' She broke a bread roll in half. 'Rationing will come eventually,' she said, smothering it in butter. 'So I intend to make the most of every mouthful. Is there any wine or have you girls drunk my meagre cellar dry?'

Marianne took a bottle of claret from the sideboard. 'The only thing in the cellar is coal, Felicia, as you well know. We've managed quite well during your absence, largely thanks to dear Elsie. She's whipped Anthea and me into shape so that we take our turns cleaning and cooking. You wouldn't believe how much we've both changed.'

'What happened to Violet and Mrs Beale? Did you sack them?'

'Of course not,' Elsie said hastily. 'Violet left to work in a munitions factory and Mrs Beale has gone to Croydon to look after her grandchildren.'

'Oh well. I suppose it is wartime.' Felicia sipped the wine that Marianne had just poured. 'I've been so used to eating round a campfire or in a soggy tent that this is pure luxury. When this dreadful war comes to an end I think we'll find the world is a very different place, and some of the changes will be for the good.'

'How do you work that out, Felicia?' Marianne asked curiously.

'There won't be a class system any longer. I read in the English newspapers that the government is telling people they shouldn't keep servants because it's unpatriotic, so from now on that's how we'll live.'

'Are you home for long, Auntie?' Anthea asked. 'We've missed you.'

'I can see that you've all got along splendidly without me but, in answer to your question, I'll be here until just before Christmas when we're planning more shows for our boys in the trenches. I'm quite a seasoned campaigner. In the meantime I'll set about raising funds for the troops. There's much to be done.'

'I'm sure the soldiers appreciate it,' Elsie said earnestly. 'I can't begin to imagine what it must have been like for you.'

Felicia shuddered dramatically. 'Awful, darling. Quite awful. And one of the worst things was being unable to have a bath. I long for lovely hot water scented with bath salts and soft clean towels to dry myself, and of course my gorgeous feather bed. It's good to be home.'

'Some of us would love the chance to go abroad and do our bit.' Marianne sent a meaningful glance in Elsie's direction. 'I'm frankly fed up with being patronised by the men in Room 40. They like to think we're all fluffy little things who only talk about kittens and embroidery and new clothes. I've put in for a transfer and one day I'll show them what I'm made of.'

'Good for you, darling,' Felicia said, smiling. 'Is there any more of that lovely stew, Elsie? I could eat a horse, and we quite often did.'

Felicia settled back into civilian life with boundless enthusiasm, throwing herself into organising charity dances and benefits in aid of the troops, and planning her next series of shows in great detail. She was rarely in the flat for long enough to do anything but eat and sleep, or came home after a long hard day simply to bathe, change her clothes and go out again to attend one of the events she had helped to organise.

As the weeks went by, spring evolved into summer, and autumn gave way to the chills of winter. Elsie continued her work with the refugees and giving classes in French, but having seen Guy off to endure the horrors of the battlefield she was even more conscious of the fact that the fresh-faced young men who stumbled over their irregular verbs would soon receive their postings. They were all sons of mothers who must be suffering nightmares even before their boys were pitchforked into hell, and some might be leaving wives and small children. The fact that her students laughed and joked and teased her mercilessly made it even harder to ignore her fears for their chances of survival.

Back in the flat the atmosphere was tense. Anthea was obviously missing Tubby and devoted herself to her work, spending her evenings at home writing letters to him or playing records on Marianne's new gramophone.

Marianne herself was a bubbling mass of contradictions. She was still trying to get Elsie a job in Room 40, but it was not as easy as she had thought. Most of the time she seemed carefree and happy, but the next moment she might sink into a deep depression. She was so volatile that Elsie would not have been surprised if she had been sacked from her job, but after months of lobbying and generally making a nuisance of herself in Room 40 Marianne was hauled up in front of Sybil, Lady Hambro, the formidable head of the secretarial section.

'I thought I was going to get the boot,' she said when she arrived home on a foggy winter evening, bringing the unmistakeable smell of a peasouper into the fuggy warmth of the drawing room. She flung off her hat and dropped her damp coat over the back of a chair. Elsie was balancing precariously on top of a ladder as she attempted to pin up paper chains in preparation for Christmas, which was just a fortnight away. 'You should have seen Hambro,' Marianne said, flinging herself down on a chair and kicking off her shoes. 'The old girl was sitting behind a huge mahogany desk smoking a cigar all through the interrogation. She grilled me like a kipper. Anyone would think I was a German spy planted in Room 40 to pass on secrets to the Boche, instead of a woman ready and eager to die for my country if need be.'

She was interrupted by Felicia who had been rushing about searching for odds and ends to pack in her suitcase as she was leaving next day for her next round of entertaining the troops in Northern France and Flanders. She delved down the side of the sofa and came up with a spectacle case. 'Ah. I knew this was somewhere in here.' She opened it and tut-tutted. 'But my specs aren't in it. Where did I leave them?'

Elsie looked down from her superior height on

the topmost rung of the wooden steps and grinned. 'On your head. You're wearing them like a tiara.'

Felicia retrieved her glasses with a sigh. 'So much to do. I know I should have started earlier but what with writing Christmas cards and sorting out all the things I need to take for a sojourn of at least a month in the awful conditions our poor boys have to suffer, I haven't had a moment to call my own.'

'You might actually see one or both of us in Paris, if you get that far,' Marianne said casually.

Anthea dropped the paper chain she was about to pass up to Elsie. 'You're going to Paris?'

Elsie wagged a finger at Marianne. 'You're not supposed to tell anyone. Lady Hambro would have you thrown in the Tower for less.'

'And shot as a traitor,' Anthea added, chuckling. 'So you managed to persuade her, did you? She's actually going to trust you to go abroad and spy for Britain.'

'Shut up, Anthea.' Marianne glanced round the room and shivered. 'You never know who's listening. Anyway, you weren't supposed to know about it.'

'No one could live in this flat and not know what you've been planning. If you're going to be a spy then heaven help us all.' Felicia left the room, closing the door behind her.

'So what will you be doing in Paris?' Anthea slumped down on the sofa. 'We all know that you're going under cover so I don't see that a little more information is going to endanger national security.'

'Well, if you must know, I'm being assigned to the department of British military intelligence in the Rue Saint-Roch.' Marianne laid her forefinger on her closed lips. 'But it's top secret.'

'All right, you've said that before, but what about Elsie?' Anthea dodged a paper chain that had come apart and drifted to the ground.

'She'll have to go through a series of interviews before they agree to her coming with me. I've told her ladyship that Elsie and I are like Siamese twins. Where one goes the other has to accompany her, and I can't work alone.'

'And what did the grand dame say to that?' Anthea retrieved the paper chain and passed it to Elsie. 'Did she tell you to go to hell?'

'We had a grown-up discussion,' Marianne said airily. 'She said no and I said then I'm going to leave here and work in a munitions factory and probably earn more, considering the hours of overtime I've put in.'

'You would. At least that part's true,' Elsie said, pinning the paper chain to the coving.

'Indeed it is,' Marianne said, frowning. 'Do you know that the men in the department get paid twice as much as we women? That's not fair and I told her ladyship so. I think it might have struck a chord because she eased up a bit after that.'

Elsie climbed down from the ladder and moved it to the centre of the room. 'Pass me another paper chain, Anthea.'

'So are you going with her or not, Elsie?' Anthea asked, holding up a length of the linked coloured paper strips. 'Marianne takes ages to get to the point.'

'I applied a couple of months ago and I still haven't heard, but if they accept me I'll have several weeks of intensive training.'

'If all goes well we'll be off to France in early spring. I can't believe that it'll soon be 1916,' Marianne said thoughtfully. 'And they said that the war would be over by last Christmas. Here we are putting up the decorations and there's no sign of an end to hostilities, but we'll change all that, won't we, Elsie? The two of us will win the war together.'

Elsie leaned over perilously to fix the drawing pin into the plaster ceiling rose. 'If you say so, Marianne.'

Marianne had, as usual and as she predicted, got her own way at last. Elsie had endured several interviews in Room 40, which at times had seemed more like interrogations, but eventually she had been given permission to accompany Marianne to Paris. Marianne congratulated her on her success but Elsie suspected that it was the striking likeness between them that had eventually swung opinion in her favour. Lady Hambro had puffed cigar smoke in the air and had eyed her thoughtfully, before giving her opinion that it might prove useful for a would-be agent to have someone who could act as their double. She had laughed heartily and said that anything which would confuse the enemy was an advantage.

Elsie had signed the Official Secrets Act and had been solemnly appointed to a very junior position in the secret service. She told Marianne afterwards that she fully expected to be presented with a mop and bucket the moment she entered their new office in Paris.

On a bitterly cold February morning Elsie woke up and for a moment thought she was back in Cromwell Road, but she stretched and her feet touched the icy cold part of the bed bringing her back to reality with a jerk. She pulled the thin coverlet up to her chin. Although the room was in almost complete darkness the first grey light of dawn was seeping through the small windowpanes and gradually everything came into focus. The sound of soft breathing reminded her that she was sharing the sparsely furnished room with Marianne.

They had left the luxury of Felicia's flat and had travelled to France in an overcrowded troop ship, although they had been afforded the comparative luxury of a cabin below deck. It had not been the most comfortable journey, but luckily neither of them suffered from seasickness. They had landed under the cover of darkness and the official who had travelled with them had organised transport to take them to the station, which was seething with men in uniform. The smell of French cigarettes mingled with the stench of unwashed bodies, smoke and engine oil. The babel of voices raised to make themselves heard over the hissing eruptions of steam from the huge iron monsters only added to the din and confusion that surrounded them. Eventually they had managed to hail a fiacre, which took them to their lodgings close to the rue Saint-Roch. The concierge, who had introduced herself as Madame Chausse, had shown them to their apartment. She had been proud of the facilities offered at such a reasonable rate, but Elsie was not impressed.

She yawned and sat up, reaching for her dressing gown with a sigh. This is where they would be for the foreseeable future. She rose somewhat unwillingly from her bed, and taking care not to wake Marianne made her away across the cold oilcloth-covered floor to the tiny room which served as a kitchen. The furnishings were basic and the only method of heating food, or obtaining any warmth at all, was a single gas ring set on a rickety wooden table next to a chipped stone sink with a single tap. The bathroom and lavatory were situated at the far end of the landing and shared by all the occupants on the fifth floor.

Elsie washed her hands and face in ice-cold water and filled the kettle before placing it on the gas ring, which lit with a sputter, flamed and then dwindled to almost nothing. At this rate it would take an hour to make a pot of tea. She had had the forethought to pack a good supply of Lyons' tea and several packets of cocoa, but the small amount of luggage they had been allowed precluded very much more than the bare essentials. Marianne had been most annoyed to discover that she could only bring a limited amount of clothes, but eventually she had been dissuaded from packing an evening gown and several silk tea gowns. Elsie had managed to convince her that warm underwear and woollen jumpers would be far more useful in the bitter winter weather.

She hurried into the bedroom and dressed quickly, but she was still shivering. She added an extra jumper in an attempt to stop her teeth chattering and pulled on her fur-lined boots. They had been warned in advance that the Parisians were suffering severe privations, but she had not been prepared for the austerity they had come across in such a short space of time. Coal, the concierge had told them grimly, was unobtainable, as what supplies there were had gone to factories and the military. Domestic boilers could not be lit and paraffin was unobtainable. 'You will turn your lights off at ten o'clock in the evening and if you want to use candles they will cost you forty centimes each.' Madame Chausse had left them to consider this as they settled into their new home.

Elsie glanced at the travelling clock that Marianne had placed on the small table between their beds. She went over and shook her gently. 'Wake up. It's eight o'clock. We don't want to be late on our first day at work.'

Marianne opened one eye and groaned. 'Go away. I want to sleep.'

'Get up. I've put the kettle on but heaven only knows how long it will take to boil, and there's no milk.'

Marianne snapped into a sitting position. 'It's freezing in here. We'll die of pneumonia.'

'Nonsense,' Elsie said briskly. 'I'm going to find the lavatory, and then I'll go out and get some milk and something for breakfast. I saw a shop a little further down the street.'

'I refuse to share a lavatory with strangers,' Marianne said, reaching for her dressing gown.

'I don't think we've got much choice.'

Marianne leaned over the edge of the bed and peered underneath. She righted herself with a grunt. 'I thought there might have been a po, but there's only dust and fluff. I don't think much of the cleaners here.'

'If you think I'm emptying a chamber pot for you, forget it,' Elsie said, giggling. 'And the only cleaners here will be you and me, so we'll take it in turns.' She took her hat and coat from the row of hooks on the door and left the room before Marianne had a chance to grumble.

The corridor was dark and the only source of light was a window at the far end. She made her way towards it, trying hard to remember which door Madame had indicated when briefly showing them round. It would be embarrassing to barge into the wrong room, but all the doors looked the same. She was getting desperate when a woman emerged from one of the rooms. Elsie hurried up to her. 'Good morning,' she said in French. 'I'm looking for the lavatory.'

'You've found it, dear.' The woman, who was not much older than Elsie herself, indicated the place she had just left. 'New here, aren't you?'

'We arrived last night,' Elsie said, edging towards the doorway.

'Jeanne-Marie.' The woman held out her hand. 'I've lived in this midden for what seems forever.'

'Denise Michaud.' Elsie shook hands. The alias still sounded strange to her ears, even though she had practised it hundreds of times during her weeks of training in London.

Jeanne-Marie brushed a strand of dark hair back from her forehead. 'You're not from round here, are you?'

Elsie was suddenly afraid that her accent had let her down. Perhaps she had been influenced by her Belgian friends, or her English overtones had betrayed her. She shrugged her shoulders. 'I'm from Provence,' she said casually. 'Now if you'll excuse me, I really need the lavatory.'

Jeanne-Marie grinned. 'Busting to go, are you? I know the feeling. I get like that on champagne, but it's in short supply these days. I like a good night out.'

'Who doesn't?' Elsie said in an attempt to sound casual.

'Aha, you are a girl after my own heart. You must

come with me some time. Most of the best places have closed down, but I know where you can still have a good time.'

'Thanks. I'll remember that, Jeanne-Marie.' Elsie darted into the small room and closed the door with a sigh of relief. The somewhat gaudily dressed Jeanne-Marie seemed like a nice friendly person, but Elsie had been warned about double agents and was only too well aware that she must be careful with whom she associated. She washed her hands in the small and grimy basin and only then realised that there was no towel. She waited for a few minutes, hoping that her new friend would have gone back to her room, before drawing back the bolt. She opened the door and came face to face with a huge bear of a man with a dark beard and moustache and bushy eyebrows. His hand was raised and she stifled a cry of fright.

Chapter Nine

'It's all right,' he said gruffly. 'No need to look scared. I don't bite.' He chuckled, a deep throaty noise that sounded more like a growl. 'Not often anyway. Have you finished in there?'

'Yes, monsieur.' Elsie slipped past him.

'Raoul Dubroc.' He held out a large paw of a hand. 'You're new here, aren't you?'

'Denise Michaud.' She shook his hand and found his touch surprisingly gentle. She managed a feeble smile.

'This isn't a safe place for a young girl to be these days, Denise.' His bushy eyebrows drew together in a frown. 'You need to be very careful where you go in Paris.'

'Thank you,' she murmured. 'I'll bear that in mind.' She hurried off, heading for the staircase, and ran down five flights to the ground floor. The grille over Madame Chausse's tiny office was closed and for a moment she was afraid that the outer door might be locked, but it opened easily and she let herself out into the chill of a frosty morning. A pale sun was attempting to squeeze its way through the clouds, but the cold air stung her cheeks and made her catch her breath. She walked briskly down the street to the bakery on the corner, but was disappointed to find that there were no croissants or pastries on sale, and only the coarsest bread was available. She purchased a loaf, thinking that it might be palatable if spread with butter and jam, but there did not seem to be a dairy in the vicinity, and she dared not draw attention to herself by asking for directions. She retraced her steps.

'What? No milk? And you call that bread? I call it a doorstop.' Marianne drew her coat closer around her body and shuddered. 'I can't eat that, Elsie, and I'm not drinking tea without milk. It's uncivilised.'

Elsie shrugged her shoulders. 'That's all I could get, and I couldn't find anywhere to buy milk or butter. I suggest you go out and see if you can do better.' She strode into the tiny kitchen to see if the kettle had boiled and found that it was barely simmering. She turned off the gas. 'This is hopeless.'

'I'm sorry.' Marianne leaned against the doorpost. 'I didn't mean to be bitchy. It's just that I like a cup of tea in the morning and I'm bloody starving. We haven't eaten a thing since that awful meal we had at the station last night, which wasn't fit to feed to pigs.'

Elsie lifted the kettle and held it out to her. 'If you want to wash in warm water you'd better use this. It's a pity to waste it.'

'Thanks, but I prefer to keep dry at the moment.

I'm afraid that water might freeze on my body and I won't be able to speak.' Marianne smiled ruefully. 'Some might say that's a good thing. Anyway, I really am sorry I was being difficult. Do you forgive me?'

'There's nothing to forgive. This isn't going to be easy for either of us.'

'I suppose we'd better set off for work. Perhaps we can get something to eat and a cup of something hot there.'

The rue Saint-Roch was lined with tall buildings facing each other across a narrow street off the fashionable rue de Rivoli. They had been thoroughly briefed before leaving London and made to study a map indicating important places such as the British Embassy, which was situated a few streets away. The official title of 41 rue Saint-Roch was the Inter-Ally Permit Office where French citizens went in order to apply for a permit to travel to Britain, but behind the rather gloomy and ordinary-looking façade the British secret service carried out its espionage in total secrecy.

Elsie found herself situated in an office crammed with filing cabinets and two large desks. She shared one with Marianne and the other with a bilingual French secretary, Andrée Dorgebray, who kept them busy all morning doing mundane filing and sorting out the pile of correspondence on her desk in order of urgency. She spoke little and only when absolutely necessary, but she did unbend slightly midmorning when she took them to the kitchen on the ground floor and showed them where the coffee and mugs were kept. There was a jug of fresh milk on a marble slab in the larder, although the temperature inside the building was only a degree or two above that outside, and close to freezing.

Clutching their mugs of hot, milky coffee they followed her back up the wooden staircase, their footsteps echoing on the bare treads. 'You will be allowed an hour for lunch,' Miss Dorgebray said with a hint of a smile. 'There is a café in the next street where you'll get good food at a reasonable price, even allowing for the fact that everything is scarce nowadays.'

'Thank you, Miss Dorgebray,' Marianne said meekly.

'Now get back to work. Lunch is from one o'clock, and I expect you both back in the office at two o'clock precisely. We finish work at five, unless there is something urgent that needs our attention and then we stay on until it is finished. I hardly need to remind you that this is wartime, ladies. I've no doubt that your lives in London were very different, but you will just have to adapt to our ways or you will be sent home. Do I make myself clear?'

'Yes, ma'am,' Elsie said hastily. She could sense the resentment building up in Marianne and she sent her a warning look.

'Yes, Miss Dorgebray,' Marianne muttered.

*

At exactly one o'clock Andrée Dorgebray rose from her desk and took her coat and hat from the stand behind the door. 'Two o'clock sharp,' she said as she left the office.

Marianne leapt to her feet. 'Let's get out of here and find somewhere to eat. I'm absolutely starving.'

'So am I.' Elsie abandoned the filing. 'Perhaps we'd better try that café that Miss Dorgebray told us about as it's near and we don't yet know our way around.'

'Agreed.' Marianne rammed her fur hat on her head. 'Let's go.'

They hurried from the office putting on their coats as they went. Outside it had started to snow. Large feathery flakes drifted from a leaden sky, coating the pavements and almost immediately turning to black slush beneath the feet of passers-by. The café was not far away and the smoky fug inside was laced with the sharp tang of wine and the heady aroma of garlic. They found a table by the window and sat down to study the handwritten menu.

'It looks like onion soup or onion soup,' Marianne said, grinning.

'I don't care. I'm so hungry that my stomach feels as though it's eating itself.' Elsie clutched her belly and groaned.

Marianne looked up as a young boy approached them with a towel looped over his arm and a serious expression on his youthful face. 'What may I get for you, ladies?'

Marianne's lips twitched but she ordered the soup and coffee as if they had selected it from a vast menu. 'He's just a kid,' she said when he was out of earshot. 'It's terrible to think that boys not much older than him are being sent to the front line and are dying every day.'

'Don't let's talk about it,' Elsie said, shuddering. 'I can't bear to think of the dreadful hardships they must be suffering.'

'Shh,' Marianne said, frowning. 'He's coming back. They must have a vat of the stuff behind the counter.' She gave the boy a brilliant smile as he placed the steaming bowls in front of them. 'Thank you.'

He bowed gravely before making his way to a customer who was calling for service.

Marianne sniffed the fragrant soup, redolent with the scent of garlic, caramelised onion and cheese. 'It looks as if this is going to be our staple diet from now on,' she said, dipping her spoon in and tasting. 'Hmm, it's very good. Food like this almost makes it worth being treated like schoolgirls by the formidable Miss Dorgebray.'

'Working there is like being back at school. I hope she relaxes a bit when she gets to know us.'

'At least she told us where to get a decent meal.' Marianne said, swallowing a mouthful of toasted bread. 'This onion soup is very good, although my breath will stink for the rest of the day. They're very generous with the garlic but I won't be kissing anyone in the foreseeable future, so I suppose it doesn't matter.'

'It's tasty,' Elsie agreed. 'And this café is near enough to the lodging house for us to come here for all our meals. I can't see myself cooking much on that gas ring.'

Marianne was silent for a few minutes while she finished her food. She looked up, wiping her mouth on her handkerchief. 'I suppose table napkins are a thing of the past,' she said with a wry smile. 'And judging by the stains on the tablecloth, soap must be in short supply too. Madame Chausse doesn't seem to use much of it in the lodging house.'

'Mrs Tranter would be horrified if she could see how dirty the place is,' Elsie said in an undertone. 'But I didn't realise that things were going to be so bad here. It's far worse than I expected.'

'And I was hoping we'd do something more exciting than filing and sorting out that woman's in-tray.' Marianne reached into her handbag and took out an enamelled compact. She stared into the mirror, dabbing powder on the tip of her nose. 'I thought we'd be doing something more useful.'

'We've got to learn the ropes, Marianne. This is our first day.'

'I know, but it's hard to be patient. I want to do something that will help to end the war.'

Elsie glanced over her shoulder to see if any of the other customers could hear. 'Don't look now,' she whispered. 'But that man who's just come in lives in our building, on the same floor. He scared me half to death this morning when I came out of the lavatory and saw him standing there.'

Marianne gazed over Elsie's shoulder. 'That man mountain with the black wiry hair?'

'I said don't look now. But yes, that's him. His name is Raoul Dubroc.'

'I didn't see a soul when I went to that ghastly little room that smells like a sewer, but I'm glad I didn't bump into him.'

'Do you think he's followed us?'

Marianne frowned. 'Of course not. I expect he works near here.'

'It's a strange coincidence all the same.'

'It's all strange to us, Elsie. Don't worry, everything will be fine. We'll become accustomed to this way of life, eventually.'

'Maybe we should have stayed in London. We were doing worthwhile jobs there.'

'And we'll be even more useful here. They have to get to know us, just as we have to get to know them.'

'You're right, of course.' Elsie pushed her plate away. 'I'm just being silly. It's all so strange and I miss everyone at home.'

Marianne reached across the table to pat her on the shoulder. 'Not everyone. Guy is here somewhere, fighting for us.'

'That makes me feel even worse.'

'And we're not entirely alone in Paris. Henri's

parents have an apartment not far from here. I thought I'd call on his mother, although it's possible she might have gone to Provence. Maybe I'll go tomorrow.'

'I hope Henri's safe and well,' Elsie murmured, looking away. 'He was kind to me when Ma died.'

'He's a darling man, and I adore him.' Marianne glanced at the large, white-faced clock on the wall above the shelves, which were crammed with bottles of all shapes and sizes. 'It's time we were heading back. I'm afraid Miss Dorgebray might make us stand in the corner with our faces to the wall if we're late returning from lunch on our first day.'

Elsie laughed and immediately felt better. It was typical of Marianne to say something ridiculous that would put all her fears into perspective. She rose from her seat. 'Let's go then.'

That evening, after a tiring day getting to know the routine in the office, it was a relief to tidy everything away and set off for the lodging house. They stopped at the café for a meal, which turned out to be a tasty stew with the tough, stringy meat cleverly disguised by the addition of wine and herbs. 'We'll have to budget carefully,' Marianne said as they left and walked briskly along the deserted street. 'I've arranged to have money transferred to a local bank but my allowance won't last long at this rate.'

'I thought you were well off,' Elsie said, pulling her collar up to her chin and screwing her eyes up against the snow, which had started to fall again in earnest. 'You always seemed to have anything you wanted.'

'I'm extravagant. It comes from being given too much too young, I suppose. Anyway, we'll be all right, but we can't exist on the pittance they pay us.'

Elsie glanced over her shoulder.

'What's the matter?' Marianne demanded. 'Why are you so edgy?'

'I thought I heard footsteps, but there's no one there.'

Marianne chuckled. 'It's probably that glass of wine you had with your dinner and there must have been a couple of bottles of claret in the stew. You aren't used to drinking that's all. The rest is your over-active imagination.'

'I suppose so.' Elsie had to quicken her pace in order to keep up with Marianne, but she was sure she had heard the heavy tread of someone not far behind them. When she looked back again moments later she thought she saw a movement in a doorway, but the gaslights were dim, forming small pools of yellowish light on the slushy pavements and creating deep areas of shadow. It must have been the wine, she decided, or the fact that she was tired and overreacting.

They arrived back at their lodgings to find that the electricity had been cut off, and the concierge offered to sell them a candle for fifty centimes. When Marianne protested that she was overcharging them,

Madame Chausse pursed her lips and narrowed her eyes. 'You can go out and buy one for forty centimes, if you can find anywhere that's selling them at this time of night.'

'We'll take it, thank you,' Elsie said, fumbling in her purse for the coins. She dropped them into Madame's outstretched hand and took the candle.

'I suppose you'll charge us for the match as well,' Marianne said crossly.

'She's joking, madame.' Elsie held the candle out to be lit. 'Thank you, Madame Chausse. Goodnight.' She headed for the stairs, cupping her hand to shield the flame from the draughts that whistled through the building.

'Old witch,' Marianne said beneath her breath as they reached the fifth floor. 'She'll be making a fortune out of the tenants.'

Elsie made her way along the corridor. 'We didn't have much choice, did we?'

Marianne's answer was drowned by a welcoming shout from Jeanne-Marie, who had emerged from her room and was heading towards them, looking ghostly in the flickering light of her candle. 'I see you've been caught out by the vampire,' she said, giggling. 'Don't worry, my dears. She catches all the new residents like that. She'll suck you dry with her little swindles. You'll learn.' She stared hard at Marianne. 'This must be your sister.'

'No, but people often remark on the likeness. This is my good friend Aimée Lalonde.' Elsie turned to

Marianne. 'This is Jeanne-Marie, she lives here as well.'

Marianne held out her hand. 'It's a pleasure to meet you, Jeanne-Marie.'

Jeanne-Marie seized her hand and shook it vigorously. 'It's nice to meet you too, Aimée. There aren't many of us single girls on this floor. There are a couple of prostitutes occupying two rooms on the first floor, but I steer clear of them. I was a dancer at the Moulin Rouge until it burned down last year, so now I serve in a bar, but I'm a respectable working girl, not like those tarts.'

'I'm sure,' Elsie said hastily.

'You must come to the bar one evening. I'll introduce you to some decent men, although most of the good ones are off fighting the Boche, but there are one or two who aren't cripples or in their dotage. Must dash now. Can't afford to be late for work.' She hurried off, teetering on her high heels.

'Well,' Marianne said, staring after her as the darkness swallowed Jeanne-Marie's departing figure except for a trail of smoke from her candle. 'We certainly get all sorts here.'

Elsie moved on to unlock the door to their room. 'I like her,' she said firmly. 'She seems a good-hearted sort of girl.'

'I suppose we might accept her invitation,' Marianne said thoughtfully. 'I can't face the thought of spending every evening stuck in this dreadful hole, and it would be heaven to go somewhere warmer than here.'

161

Elsie went inside, placing the candle on a saucer and setting it down on the small pine table beneath the window where ice was already forming on the inside of the glass panes. She shivered. 'If only we could have a fire of some sort it wouldn't seem so bad.'

'Just keep your coat and boots on.' Marianne sat down and opened her handbag. She took out a packet of cigarettes and lit one in the candle flame. 'We'll get used to all this eventually. Let's just hope we don't get flu. When you went to make the coffee this afternoon our new lady boss was telling me that there's an epidemic of it in Paris. It's just our luck to arrive here with blackouts, flu and the odd bombing raid thrown in for good measure.'

'You're the one who wanted to come here and work, Marianne.' Elsie made her way towards the kitchen. 'I'm going to put the kettle on and maybe by bedtime it will be hot enough to make some cocoa.' She lit the stub of last night's candle and went into the tiny kitchen to light the gas, returning moments later. 'It would be quicker to hold a pan of milk over a candle.'

Marianne stubbed her cigarette out in the ashtray. 'I've been thinking, would you mind having lunch on your own tomorrow?'

'No, of course not. Why?'

'I thought I'd go to the bank and then I might call at the Bellaires' apartment. I'd ask you to come with me, but I'm sure you don't want to be dragged round Paris on what might be a wild goose chase.'

'I'd like to see more of Paris than the rue Saint-Roch.' Elsie tried hard to sound casual. 'So I might tag along, if you don't mind.'

'That's fine by me. If Madame Bellaire is at home she might even let us use her bathroom. I'd kill for a hot bath.'

The bank in the rue de Rivoli was within easy walking distance, which was just as well as the snow had settled overnight, and attempts at keeping the pavements clear were patchy and had left the surface dangerously icy. Elsie's heart was pounding at the thought that she might see Henri again. She followed Marianne into the building and paused, taking in the opulence of the marble and mahogany temple of finance. White light reflected off the snow-covered rooftops of adjacent buildings and filtered through the stained glass windows, creating a kaleidoscope of patterns on the tiled floor. Bank clerks sat behind desks that would not have looked out of place in a palace or a grand hotel: not that Elsie had ever visited either, but she had seen illustrations in some of Felicia's glossy magazines. The doorman eyed them warily. 'May I help you, ladies?'

Marianne gave him her most charming smile. 'Is Monsieur Henri Bellaire in the office today?'

He shook his head. 'No, mademoiselle. He's away, fighting for his country like all patriotic Frenchmen. I'd go myself but I'm too old.'

'I'm sure you are doing an excellent job here,' Marianne said graciously. 'I don't suppose you know whether Madame Bellaire has remained in Paris?'

He shook his head. 'I believe she has gone to the country, mademoiselle. But Monsieur is in his office if you would like to see him.'

'I won't bother him today,' Marianne said airily. 'Thank you for your help, monsieur.' She took Elsie by the arm. 'I was afraid that might be the case, so I'll make a withdrawal and leave it at that.'

'But Henri might be on leave.'

'I'm sure he'd have got a message to me somehow. He knows I'm in Paris because I sent him a coded telegram. It's something we made up when we were children, and now it's come in useful.'

Elsie was bitterly disappointed, but she did not protest when Marianne marched her out into the street. After the comparative warmth of the bank vestibule the cold air took her breath away, and she clutched her hand to her mouth.

'Are you all right?' Marianne's voice was filled with genuine concern. 'You're very pale. You aren't going to faint or do anything stupid like that, are you?'

'No. I'm fine,' Elsie said slowly. 'It's so cold it took my breath away. I'm sorry you didn't see Henri. You must be worried about him.'

'I'm all right, silly. You're sweet to be concerned about my feelings, but I'm sure that Henri can take care of himself, although I'd have liked to see Selene again. Anyway, let's get something to eat. You'll feel better with a hot meal inside you.'

It felt as though their roles had been switched and that brought a reluctant smile to Elsie's lips. 'I'm supposed to be the practical one, not you.'

'I can be sensible when I want to be, and I'm starving.'

'I wonder what will be on the menu today,' Elsie said as they retraced their steps along the rue de Rivoli.

'I'll give you two guesses, but I suspect the answer will be onion soup.'

Arm in arm they walked on, slipping and sliding as they went but somehow managing to keep upright until Marianne skidded on a particularly icy patch and fell to the ground with a yelp of pain. 'My ankle,' she groaned.

Elsie made an attempt to lift her, but Marianne was a dead weight and she was obviously in too much pain to help herself. Elsie looked round in desperation but there were only a few people who had braved the icy conditions, and those who had did not seem inclined to help. 'Try to stand, Marianne. Lean on me.'

'I'll try.'

Marianne made a bold effort but every movement caused her pain and Elsie was not strong enough to lift her unaided. Then, just when she was becoming desperate, a figure loomed out of nowhere and scooped Marianne up in his arms as if she weighed no more than a sack of feathers. Elsie staggered backwards, staring at him in surprise. 'Oh. It's you.'

Raoul Dubroc grinned. 'I saw you having difficulties, mademoiselle.'

'Put me down, please, monsieur,' Marianne said angrily. 'You're making a spectacle of me.'

'Can you walk unaided?'

'I can try.'

He put her down but her ankle gave way and she would have fallen if he had not supported her. 'Now what would you like to do?' he said affably. 'Do you want to stand here and turn into an icicle, or would you like some assistance.'

Elsie tapped Marianne on the shoulder. 'Monsieur Dubroc has a room on the same floor as us, I think I might have told you?'

'I'd be grateful for some help,' Marianne said stiffly.

Raoul scooped her up in his arms and marched off, with Elsie desperately trying to keep her balance as she hurried after them.

'Where are you taking me?' Marianne shot him a sideways glance. 'I think perhaps I could walk now.'

He said nothing as he headed into the rue de l'Echelle, leaving Elsie little alternative but to follow them. 'Where are you going, Raoul?' she demanded breathlessly, but either he had not heard or he chose to ignore her, and he continued on his way as if carrying a young woman through the streets of war-torn Paris was an everyday occurrence.

Even in such circumstances, Elsie could not but admire the wide avenue of terraced seven-storey buildings. The elegant façades, embellished with wrought-iron balconies, were a haunting reminder of times before the war when the carriages of the rich and famous thronged the fashionable street. Maybe those days would return when the war ended, but Elsie suspected that life might never be the same for any of them. It was easy to imagine how wonderful it must look in the spring, when the sun warmed the pavements and the stark bare branches of the trees burst suddenly into leaf.

She dragged her thoughts back to the present as Raoul turned left into the rue d'Argenteuil, a much narrower street which, Elsie realised, getting her bearings at last, would lead into the rue Saint-Roch. He stopped suddenly outside a small café. 'I know the proprietor,' he said brusquely. 'He'll look after you.' He jerked his head in Elsie's direction. 'Would you open the door, please?'

The outside looked decidedly seedy and run down. The windows were filmed with condensation and the name above the door, Café Goulet, was barely visible beneath a coating of city grime. Elsie opened the door and was greeted by the now familiar waft of tobacco smoke and the heady tang of red wine, but the pervading aroma was of meat roasting on a charcoal brazier. She could hear the hiss and sizzle of the exploding juices and her mouth watered in anticipation. Raoul carried Marianne to a table close to the bar and set her down on a chair. 'My friend's wife will take a look at your ankle. She is a nurse.'

'Thank you. I'm very grateful for your help, monsieur.'

'It's Raoul,' he said gruffly. 'Just Raoul.' He bowed from the waist, looming over her like a giant. 'Think nothing of it. I was just passing by.' He signalled to the proprietor who scuttled out from behind the bar, wiping his hands on a cloth.

'What can I do for you, Raoul?' His dark eyes flickered over Marianne and Elsie. 'Are these friends of yours?'

Raoul drew him aside, speaking in a low voice. Elsie had to strain her ears to hear what was being said. 'They are all right. You need not worry, Raimond.' He nodded his head in Marianne's direction. 'The young lady had a fall. Is Honorine at home? Perhaps she could take a look at the injury and see if there are any bones broken.'

Raimond turned his head. 'Honorine,' he bellowed. 'Get yourself out here at once. We have an emergency.'

'No, really,' Elsie protested before Marianne had a chance to argue. 'I'm sure it's just a simple sprain.'

'My wife is an expert in these matters.' Raimond draped the grimy cloth over one shoulder. 'What can I get you, ladies? A glass of cognac, perhaps?'

Elsie opened her mouth to refuse but Marianne forestalled her. 'No, thank you. We have to get back to work very soon. It would not look good to turn up the worse for drink.'

Raoul gave a deep belly laugh that rattled the glasses on the shelf behind the bar. 'The young ladies have only to go as far as the rue Saint-Roch. The British permit office, I believe.'

'How did you know that?' Elsie demanded, immediately suspicious. 'I didn't tell you where we worked.'

He shrugged his shoulders. 'Perhaps Jeanne-Marie mentioned it, or even Madame Chausse. Word gets round in a small community.'

Elsie was about to deny ever having disclosed their place of employment to anyone when Honorine Goulet erupted into the bar. 'Why are you shouting like a wounded bull, Raimond? I'm busy and I have to be at the hospital in an hour.'

'Your expertise is needed, my love,' he said smoothly. 'This young person has had a fall in the snow and hurt her ankle.'

Honorine marched over to Marianne. 'Let me see.' She rounded on her husband and Raoul. 'Look the other way. Give the poor girl some privacy.' She waved her hand to encompass the male customers who were seated at the small tables. 'That goes for all of you.' She slid a stool beneath the affected limb and went down on one knee in front of Marianne. 'I will have to take your boot off.'

'That's all right,' Marianne said, wincing as Honorine proceeded to untie the laces and ease the boot off. 'I think it is just a sprain, as Denise said.'

Honorine glanced up at Elsie with a challenge in her grey eyes. 'You are a nurse?'

'No, madame. It was just a guess.'

Marianne grimaced as Honorine manipulated the injured ankle. 'That hurt.'

'It is just a sprain.' Honorine rose to her feet. 'I will bind it up for you, but try to rest it as much as possible.' She went behind the bar and returned with a small black bag. 'This won't take a moment.' She looked up at her husband. 'Don't stand there like a fool. Hot coffee is needed here, with sugar, and whatever the ladies wish to order for their meal. We all have work to do, Raimond. We can't stand about chatting to our friends all day, like some I could mention.'

Raoul backed towards the door. 'I'll leave you in Honorine's capable hands.' He left with a wave of his hand and a gust of cold air blew in from the street.

Raimond bustled behind the bar and poured the coffee while his wife expertly bandaged Marianne's ankle. 'There,' she said, closing the bag with a snap. 'That should help, but remember what I said about keeping the weight off it.'

'Thank you very much, madame.' Marianne took her purse from her pocket. 'How much do I owe you?'

Honorine threw up her hands. 'It is just a bandage. I wouldn't take your money for such a small service.'

'Well, I'm very grateful,' Marianne said sincerely.

'We would like to buy some lunch,' Elsie added. She eyed the prices of the beefsteaks on the blackboard and thought of their dwindling supply of money. 'Maybe a bowl of soup.'

Raimond served them their coffee. 'You need sustenance, young ladies. Any friends of Raoul are friends of mine and my good wife.' He went behind the counter and returned moments later with two helpings of grilled meat, fried onions and a generous portion of freshly baked bread. 'Eat and enjoy,' he said, beaming. 'Raimond Goulet's beefsteaks are the best in Paris. War or no war, we aim only to please.'

'And he has the biggest mouth in France.' A working man who had been sitting at a nearby table rose to his feet and took some coins from his pocket. He handed them to Raimond, grinning broadly. 'And he overcharges, ladies. Be warned. He will lure you in with a discount on your first meal, and then he will charge you extra each time you return.'

'If what you say is true why do you come here every day for your food?' Raimond demanded cheerfully. 'He is a liar. Don't pay any attention to Maurice.'

Elsie managed a smile as she concentrated on eating. The food was delicious and more than welcome. Marianne was also demolishing her meal as if she had not eaten for weeks, but a quick glance at the clock on the wall reminded Elsie that it was time to return to the office. Mademoiselle Dorgebray would not be amused if they were late. She would, no doubt, expect Marianne to crawl back to work even had she broken her ankle. Elsie chewed and swallowed the last morsel, wiping the plate with bread in the French fashion. She smiled to herself. Ma would be horrified if she could see her now. She had taken pains to ensure that Elsie grew up with acceptable table manners and she would consider this behaviour quite reprehensible.

'Come along, Denise,' Marianne said, rising to her feet. 'We've got to get back to the office. Stop daydreaming and put your skates on.' She limped over to the bar. 'What do I owe you, Monsieur Goulet?'

Chapter Ten

They just scraped into work on time. Miss Dorgebray was already at her desk and she glanced at the clock but said nothing. If she noticed that Marianne was limping she did not mention it, and she bent her head over her sheaf of papers with a frown puckering her brow.

Elsie tried to concentrate on translating a report from an agent in Belgium, but now that she had time to herself all she could think about was Henri. He might be anywhere, fighting in the front line and enduring the terrible conditions that Felicia had described in such agonising detail. He might be racked with trench fever or dying from his injuries in a military hospital. He would be just a number to the orderlies on duty: he would be one of many with no one to hold his hand and whisper words of comfort.

She realised with a sudden pang of conscience that she had given little thought to how Guy must also be suffering in the trenches, and that made her feel even worse. She had rejected him because she loved Henri, but she had made Guy suffer as she was suffering now. If she could turn back the clock she might have been able to let him down more gently. She could still see the pain in his eyes when she refused to accept his ring. The closely written lines of handwriting danced up and down in front of her eyes like tadpoles in the village pond, and she blinked back tears. She gathered her scattered thoughts with a concentrated effort. Men's lives depended on the intelligence gathered here and she had an important job to do. She steeled herself to carry on.

They worked in silence with only the ticking of the clock to mark the passage of time, and the occasional rustle of paper or scratch of a pen nib to prove that the three occupants of the room had not fallen asleep.

At three o'clock precisely, Andrée announced that she was going downstairs to make herself a cup of coffee. Marianne leaned over to put her arm around Elsie's shoulders. 'Cheer up. I know you're worried about Guy, just as I'm worried about Henri, but at least I know that he's still alive.'

'How do you work that out?'

Marianne gave her a sympathetic smile. 'Because, you ninny, the staff at the bank would be the first to know if anything had happened to him.'

'I didn't think of that.'

'The same goes for Guy. We would have heard if there was bad news, so stop worrying and cheer up. It's bad enough having to plough through all these handwritten notes without you acting as though the end of the world is about to happen.'

'I just wish we were doing something more active.'

'We're doing all we can. Remember that.'

'You sound so casual about it, Marianne. Aren't you worried about Algy and all your other gentlemen friends who've enlisted?'

'Of course I am, but turning myself into a nervous wreck isn't going to help them. What we're doing might be a bit dull but we might just stumble across a crucial piece of intelligence that will save lives.'

Elsie cocked her head on one side. 'Shh. She's coming. Better not get caught chatting.'

That evening, in the chilly confines of their lodgings, Marianne sat at the table by the window wrapped in her fur coat and the counterpane from her bed. Elsie was attempting to darn a hole in her stocking by candlelight as the electricity supply had failed yet again. Marianne gave a sudden start and peered out of the window, wiping the frost off the inside with her sleeve. 'I'll swear there's someone watching us,' she said in a low voice. 'I thought I was imagining things at first because the gaslight is so dim, but then he lit a cigarette and I saw the flicker of a match.'

'Where?' Elsie put down the stocking and leaned across the table. 'I can't see anyone.'

'In the shop doorway on the other side of the street, directly opposite. Wait until he takes a drag and you can just make out the glowing tip of the cigarette.'

Elsie peered into the darkness. 'Why would anyone be watching this building?'

'I think it's us he's watching.' Marianne's voice throbbed with suppressed excitement. 'We're agents of the British government. He could be a German spy.'

'Or maybe he's got a girlfriend living here, or perhaps he's a client of the girls on the first floor that Jeanne-Marie mentioned.'

'There,' Marianne said, pointing excitedly. 'The cigarette. Did you see it?'

'No, but a man stopping for a smoke doesn't mean he's spying on us.'

'I wish I had some cigarettes left, but I can't stand the French tobacco.' Marianne rose to her feet and limped over to her bed. 'My ankle aches and I'm chilled to the marrow. I'm going to bed.'

Elsie abandoned her darning. 'I can't see well enough to finish this. I'm going to the bathroom, and hopefully when I get back the water in the kettle will be hot enough for a cup of cocoa.' She stood up, taking one last look out of the window. 'Whoever it was seems to have gone, Marianne. You can rest easy.'

'I won't sleep a wink,' Marianne said, yawning.

Elsie left the room and headed for the lavatory. She longed for a hot bath, but there was no chance of that. She had not properly understood Felicia's desire for such a luxury when she returned from entertaining the troops, but now she could sympathise. Wallowing in hot, scented water was one of the things she missed the most, as well as freshly laundered sheets and clothes, not to mention a nice cup of tea. These headed a long list that she added to mentally each day.

There was only one person waiting outside the bathroom and Elsie exchanged nods and pleasantries with the middle-aged woman, who apparently worked as a cleaner at the Louvre, but then the occupant emerged and Elsie was left on her own. She heard approaching footsteps and glanced over her shoulder to see Raoul wearing his heavy great-coat and a fur hat which made him look even more bear-like than usual. He raised his hand in a salute. 'Good evening.'

She smiled in acknowledgement. 'You're home late.'

'I've only just finished my shift at the Gare du Nord.'

'What do you do there, Raoul?'

'I'm a signalman. I've worked for the railway for twenty years, man and boy.' He was about to walk off when the bathroom door opened and the cleaning lady emerged. She scuttled off, swinging her wash bag. Elsie was about to enter when she had a sudden thought and called out to Raoul. 'Just a minute.'

He paused, turning his head. 'You wanted something?'

'Were you watching our window from the street just now?'

His deep laugh reverberated off the walls in the narrow corridor. 'Why would I do such a thing?'

'I don't know. Maybe we were mistaken, but you always seem to be popping up in the most unexpected places.'

'A coincidence,' he said casually. 'You make too much of it.' He strolled off, leaving Elsie staring after him. There was something about Raoul Dubroc that did not add up – but they were living in the twilight world of the secret service – sometimes nothing made sense. She must not allow herself to become so entangled in its web that she could not tell the difference between fact and fiction.

When she returned to the room she found that the kettle had almost boiled and she was able to make cocoa, but Marianne had fallen asleep beneath a pile of blankets and clothing and it seemed a pity to wake her. Elsie went to sit by the window, sipping the cocoa, which she had sweetened with condensed milk. She watched the street for some time, but there were only a few passers-by and there was no sign of anyone loitering below. Perhaps Marianne had imagined it after all, or else it had been a completely innocent person simply stopping to enjoy a smoke before going on his way. She went to bed and slept soundly, exhausted both emotionally and physically.

The weeks went by and Elsie's days fell into a strict routine centred on work at 41 rue Saint-Roch. She and Marianne went to the Café Goulet every day for their lunch, as it was near enough to make it the most convenient place to eat, and Raimond always made them welcome. The formidable Honorine greeted them warmly whenever she happened to be in the bar, but more often than not she was at the hospital. The locals seemed to accept them without question, and Elsie was convinced that this was thanks to Raoul, who occasionally breezed in for a drink and a chat with Raimond. Elsie was still slightly suspicious of Raoul, and her fertile imagination had him alternately as a German spy or a Russian émigré. His shifts at the railway station seemed to vary, which might explain his sudden and unexpected appearances, but on the rare occasions when she ventured out alone she could not shake off the feeling she was being followed.

One evening Jeanne-Marie took them to the bar where she worked, but it was gloomy, damp and smoky in the cellar and the customers were mostly men who were too old to enlist or exempt on medical grounds. Elsie sat in a corner sipping a glass of red wine while Marianne chatted to a young soldier who had been badly wounded and sent home to recuperate. Elsie tried not to stare at the empty sleeve where his left arm should have been, but Marianne did not seem perturbed by that or the livid scars on the soldier's face. Elsie could only admire her friend for being able to cope with such obvious disabilities without being patronising or overly sympathetic, but she herself felt like crying every time she looked at him.

After the first visit Marianne went to the bar on several occasions, but Elsie chose to stay in the lodging house and keep up to date by reading the English newspapers which had been discarded in the rue Saint-Roch. She tried not to think about either Henri or Guy, and to distance herself from the terrifying accounts of the fighting at Verdun. Terrible losses were reported, with hundreds of thousands of casualties, and although the battle had begun in February there seemed to be no end in sight. The advance of the German army might have been halted, but Paris was by no means immune to terror from the skies, although according to the newspapers, the French capital fared better than London when it came to death and casualties caused by incendiary bombs.

Life grew a little easier when winter finally lost its grip and a warm spring heralded the balmy days of summer. Elsie began to feel more at home in Paris and she used her free time to explore and admire the sights or to walk in the Tuileries gardens or the Place du Carrousel. She sometimes found herself walking past Henri's bank but she did not go in, although she had a vague hope that perhaps he might be on leave and they would suddenly come face to face. She imagined their reunion in a hundred different ways, but it always ended in a passionate embrace and they walked arm in arm along the Quai des Tuileries, into the future, together forever. He had never given her any reason to suppose that he might feel the same, but she had built a dream world around him, and it was here she chose to escape from the monotony of her work.

'Oh, I beg your pardon, madame.' Elsie had been miles away when she collided with a woman who had stepped out of the Bellaires' bank onto the pavement. She stared at the lined but still beautiful face. 'Madame Bellaire. I am so sorry. I wasn't looking where I was going. Are you all right?' She knew she was gabbling, but the shock of seeing Henri's mother was too much for her. 'Are you hurt?'

Selene Bellaire stared at her blankly. 'I'm sorry. Do I know you?'

Elsie realised her mistake too late. She dared not break her cover. 'N-no. I've seen your photograph in a fashion magazine, madame. I'm so sorry.' She backed away, panicked. 'Please excuse me.'

'Who are you?' Selene stared at her, frowning. 'You do look familiar and yet I can't quite place you.'

'You wouldn't know me, madame. I apologise for not looking where I was going.' Elsie turned to go but Selene caught her by the sleeve.

'I never forget a face. What is your name?'

'Denise Michaud,' Elsie said in desperation. 'You must have mistaken me for someone else, madame.'

'You remind me of someone very dear to me.'

'Excuse me, madame. I have to get back to work.'

'I have it at last. You are Marianne's maidservant. I'll never forget that evening in Darcy Hall when my son mistook you for Marianne, and the embarrassing debacle of the dinner party.'

It was strictly against the rules and Elsie knew that she should leave now before things became even more complicated, but she was desperate for news of Henri and who better to tell her than his own mother. 'I can't reveal my identity, madame.'

'These are difficult times,' Selene said slowly. 'Assure me that you are doing nothing wrong and we will say no more.'

'I promise you that I am not doing anything that would harm your country or mine.'

Selene inclined her head slightly. 'Then I wish you well.' She was about to walk away but Elsie could not allow her to leave without asking the question that was uppermost in her mind.

'Madame Bellaire. A moment, please.'

'What is it?'

'Have you news of Henri? Is he safe and well?'

A flicker of emotion crossed Selene's classical features. 'He is at the front, fighting for his country.'

'But he is alive.'

'Yes, thank God. I saw him briefly in January and he was in good spirits, but very thin.' Selene's dark eyes brimmed with tears. 'He was so tired that he slept for most of his leave, and I used to creep into his bedroom just to look at him and to reassure myself that he was real and not a figment of my imagination.' She dashed her hand across her eyes. 'When you become a mother you will understand.'

Elsie realised that she was crying too. Whether it was sympathy or the sheer relief of knowing for certain that Henri had survived thus far she did not know, but the guilt she had felt on betraying her own identity was a small price to pay for peace of mind. She would return to the office and continue her mission with at least a small hope that Henri would be spared the fate of so many good men. She laid her hand on Selene's arm in a mute attempt to comfort her, and then hurried away. If she stayed a moment longer she would give herself away.

She returned to the rue Saint-Roch and took her place behind her desk. Marianne and Andrée had not yet returned from their lunch break and for that Elsie was grateful. It gave her time to compose herself, but she had reckoned without Marianne's sharp eyes and intuitive response to her moods. 'What's up with you?' she demanded as she took her seat. 'You were happy as a sandboy earlier and now look at you.'

Elsie turned her head away. 'I'm fine.'

'No, you're not. You've been crying and the tip of your nose is red. Something or someone has upset you.'

'I made a big mistake,' Elsie whispered, gazing anxiously around although there was no one else in the room. 'I didn't mean to tell her but she knew me, Marianne. She actually recognised me.'

'Stop talking in riddles. Who recognised you and what did you tell her?'

'I literally bumped into her as she came out of the bank.'

'Who?' Marianne took her by the shoulders and shook her. 'Tell me quickly before Andrée gets back from lunch.'

'Madame Bellaire. I almost knocked her down.'

'And she recognised you?'

'Not at first, but she kept on saying that she never forgot a face and she wanted to know my name.'

'You didn't tell her?'

'I didn't mean to but it just slipped out.'

'You idiot,' Marianne said, frowning. 'But you didn't tell her your real name?'

'No, of course not.'

'And you didn't tell her what you were doing here?'

'No. Although I think she guessed. She's not stupid.'

'I suppose you asked her about Henri and completely gave the game away?'

'He's alive. I was going to tell you when I had the opportunity.'

Marianne cocked her head on one side. 'Shh. Someone's coming. We'll talk about this later, but I think you'll have to warn our friend Andrée that there's been a breach of security. Heaven help us both.'

Andrée Dorgebray went straight to Major Kirke, the head of operations, and Elsie was summoned to his office. In an interview that made her feel like a silly schoolgirl she was compelled to admit her connection with the Bellaire family. She gave him an exact account of what was said outside the bank in the rue de Rivoli and Major Kirke sat in silence, his unwavering stare seeming to bore into her soul. She finished with an apology, but she could see that he was unmoved. He leaned across his desk. 'You are a danger to us all while you remain here. You will be moved on.'

'Are you sending me home, sir?'

'I haven't decided what course to take.'

'You mustn't blame Marianne, I mean Aimée. She had nothing to do with it.'

'If you are to have an alias you should think of yourself as that person. You eat, sleep and breathe as that person. You, it seems, cannot put your personal feelings aside and that's dangerous.'

'I'm sorry, sir.' Elsie raised her chin and looked him squarely in the eyes. 'But I want to serve my country. I don't care what you ask me to do. I know I made a mess of things but I'll go anywhere and do anything you want so that I can make up for what I've done.'

'I believe you. Go back to your office.' He dismissed her with a wave of his hand. 'Send Mademoiselle Dorgebray to me.'

That evening Elsie and Marianne sat in their room at the lodging house with their bags packed, waiting for orders to move on. 'I can't believe that you were so stupid,' Marianne said angrily. 'We were just beginning to get somewhere in the rue Saint-Roch and you had to spoil it all.'

'You don't have to come with me. I told Major Kirke that it was entirely my fault. I deserve to be sent home in disgrace but you've done nothing wrong.'

'Come off it, Elsie. You know we're a team. We work together and I told Major Kirke so. Perhaps they can find something for both of us back at Room 40. We could be part of Blinker's Beauty Chorus and live in luxury in Felicia's flat.'

Elsie was about to reply when someone banged on their door. They both jumped. 'It's time to go, Marianne.' Elsie stood up. 'But you can still change your mind.'

'I told you, we're in this together.' Marianne rose to her feet and picked up their suitcases. 'Let's see what they've got in store for us.'

Elsie opened the door and found herself looking up into Raoul's whiskery face. 'Not now,' she said abruptly. 'We're going out.' She made an attempt to close the door but he put his foot over the threshold.

'Come with me and don't make a noise. We don't want to alert the whole building.'

Marianne hurried to Elsie's side. 'What do you mean?'

He grinned. 'Major Kirke sent me.'

'But you work for the railways,' Elsie said slowly. 'You're a signalman.'

'Don't waste time, girls. We have a train to catch.'

'How do you know Major Kirke?' Marianne

dropped the cases on the floor and stood glaring at Raoul, arms akimbo. 'Are you a German spy?'

He threw back his head and laughed. 'Do you think I'd admit it if I were a spy?' He was suddenly serious. 'There's no time to lose. We have a connection to make and we can't afford to miss it.'

'How do we know you're telling the truth?' Marianne demanded.

'All right,' he said slowly. 'I'm trusting you with this information because I've come to know you quite well since you came to Paris. I'm Belgian and I'm an agent for the British government.'

'So that's why you kept popping up every time we were in trouble,' Elsie said incredulously. 'That's why you took us to the Café Goulet.'

'We must leave now,' he said, glancing over his shoulder at the sound of footsteps. He stepped into the room and waited a moment before looking out. 'It's all right, they've gone. Come along, we're wasting time.'

'Where are you taking us?' Elsie asked nervously.

He snatched up their cases. 'I'm just following orders, and I only know that I'm taking you to the Gare du Nord. Come.'

Elsie and Marianne exchanged puzzled glances but Raoul had their cases and was disappearing in the direction of the stairs. 'We haven't much choice,' Elsie said in a whisper. 'We can't stay here, and if Raoul knows Major Kirke then he must be on our side.'

'Agreed. Let's go.'

Elsie took one last look round the shabby room that had been their home for the last six months. They had almost frozen to death in the winter and now, in summer, it was hot and stifling. It was not a memory that she would cherish. She closed the door.

They were not challenged as they walked out of the building. Madame Chausse, who usually sat in her small office like a spider in the middle of its web, was nowhere to be seen as they followed Raoul into the silky dusk of a summer evening. If it had not been for the rumble of guns in the distance, and the muffled sound of a bomb exploding too close for comfort, it might have been the sort of evening when in peacetime people would be promenading after dining out, or making their way to the Paris Opéra. Elsie looked up into the darkening sky and wondered what terror would rain down on the city that night.

'We're not travelling in that, are we?' Marianne pointed at a farm cart with a swayback nag in the shafts. It turned its head at the sound of her voice and gave her a baleful look.

Raoul tossed their bags onto a pile of rotting straw and manure in the back of the cart. 'Get on,' he said tersely. 'The sooner we get away from here the better.' With surprising agility for such a big man he vaulted onto the driver's seat, barely waiting for them to climb up beside him before flicking the reins and urging the old horse into an ambling walk.

'Have you any idea what they plan for us?' Elsie tried again.

'You'll be met at the station. The agent will give you your papers and your instructions. I don't know where they're sending you, but I don't think you're going home.'

They travelled in silence through the quiet streets, stopping eventually outside the Gare du Nord. 'Jump down, ladies,' Raoul said gruffly. 'This is where we say goodbye.'

Elsie seized his hand and shook it. 'Thank you for being our friend, Raoul.'

'Go into the station,' he said gruffly. 'You should hurry.' He climbed down and retrieved their cases from the back of the cart. 'Goodbye and good luck.'

They stood for a moment, staring after him as he drove off. 'I suppose we'd better go into the station and see what happens,' Marianne said, glancing round nervously. 'Do you get the feeling we're being watched?'

'I do.' Elsie picked up her case. 'Let's go and find out what they're going to do with us.'

Marianne retrieved her bag, wrinkling her nose. 'This smells disgusting, and I've got a funny feeling that whatever they have planned for us isn't going to be good.'

Arm in arm, they walked into the station.

Chapter Eleven

'What now?' Elsie murmured as they came to a halt in the main concourse.

'We just loiter and hope that our contact will find us.'

Elsie glanced at the station clock. 'It's half past ten. Let's hope they come soon, because I don't fancy sleeping in the waiting room.'

'I don't think there's going to be any need for that.' Marianne nudged her, nodding in the direction of a young woman who was walking purposefully towards them. 'I think I know that person. I've seen her in the rue Saint-Roch.'

Their contact smiled at them as if greeting old friends. 'I am Chantal,' she said in a low voice. 'Your train leaves in ten minutes so we haven't much time.'

'Where are we going?' Marianne demanded. 'We haven't been told anything.'

'Your papers and tickets are in this bag,' Chantal said, slipping it off her shoulder. 'You will take the train to Calais and you will be met on the station. You will receive further instructions there. Good luck.' She handed the bag to Marianne and walked off without giving them a chance to question her.

'I wonder if we're really going home.' Elsie stared after her with a puzzled frown. 'Why couldn't she tell us?'

Marianne opened the bag and pulled out a couple of passports, two rail tickets and two permits to travel. 'We're going to Calais, so maybe they are sending us home.'

'I hope so,' Elsie said with a sigh. 'Being a secret agent isn't as exciting as I thought it would be.'

Marianne grabbed her by the hand. 'According to the notice board our train is due to leave in a few minutes. We'd better get a move on.' She began to run in the direction of the platform, where the engine was already building up a head of steam.

They raced along the platform looking for an empty compartment, but all the carriages were packed with troops, and they had to leap on board as the train started to pull out of the station. Elsie tumbled headlong onto the lap of a sleeping soldier who awakened with a start. She apologised profusely and moved away quickly as he slid his arm around her waist with a sleepy grin. 'I thought I was dreaming,' he murmured. 'You can sit on my lap if you want.'

'Get up and make room for the lady.' A soldier sitting opposite had roused himself and staggered to his feet. 'Take my seat. We aren't all animals.'

'You need your rest, soldier,' Marianne said, smiling. 'Perhaps we could squeeze in the corner. We don't take up much room.'

'It's all right.' He tossed their cases onto the luggage rack. 'I'll sit on the floor, and so will my friend over there.' He tapped a sleeping soldier with the toe of his boot. 'Be a gentleman and let the ladies have your seat.'

The young soldier awakened with a start and slid to the floor with a vague attempt at a salute. 'Yes, sergeant.'

'Thank you.' Elsie sank down in the corner of the carriage. 'You're very kind.'

'Yes, indeed.' Marianne took the seat vacated by the sergeant. 'We're very grateful,' she added, settling herself in between two other soldiers who had slept through it all.

The men made themselves as comfortable as possible on the floor, curling themselves around the feet of those lucky enough to be seated. Marianne flashed them a grateful smile and closed her eyes, but Elsie was wide awake. She gazed out of the window, straining her eyes in order to see, but it was dark now and there were very few lights to show that they were still within the city boundaries. The steady breathing of the others in the compartment was punctuated by snores, and the rhythmic clickety-clack of the iron wheels going over the points drummed in her ears, but gradually the gentle swaying motion of the carriage made her feel drowsy and she closed her eyes. Her last waking thought was of home. Would they be in England by morning? She drifted off into the comforting arms of oblivion.

She was awakened by someone shaking her vigorously and she opened her eyes. At first she thought she was back in her bed at Madame Chausse's lodging house, but she realised dimly that there was movement all around her. It was still dark but a glimmer of light filtered in from the platform and she could hear someone shouting. 'Calais.'

'We get off here,' Marianne said impatiently. 'Wake up, Elsie.'

'I fell asleep.'

'Of course you did.' Marianne stood aside as the last soldier left the compartment. 'Thanks again,' she called after him.

'I wanted to thank them too,' Elsie said, yawning.

'I thanked them for you.' Marianne pulled her to her feet. 'We've got to find our next contact.'

Elsie's limbs were cramped and she had slept at an awkward angle, resulting in a stiff neck. She pulled her case down from the rack, but as she stepped out onto the platform to join Marianne they were caught up in a great wave of soldiers who were heading for the ticket barrier. Swept along on a mixed tide of British khaki uniforms and the blue-grey recently adopted by the French army, they reached the main concourse, where they looked for a quiet spot where they could wait unnoticed.

This time it was a much older woman who approached them. She embraced each of them in turn. 'Try not to look so surprised,' she whispered.

'Act as if you are pleased to see me. We don't want to draw attention to ourselves.'

'It's all very well but we want to know where we're going,' Marianne said with a fixed smile.

'You will be given information as and when you need it.'

'So what are we going to do now?' Elsie demanded. 'We need to know.'

'Follow me,' the woman said calmly. 'Look casual and just walk out of the station. I have a fiacre waiting.' She quickened her pace, heading towards the exit. The horse-drawn vehicle was waiting for them as she had promised and she climbed inside.

'This is a step up from Raoul's cart,' Elsie whispered as she followed Marianne into the carriage. 'At least it doesn't smell of dung and rotting straw.'

Marianne threw herself down on the seat. 'We're in private now, madame. What are our instructions?'

'Yes, please tell us what you know.' Elsie closed the door and took a seat beside Marianne.

The woman tapped the roof of the fiacre with the ferule of her umbrella and the vehicle lurched into motion. 'There is a vessel waiting for you at the docks. You must do exactly as the captain tells you.'

'Are we going home?' Elsie could not keep a tremor of excitement from creeping into her voice.

'You will be taken to Antwerp.'

'Antwerp?' Marianne sighed. 'And I suppose we will get further information there. Is there no one who can tell us what will be expected of us?'

'That would be unsafe.'

'But we are being sent to Belgium. We're British citizens and we have a right to know.'

'La Dame Blanche. That's all I can safely tell you. The rest will become clear when you receive your orders in Antwerp.' The woman settled back against the squabs. 'We will be at the docks shortly. Be prepared to alight quickly and . . .'

'Someone will be waiting for us,' Marianne said, finishing the sentence for her. 'We're getting used to that, madame.'

The vessel that was waiting for them at the docks proved to be a rusting motor boat that even in a poor light looked as though it should have been sent to the scrap yard. They had been met by a crewman who introduced himself as Adams, and he took them to meet the captain. Elsie was accustomed to speaking French but it was wonderful to hear her native tongue again. She could have hugged each one of the crew in turn as she boarded the vessel, but she managed to restrain herself.

The master welcomed them brusquely. 'This isn't a luxury yacht, ladies. But every seaworthy vessel has been commandeered for some sort of duty and my orders are to transport you safely to Antwerp.'

'How long will it take?' Marianne asked anxiously.

'We go as close to the coast as we dare, and it depends on the wind and weather but I'd say ten or twelve hours, maybe less. We have to be particularly careful outside Zeebrugge and Ostend where the Germans have laid minefields.'

'Minefields?' Marianne said faintly.

He grinned. 'Don't worry. We've done it before and we can do it again. You're in good hands.'

'I'm sure we are,' Elsie said stoutly. 'But I don't suppose you know anything about our mission, do you, captain?'

He shook his head. 'I'm just here to do my part, miss.' He beckoned to Adams, who was busy stowing the mooring rope. 'Take the young ladies to the cabin and make them comfortable.'

'Aye, aye, sir. Come with me, ladies.'

He led the way to the cabin, which was surprisingly neat and tidy, but the accommodation was spartan to say the least. He glanced at them with a worried frown. 'We don't normally carry passengers but you might be able to stretch out on the benches and get some shut-eye. We should have a reasonable trip.'

'I'm sure we'll be fine,' Elsie said hastily.

'Yes, absolutely.' Marianne put her case under the table and sat down.

'I could make you some cocoa,' he said, moving to the back of the cabin which seemed to serve as a small galley.

'That would be lovely.' Elsie stowed her case and sat down opposite Marianne. Outside it was still dark and the cramped confines of the cabin seemed like another world. The smell of salt water and engine oil mixed oddly with the comforting aroma of hot chocolate as Adams made the cocoa. He placed a mug in front of each of them.

'Thank you,' Elsie said, sipping the hot drink, which was thick and sweet with the addition of condensed milk.

'It's most welcome,' Marianne added. 'Thank you, Adams.'

'If there's anything you want just give me a shout,' he said, backing out of the doorway. 'You might just get forty winks if you're lucky.' He closed the door and they were left alone in the cabin, which had started to rock gently as the boat glided out of the harbour. The motion changed as they emerged into the Channel. 'I can't imagine sleeping on this,' Elsie said, patting the hard leather upholstery.

'I think I'd nod off on a bed of nails.' Marianne stirred her drink, frowning thoughtfully. 'I wonder what's going to happen when we get to Antwerp.'

'That bothers me too, and what was all that about a white lady? Our elderly friend seemed to think that we ought to know. Is it code?'

'If it is I haven't come across it.' Marianne put her mug down on the table, and stretched out on the narrow bench. 'Anyway, I'm going to get some sleep. Wake me up when we get there.'

Elsie finished her drink in silence. She peered out of the salt-encrusted porthole but the sea and the sky seemed to merge in a mass of greyness. Then, suddenly, as if an invisible hand had drawn a line across the horizon, she could see a faint glimmer of light to the east, the start of a new day, she thought tiredly. Where and how will it end?

They were met on the docks in Antwerp by a woman who introduced herself as Adèle. She took them to a small café in a side street where the proprietor seemed to know her, although his greeting was less than warm. They were ushered into a back room, and, as her eyes grew accustomed to the gloom, Elsie realised that they were in a storeroom. Crates and boxes were piled up beneath the barred window, almost obliterating what little light filtered in from the street. The air was thick with the smell of must and damp rot and the flagstone floor felt gritty beneath her feet.

Adèle took a packet of cigarettes from her handbag and offered them round. Marianne accepted one, but Elsie shook her head. 'No, thank you,' she said politely. 'I don't smoke.'

Adèle struck a match and lit Marianne's and then her own. 'You will, my dear. When you've been living for a while under the watchful eye of the Boche you might need something to calm your nerves.'

Marianne exhaled smoke into the air above their heads. 'Why are we here? Where are they sending us?'

Adèle became suddenly businesslike. 'You will travel to Brussels by train.' She delved once again into her handbag and produced a manila envelope, which she handed to Marianne. 'These are your tickets and travel permits. There is also a small amount of currency for your immediate needs.'

Marianne stared at the envelope as if it were a ticking bomb. 'What do we do when we arrive in Brussels?'

'You will be met at the station and taken to a school run by two sisters, Laure and Louise Tandel. Unfortunately Laure is currently in a German prison, serving a sentence for defying the authorities.' Adèle took a long drag on her cigarette, eyeing them thoughtfully. She exhaled with a sigh. 'This is a dangerous business, and you are foreigners. To be caught means the firing squad.'

'We know that,' Elsie said stoutly. 'We'll do whatever is required of us.'

'The women agents in Battalion III of the organisation known as La Dame Blanche, the White Lady, as you say in English, are scattered throughout the country, gathering military intelligence and sending it back to London.' She gave them an appraising look. 'But you are perhaps too young and inexperienced for that kind of work. However, I'm sure that Louise will find something for you to do.'

'When do we leave for Brussels?' Marianne asked wearily. 'We seem to have been travelling for days; first by train and then on a very small boat. We're tired and we're both in need of a bath and a change of clothes.'

Adèle smiled for the first time since they had met. 'I can sympathise, but you will have time to rest in Brussels before you are sent to your post.' She made for the door. 'Wait here and someone will come to take you to the railway station.'

'Are you leaving us?' Elsie asked anxiously.

'You will be in good hands.' Adèle left, closing the door behind her.

Marianne sat down on an upturned crate. 'I'm actually beginning to miss our ghastly room at the lodging house. At least we could get a decent night's sleep there.'

'But only if you could ignore the noise from the street below, and the constant thud of footsteps in the corridor outside our room.'

'Anything is better than that dreadful boat.' Marianne dropped the cigarette end onto the floor and ground it beneath the heel of her shoe. 'I'm starving. Do you think they'll feed us?'

Elsie perched gingerly on a pile of cardboard boxes. 'I keep thinking of the meals that Mrs Beale cooked for us. I'm so hungry that my stomach hurts.' She turned with a start as the door opened and the proprietor sidled into the room with a laden tray in his hands.

'It's not much,' he said gruffly, 'but it's all we have.'

Elsie jumped up and took the tray from him. 'Thank you. We're most grateful for anything.'

He grunted and backed out of the room. Elsie put

the tray on the floor between them. 'Bread, sausage and beer.'

Marianne bent down to pick up a hunk of coarse rye bread and a piece of sausage that reeked of garlic. She took a bite, chewed and swallowed. 'It's better than nothing.'

'I could eat almost anything, and we're probably taking food from their mouths, so we should be grateful.'

Marianne closed her eyes and took another bite. 'I'm pretending it's one of Madame Aubertin's freshly baked croissants, spread with butter and apricot conserve.'

'Who is Madame Aubertin?'

'She is the Bellaires' housekeeper in le Lavandou. She is the most amazing cook, but she is a frustrated opera singer and sings all day long. You can tell her mood by her choice of aria.'

'Do you think she's still singing?'

'I don't think anything short of death would silence Madame.' Marianne drank thirstily. 'This stuff is all right, but you should taste the wines of Provence. They are like nectar.'

Elsie sipped her drink. 'You speak so fondly of the time you spent there. Would you like to go back to le Lavandou?'

'It was heaven,' Marianne said with a sigh. 'They were the happiest days of my life.'

They finished their meal in silence and settled down to wait for the guide who would take them

201

to the railway station. Elsie felt herself nodding off but came quickly to her senses at the sound of footsteps. She cocked her head on one side. 'Someone's coming.'

Moments later the door opened and the space was filled by the proprietor's considerable bulk. 'Come,' he said abruptly. 'It's time for you to leave.'

The train was packed with soldiers as well as ordinary Belgians going about their day to day business. The sight of so many German uniforms made Elsie nervous, and suddenly the magnitude of their task dawned upon her. When they were in Paris the war had seemed far away, and the shortages of food and fuel had been inconvenient but not life-threatening. Now they had come face to face with the enemy, and that in itself was confusing. Most of the soldiers were young men, and many of them were little more than fresh-faced boys. They were fellow travellers, chatting, laughing and joking as if they had not a care in the world. It was hard to imagine them as individuals, wielding weapons – prepared to kill or be killed – but this was what they must and would do when they came face to face with the opposing armies.

She sat quietly, in a seat by the window, pinned to the wall of the carriage by the weight of a country woman who was hugging a basket filled with potatoes. Marianne sat on the hard wooden seat opposite, next to a small boy who seemed to be having difficulty in keeping awake. His head kept nodding until he fell asleep and slumped against Marianne. 'Victor, wake up.' The woman seated next to Elsie leaned over to tap him on the shoulder. 'You are annoying the lady.'

The child jumped and opened his large blue eyes, mumbling an apology.

Marianne rose to her feet. 'Would you like to sit next to him, madame?'

With a lot of manoeuvring they managed to change places and Marianne took the woman's seat beside Elsie. 'We should be there soon,' she said in a low voice.

Elsie glanced at the soldiers seated on the other side of the aisle. One of them looked up and winked at her. She felt the blood rush to her cheeks and she looked away. 'The sooner the better,' she whispered.

'Try not to look so scared,' Marianne hissed. 'Act normally.'

'What is normal in a situation like this?'

Marianne fumbled in her handbag and then closed it again. 'Hell and damnation.'

'What's the matter?'

'I forgot my hanky,' Marianne said loudly. She lowered her voice. 'The other day I was desperate for a cigarette and I bought a packet, but they're French, and although I'd do almost anything for a smoke I simply can't risk it.'

'I doubt if they'd notice,' Elsie said, chuckling.

The air in the compartment was already fuggy with tobacco smoke, and a thick blue haze floated above their heads. 'You'll just have to give up again.'

'You can laugh. You don't indulge in the habit.'

'No, thank goodness, or I'd be in a state like you. Let's hope we get there before you starting chewing your fingernails. And you told me to act naturally.' Elsie leaned back in the seat and closed her eyes. 'Wake me up when we get there.' She was only pretending to sleep, but she realised that she must have dozed off when Marianne nudged her in the ribs as the train lumbered to a halt. All around them there was movement as passengers gathered their belongings and made their way to the end of the compartment.

'This is where we get off too.' Marianne stood up, shaking out the creases in her cotton skirt.

Elsie rose stiffly to her feet and followed Marianne as she edged towards the open carriage door. In moments they were on the platform, caught up in the throng of civilians and army personnel who were surging toward the exit. 'I wonder who will meet us this time?' she said in a low voice. 'Adèle didn't tell us who to look out for.'

Marianne came to a halt in the main concourse. 'We'll just have to wait and hope they find us.'

Elsie turned with a start as someone plucked at her sleeve. She looked round to see a schoolgirl standing at her side. 'Yes? Can I help you?'

'My name is Marie. Miss Tandel sent me to fetch

you.' The girl spoke in perfect English with only a slight trace of an accent.

'We speak French,' Elsie said hastily.

'Come.' Marie took her by the hand. 'It is not too far to walk.'

Elsie decided that a twelve-year-old's idea of a short walk differed somewhat from her own, and it was mid-afternoon by the time they arrived at the school. They were admitted by one of the older girls, who led them through a maze of corridors, stopping outside a door marked *Principal*. 'I'll tell Mademoiselle that you are here.' She knocked and entered, reappearing almost immediately. 'She will see you now.'

Elsie followed Marianne into the book-lined office. Louise Tandel was seated behind a cluttered desk, but she stood up as they entered and came towards them with her hand outstretched. 'Welcome to La Dame Blanche,' she said, smiling. 'Do sit down. You must be tired after all that travelling.' She tugged at a bell pull. 'I'm sure you could do with some refreshment.'

'Thank you. That would be lovely.' Marianne sank down on the hard seat of an ornately carved chair.

Elsie sat down beside her. 'Perhaps you could tell us why we've been sent here, mademoiselle.'

'You are much younger than most of our agents in Battalion III, but I have something in mind for you.' Louise eyed them thoughtfully. 'Now we've met, I think you would be ideally suited to this kind of work.'

Elsie was mystified. 'What would that be?'

A timid tap on the door halted the conversation. 'Enter.' Louise took her seat behind her desk, sitting upright and looking every inch the schoolmistress.

The door opened and a young maidservant entered the room. 'You rang, mademoiselle.'

'Yes, Nina. Would you bring coffee, please? And the ladies are hungry. See if you can find something for them in the kitchen.'

'Yes, mademoiselle.' Nina bobbed a curtsey and left.

'I'm afraid it will be ersatz coffee,' Louise said apologetically. 'Real coffee is very expensive and hard to come by these days. I expect it is the same in England.'

'We've been away from home for some time, but I believe it's getting that way.' Marianne leaned forward on her chair. 'Why are we here, Mademoiselle Tandel?'

'Yes,' Elsie said, taking up the subject that had been nagging away at her ever since they left Paris. 'What will be required of us?'

'We have a network of agents whose job is to keep a twenty-four hour watch on the trains that pass through their area. They keep a count of the number of troops, horses and cannons on each train and, once a week, they pass this information on to their contact.'

'But we will be working together, won't we?' Elsie asked anxiously.

'Yes, you will. Watching the trains night and day is an exacting task, and you will have to work out a rota between you. We have whole families doing similar work.'

'That's all we have to do?' Marianne opened her handbag and took out her cigarettes. 'Do you mind if I smoke?'

Louise stared at the packet and shook her head. 'You must dispose of those immediately. French cigarettes have been unobtainable since the start of the war. It's small details like that which would give you away immediately.' She held out her hand. 'Give them to me and I'll dispose of them.'

Marianne handed them over and closed her bag with a sigh. 'It seems such a waste. Surely we are safe within these walls?'

'I do not allow smoking on the premises. It's a bad example to the girls.'

'When will we start our duties, mademoiselle?' Elsie shot a warning glance at Marianne, who looked as though she was about to protest.

'You will be my guests tonight. After dinner we will talk, and I will tell you everything you need to know. Tomorrow you will assume your new identities and you will travel to your posting.'

'Where, I suppose, we will be met by yet another agent,' Marianne said impatiently.

Louise shook her head. 'Not this time. When you

leave here you are on your own. You will be agents of La Dame Blanche, and many lives will depend upon the information you gather. Belgium may have been overrun by the Germans, but we are fighting back in the only way left open to us.' She opened a drawer in her desk and took out a packet of cigarettes, tossing it to Marianne who caught it deftly in one hand. 'My sister also smokes, although she thinks she does it in secret when she takes a walk in the garden after dinner each evening.'

'Thank you, mademoiselle,' Marianne said with feeling. 'You've saved my life.'

A faint smile curved Louise's lips. 'Don't let the girls see you.'

Chapter Twelve

In their new identities as sisters, Lotte and Anouk Peeters, Elsie and Marianne arrived at their destination next day. They had been fully briefed by Louise and had memorised their parts as if rehearsing a play, repeating their new names again and again and testing each other on their combined past.

'Our parents are dead,' Elsie murmured as they alighted onto the platform of a small station between Audenarde and Courtrai. 'We have come to stay with Aunt Valentine who lives in the Merchant's House on the edge of the village. We used to spend our holidays there when we were children.'

'And we've been working as typists in Brussels, but our aunt is unwell and we have given up our jobs to look after her,' Marianne added, grinning.

'If we keep repeating the story we might come to believe it.' Elsie noted the deserted platform and sighed. 'It doesn't seem to be very busy here. I can't imagine that we'll have much to do.'

'I hope it's not going to prove deadly dull.' Marianne shifted her suitcase from one hand to the other. 'Let's go and find the Merchant's House and introduce ourselves to our ailing aunt.'

'I hope she's got something for supper,' Elsie said wearily.

Marianne took a scrap of paper from her pocket and studied it. 'According to Louise we turn left when we leave the station. The Merchant's House is a little way down the street. It shouldn't be too hard to find.'

'I'm tired and hungry, and I didn't sleep very well last night.' Elsie set off towards the exit with a purposeful step. 'The sooner we get started, the better.' Outside the station she turned left, and found herself facing a terrace of tall, narrow town houses, huddled together as if forming an alliance against the smaller, whitewashed cottages in the village. These modest dwellings seemed to have been tossed at random on either side of a lane, at the end of which Elsie could just make out the shape of barges moored alongside a landing stage and a shimmer of water from the river beyond.

'Don't dawdle, Lotte,' Marianne said impatiently. 'That must be the Merchant's House.' She pointed to a building that might have been plucked from a street in Brussels and deposited in a prominent position at the end of the terrace. The five-storey house was twice the size of any of its neighbours, and the traditional stepped gables were decorated with ornate pinnacles. 'Obviously the wool merchant made a lot of money and he wanted to show off,' Elsie said, grinning. 'Aunt Valentine must be filthy rich.'

'We'll soon find out.' Marianne linked arms with her and started walking. 'Best foot forward.'

'Where is everyone?' Elsie murmured as they crossed the deserted street. 'Has the village been evacuated?'

'They're probably having their evening meal,' Marianne said, glancing over her shoulder. 'But I must admit it's a bit strange.'

Elsie was apprehensive. What, she wondered, have we let ourselves in for? Working in the comparative safety of the rue Saint-Roch was one thing, but they were now in occupied Belgium, and about to step into the unknown. Marianne did not seem to be troubled by doubts as she hammered on the heavy oak door. 'That should raise the ghosts of the past,' she said, chuckling.

Moments later the door was opened by a thin woman who might have been any age from forty to sixty. Her greying hair was scraped back into a tight bun, emphasising her sculpted features and high cheekbones. She wore the unrelenting black of widowhood with an air of understated elegance, and was obviously someone to be reckoned with. 'Welcome to my home. Come in.' She stood aside to allow them to enter, closing the door as soon as they were safely inside the echoing entrance hall. 'I am Valentine Peeters. Which of you is Anouk?'

Marianne stepped forward. 'I am.'

Valentine turned her attention to Elsie. 'And therefore you must be Lotte.'

'Yes, madame.'

A glimmer of a smile lit Valentine's pale blue eyes. 'You must call me Aunt Valentine, even when we are alone. It must become a habit so that you don't give yourselves away in front of those who are less understanding of our cause.'

'Of course,' Elsie said hastily. 'I'm sorry, Aunt Valentine.'

'Leave your cases. Hendrick will take them to your room.'

'Hendrick?' Marianne raised her eyebrows. 'We understood you lived alone.'

'Hendrick has been with me for many years. You might say I inherited him with the house, and I trust him implicitly.' Valentine moved across the black and white tiled floor with the grace of a prima ballerina. 'Come into the dining room. I'm afraid I can't offer you the hospitality we were used to, but we will not starve while there are eels in the river.'

'Eels,' Marianne whispered as she followed Elsie and their hostess into the room. 'I don't think I'm that hungry.'

'I am,' Elsie said stoutly. She took her seat at a carved oak table that would have seated at least ten people. The wainscoted walls and beamed ceiling might give the impression of cosiness in winter, but despite their size the windows allowed in only the minimum of light, creating an atmosphere that reminded Elsie forcibly of paintings by Dutch masters. She was not particularly interested in art, but Guy had once taken her to the National Gallery where she had seen works by Vermeer and Jan Steen.

She shifted to a more comfortable position on the hard wooden seat and waited while Valentine and Marianne settled in their places. The only food in sight was a platter of coarse rye bread and a bowl of wrinkly apples which must have been stored since the last harvest. At first she thought that must be their supper, but after a moment the sound of heavy footsteps was followed by the creaking of the door and an elderly man shuffled in with a large tureen clutched in his gnarled hands. He placed it on the table in front of Valentine. She lifted the lid and sniffed appreciatively. 'This smells wonderful, Hendrick.'

'It should be,' he said gruffly. 'It took me long enough to skin the slippery little devils.'

'Waterzooi,' Valentine said, dipping a ladle into the aromatic fish stew. 'Hendrick is a master chef when it comes to making this dish.'

He muttered something under his breath, glaring at Elsie beneath shaggy grey eyebrows. 'Who are you, young lady?'

She half rose in her seat in deference to his age. 'I am Lotte Peeters.'

He snorted derisively. 'You are not one of the family. I may be old but I am not a fool.'

Valentine laid her hand on his arm. 'I told you about these young ladies. Have you forgotten already?'

He shook his head and his grey mane wafted around his face like a dandelion clock. 'I am not senile, madame. I know why they are here, but they are not family.'

'No, Hendrick,' Valentine said gently. 'They are not, but they will become part of our little family, and they will take over the work that Jens and Yannick did so well.'

'They will not replace your sons, madame. They are just girls.'

'I was just a girl when I came here,' Valentine said, smiling. 'You were a great help to me then, Hendrick. I expect nothing less from the brave English girls who have come such a long way to help us win the war.'

Hendrick grunted. 'I suppose so. But they don't know our ways.'

'We will soon learn,' Elsie said firmly. 'But we will need all the help you can give us.'

'May I have some of the delicious-smelling stew?' Marianne gave Hendrick one of her most charming smiles. 'I can't wait to taste it.'

Valentine ladled a generous helping into a bowl and passed it to Marianne. 'Help yourself to bread.' She filled another dish, handing it to Elsie. 'This is the best waterzooi in the whole of Flanders.'

'You won't get better anywhere else.' Hendrick watched them closely as they raised their spoons to their lips.

Elsie swallowed a mouthful and nodded. 'Yes, it's very good indeed. Delicious.'

'Well?' Hendrick stared hard at Marianne.

She nodded her head. 'What else can I say? I've never tasted anything like it.'

'Thank you, Hendrick. That will be all for now.' Valentine sent him off with a wave of her hand and a sympathetic smile. She waited until the door closed behind him. 'He's very loyal, and he was extremely upset when my sons left for England.'

'When was that?' Marianne said, frowning. 'How did they escape?'

'My boys left before the German invasion. They were only sixteen and fourteen, but I sent them to England. I haven't had word from them for two years, so I can only hope they are safe.'

'Hendrick seemed to think they had just left.' Elsie exchanged puzzled glances with Marianne, but Valentine seemed unperturbed.

'Hendrick gets a bit muddled at times, but he loved the boys as if they were his own. He was like a second father to them after my husband died.' Valentine dipped a chunk of bread into her soup. 'Hendrick's memory isn't what it used to be, which is why I asked Louise to send me someone younger to help watch the trains. I'm finding it hard to keep awake at night, and the poor fellow was always falling asleep even in the daytime. I can't tell you how grateful I am that you have come here to help us.'

'When do we start?' Elsie said, swallowing a mouthful of the stewed eel, which she found surprisingly tasty.

'Tonight, if you feel up to it? As there are two of you I suggest you take it in turns to do the night duty. It can get very tedious and sometimes it's difficult to keep awake.'

'I'll volunteer for the first watch then,' Marianne said cheerfully. 'I'm a night owl, aren't I, Elsie? I mean, Lotte.'

Valentine's winged eyebrows drew together in a frown. 'You must never slip out of character, not even in the house. You must eat, sleep and think like Anouk and Lotte Peeters. After supper I will show you family photographs and from now on they will be as real to you as those back home.'

Elsie nodded silently, but Valentine's words had struck a chord. Henri still haunted her dreams, but her memories of their brief moments together were fading fast. His features had become blurred, and she was afraid she might be forgetting him. Sometimes she wondered if her feelings for him were real or imagined. It shocked her to realise that it was easier to remember Guy, and the good times they had shared. She knew that she had taken him for granted, but she remembered the many kindnesses he had shown her and others, and she missed his wry humour. Henri had thrilled her and made her pulses race, but Guy had made her laugh.

'Lotte?' Valentine's voice shattered Elsie's reverie and she came back to earth with a jolt.

'I'm sorry, Aunt Valentine. What did you say?'

'I was telling you both that you must remember

that we are an occupied country. The Germans are everywhere, and although we don't see very much of them in the village that doesn't mean that we can act and do as we please. If anyone is suspected of spying they're arrested and imprisoned; many have been executed by firing squads.'

'We will be careful,' Marianne said hastily. 'We've been trained well, and we won't make stupid mistakes.'

Valentine turned her head to give Elsie a searching look. 'You do understand, don't you?'

'Yes, of course.' Elsie nodded emphatically. 'Might I have a little more stew?'

After supper Valentine showed them up to the fourth floor. She paused at the foot of a narrow staircase. 'The top floor is where the servants were housed in the old days. Hendrick used to sleep there but he finds the stairs a bit of a trial, and he has a room on the ground floor close to the kitchen.' She walked on. 'These two rooms at the front of the house are yours. They overlook the station and the railway sidings, giving you an excellent view of the troop trains. They stop here to take on water, giving you time to make a note of the numbers of soldiers, horses and cannons on board. The code we use is quite simple. The soldiers are dried peas, the horses are potatoes and guns are cabbages. You will find pen and ink in your rooms and you make the lists on tissue paper.'

'What happens to them then?' Elsie asked.

'They are rolled up and inserted into hollowed-out broom handles, and once a week Hendrick takes them to the agent. You don't need to know any more than that.' Valentine opened the first door. 'You may choose which room you prefer. The bathroom is at the end of the passage.' A smile curved her thin lips. 'Don't look so surprised, Lotte. My late husband was very particular about keeping up to date with things like indoor plumbing. We are one of the few houses in the village to have hot and cold running water. It is one luxury that so far has not been taken away from us. Now, I'll say goodnight and leave you to settle in.' She walked slowly towards the staircase.

Marianne took a quick look in both rooms, and having tested the beds she made her choice. 'I'll take this one. It's nearest to the bathroom and the mattress is a little less lumpy than the one in your room.'

Elsie went to the window and looked out. 'Are you sure you want to do the night watch, Marianne? I don't mind doing it if you're tired.'

Marianne threw herself down on the bed and stretched out. 'Actually, I am a bit sleepy. Would you mind awfully?'

'Of course not. I wouldn't have offered if I didn't think I could stay awake. I'm not sure I could sleep anyway. It's all so strange and new.'

'You've got too much imagination for your own good, darling.' Marianne closed her eyes. 'I could sleep on a bed of nails.'

'I'm going to my room to unpack.'

'I'm just going to fish my nightie out of my case and then I'm going to bed,' Marianne said, yawning. 'I'll do the rest in the morning. Night night.'

Elsie went next door to her room. It was identical in size and shape and furnished simply with a single bed, a wardrobe and a chest of drawers. A desk and chair set beneath the window were obviously intended for the person keeping watch, and she was already beginning to regret her offer.

The room was filling with shadows as the daylight faded into dusk, and by the time she had unpacked her case and put her clothes away it was almost dark, but she could not light a candle for fear of someone spotting her at the window. What had seemed like an easy task was beginning to feel like an uphill struggle as tiredness threatened to overwhelm her.

She opened the window and sat down to wait for the first train to rumble into the station. An hour passed and she was beginning to nod off when the silence was shattered by the sound of an approaching steam engine. She was suddenly wide awake, and her heart was pounding as she sat with the pen poised. The train drew to a noisy halt with screeching brakes and a burst of steam, followed by the banging of carriage doors and the rumble of male voices. It was obvious that the Germans paid little heed to the fact that their activities might wake the sleeping population. Lights blazed and Elsie worked frantically, noting down the numbers on a small sheet of flimsy paper, taking care to put it in code as Valentine had instructed.

Eventually the train pulled out and there was silence again, but not for long, as another one followed in quick succession, and then a third. Elsie was beginning to lose concentration and her eyes were sore. She wondered how many troop trains would pass through that night, and whether she would be able to cope with such a long vigil, but then all was quiet again. She was cramped and rose from her seat, pacing the room in an attempt to keep awake. The bed with its snowy coverlet looked more and more inviting, and she was tempted to lie down and rest her weary body. She went to sit in front of the window, taking deep breaths of the cool night air. The smell of soot and hot engine oil still lingered, but there was no sign of movement on the platforms. She rested her chin on her cupped hands, focusing her eyes on the starry sky. It was eerily quiet. And then, in the early hours of the morning, she heard what sounded like footsteps on the floor above. She was suddenly wide awake and alert. She stiffened, straining her ears, thinking it must have been the old wood contracting in the cool of the night, or perhaps she had drifted off to sleep and had been dreaming.

Then it came again. The sound of someone pacing the floor overhead was unmistakeable. The house might have its ghosts but this one wore boots. She stuffed her hand into her mouth to prevent herself from crying out and leapt to her feet. She ran to the door and wrenched it open. The footsteps were even louder, and directly overhead. Whoever it was seemed to be heading for the stairs. She was about to rush into Marianne's room and wake her up when the sounds stopped, and once again the house echoed with silence. She stood in the doorway, trembling from head to foot. She was overwrought and exhausted. Perhaps it was her imagination. She closed the door softly, turning the key in the lock before returning to her position at the desk. Now she was wide awake. She sat very still, stiff and upright as she waited and listened, but all she could hear was the thudding of her own heart.

'Why on earth did you lock your door?' Marianne demanded when Elsie rose stiffly from her seat at the desk to let her in next morning. 'Did you think the bogeyman was coming to get you? Or maybe a couple of German storm troopers.'

'That's not funny,' Elsie said wearily.

Marianne took her by the shoulders, staring into her face with a worried frown. 'Are you all right, darling? You look terrible.'

'Someone is up there in the attic,' Elsie said breathlessly. 'I heard them moving about last night. I didn't know what to do.'

'I knew I should have taken the night shift. You were overtired and imagining things. Valentine would hardly be roaming round her attic rooms in the small hours, and poor old Hendrick can hardly get from the kitchen to the dining room, so I don't think it was him.'

Elsie shook her head. 'I know what I heard, Marianne. Someone heavy-footed was pacing the floor. I'm surprised you didn't hear anything.'

'I was out for the count.' Marianne moved to the desk and picked up Elsie's notes. 'No wonder you were hearing things. You had a busy night.'

'There were three troop trains close together, and then a big gap before they started up again just before dawn.'

'Well, it's my turn now. Have a wash and get some breakfast before you go to bed. I'll take over in my room, and then perhaps we'll split the night shifts. It's too much for one person to do twelve hours at a stretch.'

Elsie nodded tiredly. 'I'm all in, but I suppose I'd better eat something.' She made her way to the bathroom. After splashing cold water on her face and cleaning her teeth, she went downstairs to the dining room.

Valentine was seated at the table, reading a newspaper and drinking coffee. 'Sit down and have some breakfast, Lotte.' She picked up a silver coffeepot and filled a cup, passing it to Elsie. 'This is real coffee. Heaven knows when I'll be able to get more, but I intend to enjoy it while I can.'

Elsie sat down and took a sip. She would have

much preferred a nice cup of tea, but she did not want to offend Valentine. 'Delicious,' she said politely.

'How did you get on last night?'

'I managed, but I was very tired.'

'Of course you were, but you'll find it gets easier as you go along. The information we gather might seem trivial to us, but it goes back to London, and apparently they make good use of it.'

Elsie helped herself to a slice of bread and a sliver of cheese. 'I may have been imagining it, but in the middle of the night I thought I heard someone moving about in the attic.'

Valentine paused with her cup halfway to her lips. She shook her head. 'No one goes up there these days. It was probably bats flying in and out. I believe there are some panes of glass missing, so that would account for how they got in.'

Elsie accepted this without comment. She had the feeling that Valentine was keeping something from her, but she was too tired to pursue the matter further. She finished her meal. 'If you'll excuse me, Aunt Valentine, I'll go to my room.'

'You'll feel better when you have had some sleep, my dear. And don't worry about anything you might hear coming from the attics. This is a very old house and the timbers expand in the day and contract at night, making all sorts of odd noises. I suppose I'm used to it and take no notice.'

Still unconvinced, Elsie shared the watch that

night with Marianne, but there were no strange sounds to distract her and she began to think she must have been mistaken. Perhaps it had been simply the creaks and groans of old timbers, or even bats flying around as Valentine had suggested, but she could not quite suppress the doubts that niggled at the back of her mind.

Their first few weeks in the Merchant's House passed uneventfully, and their task became routine. The days were long and the nights seemed even longer. Splitting their shifts was less exhausting, but then boredom began to set in. Elsie would have liked to do much more than merely keep a tally of troop movements, and she was beginning to feel like a prisoner, but she did not complain. Marianne had no such scruples and she made her feelings clear.

Eventually, and somewhat unwillingly, Valentine allowed them to go into the village, one at a time, and only when accompanied by herself or Hendrick. These forays to the local market made a welcome break from keeping a constant watch on the movement of troops and munitions, but Elsie was uncomfortably aware that they were the object of much speculation. Valentine's friends and acquaintances seemed eager to meet her nieces from Brussels. 'They are just nosey,' she said, steering Elsie away from a group of women who had stopped haggling over the price of potatoes on a farmer's stall to wave and beckon to them. 'Move on quickly, Lotte.'

She smiled and nodded at the village priest who was heading towards them. 'Good day, Father. You must excuse us if we don't stop to chat. I've left Hendrick watching over the oven and his memory isn't what it was. If we don't hurry back I'm afraid the bread will be burnt to ashes.'

The priest came to a sudden halt, staring at Elsie with a downturn at the corners of his mouth. 'I was hoping to meet your nieces, Valentine. I was expecting to see you all in church.'

Valentine placed herself squarely between them. 'You know me, Father. I attend as and when the mood takes me. I talk to God in my own way and on my own time.'

He shook a finger at her. 'God loves us all, Valentine. But perhaps a little more effort on your part would set a good example to the young ladies.' He peered over Valentine's shoulder and beamed at Elsie.

She smiled vaguely and tugged at Valentine's sleeve. 'The bread, Aunt. Perhaps we should hurry?'

'The bread!' Valentine uttered a shriek and grabbed Elsie by the hand. 'Goodbye, Father. I will attend mass one of these days.' She hurried off in the direction of the Merchant's House, slowing down when she spotted a group of German soldiers who were standing outside the inn, smoking cigarettes and chatting. 'Ignore them,' she hissed. 'Walk past but never look them in the eye. We don't consort with the enemy.'

There was a momentary lull in the soldiers' conversation and Elsie sensed that they were watching them closely. She hurried past but one of them called out and she glanced over her shoulder. He smiled and winked at her and she looked away, blushing. 'I can see now why you don't want us to go out alone,' she said breathlessly.

Valentine shot her a sideways glance. 'These men are far from their homes and families. We are forced to tolerate their presence, but we have as little to do with them as possible.'

'Why are they in the village? Why aren't they fighting the war in France?'

'They're here to remind us that we are an occupied country, and that we must obey their rules or suffer the consequences.' Valentine walked on, coming to a sudden halt at the top of the lane which led to the river. 'The big house on the riverbank is where the doctor lives. Hopefully you will never need his services, but it's useful to know your way around. Now we must hurry home. You need to catch up on your sleep.'

Elsie gazed longingly at the river. The sun reflected off its surface in pools of molten gold, and she had a sudden longing to feel the cool, silky caress of the water on her bare skin, but going for a swim was out of the question. She had work to do. The newspapers had been filled with accounts of the fighting on the Somme, and that made the task that she and Marianne had taken on seem even more important than before. She followed Valentine back to the house. This was to be her life until the end of the hostilities. She could only hope and pray that the war would end soon.

That evening Marianne was suffering from a severe headache and Elsie offered to take both shifts. 'It's probably the heat,' she said sympathetically. 'And you've been stuck indoors for a whole week. At least I had a breath of fresh air this morning when we went to market.'

Marianne sank down on her bed. 'Are you sure, Elsie? It's such a long night, especially when it's so damned hot.'

'I'll be fine. You get some rest and try to sleep.'

Marianne lay back and closed her eyes. 'Valentine gave me some herbal concoction she'd brewed, and it's beginning to have an effect.'

Elsie left her and went to her own room. She took up her position at the window, staring out at the now familiar view of the station and the railway sidings. She knew every inch of the platform and the iron rails that carried the locomotives and their rolling stock. She was familiar with the faces of all the station workers, and the drivers of the roaring monsters that thundered along the tracks belching smoke and steam. The most difficult part of the whole procedure was keeping awake, especially in the small hours when all she wanted to do was lie down and go to sleep. She kept alert by drinking copious cups of ersatz coffee. Valentine's supply of real beans had run out, and now they were compelled to drink a bitter brew made from ground acorns. She found herself longing even more for a cup of tea, and she dreamed of bacon and eggs served with little triangles of fried bread, or a plate of bangers and mash with thick brown onion gravy. It was odd, she thought, gazing out of the window at nothing in particular, that the things she missed most were not the luxury meals she had eaten in posh London restaurants, or the delicacies that Mrs Beale had cooked with such expertise. It was the treats from a fondly remembered childhood that she missed the most. Money had always been in short supply, but sometimes the cook at the manor house had allowed Ma to bring home the leftovers from the servants' meals. It was better, Ma had always said, than feeding good wholesome food to the pigs. On those occasions they had gone to bed with full stomachs. She chose to forget the many occasions when she had lain down to sleep with her belly growling with hunger.

She laid out the thin sheets of paper, pen and ink. Dusk was falling fast and soon it would be dark. The lights in the station only came on for the arrival of each train and went out again at its departure. They would enable her to see well enough to make the necessary notes, but in the meantime it was too dark to read or sew or do anything other than sit and think. She stood up and stretched, taking deep breaths of the rose-scented night air as yet untainted by soot and smoke. There was just time, she thought, to go down to the kitchen and heat up some coffee. Valentine always left a pot on the range, which retained its heat well into the night, and there would be bread and cheese in the larder in case she felt peckish. Valentine was a generous and considerate hostess, and Hendrick might appear surly, but he often left a punnet of blackberries on the kitchen table, or some peaches that he had obtained somewhere on his travels when he delivered the intelligence to their agent.

Elsie felt her way down the stairs, treading softly so that she did not disturb Marianne or Valentine, whose room was on the first floor. She had expected the kitchen to be in darkness, but when she opened the door she was met by flickering candlelight. For a second or two she thought it was Hendrick who sat at the kitchen table, hunched over a plate of food, but it was a stranger in mud-spattered British army uniform who leapt to his feet. His eyes were dark hollows in a gaunt unshaven face, and he backed away from her.

Chapter Thirteen

'Who are you?' Her voice shook but she stood her ground.

He swallowed, wiping his lips on the back of his hand. 'Don't scream. I won't hurt you.'

'You're English,' she said with a sigh of relief. 'But you're hurt.' The sleeve of his tunic had been cut away and his left arm was roughly bandaged. It was caked with blood and dirt, and she could smell the suppurating wound from where she stood. She felt nauseous and faint, but she steeled herself to meet his frightened gaze with an attempt at a smile. 'Sit down, please. I'm English too and I promise not to call for help.'

He sank onto the seat, holding his head in his hands. 'Sorry, miss. Feeling a bit seedy to tell the truth.'

'Does Valentine know you're here?'

He shook his head. 'I dunno where I am, and that's no lie. I was brought here by an old chap. He's gone to lock up, or something. He'll be back any moment.'

'So it was Hendrick who brought you here,' she said thoughtfully. 'What's your name?'

He shot her a wary glance. 'Private Smith, miss.'

'Have you got a first name? I can't call you Private Smith if I'm going to see to that arm of yours.'

'My friends call me Jim.'

She took the kettle from the range and searched the cupboards for a bowl, which she filled with hot water. 'I'm not a nurse but I can change a bandage.' She opened a drawer and took out one of Valentine's spotless linen tablecloths. 'I don't suppose she'll mind if I tear this up. Anyway, it's too bad if she does.' She ripped it into narrow strips and was about to undo the filthy rags around the soldier's arm when Hendrick burst into the kitchen.

'What's going on? Why are you down here? There's a train due soon.'

'I know,' Elsie said calmly. 'But this poor man looks to be in a bad way.'

Hendrick eyed the torn tablecloth, shaking his head. 'Madame won't be pleased.'

'She'll understand. But what this man needs is a doctor.'

'Impossible. No one knows what we do here. One word in the wrong place and we'll all be for the firing squad.'

'I can't speak the lingo, so I dunno what you're talking about,' Jim said weakly. 'But if I'm putting you in danger I'd best be on my way.' He half rose from his seat but Elsie pressed him down with a gentle hand.

'I was just telling Hendrick that you ought to get

231

proper medical care, but he says it's too dangerous.' She glanced at Hendrick's gnarled hands. Somehow she did not see him as a male nurse. 'I'll dress his wound, but you'll have to take over then. I've got to be in my room when the train arrives.'

Hendrick scowled at her, his eyebrows meeting over the bridge of his nose. 'That's not right. Madame wouldn't approve.'

She would have laughed if the situation had not been so serious. 'What do you expect him to do? He's so weak he couldn't hurt a fly.' She gave Hendrick a searching look. 'He's not the first one you've helped, is he?'

Hendrick shrugged his shoulders. 'I'm saying nothing.'

'You've been hiding escapees in the attics, haven't you?'

'Maybe we have, and maybe we haven't.' Hendrick moved swiftly round the table and helped Jim to his feet. 'The young lady is going to see to you later. Come with me.'

Jim cast a helpless look in Elsie's direction. 'What did he say?'

'He said he'd take you upstairs. I'll dress your wound when he's settled you in one of the attic rooms. You'll be safe up there, and I'll get to you as soon as I can.'

She stood aside as Hendrick helped the young soldier to his feet. He looped Jim's good arm round his shoulders, supporting his weight as they made their way out of the room. Hendrick's infirmities seemed to have been forgotten, or perhaps, she thought with a wry smile, it had all been an act. She gathered up the bandages and the bowl of hot water and took them to her room.

She did not have long to wait before the train arrived and she settled down to make notes in the code that was now ingrained in her memory forever. She knew she would never see a German uniform without associating it with dried peas. She forced herself to concentrate, but her hand trembled and she had to focus all her energy in order to complete the task. She waited until the train had pulled out of the station before venturing up the narrow flight of stairs into pitch darkness. She had to feel her way along the walls until she came to a room with just a sliver of light showing beneath the closed door. She opened it and went inside.

The room beneath the eaves was empty of furniture apart from a single bed and a wooden chair. A bare light bulb dangled from the rafters, shedding a dim light on the bare floorboards, and the air was still and stifling. Elsie's first instinct was to go to the small window and open the shutters, but she realised in time that this might arouse the curiosity of the soldiers who patrolled the streets at night. She went to kneel by the bed where Jim lay propped up on a couple of pillows. 'Jim,' she said softly. 'I've come to dress your wound.'

'It's hot in here, miss.'

She felt his forehead and her worst fears were confirmed. 'You've got a touch of fever, but that's only to be expected.' She adopted a brisk, no nonsense tone. 'Now I'm going to take off the old dressing. I'll try not to hurt you.' She peeled off the filthy bandage. 'I'm sorry,' she added when he winced with pain. The stench of suppurating flesh was almost unbearable, but she braced herself to bathe the ugly wound. It took all her willpower to remain outwardly calm, and her stomach roiled as if she were still at sea in the small boat, but she was determined to do what she could to make him more comfortable. 'How did you get here?' she said in an attempt to take his mind off the pain. 'Where did you come from?'

'I can hardly remember,' he said dazedly. 'We were in the trenches and then we went over the top. I got hit and the next thing I remember was coming to in the dark. I couldn't move and then I realised there was a dead body pinning me down. I don't know how I did it, but somehow I managed to get free and crawl to the edge of a village. A French farmer found me lying under a hedge. He could have turned me in, but instead he took me home and his wife dressed my wound.'

'You were very lucky,' Elsie said, wrapping the strips of linen around his arm. 'You might have been captured by the Germans and taken prisoner.'

'I'll always be grateful to that couple. They saved my life.'

'But that must have been miles away. How did you get here?'

'It's all a bit of a blur, but I was passed from one person to another. They seem to have a network of people willing to risk their own lives to help British and French soldiers escape. I ended up on a barge and we came by river. Your man was waiting for me at the landing stage. I – I'll always be grateful for this.' His head lolled to one side and his eyes closed.

Elsie scooped up the soiled dressings and the bowl of bloodied water. 'I'll be back,' she whispered. 'You're safe here, Jim Smith.' She left the room and went downstairs to the kitchen where she found Hendrick. He had tidied away all traces of their visitor and was seated at the table with a glass of beer in his hand. He did not look up.

'How often do you give shelter to these men?' Elsie asked as she emptied the bowl into the sink. 'I knew I wasn't imagining things when I heard someone in the attics on my first night here.'

'The less you know the better.' He lifted the glass to his lips and drank.

'But I know about this man, and he needs a doctor. He has a fever and his wound is infected. He could lose his arm if gangrene sets in.'

'Madame will know what to do.' Hendrick put the empty glass down and stood up. 'I'm going to my bed.'

'Valentine knows about this?' Elsie barred his way as he made for his room at the back of the kitchen.

'Tell me what's going on, Hendrick. Why is nothing as it seems?'

He looked down on her from his great height. 'That's just the way it is. They come and they go. It's as simple as that. We do what we can.' He side-stepped her and crossed the flagstone floor to his room.

'As simple as that,' Elsie repeated, shaking her head. She washed the bowl and tossed the telltale dressings into the fire, raking the embers until the soiled bandages had burned to ash. She poured herself a cup of coffee and returned to her room to await the arrival of the next train. She checked on Jim several times during the night. It was obvious that he needed medical attention, but there was nothing she could do until morning.

Valentine was an early riser and she usually took her bath first thing. Elsie listened for the rattle of the plumbing as the water rushed through the lead pipes. She waited impatiently for Valentine to complete her ablutions, but eventually the sound of splashing ceased and she heard the bathroom door open and close. After a few minutes she went downstairs, and rapped on Valentine's bedroom door, barely allowing her time to answer before she entered. 'I must speak to you urgently.'

'Whatever is the matter, Lotte? You look flustered.'

'I know all about the escape route that you and Hendrick have been organising,' Elsie said breathlessly.

'I suppose it was inevitable that you would find out.' Valentine clutched her dressing gown around her thin body. 'How much do you know?'

'Hendrick didn't tell me anything, if that's what you're thinking. I went downstairs to make myself some coffee and found an injured man in the kitchen.'

'Where was Hendrick? He should have been more careful.'

'I'm sure he was doing his best, but the young soldier has a badly infected wound. I'm afraid he might die, or at the very least lose a limb.'

'This isn't your problem,' Valentine said firmly.

'He's not the first one you've helped, is he?'

'We do what we can.'

'I think you're very brave to risk everything in such a way, but this chap really does need a doctor.'

'That's out of the question, I'm afraid. I'll go up and see him as soon as I'm dressed.'

'But his wound is festering and he has a fever.'

Valentine moved towards her, placing a firm hand on Elsie's shoulder. 'I said I will see to him, Lotte. You're tired and overwrought. Go downstairs and have something to eat and then you must rest. I am perfectly capable of dressing a wound and treating a fever. Now do as I say and then you must get some sleep. Anouk should be perfectly all right to take over from you.'

'May I tell her what you're doing? She'll find out sooner or later.'

'It is dangerous knowledge, but perhaps she should be told.' Valentine moved to the dressing table and picked up a silver-backed hairbrush. 'No one in the village must find out about this. So far our exploits have been kept secret, but one word out of place could prove fatal.'

'I understand. I won't breathe a word of it, and neither will Marianne. I can promise you that.'

Valentine sat down and began brushing her long grey hair. 'A single ill-judged remark is all it takes, Lotte. You've just called your friend by her real name. That would be enough to incriminate us all.'

'I'm sorry, but we're on our own. No one would know.'

'You have to live your part. It has to become more real than the life you led before. Go downstairs and get something to eat and then sleep. Don't worry about our new friend. He will be taken care of.'

Summarily dismissed there was nothing Elsie could do other than obey Valentine's instructions. She went to the kitchen and was met by Hendrick. 'I have something for you. Hold out your hand.' He placed a brown hen's egg on her cupped palm, closing her fingers over its smooth shell. 'You did well last night.'

She looked up and realised that beneath the shaggy eyebrows his grey eyes were smiling. 'Thank you,' she murmured. 'I'll share it with Anouk.'

'No, it is for your breakfast only. I saved it for you, but if you don't want it . . .' He made as if to take it from her, but she snatched her hand away, hiding the egg behind her back.

'I do want it, Hendrick. It will be a treat. Thank you.'

He grunted and walked out into the back yard, allowing the door to swing shut of its own accord.

Elsie weighed the egg in her hand, wondering whether to have it boiled, fried or scrambled. She was not sure that she deserved to be singled out for such an honour, but she understood the meaning of the gift – Hendrick had accepted her at last. She was no longer an outsider. She decided to celebrate by having a boiled egg and soldiers for breakfast, something she had not had since she left England. But even as she enjoyed her meal she suffered pangs of homesickness. Perhaps it was the arrival of the young British soldier that had brought home a little closer, or maybe it was Hendrick's unexpected act of kindness that brought tears to her eyes as she dunked the last sliver of toast in the golden egg yolk. She dashed them away when Valentine bustled into the kitchen.

'I've seen the young man,' she said, taking a cup from the dresser and filling it with coffee. 'I'll need some carbolic acid, which I can only get from our good doctor.' She sipped her drink, frowning. 'Have you seen Hendrick this morning? I want him to go immediately to the doctor's house.'

'He went out. He didn't say where he was going.'

Valentine slammed her cup down on the table.

'He's impossible. He should have checked with me first.'

'I could go for you,' Elsie volunteered. 'I know where the doctor lives and it won't take me long.'

'You should be resting.' Valentine eyed her thoughtfully. 'But Anouk is fully occupied. It seems as if the entire German army is on the move.'

'I could be there and back in ten minutes,' Elsie said confidently.

'All right, but if anyone wants to chat you must make an excuse and move on quickly.'

'I understand.'

'You must ask to see the doctor in person. His busybody of a wife will probably tell you that she is able to dispense medicines, but she is a gossip and can't be trusted to keep her mouth shut. Tell the doctor that Hendrick has a recurrence of his old problem and that I require a bottle of the usual strength carbolic acid. He will know what you mean.'

'I'll go at once.' Elsie picked up her plate and took it to the sink. 'Do I need any money?'

'He will put it on my account.' Valentine glanced at the eggshell and smiled. 'I see that Hendrick has been making a fuss of you. You are honoured, Lotte. He doesn't take to many people.'

'I understand, and I'm very grateful. The egg was delicious.' Elsie left by the back door and set off for the doctor's house. It was still early but the station was alive with movement and noise as the next troop train drew to a halt. As she walked down the street she realised that very few of the villagers were about, and she wondered if they went to ground, like a fox pursued by the hunt, when such trains pulled into the station. This was the first time that she had been out alone, and she was suddenly nervous. She walked quickly, looking neither left nor right, until she arrived at her destination. To her relief it was the doctor himself who opened the front door and ushered her into the surgery, telling her to wait while he dispensed the antiseptic. 'Give my regards to your aunt,' he said when he saw her out. 'I'm glad she's keeping well.'

'Thank you, doctor. I'll pass on your good wishes.' Elsie hurried on her way, although she would have loved to linger by the river and take deep breaths of the country air. The earthy smell of the muddy banks mingled with a hint of woodsmoke and the leaves were already burnished with the colours of autumn, but she had a mission to fulfil and she walked on. She did not see the German soldier until it was too late. He stepped in front of her, barring her way.

'Good day, mademoiselle,' he said in heavily accented French. 'Why are you in so much of a hurry on such a beautiful day?'

She recognised him as the soldier who had tried to attract her attention when she was out walking with Valentine. She forced a smile, hiding the bottle of carbolic acid in the folds of her full cotton skirt. 'I was running an errand for my aunt.'

'You do not come out very often,' he said, falling into step beside her. 'It does not seem right for a young lady to be shut up in the house all day.'

'I am kept very busy. My aunt is not a well woman.'

'I have seen her striding about the village. She looks very healthy to me.'

'She has a weak heart,' Elsie said, improvising wildly. 'She has to be careful.'

'She is a lucky woman to have a devoted niece like you.'

She shot him a suspicious glance, but there was no sign of mockery in his blue eyes. 'She does not complain.' They were nearing the station and Elsie came to a halt. 'It was nice to talk to you, but now I must say goodbye.'

He seized her hand and held it, looking into her eyes with what seemed to be a genuine smile. 'My name is Dieter. May I know yours?'

'Lotte Peeters.' She snatched her hand free, hoping that Marianne had not seen them from her vantage point at the window. The train was about to depart, and she would have to complete her notes before the next one arrived. Dieter was saying something, but his words were drowned by a blast of steam and the screech of metal against metal as the train began to move. Elsie seized the opportunity to smile and walk away, praying silently that he would not follow her. She did not look back, but as she entered the house she had the feeling that he was still there, watching her. She was aware of conflicting emotions as she went in search of Valentine. The young man she had just met was far from home and probably lonely. In another life she might even have liked him and wanted to know him better, but their countries were at war placing them on opposing sides.

She hurried upstairs to the attic room and found Valentine tending to the injured man. His eyes were closed and he was babbling incoherently. 'How is he?' Elsie asked anxiously. 'Will he be all right?' The smell in the stuffy room was almost too much to bear, and she covered her nose and mouth with her hand, but Valentine worked on apparently unperturbed by the rank odour. She had already stripped Jim of his tunic, and had begun to clean off the layers of dirt that had accumulated on his body.

She dipped a flannel in a bowl of water and wrung it out. 'I've seen worse. Did you get the antiseptic?'

Elsie placed the bottle on the floor beside her. 'Is there anything else I can do?'

'I think you'd better put Anouk in the picture before you do anything else.'

'I will, but please call me if you need help.'

'I will.'

It was a relief to leave the room and breathe air that was musty but uncontaminated by human suffering. Elsie went downstairs to Marianne's room. She had barely crossed the threshold when Marianne turned her head to glare at her. 'Why were you chatting to a German soldier? Are you out of your mind? Are you completely crazy? You know what Valentine said about fraternising with the enemy.'

Elsie slumped down on the bed. 'If you'll shut up for a moment I'll tell you.'

'All right, but it had better be good. I've just finished counting hundreds of dried peas, potatoes and cabbages, and I'm heartily sick of them. This stuff is driving me mad and there you were, out walking with a bloody Hun as if you were on a date.'

'It wasn't like that,' Elsie said tiredly.

'I'm listening.' Marianne sat back in her chair, folding her arms. 'This had better be good.'

'The first night we were here I heard noises coming from the attics. Last night I went down to the kitchen and found a British Tommy sitting at the table.'

'What?' Marianne's lips formed a circle of surprise.

'Hendrick and Valentine are part of an escape route organised by La Dame Blanche. Jim Smith seems to be one of many they've helped, and he's in a bad way. That's why I went to the village. I had to get some antiseptic from the doctor.'

'So this is a safe house. They're taking a terrible risk.'

'No more than having us here and passing weekly reports to a British agent.'

'But that doesn't explain why you were getting so pally with Fritz.'

'He just appeared in front of me, and I had a bottle

of carbolic acid clutched in my hand. Luckily he didn't spot it or I'd have had some explaining to do.'

'Didn't this nice polite German want to know where you'd been?'

'He didn't ask. I know it's irrational, but I felt quite sorry for him.'

'Don't waste your sympathy on the Boche. Just remember that they're the ones who'll man the firing squad if we're caught spying on them.'

'I know that, but Dieter is a human being. I can't hate him simply because he's on the wrong side. Anyway, I won't see him again so it doesn't matter.'

'You might find that difficult,' Marianne said, turning her attention to the street below. 'The bastard is still hanging around out there.' She leapt to her feet. 'I'll put a stop to his little game. He's probably spotted you for an innocent and thinks you're easy prey.'

'What are you going to do?'

'Take off your frock and give it to me. He's only met you briefly, and I'm almost as good an actress as Felicia when I put my mind to it. I'll go out there and put him straight.'

'No, Marianne. It's a huge risk and it's really not necessary.'

'Yes, it is. You're too nice, Elsie. You don't like hurting people, but I'm not so tender-hearted, especially when it's a German. Take it off and give me your hair band.'

'I'm not sure about this.'

'But I am, and it's the only way. These men are predators and he's got his eye on you. I'll sort him out once and for all.'

'I can handle it on my own.'

Marianne cocked her head on one side, curling her lips in a cynical grin. 'Oh, yes? Elsie darling, you have a heart the size of the Pacific Ocean. You felt really sorry for the chap. I know, because you're as transparent as glass.'

'I just saw him as someone who was far away from his home and family, but if you're determined to speak to him you should clear it with Valentine first.'

'Sometimes one has to take the initiative.' Marianne held out her hand. 'We'll swap places for the first and last time, I promise.'

'You will be careful, won't you?' Elsie said as she slipped off her frock and handed it to Marianne. 'You won't do anything rash.'

'Don't worry. I'll be the soul of tact and diplomacy, but I'll make certain he won't bother you again.'

'I'm really not sure about this,' Elsie protested, but Marianne had already left the room. She ran to the window and looked out, hoping that Dieter might have gone, but to her dismay he was still there, leaning against a lamp post, smoking a cigarette. She waited, hardly daring to breathe. Her heart was pounding and she felt sick with apprehension as she saw Marianne emerge from the house and cross the street. It was like watching a film at the pictures in which she was the leading lady, only it was Marianne who had taken her role, and she was playing a dangerous game. Elsie was tempted to open the window and call her back, but she knew that would be a fatal mistake. She leaned forward in an attempt to get a better view.

Dieter had discarded his cigarette and he drew himself up to his full height. She was too far away to see the expression on his face, but they were standing close together; too close, Elsie thought, crossing her fingers and praying silently that Marianne would resist the temptation to claim yet another heart. Making men fall in love with her seemed to come naturally to Marianne. Elsie had seen it happen on too many occasions in London. She breathed a sigh of relief when the encounter seemed to come to an amicable conclusion. Dieter snapped to attention and bowed from the waist and Marianne blew him a kiss as she walked away.

Elsie ran from the room and tore downstairs to meet her in the entrance hall. 'What did you say to him?'

Flushed and smiling, Marianne gave her a hug. 'Don't worry. He won't bother you again.'

'What did he say?'

'He asked me if I would like to take a walk by the river. He offered to bring a picnic, and I was actually tempted to say yes. I wasn't expecting that.'

'But you didn't.'

247

'No, of course not, silly. I told him how strict Aunt Valentine was and that I was rarely allowed out, so it would be impossible for us to meet again, and he said that he was very sorry, but he understood perfectly.' Marianne stripped off Elsie's dress and tossed it to her. 'I suppose he can't help being a German, and he's probably a nice enough chap, but I think he might be gentleman enough to leave you alone.' She slipped on her own clothes, checking her appearance in the mirror with a satisfied smile, and patted her hair into place.

'I hope you're right. We're in a dangerous situation here, Marianne.'

'It's exciting, isn't it? I love this work.'

'You said you hated it a few minutes ago.'

'I was bored with counting vegetables, but things have taken a turn for the better. We've got a wounded soldier to hide, and a German officer to confuse and keep at bay.'

'Don't. You make it sound like a game, and it's anything but.'

Marianne gave her a hug. 'I know that, Elsie my love. But now we're not simply stuck in a backwater waiting for the next train to pull into the station; we're really in the middle of things.' She walked purposefully to the window and looked out. 'He's gone.' She slumped down on her chair. 'Oh, well, I suppose that's that.'

'Marianne, don't.'

'Don't what?'

'Don't give me that innocent look.'

'Honestly, darling, I don't know what you're talking about.'

'Yes, you do. You're bored and you'd enjoy flirting with him just for the hell of it.'

'Who me?' Marianne pulled a face. 'What nonsense you talk, Elsie. Do you really think I'd do anything so foolhardy and downright dangerous? That's crazy talk.'

Chapter Fourteen

Elsie went to her room and lay on her bed, but she could not sleep. She had seen the sparkle in Marianne's eyes and she was uneasy. Eventually she got up and went to the bathroom. She ran the water, undressed and climbed into the cast iron tub, careful to avoid the rough patch where the enamel had worn away. She closed her eyes, shutting out the clinical white tiles, and imagined herself back in Felicia's luxurious bathroom, where hot water gushed from gold-plated taps, and fluffy Egyptian cotton towels hung from a heated towel rail. She opened her eyes and sighed. The water was tepid and there was no soap. She stepped out of the bath onto bare linoleum and dried herself on a threadbare towel that felt like sandpaper on her skin. She had hoped a hot bath would make her sleepy but now she was refreshed and wide awake. She knew she could not rest until she had checked on the patient and she dressed quickly before making her way upstairs to the attics.

There was no sign of Valentine as she entered the room, but Jim opened his eyes and managed a weak smile. Elsie pulled up the chair and sat down. 'How are you feeling?'

He ran his hand over his clean-shaven chin. 'A lot better than I did, ta.'

'I'm glad. I was worried about you.'

'I'm tough, miss. I've come this far so I don't think a scratch on me arm is going to stop me now.'

'Can I get you anything?'

'No, ta. The Belgian lady gave me some soup.' He reached out his hand. 'You was the one what helped me last night, wasn't you?'

'I didn't do much, Jim.'

'Just hearing an English voice helped me more than you'll know. I knew I was getting close to home.' He squeezed her fingers. 'I dunno what you're doing here, but good for you, miss.' He closed his eyes.

Elsie withdrew her hand gently and pulled the sheet up to cover his naked chest. She stood up and tiptoed out of the room, wiping away tears. His heartfelt thanks had touched her deeply: she had done little enough, but simply being there and speaking to him in his own tongue had obviously helped. She closed the door quietly, and went downstairs to the kitchen.

Valentine was standing in front of the range, stirring the contents of a large saucepan, and its savoury aroma filled the room. 'You should be asleep,' she said sternly. 'Wearing yourself out won't help anyone and you might make mistakes.'

'I went to check on Jim. He seems much better, thanks to you.'

Valentine frowned. 'I'm afraid he'll lose that arm,

but I've done all I can. I just hope he'll get back to England before gangrene sets in.'

'But surely he's not well enough to move on?'

'It's not up to me, Lotte. We do what we can for them, but it's safer for all concerned if the chain remains unbroken.'

'He's so weak.'

'The boy is in better shape than when he arrived last night. We can't afford to get involved with individuals. We're professionals and we have a job to do. You must remember that at all times.'

'I'll try, but it won't be easy.'

Valentine replaced the lid on the pan. She smiled and waved the spoon at Elsie. 'You'll have to guard that tender heart of yours, my dear. You will have to grow a protective shell around it and try to be more like your friend. Anouk has the makings of a ruthless espionage agent.'

Elsie knew that was not true but there was no point in arguing. Valentine might think that Marianne was tough and heartless, but Elsie had seen the softer side of her friend, and she knew that her blasé attitude to life was just an act. She had a picture of Marianne and Dieter fixed in her mind and she was afraid. One day she knew that Marianne would fall deeply and irrevocably in love. Elsie prayed that it would not be the handsome young German who proved to be Marianne's Nemesis.

When Elsie went to see Jim next day his bed was empty and had been stripped down to the flock-filled mattress. There was no sign that the room had been occupied recently. She felt quite ill at the thought of a sick man being moved from one safe house to the next, but it was not just his life that was at stake. They were all in danger. She laid her hand on the pillow and silently wished Jim Smith a safe passage home.

In the months that followed there was a steady trickle of British and French soldiers who came in the night, were fed and given a bed, and were gone as soon as darkness fell the following day. Valentine and Hendrick saw to their needs and Elsie was not involved with them on a personal level, apart from helping in the washhouse when Valentine was otherwise occupied. Their lice-ridden shirts and undergarments went into the copper, and Hendrick had the unenviable task of running a candle flame down the seams of the filthy tunics and trousers in an attempt to kill off the chats, as the soldiers called the lice. Elsie hated handling the verminous garments but she felt it was the least she could do for the poor devils who occupied the attic room. It was hard to imagine the dreadful conditions in the trenches and the privations the men had to endure, but at least they would travel on without suffering the torment inflicted by ravenous parasites.

The Somme offensive had begun on the first of July and news filtered through in November that it had at last come to an end, but the war raged on.

The days were growing ever shorter, but Elsie had not ventured into the village since her encounter with Dieter. Valentine had offered to take her to market and she had refused politely, although she was running out of excuses. Marianne was always eager to go in her stead, even if it meant that she had to lose sleep, and Elsie was beginning to suspect that she had an ulterior motive: her worst fears were confirmed one evening when she was on duty watching the railway station. The continuing hostilities had meant that trains transporting troops and supplies to the front line were more frequent, and timetables were of little use.

She was seated at the desk in her room, staring out into the darkness. She rarely allowed herself the luxury of thinking about Henri, but the melancholy winter evening had evoked a feeling of loss and longing. The last soldier they had sheltered had been a Frenchman and she had found herself wishing that it was Henri they were helping on his way to neutral Holland and freedom. Guy was also in her thoughts and she made a point of asking the British soldiers who passed through their hands if they knew him, but so far without any success. She still suffered pangs of remorse when she remembered their last meeting, and the sight of him walking off and disappearing into the crowds in Piccadilly still haunted her dreams.

She was about to sip her rapidly cooling coffee when a movement below caught her eye. She leaned forward to get a clearer view and her heart lurched against her ribs. Marianne was supposed to be catching up on her sleep in readiness to take over the watch at midnight, but she was crossing the street, walking with a swing in her step as if she were going to a party. There was no reason for her to be out when everyone in the village was obeying the curfew, and she could be shot for disobeying the law or sent to a prison camp. Elsie was tempted to go after her, but even as she rose to her feet she saw a shadowy figure emerge from the station. She knew instinctively that it was Dieter who enveloped Marianne in a passionate embrace and drew her into the deep shadows. Elsie's knees buckled and she sat down again. Her heart was racing and her palms were clammy with sweat. Marianne must have lost her mind to risk all their lives for a romance that was doomed from the start.

She sat, rigid with fear, waiting for the couple to reappear for what seemed like hours. Eventually they stepped out of the shadows, parting with one last kiss. 'You fool, Marianne,' Elsie cried angrily. 'You idiot.' She jumped to her feet and raced downstairs, waiting impatiently to confront Marianne as she entered the house. She dragged her into the dining room.

'What the hell? What d'you think you're doing, Elsie?' Marianne demanded breathlessly. 'You gave me the fright of my life.'

Elsie closed the door and leaned against it. 'Don't

act the innocent. I saw you and him. I saw you, Marianne.'

'It's just a bit of harmless fun, darling. Heaven knows we get little enough of that.'

'Harmless fun? Not only were you breaking the curfew, but you were consorting with the enemy, and you were pretending to be me. I'll be the one who goes before the firing squad if you're caught, not you.'

'Don't be ridiculous.' Marianne faced her with a defiant toss of her head. 'You're over-dramatising the whole thing. Dieter won't betray us. He's in love with me.'

'And I suppose you're madly in love with him.'

Marianne shrugged her shoulders. 'Maybe, although I'm not sure I know what love is.'

'You're in love with the idea of being in love, Marianne. You're bored with what we're doing even though you know it will save lives. You're a selfish, stupid girl and I've a good mind to tell Valentine.'

Marianne's face was a pale oval as the lights from the station shone into the room. 'You wouldn't dare. She'd blame you as much as me.'

'You'll get us all killed. Don't you care?'

'I'm not having this conversation, Elsie. I'm going to my room, so move out of the way.'

'I'm not letting you go until you promise not to see him again.'

Marianne's defiant expression was replaced by a pleading look. 'I know it's dangerous and that I'm being foolish, but this could be the real thing, Elsie. It might be what I've been waiting for all my life, and if it is then nothing will keep us apart.'

'Death will, Marianne. He'll end up with a court martial and you'll be shot along with the rest of us. A whole unit of La Dame Blanche will be at risk because you want thrills. You don't love him – it's all a game to you.'

'I need a cigarette,' Marianne said crossly. 'Move out of the way, Elsie. I've got to get some sleep before I take over from you.'

'I'm only letting you go because there's a train due to arrive at any minute, but you'd better think about what I said. If you don't tell the German that you've been deceiving him, I will.'

'Go to hell.' Marianne flung out of the room.

There were three troop trains in quick succession and it was closer to one o'clock in the morning when Marianne put in an appearance. Her hair was tangled and she had the crumpled look of someone who had fallen asleep fully dressed. 'I'm sorry,' she muttered. 'I meant to relieve you at midnight but I fell asleep.'

Elsie stood up and stretched. 'It's been busy. The Germans seem to be throwing everything they've got at our boys. I hope to God it ends soon.'

Marianne hesitated in the doorway, a worried frown creasing her brow. 'Are we still friends?'

'Of course, but you know what you have to do. You have to put an end to this business with Dieter.'

257

Elsie brushed past her. 'I'm going downstairs to get something to drink. D'you want anything?'

Marianne shook her head. 'I'll think about what you said, but I'm not making any promises. I do like him a lot. He makes me feel special.'

Elsie said nothing. She would give Marianne until morning to decide whether or not to end her involvement with the German, and if all else failed she might have to seek Valentine's help. She hated the thought of revealing Marianne's ill-judged affair, but all their lives were at stake. She was halfway down the second flight of stairs when she heard footsteps coming towards her. Someone was in a hurry. She reached the landing at the same time as Valentine. 'What's the matter?' Elsie asked anxiously.

'We've got a seriously injured man and I need someone level-headed to assist me. I'm afraid that excludes Anouk.' Valentine brushed a stray lock of hair back from her forehead. 'I know it's your rest period, but . . .'

'You don't have to ask. Of course I'll do anything I can.'

'Hendrick is with him.' Valentine turned on her heel and retraced her steps with Elsie following close behind.

In the kitchen Hendrick was standing over a soldier who was stretched out on the table as if he were in an operating theatre. The stench of blood and suppuration filled the room, and even by candle-light Elsie could see that the man was barely breathing. Hendrick looked up and his expression was grim. 'I'm surprised he made it this far. He's in a bad way.'

'Stoke the fire, Hendrick,' Valentine said briskly. 'We'll need plenty of hot water.' She turned to Elsie. 'Go into the parlour and fetch my sewing box. I want a darning needle and thread and scissors. All of which you must sterilise in carbolic. It's fortunate that I persuaded the doctor to give me a fresh supply.' She started to unbutton the soldier's mud-encrusted tunic.

Looking for something in almost complete darkness was not easy but eventually Elsie found the polished rosewood box and took it to the kitchen. Hendrick and Valentine had managed to peel off the man's clothing, which now lay on the floor in a muddy heap. A clean towel covered his legs, one of which was roughly splinted, but the sight of the gaping hole just below his left shoulder made Elsie want to retch. If the smell was anything to go by infection had already set in and his condition was critical. 'Sterilise the needle, thread and scissors,' Valentine said calmly. 'Hendrick, tear up my last tablecloth. I don't know what we'll do when this one is gone, but perhaps some kind soul in the village will sacrifice some of their linen.' She started to clean the flesh surrounding the wound, working swiftly and methodically.

Elsie's hand was shaking as she poured carbolic into a dish. 'What else do you want me to do?'

'I've a small amount of chloroform left. I keep it

for the most serious cases and this is one of them. I'm going to have to probe the wound to make sure there are no fragments of the shell left in it before I begin suturing. If he starts to come round I want you to pour a little of the chloroform onto a pad and hold it over his face. I'll tell you when to do it and when to stop. We don't want to send him to meet his maker before his time.'

Hendrick placed a pile of clean linen on the table. 'Is that enough?'

'For the moment.' Valentine probed the man's flesh, uttering a cry of triumph as she retrieved a sliver of metal. She glanced at Elsie. 'Don't you dare faint, my girl.'

'I'm all right. He doesn't seem to need anaesthesia, so is there anything else I can do?'

'Thread the needle and pass it to me. I'm going to swab the wound with carbolic and sew him up.'

'Have you done this before?' Elsie asked anxiously.

Valentine gave a short bark of a laugh. 'I've trussed many a capon and turkey. Flesh is flesh whether it's animal or human.' She turned to Hendrick. 'I'll need the hot water to wash him when I've finished my bit of expert darning.'

'Yes, madame.' Hendrick nodded and grinned. 'He's a lucky fellow.'

'Stand by his head, Lotte,' Valentine ordered. 'This will hurt and might bring him round before I'm done. Be ready with the chloroform. He might need it after all.'

Elsie moved into position. She watched in admiration as Valentine closed the jagged edges of torn flesh with neat sutures. 'Where did you learn to do that? I'm sure no one uses such expertise to truss poultry.'

Hendrick looked up. 'Madame's father was a doctor,' he said proudly. 'She is as good as, or maybe better than the one we have now.'

'I did two years in medical school.' Valentine snipped the thread. 'Then I met the man I was to marry and gave up my career to be his wife.' She met Elsie's questioning gaze with a smile. 'I've never regretted my decision. I was lucky to marry such a wonderful man.' She tossed the needle into the antiseptic. 'Now I will clean him up before Hendrick takes him up to the attic.'

Elsie abandoned the chloroform with a sigh of relief. She had not wanted to risk killing the soldier with an overdose of anaesthetic. 'I can help with that.'

Valentine wrung a flannel out in warm water and tossed it to her. 'Wash his face, and check his head for lice.'

Elsie took a deep breath. Searching men's hair for parasites was one of the things she hated most when helping care for the injured soldiers, but it had to be done. After a cursory examination she smiled. 'He's clean,' she said, breathing a sigh of relief. The man's face was in deep shadow and he had several days' worth of stubble covering the lower part. 'He

261

needs a shave,' she said, dipping a flannel in warm water and wringing it out. She was about to start washing the dirt off his face when he opened his eyes. He stared at her dazedly. 'Elsie? Is it really you?'

'Guy?' She leaned closer. 'Is it really you?'

Valentine stopped what she was doing to stare at Elsie. 'Do you know this man?'

A gurgle of hysterical laughter escaped Elsie's lips. 'It's my friend Guy. We knew each other in London before the war.'

'Where am I?' Guy whispered. 'Am I dreaming?'

'You're safe.' Elsie held his hand to her cheek. 'It's a miracle that brought you to us. I can hardly believe it.'

'Don't tire him,' Valentine said sharply. 'He needs to rest.'

'I'll look after you, Guy,' Elsie said softly. 'You're safe now.'

His eyelids fluttered and closed. Elsie experienced a moment of panic, thinking that he had slipped away, but the gentle rise and fall of his chest proved that he was still clinging to life. It was only when she felt the tears rolling down her cheeks that she realised she was crying.

Valentine drew her aside. 'I want you to go to the attic room and make up the bed. Hendrick will bring the young man up when we've finished here.' She lowered her voice. 'You do realise that this is a dangerous situation, don't you?'

Elsie sniffed and wiped her eyes on the back of her hand. 'No more so than all the rest, surely?'

'You're obviously involved in some way with this man, and he knows your true identity. Such knowledge if it got into the wrong hands would cause irreparable damage.'

Elsie glanced anxiously at Guy, but he had lapsed into unconsciousness. 'He would never betray me.'

'We can't take that risk. He will have to be moved on and you must go with him.'

'But we're doing good work. You won't be able to manage without us.'

'You and Anouk have done a wonderful job, but now you've both become a danger to us all.'

'You know about the German officer?'

'It is my house. I have to know everything that goes on within its walls. I was going to speak to her about it in the morning.'

'Are you sending us away?'

'Yes, but you will have to travel separately. I haven't made a plan as yet, but I will.'

Next morning Valentine insisted that Marianne and Elsie came down to breakfast together. She sat at the head of the table, pouring coffee as if it were an ordinary day. She waited until they were seated. 'Lotte knows why I wanted to see you together,' she said calmly. 'Has she said anything to you, Anouk?'

'Nothing.' Marianne shot a dagger's glance at Elsie, who shook her head.

'I knew about your affair,' Valentine added hastily. 'Lotte didn't tell me, if that's what you're thinking.'

Marianne shrugged her shoulders. 'Nothing you say will make any difference, and nothing will stop me seeing Dieter.'

'And you must continue to meet him,' Valentine said smoothly. She raised her hand as Elsie was about to protest. 'Things have changed overnight. The young soldier in our care is known to both of you and that will endanger all La Dame Blanche agents on the escape route. Lotte and the soldier will be leaving tonight, but you, Anouk, will have to remain here until I think it is safe to move you on.'

'That suits me,' Marianne said smugly.

'This is only a brief reprieve.' Valentine fixed her with a stern stare. 'If you disappear suddenly it will make the German suspicious. You will continue your sordid little liaison until I tell you to bring it to an end.'

Elsie stared at her in surprise. 'Isn't that putting Anouk in a dangerous position? What if Dieter reports her to the authorities?'

'He's hardly likely to do that. The German army disapproves of fraternisation as much as we do. His whole career would be in jeopardy.'

'And what if I refuse to go?' Marianne demanded angrily. 'You're playing with my life as well as his.'

Valentine fixed her with a hard stare. 'Perhaps you would rather face the firing squad?'

Elsie sent a warning look to Marianne. 'Don't be

a fool. You know that there's no future in such a relationship. How would you feel if they sent him to the front and he was killed? It would be your fault.'

'It won't happen that way. We've been careful not to attract attention.' Marianne raised her cup to her lips and drank thirstily. She stood up. 'Say what you like, Aunt Valentine, I won't stop seeing him. I'm going to bed.' She stormed out of the room.

Elsie half rose from her seat but Valentine motioned her to sit. 'Let her go. She's got to realise that she can't always have her own way.'

'She thinks she's in love with him,' Elsie said earnestly. 'Let me talk to her and make her see sense, and then we can move on together. I don't want to leave her like this.'

'Hmm.' Valentine frowned. 'I know very little of your past, but it won't hurt her to be on her own for once. She might not be so foolhardy without you there to pick up the pieces.'

Elsie was genuinely shocked. 'No, I can assure you that she's done a lot for me.'

'And she's traded on it ever since,' Valentine said shrewdly. 'It's none of my business, but I'd say that time spent apart will do you no harm. From what I've seen of you two, it's Anouk who is the dependent one. She relies on you more than you know.' She folded her table napkin and laid it neatly on the table. 'Anyway, you and your soldier friend will be leaving tonight. I need you to take the first four-hour watch, and then you must get some rest.'

'I don't think Anouk will be able to cope with a double shift.'

'I don't expect her to. I've done it before and I'll continue until Louise Tandel finds me suitable replacements.'

'And then you will send Anouk to safety?'

'I will, and the sooner the better, but my first concern is to get you away. Now enjoy your breakfast, such as it is.' Valentine was silent for a moment, staring into her coffee cup. 'There is one thing you can do for me, if you will.'

Elsie swallowed a mouthful of the coarse rye bread which she had smeared with a little apricot jam. 'Anything.'

'My sons, Jens and Yannick, are in England somewhere. I'd be grateful if you could give them a message from me, should you be able to trace them.'

'That shouldn't be too difficult. I used to work with the Belgian refugees in London.'

'Just tell them that I am well and thinking of them constantly, and that I can't wait to see again. God willing, the war will soon be over.'

'If I ever get home safely it's the first thing I'll do. I promise.'

Chapter Fifteen

It was dark and bone-chillingly cold. The moon and stars were obscured by a thick blanket of clouds. Guy had been dosed with one of Valentine's herbal concoctions and was heavily sedated, but somehow Hendrick managed to carry him to the riverbank where a fishing boat was waiting to take them on the start of their journey. Elsie followed, praying silently that no one would see them making their escape. They were breaking the curfew, but Hendrick had made this trek many times and knew all the short cuts. When they reached the jetty he carried Guy onto a boat, aided by the skipper and his mate. Hendrick stepped ashore, proffering his hand to Elsie. She squeezed his fingers and stood on tiptoe to kiss his whiskery cheek. He mumbled something unintelligible as he helped her to board the vessel. She whispered her thanks and he shambled off, his ungainly outline blurring until he was just a shadow and then he was gone. Her last link with Marianne and Valentine and the Merchant's House had vanished into the night.

She turned to see the skipper standing at her side. He pointed to where the mate was making Guy as comfortable as possible on a pile of sacks, and she made her way across the deck to sit beside him. The smell of fish was overpowering, but Guy was in a drug-induced stupor, and unlikely to complain. She cushioned his head on her lap and prepared herself for a long night as the boat glided away from the shore. The limp sails caught a sudden gust of wind, filled and billowed and the vessel scudded along as silently as a swan on a glassy lake. The landing stage and the village houses dissolved into the darkness, and Elsie breathed a sigh of relief. For the moment at least they were safe. She leaned back against the gunwales, closing her eyes.

She was awakened by a rough hand clamped over her mouth and a gruff voice close to her ear. 'Don't make a sound.'

She opened her eyes, acknowledging the skipper's order with a nod of her head.

He took his hand away. 'German checkpoint,' he whispered. 'Keep quiet and don't move.' He reached for a sheet of tarpaulin and spread it over them.

Elsie dared not move a muscle. She curled up beside Guy, wrapping her arms around him. It was dark and stuffy and the fishy smell made her feel sick, but the smallest sound might give them away. She froze, hardly daring to breathe. She could feel the boat tacking and slowing down until the wooden hull ground against what she assumed must be a landing stage. She could hear a voice shouting orders in German, and the skipper's monosyllabic responses. There was a sudden lull and then, to her immense relief, the boat rocked gently into motion. She lay very still, but Guy was stirring and she whispered words of comfort in his ear, hoping that they would register in his fevered brain. There was no way of knowing what was going on above them or how long they must remain concealed. She was hot and thirsty, and it seemed as though they had been forgotten when suddenly the tarpaulin was lifted. The winter sunlight was cold and white, and the fresh air had a bite that made her cheeks tingle. She struggled to a sitting position.

'We got away with it,' the skipper said, grinning. 'If they had decided to search the boat it would have been a different matter, but they must have been eager to change shifts and were careless.'

'Thank God for that,' Elsie said, sighing with relief. 'Thank you, captain. We owe our lives to you and your crew.'

He shrugged his shoulders, and glanced down at Guy who was mumbling incoherently. 'How is he?'

'He's feverish, and the sedative is wearing off. He needs proper medical attention.'

'We're only taking you as far as Ghent, where you'll be transferred to a barge. It will be more comfortable for you, but until then you must keep your head down. You must not be seen.'

'I understand.'

He nodded. 'We'll put ashore soon.'

'Why? Won't it add unnecessary time to our journey?'

'We all have to eat and you need to keep your strength up. You have a long way to go and it's better to travel on a full stomach.'

Elsie glanced anxiously at Guy who was now babbling and tossing about on his makeshift bed. 'I suppose you're right,' she said reluctantly.

'Don't worry. We'll be in good time to make our rendezvous. Things move slowly on the river, but we get there all the same.'

An hour later the flat-bottomed boat was hauled up on shore in a narrow inlet. The shingle beach was sheltered on three sides by woodland, and there was no obvious sign of habitation. Elsie made Guy as comfortable as possible before climbing out onto the shingle. Her limbs were cramped after a long night sitting on deck and it felt wonderful to walk about, taking deep breaths of fresh air. A shout from the skipper made her stop and turn to see him beckoning to her. 'Breakfast,' he called. 'Hot coffee and fried eel.'

She walked back slowly, wondering how she could refuse to share their food without offending the mate. She had eaten and enjoyed the waterzooi prepared by Hendrick's expert hands, but this was different. The mate had been fishing as the boat glided over the water, but seeing live eels slithering about on the wooden planks reminded her of the grass snakes that were a common sight on the rolling Dorset downs. No one at home would dream of eating a snake, she thought, as she eyed the soot-blackened frying pan with a sinking feeling. She had made herself scarce while the ugly process of killing and skinning the slippery creatures was in progress, but now she must try to eat the cooked flesh, which the skipper assured her was a delicacy.

'Eat and enjoy,' the mate said, handing her a tin plate and a fork. 'You won't taste better in the whole of Belgium.'

The skipper poured steaming liquid into a mug and placed it on the stones beside her. 'It is real coffee,' he said proudly. 'We liberated a supply from a drunken German soldier who could not find his way back to camp.'

They were both watching her and waiting for her to taste the food. She speared a piece of the white flesh with her fork and bit into it. To her astonishment it was delicious. She smiled. 'It's very good. Thank you.'

'You see,' the skipper said, nodding. 'You should not be afraid to try new things. Now eat up and we'll be on our way again.'

It was a long and exhausting day but they managed to pass through the various checkpoints with surprising ease. There had been tense moments beneath the smelly tarpaulin when Elsie was afraid that Guy would give them away, but she had managed to calm him by stroking his hot forehead or simply holding his hand. He seemed to draw comfort from knowing that she was near, and whenever possible she continued to bathe him with rags wrung out in river water.

It was dusk when they hove to beside the barge that was to take them on to Antwerp. Matters were swiftly taken out of her hands as crew from the vessel leapt on board with a makeshift stretcher. Elsie said her goodbyes, thanking the skipper and his mate for their help and kindness. The captain blushed beneath his tan and muttered something into his beard, but the mate was less shy when it came to showing his feelings and he kissed her hand, wishing her good luck. Guy was lifted onto the barge and Elsie climbed on board, helped by one of the crew. She paused on deck watching the fishing boat sail away with a feeling almost akin to panic. She was once again amongst strangers and facing the unknown. No one had told her what was to happen when they reached Antwerp, or how she would travel on from there, but her main concern must be for Guy, who was in urgent need of medical attention. Once again she had to put her trust in the agents of La Dame Blanche.

She discovered with some embarrassment that they had been given the captain's cabin. 'This is very kind of you,' she said shyly.

The bargee gave her a curt bow. 'We must all do what we can for our allies.' He glanced at Guy, shaking his head. 'He looks to be in a bad way, but you are welcome to take what you need from my medicine chest. We will not reach Antwerp until tomorrow, so I suggest you make him as comfortable as possible.' He unlocked a small cupboard and handed her the key.

'I can't thank you enough,' Elsie began, but he cut her short with a wave of his hand.

'No thanks needed, mademoiselle. I will leave you now but you must keep out of sight, especially if we should be stopped by a German patrol boat.'

Guy was groaning softly and when Elsie laid her hand on his forehead she was alarmed to find him hot and feverish. She examined the contents of the medicine chest, but it contained very little that would be of use to her other than a bottle of laudanum. She mixed a few drops in water and held the cup to Guy's lips, encouraging him to take small sips.

It was some time after she had settled him for the night that she realised the barge had stopped moving. She went out on deck to find out why. The captain gave her what her mother would have called an old-fashioned look. 'All traffic must cease at night, even on the river,' he said as if speaking to a small child. 'There is a curfew, you know, and I told you to remain in my cabin.'

'I – I didn't realise it affected river traffic,' she said humbly. 'When will we arrive in Antwerp?'

'All things being equal we will be there by mid-afternoon tomorrow.'

'Do you know what will happen to us then?'

He shrugged his shoulders, a gesture with which she was now familiar. 'Who knows? But you will be told when the time comes. Now, I suggest you get some sleep.'

'But it's your cabin, captain. Surely you will want it for yourself?'

'I would not expect a young lady to share with the crew. Don't worry about me. You have enough to do taking care of the injured man.'

Elsie acknowledged this with a smile and returned to the cabin. The laudanum had done its work, and she made herself as comfortable as possible on the padded leather bench. She did not think she would sleep, but gradually her eyelids grew heavier and heavier and the gentle rocking motion of the barge had its effect.

She was awakened by a tap on the door. She opened her eyes, blinking as sunlight streamed in through the window. 'Come in.'

The door opened and a boy of about fourteen breezed in carrying a tray. He placed it on the captain's desk. 'Coffee and hot rolls,' he said cheerfully. 'We live well on the *Wilhelmina*.'

Elsie struggled to a sitting position. 'I can see you do,' she said, smiling. It was lovely to be awakened by someone who looked as though he was enjoying life despite the constraints of living in an occupied country. She sniffed the aroma of freshly baked bread. 'Is that real butter?'

He puffed out his chest. 'We do a little trade here and there when we pass through the countryside. The Germans don't get it all their own way.' He grinned and winked and left her to enjoy her breakfast.

She stood up and stretched. She felt refreshed but crumpled and in desperate need of a wash, but her discomfort was nothing when compared to Guy's condition. She moved to his side and felt his brow. He was definitely cooler, and the wound beneath the dressing seemed to have stopped bleeding. She pinned all her hopes on finding a doctor to treat him when they reached Antwerp. Until then she would do what she could, although it was little enough. He opened his eyes which were clouded with fever and his eyelids drooped, but he managed to sip some water laced with laudanum. 'Well done.' She gave him an encouraging smile. 'You'll soon be better, Guy. When we reach Antwerp I'll find a proper doctor for you. We'll have you up and about in no time.'

She sat down to eat her breakfast, savouring the crisp rolls spread with butter and jam. The barge captain and his crew obviously lived well, and she discovered the reason later that morning when they were boarded by a German patrol. No one had warned her of their approach and she almost panicked, looking round instinctively for something akin to the fishermen's tarpaulin, but commonsense reasserted itself. The captain would not take such risks unless he was absolutely certain that his cabin was sacrosanct, even from the Germans. She sat beside Guy, hardly daring to breathe until the sound of booted feet faded as one by one the soldiers left the vessel. She could have cried with relief but she had to wait until the boy brought her midday meal before her curiosity could be satisfied. 'Why didn't they make a full inspection?' she asked eagerly. 'I was afraid they would find us.'

'We carry cargo for the German army,' he said casually. 'They think they have beaten us, but we know different. We humour them and we laugh at them behind their backs. They will never break our spirit.'

Elsie glanced at the ample serving of food on her plate and smiled. 'I can see that. It's good to know that we are in safe hands.'

'The safest.' He saluted her and swaggered out of the cabin.

It was late afternoon when they finally arrived in Antwerp. Elsie had been expecting someone to come for them the moment they tied up at the jetty, but they seemed to have been forgotten. Peering through the small window she could see cranes lifting cargo from the hold and she realised that they would have to wait a while longer to discover their fate.

It was growing dark when the cabin door opened to admit a short, stocky middle-aged man who wore a suit and carried a briefcase. He looked oddly comic

276

and out of place on a working vessel, but Elsie did not feel like laughing. 'Who are you?' she asked nervously.

'I've come to escort you to your destination,' he said curtly. 'Don't be alarmed.' His expression softened. 'You and your companion will be quite safe.'

'Can you tell me where we're going?'

He opened his briefcase and took out a set of papers, handing them to her. 'These are your documents. You are Elsie Mead and the gentleman is Guy Gifford.'

She stared at him in amazement. 'But those are our real names.'

'Quite so, although you must not use them until you are safely over the border, so keep them well concealed.' He cleared his throat, adopting an official tone. 'We have to get you and your companion to the place where you will rest tonight before the curfew comes into force. All I can tell you is that very soon, God willing, you will be in Holland and on your way back to England.'

'I'm going home?' Elsie could hardly believe it. She had thought her task was to see Guy to safety, and then she would return to La Dame Blanche with another identity, but it seemed that she had been mistaken.

He nodded and a hint of a smile played on his tight lips. 'Come with me now. My men will bring the injured man.'

Yet again their lives were in the hands of nameless people who operated the escape route, but this time their destination was a hospital. The smell of Lysol permeated the whole building as they entered through the staff entrance at the rear of the building. Guy was stretchered from the wagon and carried to a private room on the ground floor. Elsie was allowed to accompany him as far as the door but she was prevented from entering by a young nurse who introduced herself as Nurse Bosmans. 'Come with me,' she said, bristling with efficiency. 'You may return when the doctor has finished examining the patient.'

'But I should be there in case my friend wakes up and is alarmed to find himself in a strange place.'

'He is in the best of hands, but you look as though you could do with a bath, if you don't mind me saying so.'

Taken aback by this blunt approach, Elsie stared at her open-mouthed. 'I've been travelling for two days,' she protested.

'There is a strong smell of fish on your person, mademoiselle. There are clean clothes for you in the bathroom. You will need them for your journey.' She walked off, leaving Elsie no alternative but to follow her to the bathroom along the corridor. 'You will find everything you need in there,' she said. 'I will return soon.'

Stepping inside Elsie found that someone had run the water for her. Steam condensed on the clinical white tiles and trickled like tears onto the flagstone floor. She needed no encouragement to strip off her clothes and climb into the deep tub, scrubbing herself with soap and flannel until her pale skin glowed pink. Mindful of the nurse's promise to return swiftly, she dried herself and dressed in the clean garments that had been laid out for her on the towel rack. The skirt was too big, but someone had thoughtfully provided a leather belt, and the white cotton blouse was also on the large side but it was freshly laundered and smelled of lye soap, which was a great deal better than rotten fish. A rather shapeless woollen cardigan in a muddy shade of brown came almost to her knees. It completed the outfit, but there were no mirrors in the room to confirm Elsie's suspicion that she looked frumpish and nondescript. She felt guilty for even thinking about her appearance when men were dying in battle, but she would certainly pass unnoticed in such a get-up.

'Are you ready?' Nurse Bosmans rattled the handle and opened the door. 'You look . . .' she hesitated and her expression said it all, 'clean and tidy. You may leave your soiled clothes. We will distribute them to the poor and needy. Come with me, please.' She led the way to Guy's room and ushered Elsie inside. 'The doctor has given him something to ease the pain. He should sleep now. You may stay with him if you don't mind sitting up all night.'

'I'll be fine.' Elsie sank down on the chair beside

Guy's bed. She patted his hand as it rested on the spotless white coverlet. 'He looks better already.'

'If his condition should worsen just ring the bell and someone will come.' Nurse Bosmans turned on her heel and left the room.

Elsie knew that she faced another uncomfortable night. She sat back in the chair and closed her eyes, thinking of home. It seemed too good to be true that soon she might be back in England, but on thinking it through she began to worry. She had enjoyed the time she had spent in Felicia's flat, but she wondered what sort of welcome she might receive if she turned up without Marianne. Would she still have a job in Room 40, or would she be sacked because Marianne's affair with a German officer had endangered their operations? There were so many questions that she was unable to answer, but her main concern now had to be for Guy. She was determined to get him home where he could have the best medical treatment. He moved and murmured in his sleep and she was suddenly alert. 'We'll be home soon, Guy,' she said in a low voice. 'You'll be well taken care of in a proper hospital. I won't leave you until I know that you're on the road to recovery.' She watched him as he slept. He had always been slim, but now he looked positively skeletal. She could only imagine the horrors he had seen and the suffering he had endured before he reached the Merchant's House. The initial signs of improvement in his condition had convinced her that he would recover, but now as he lay in the pristine hospital bed she was not so sure. His bones protruded beneath his skin, his cheeks were hollow and his eyes seemed to have sunk into his skull. He looked nothing like the well-dressed young man she had first met in London. She could almost see the angel of death hovering above the bed, but she told herself that she was being morbid, and that he was in good hands now. Resting her head against the wall she closed her eyes.

She was awakened by the sound of stertorous breathing, and she snapped into an upright position. Guy seemed to be struggling for each laboured breath. She leapt to her feet and reached for the bell, pressing it with all her might. 'Don't die,' she pleaded. 'Please don't leave me.'

For three days Guy's life hung in the balance. Elsie remained at his bedside, leaving only when sent out of the room by the doctor. Her meals were brought to her by a young ward maid who liked to stop and gossip but was shooed away by Nurse Bosmans, who never seemed to be off duty. Elsie could only admire the nurse's stamina and dedication to her work. She was always immaculate and seemed to be unflappable: Elsie suspected that beneath the starched white apron there was an automaton void of human emotions. There must, she decided, be a key concealed in the folds of Nurse Bosmans' blue cotton dress that Matron wound up every day before the young nurse went on duty.

It came as a shock one morning to find Nurse Bosmans in the bathroom, bathing her swollen eyes with cold water. She looked up, startled by Elsie's sudden appearance, and turned her head away.

'I'm sorry,' Elsie murmured. 'I didn't know anyone was in here. You didn't lock the door.'

'There is no lock.' Nurse Bosmans seized a towel and dried her eyes. 'We can't risk patients locking themselves in.'

'Are you all right?' Elsie asked anxiously. 'I don't mean to pry, but you seem upset.'

'I'm fine.'

Elsie shook her head. 'That's not true, is it?'

'I just need a few moments.' Nurse Bosmans' mouth drooped at the corners and her eyes filled with tears. 'I had some bad news. Please go away.'

'I can't leave you like this.' Elsie took her by the shoulders and guided her towards a chair. 'Sit down for a moment.'

'I'll be all right. I just need to compose myself.'

'Would it help to tell me about it? Sometimes it's easier to talk to someone you hardly know.'

'My fiancé was fighting with the French army . . .'

'The Somme?'

Nurse Bosmans nodded, burying her face in her hands with a muffled sob.

'I am so sorry.' Elsie stood awkwardly, not knowing whether to give the young woman a hug or to leave her to her grief. At home it would have been much simpler; she would have rushed to the kitchen and made her a cup of strong, sweet tea. What did foreigners do in such circumstances? She followed her instincts and gave the starchy nurse a cuddle, holding her and allowing her to cry on her shoulder.

'Nurse Bosmans.' The ward sister's voice echoed off the tiled walls.

'Stay there.' Elsie moved swiftly to the door, opened it and stepped outside coming face to face with the ward sister. 'If you're looking for Nurse Bosmans I believe she went to the dispensary to collect some medicine for my friend.'

'Tell her to come and see me when she returns.' The senior nurse strode off, leaving Elsie with the distinct impression that Nurse Bosmans would receive little sympathy from that quarter. No wonder the poor thing was hiding away in the patients' bathroom. She went back inside and closed the door. 'I suppose you heard?'

Nurse Bosmans nodded. She sniffed and wiped her eyes on the towel. 'Thank you.'

'You ought not to be working,' Elsie said sternly. 'You need some time to yourself.'

'That's impossible. We're short-staffed as it is, and my patients come first.' She folded the towel neatly and hung it on the rail. 'I must get back to work.'

Elsie took her hand in a firm clasp. 'You're a brave woman, Nurse Bosmans.'

'Axelle,' she said, smiling shyly. 'My name is Axelle.'

'That's lovely. I'm . . .' Elsie just managed to stop herself blurting out her real name. 'I'm Lotte.'

Axelle held her finger to her lips. 'It's best that I know nothing about you or the man you brought into my care. Tomorrow you will be moving on. I don't know any more than that, but I'm telling you so that you are prepared.'

'You don't know where we're going?'

'It's safer that way. We are told only what we need to know.' Axelle stood up, peering into the mirror above the washbasin. 'I'll report to Sister now. She'll know that something is wrong but she won't enquire. We are not allowed to have private lives or feelings of our own. That is how it has to be.' She turned to Elsie, holding out her hand. 'I will probably be sent to another ward, so I won't see you before you leave. Good luck, Lotte.'

Elsie held the small, work-worn hand and gave it a gentle squeeze. 'Thank you for everything you've done for my friend. I'm very sorry about your fiancé.'

Axelle bit her lip and her eyes brimmed with tears but she brushed them away. 'Goodbye.' She fled from the room and Elsie stood silently, listening to the patter of Axelle's feet on the flagstone floor. She realised now that she had misjudged her completely: she had made assumptions that were wrong, and she was ashamed. These people were risking their lives by hiding and treating fugitives. She and Guy owed them a debt of gratitude that could never be repaid. She walked slowly back to his room and took her place at his bedside.

He opened his eyes, as if sensing her presence, and he attempted a smile. 'I thought I'd been dreaming and that you weren't really here at all.'

She took his hand and held it to her cheek. 'I am here, and I'm not going to leave you, Guy. We'll see this through together.' She held his hand until she was sure that he was asleep, and only then was she able to relax and allow herself to drift off.

She was dreaming of home. She was a child again, living in Tan Cottage, and Ma was on her way back from working at the manor house. Soon she would walk up the garden path with a basket of leftovers from the manor kitchens. She was about to get up and go to the window to see if Ma had arrived, but someone was shaking her by the shoulder. She opened her eyes. 'Ma? Is that you?'

'It's Axelle.' The familiar voice was close to her ear. 'There's a change of plan. You have to leave right away.'

Chapter Sixteen

Elsie was suddenly wide awake and her heart was racing. She could tell by the urgency in Axelle's voice that the danger was real, and an orderly was leaning over Guy, waking him gently. A wheelchair stood beside the bed.

'What's happening? Where are we going?' Elsie demanded anxiously. 'He's too ill to be moved.'

'Shh.' Axelle leaned closer. 'There is a German inspection in progress. They do this periodically and they descend upon us without warning. You must be quiet and leave the rest to those who know what they're doing.' She thrust a parcel into Elsie's hands. 'Medicine and dressings. Now go, and good luck.' She whisked out of the room before Elsie had a chance to thank her.

The orderly lifted Guy into the wheelchair, covering him with a blanket. Elsie shrugged on her jacket and scooped up Guy's uniform, hurrying after them as the orderly set off at a brisk pace. Negotiating the narrow corridors was like making their way through a rabbit warren, and Elsie had to run in order to keep up, but the smallest sound made her glance nervously over her shoulder to see if they were being followed. The orderly took them through the silent kitchens and outside into the darkness of the back yard. The chill of the night took Elsie's breath away but she wrapped her jacket closer around her body and quickened her pace as they skirted the building, heading for a gateway which led into a service alley. They were in almost total darkness; the only sound was the soft thud of their footsteps and the crunch of the wheelchair's rubber tyres on the gravel as they sped along narrow streets. Windows were shuttered and the street lamps were unlit. She had the eerie feeling that they were the only three people left in a deserted city and the rest of the population had fled.

Eventually, just as Elsie was beginning to tire, they emerged from the back streets into a wide square and the clouds parted, allowing the moon to cast its silvery light on what appeared to be a more prosperous part of the city. Large houses, outlined against the night sky, sat solidly behind iron railings that glinted with frost. The orderly stopped outside the grandest of these and opened the wrought-iron gates. He motioned Elsie to follow him as he pushed the wheelchair across the courtyard, and for a moment she thought he was going to knock on the front door, but then she realised that he was making for the rear of the building.

A figure emerged from the deep shadows as they crossed the stable yard. It was too dark to see her face, but it was a woman who took the wheelchair from the orderly and with a brief word sent him on his way. Elsie opened her mouth to thank him, but he had already disappeared into the gloom.

'Come with me.' The woman spoke in English with only the slightest trace of an accent. She pushed the wheelchair towards the stable block. 'Close the door,' she said when they were safely inside. 'I'll light a lamp.'

Elsie did as she was told and for a few seconds they were plunged into darkness. A scraping sound followed by a flash of light and the smell of sulphur was succeeded by the warm glow from a paraffin lamp. A whicker from one of the stalls made their new host turn to give the horse a comforting pat on the neck. 'It's all right, boy. They're friends.' She regarded Elsie with a hint of a smile. 'I am known simply as the baroness, and I am going to look after you until your friend is well enough to be moved on.'

Guy's head lolled to the side and Elsie leaned over him in alarm. 'Are you in pain, Guy?' She laid her hand on his forehead, uttering a sigh of relief. 'He's not feverish.'

'He's drugged,' the baroness said in a matter-of-fact voice, as if having guests in such a state was an everyday occurrence. 'It is for the best.' She hung the lamp on a hook, wiped her hand on her baggy skirt and held it out to Elsie. 'You are welcome, and you will be safe here until we can get you across the border into Holland.' She glanced round the stable with a shrug of her broad shoulders. 'It is basic, but we will make you as comfortable as possible.'

Elsie found herself slightly in awe of this imposing woman, who even in her shapeless garments, with her grey hair confined in two long plaits, was quite obviously someone of importance. 'We are very grateful, madame, and greatly in your debt.'

'Nonsense. We all do what we can to help our allies.' She indicated the next stall with a wave of her hand. 'A bed has been made up in there for the young man, and in the next one there is all you need for now. I'll leave you to get some rest and I'll be back first thing. I'll have to lock you in because you mustn't been seen outside these walls.'

'I understand.'

'In the morning we will see what can be done for your friend.' The baroness rolled up her sleeves. 'But first I'll help you get the poor boy out of that contraption, and then I'll leave you to tend to him. Nursing the sick isn't my forte, unless it's horses or dogs, and then I know what I'm doing.' She looked Elsie up and down with a critical eye. 'You're probably stronger than you look. Let's see if we can get him to bed without doing irreparable harm. Heave ho.'

Together they managed to ease Guy from the chair and laid him down on the straw-filled palliasse. He groaned but did not awaken from his drugged stupor, and for that Elsie was grateful. 'Thank you, once again, madame.'

'Get some rest, my dear. You'll need all your strength in the coming days. You've still got a long road ahead of you, but La Dame Blanche will do its best to get you home safely.' She left, locking the stable door behind her.

Having made Guy comfortable, Elsie went to the next stall and lay down, although she did not expect to get much sleep in such strange surroundings. The horse shifted about in his stall and the stable smelled strongly of urine and damp straw. It was a stark contrast to the clinically clean atmosphere in the hospital.

She awakened next morning to find sunlight filtering through the windowpanes. Her first thought was for Guy and she struggled to her feet, stumbling over her long skirts in her hurry to reach him. He lay very still and for a terrifying moment she thought that he had stopped breathing. She threw herself down on her knees at his side and seized his wrist, feeling for a pulse as she had seen Nurse Bosmans do on numerous occasions. The steady throbbing of blood through his veins reassured her and she sat back on her haunches. 'You gave me a fright,' she murmured.

He opened his eyes, blinking dazedly. 'Elsie.'

'Yes, it's me.'

He sniffed the air. 'I can smell horses.'

'We're in a stable,' she said, chuckling. 'I don't know where we are exactly, but the hospital orderly brought us here last night because the Germans were doing a spot inspection at the hospital.'

'But why are we in a stable?'

Elsie turned her head at the sound of the door being unlocked and opened. 'I think we're about to find out.' She stood up as their new host entered, carrying a tray of food. In daylight she could see that her first impressions of the baroness had been correct. This was a woman used to giving orders and having them obeyed. 'Good morning, madame,' Elsie said, shaking out her skirts.

'Good morning. I hope you slept well.'

'Yes, thank you.'

'I've brought you some coffee and rolls. I'm afraid there's no butter or jam, but food is scarce these days.'

'We're very grateful for anything, madame.'

'How is the patient?'

'I'm able to speak for myself.' Guy raised himself on one elbow. 'May I know who you are, madame?'

'I am the baroness, and my job is to see you and your companion on your way to the Dutch border.'

'We're very grateful that someone of your standing would want to risk everything by helping us,' Elsie said earnestly.

A grim smile hovered about the baroness's lips. 'I am extremely unimportant these days. A title is more of a hindrance than a help, but fortunately the German official in charge of this area is easily impressed, and it does carry a little weight with him at least.' She set the tray down on a bale of hay. 'Eat your breakfast. I will return later and answer any questions you may have. There is a pump in the yard and an outside lavatory. I suggest you make use of them now. I trust my servants, but there are things it is best for them not to know.'

Elsie waited until the baroness had left them before sitting down to share the meal with Guy. He sipped the strong black ersatz coffee without complaint and managed to eat some of the bread. He pulled a face. 'What I wouldn't give for a dollop of butter and some Cooper's Oxford Marmalade.'

'You're feeling better. I'm so glad.' Elsie reached out to cover his hand with hers. 'I thought I'd lost you.'

His eyes darkened. 'Would you care very much?'

'Of course I would, Guy. Don't be so silly.'

'You don't have to do this, you know, Elsie.'

She stared at him nonplussed. 'What are you saying?'

'You ought to go on alone. Let them take you to safety. I'm just a hindrance, and I'm holding you back.'

'I won't listen to such nonsense. I'm not going anywhere without you. What sort of person do you think I am?'

He smiled and raised her hand to his lips. 'A very brave woman and I don't deserve such a friend.'

She snatched her hand away. 'And you won't have one if you keep talking such tripe.' She scrambled to her feet. 'Now, if you've had enough to eat I'm going to try to get you outside to the lavatory.' She went to fetch the wheelchair and pushed it closer to the stall.

Guy bent one leg, keeping the splinted limb straight. 'Give me a moment and I'll be fine.' He looked up with an apologetic grin. 'I'm just a bit weak.'

'Of course you are,' she said sympathetically. 'Take a breather, and then we'll have another go.'

Eventually, after a considerable struggle, she managed to get him into the chair and across the yard to the outside lavatory. She was too intent on helping him without causing him additional discomfort to feel any embarrassment, and Guy suffered her ministrations without complaint. He even managed to hobble a few paces, but he sat down again quickly, leaving Elsie to get him to the pump. She washed his face and hands with a scrap of cloth torn from her petticoat. 'I don't think I'd make a very good nurse,' she said, mopping the excess water as it trickled down his neck and soaked his shirt. 'Sorry.'

'You're coping magnificently,' he said manfully. 'I'm the useless one. I'm as weak as a kitten and my right leg is useless.'

'You'll get stronger every day.' Elsie paused for a moment to look round and was even more impressed by their surroundings when seen in daylight. 'The baroness must be very wealthy to own such a place.

She has such a lot to lose by helping us and others in a similar position. You've got to admire her.'

'I just wish I wasn't so bloody helpless.' A note of bitterness had crept into Guy's voice and he turned his head away. 'Don't take any notice of me, Elsie. I'm just feeling sorry for myself.' He shot her a sideways glance. 'I should be looking after you, not the other way round.'

'And you would if our situations were reversed. You're lucky to be alive, Guy Gifford.' She realised that she had spoken more brusquely than she had intended and she leaned over to drop a kiss on the top of his head. His hair had been savagely cropped in the hospital, and now stood up in tiny hedgehog spikes, making him look younger and even more vulnerable. She brushed a trickle of water from his cheek. 'You've survived – that's all that matters. We'll get through this together.'

He smiled weakly. 'You're a wonderful girl, Elsie.'

There was no doubting his sincerity and she was touched, but she turned away. This was not the time to weaken; she must be strong for both of them. She splashed water on her hot cheeks. It was ice-cold but invigorating and she dried her face on her skirt. 'I'd give anything for some decent clothes,' she said, steering the subject to safer ground. 'I must look an absolute fright.'

'You look beautiful,' Guy said seriously. 'I'll always remember you like this. You're the bravest woman I've ever met, and the loveliest.'

'You're obviously feverish,' she said, laughing. 'Let's get you back to the stables before the baroness spots us and tells us off for loitering.' There were tears in her eyes as she seized the handles and began to push the wheelchair across the cobblestones. Guy was completely dependent upon her and she had to be brave, but deep down she was terrified. At any moment they could be discovered and shot as spies or at the very least thrown into prison for the duration of the war. Home seemed a long way away, and getting to the Dutch border was not going to be easy. They had just reached the stable door when she spotted the baroness hurrying towards them. She could tell by her tense expression that all was not well. 'Is anything wrong, madame?'

'There's been a change of plan. You were supposed to remain here for a few days, but I've just been informed that my home has been commandeered by the Germans. They are going to billet some of their most important officers here.'

'But that's terrible, baroness. What will happen to you?'

'I'll be treated well enough, but for the time being my work for La Dame Blanche will have to cease. It would be too dangerous to carry on.'

'So we must move on tonight?'

'No, my dear. I'm afraid we will have to take a great risk. You will leave within the hour.'

'How will we travel? Guy is too weak to walk.'

'My maid's husband is a farmer. It's fortunate that today is market day, and he is already in town unloading his produce. He'll be here shortly and will take you to one of our agents closer to the Dutch border. You'll remain there until we can organise the next part of your journey.'

'You are all taking such enormous risks,' Elsie said softly. 'I can't thank you enough.'

'We do what we can. Now go inside and be ready to travel. I'll bring your documents to you before you go, but stay inside until I tell you it's safe to come out. My unwelcome guests will be arriving shortly.' She strode off in the direction of the house, leaving Elsie staring after her in awe.

'What a woman,' Guy said in a low voice. 'I wish we'd had time to get to know her better.'

Elsie manoeuvred the chair into the stables and the horse whinnied as if in greeting. She paused outside his stall, stroking his satiny nose. 'You'll be glad of some peace and quiet, no doubt.'

'I wish I could help,' Guy said as he watched her clearing away evidence of their stay.

'I can manage,' she said cheerfully.

Guy watched as she rolled up his palliasses and tidied the stall. 'So we're going on a hayride.'

She looked up and forced a smile. 'I don't think this is going to be much fun.'

It was hot and airless beneath the canvas sheet that covered the cart, and the wooden wheels jolted over the cobblestones in town and bounced over the rutted lanes when they reached the country. The farmer had not had time to sweep the mud off the boards, and the smell of manure was suffocating, but Elsie lay huddled up against Guy, trying to shield him from the worst of the bumps with little success. He did not complain or cry out, but she felt the tremor go through him each time the jolt was severe enough to cause him pain. 'It's like a game of sardines,' she said in an effort to make light of their discomfort.

'Let's hope no one finds us,' he whispered, and even in the dark she sensed that he was smiling.

She gave him an encouraging hug. 'I think we're slowing down. Better keep quiet in case it's a German checkpoint.'

The cart drew to a lumbering halt and Elsie held her breath. She tightened her hold around Guy and she felt his muscles tense. She could hear noises but she could not make out what was happening until the cover was drawn back, and they were in the cold light of a snowy landscape. She shielded her eyes and found herself looking up into the farmer's weathered face. He held out his hand. 'We're here,' he said, helping her to a sitting position. 'Get out, mademoiselle, and I'll do the rest.'

She jumped to the ground and found herself standing on hard-packed snow beneath the huge sails of a windmill. They seemed to be in the middle of nowhere, surrounded by flat fields with a silver ribbon of a river glinting in the distance. 'Is this where we'll be staying?'

The farmer helped Guy to the ground. He nodded. 'You are only fifteen miles from the Dutch border. The miller will take care of you from now on.'

Elsie followed his gaze, which rested on a small cottage at the rear of the mill, and even as he spoke the front door opened and a tall, muscular man emerged. He strode purposefully towards them, stopping to speak to the farmer in Flemish. After a rapid exchange he turned to Elsie and Guy with an expansive gesture. 'Welcome,' he said in a guttural accent. He took Guy's arm and placed it around his shoulder. 'Come.' He nodded his head in the direction of the cottage.

The farmer patted Elsie on the shoulder. 'You will be safe here. Now I must leave you. Good luck.' He climbed up onto the driver's seat, and making encouraging noises he flicked the reins and the horse shambled off.

Elsie followed the miller and Guy into the cottage where they were greeted by the miller's wife, who hurried them upstairs to a small attic room. She spoke only Flemish, which made conversation difficult. Elsie had to rely on sign language, much to the amusement of the kindly woman, who seemed to find Elsie's attempts at miming hilarious. She brought them freshly baked bread, cheese and mugs of pale-coloured beer, which Elsie found refreshing after the long and uncomfortable journey in the cart.

Guy ate little but drank thirstily and fell asleep almost immediately, lying on a bed of flour sacks stuffed with hay. The scent of the fields filled the small room beneath the eaves, and after a while Elsie began to relax. She was exhausted by the chaotic events of the past few days, and when she was not worrying about Guy her thoughts had been with Marianne. She was deeply concerned about Marianne's liaison with the German officer, and she hoped that Valentine would put an end to the affair and send her, as she had promised, to another assignment far away from temptation.

She was growing sleepy and she lay back on the pile of brightly coloured cushions that had been laid on the floor. She covered herself with a blanket and was drifting off when a sudden grinding noise brought her to her senses. She raised herself on her knees and peered out of the window to see the mill sails catching the wind. They spun round and round, gathering speed, but it was another and more sinister sound that made her hold her breath. She craned her neck to see better as a motor vehicle drew up outside. Two German soldiers climbed out and headed for the cottage door.

It seemed as though the world had stopped. The sails might be turning but Elsie's heart had stilled in her chest and she was finding it difficult to breathe. She drew back from the window, hoping and praying that their hiding place would remain undiscovered, but it seemed that her prayers had been in vain when she heard footsteps on the bare wooden treads of the narrow staircase. She was about to wake Guy when the miller's wife clattered into the room. Elsie gazed down at the woman's clogs and felt a bubble of hysteria rise in her throat, but her relief was short-lived. Outside the mill the sound of raised German voices made her tremble with fear and she raised her head, sending a mute plea for help to the plump woman, who seemed oblivious to anything other than the need to tidy the room. She swooped on the dirty crockery and piled it onto a tray.

Elsie tugged at her skirt and pointed to the stairs. 'Germans?' she said urgently. 'Allemand – Deutsch.'

The miller's wife frowned, shaking her head. She said something in rapid Flemish, and then her expression softened. She smiled, murmuring something that was obviously meant to be comforting, and left the room with the tray clutched in her hands.

Guy slept on, apparently undisturbed by the commotion, but Elsie still feared discovery. She waited for the inevitable, despite the seeming unconcern of their hostess. Then, above the noise of the sails and the rumble of the grindstone, she heard the sound of doors being slammed followed by the cough and splutter of an engine starting up. She raised herself to take a peek out of the window, and could have cried with relief when she saw the vehicle begin to move. It backed out of view and she heard it drive away, the noise fading into the distance, leaving just the gentle humming of the mill in action.

She lay down and allowed herself to drift off into a dreamless sleep.

The months passed. Christmas came and went with barely a change in their daily routine, and the seasons changed, but there was no question of making the final move until the fractured bones in Guy's leg had knitted together. His chest wound had healed, thanks to the attention of the doctors at the hospital and Axelle's devoted nursing, and he was growing stronger each day. The miller's wife kept them well fed, and, under the cover of darkness, Elsie was allowed outside, although it was made clear to her that she must not stray far from the mill. When the weather permitted the miller helped Guy down the stairs so that he could take advantage of the fresh air, and exercise muscles that had become weak from lack of use. Elsie was delighted with his progress, but she was well aware that their continued presence was putting their kind hosts in great danger.

They were so close to the border that she could almost taste freedom, and now that Guy was regaining his strength she was eager to leave, but they had to wait until they received word from La Dame Blanche. As far as Elsie was concerned it was the enforced idleness that was the hardest thing to bear. She did her best to be useful around the cottage, but although the miller's wife did not complain, Elsie suspected that she was more of a hindrance than a help.

Spending days, weeks and months confined in the small space beneath the eaves, listening to the hypnotic sound of the mill sails whirring and the grindstone rumbling was enough to drive an active person out of their mind. Elsie fretted, but Guy was ever patient. He invented word games in an attempt to keep her amused, and regaled her with stories of his childhood. He had the ability to see the humorous side of even the most mundane events, and he made her laugh until her sides ached and she forgot that they were virtually prisoners, if only for a few minutes.

In turn she told him about life in her village, although she made light of the hardships that she and her mother had endured and the unrelenting poverty that had come upon them after her father's untimely death. Then, one evening, having drunk a little too much of the local beer, she admitted her feelings for Henri.

Guy did not seem surprised. 'I knew there was something,' he said slowly. 'I sensed that there must be someone else in your life, and I've waited all this time for you to tell me.'

'I couldn't,' she said sadly. 'It was my problem.'

'Did he feel the same?'

She shook her head. 'I don't know. He never gave me any encouragement. He was kind to me when Ma died, and he singled me out for attention, but then he went off to war and that was that.'

'I know it must be hard for you, Elsie, but I'm

glad,' Guy said, smiling. 'I'd have had to challenge him to a duel if I thought he'd been toying with your affections. It would have been pistols at dawn.'

She looked up with a gurgle of laughter. 'You're barmy, you really are.'

'But I made you laugh. I bet Henri couldn't do that.'

'No,' she said thoughtfully. 'I don't think he could.' She snuggled up against him, closing her eyes, safe in the knowledge that the closeness they shared was something special and priceless. She was comforted by his nearness, and he made her feel needed and safe in a world torn apart by war.

In some ways their enforced stay with the miller and his wife were halcyon days, but Marianne was never far from Elsie's thoughts. She was afraid for her and for Dieter too. Their affair was bound to end badly. Sometimes at night, when she was alone outside, staring up into the black velvet sky, Elsie chose a star and wished on it. She kept the secret to herself, hoping that it might come true.

Chapter Seventeen

With each day virtually the same Elsie gradually lost track of time, but summer was drawing to an end. The miller and his wife went to market once a week and brought back newspapers, but these were printed in Flemish and with only a few words in that language Elsie was unable to make sense of the text. Photographs taken at the front were another matter, and needed no explanation. The names Ypres and Passchendaele leapt out at her and brought tears to her eyes, and she could see that Guy was also deeply affected. 'My wounds are healed,' he said, looking up from the latest newspaper. 'I should be back there with my unit, fighting the Hun.'

Elsie felt a cold shiver run down her spine. 'Your broken bones might have healed but you need time to recuperate at home. You won't do anything silly, will you?'

He met her anxious gaze with a gentle smile. 'I won't limp off into the sunset, if that's what you think. I intend to see you safely home before I report for duty.'

'They might not send you back to active service.'

'I'll have a damn good try, Elsie.'

'It would be madness. I won't let you do anything so foolhardy.'

He turned to her with a question in his eyes. 'Do you care so much what happens to me?'

'Of course I do.' She met his gaze with a steady look. 'No one could have a better friend or a kinder companion than you.'

'I'm not sure that's a compliment,' he said with a wry smile.

She scrambled to her feet. 'You know what I mean, Guy. Anyway, I'm going downstairs to help with the supper. This inactivity is beginning to get me down.'

He reached out to catch her by the hand. 'You've stood by me all this time, Elsie. You could have gone home long ago if it weren't for me.'

'We're getting maudlin. I'm going to speak to the miller and ask him to hurry things along. Heaven knows they must be eager to get rid of us. We're endangering their lives every moment we're here.'

The miller was in the kitchen, sitting in a chair by the range, smoking a pipe. Elsie put the request to him without any preamble. Although his first language was Flemish, he spoke a little French and they were able to communicate after a fashion, but he could not give her any information. All he would say with a shrug of his shoulders was 'La Dame Blanche. We will have to wait.'

One evening in September when it was too wet to go outside, Elsie sat very still on her pile of cushions, listening to the steady pitter-patter of the rain on the roof tiles.

'A penny for them.' Guy's voice broke into her thoughts, making her jump.

She turned her head to give him a vague smile. 'I was thinking of home and wondering where I'll go when we do get back to England. I can't go back to Sutton Darcy, and I'm not sure how long I can stay with Felicia. I'm afraid I'm getting used to being a virtual prisoner and the outside world seems a strange and frightening place.'

'I know what you mean.' Guy sat up, leaning his shoulders against the roughly plastered wall. 'But I'm sure it won't be much longer, Elsie. They'll move us on as soon as humanly possible.'

'I know, but it's so hard not knowing what's happening in the outside world, and I wish I knew what had happened to Marianne.'

'I realise she's doing a dangerous job, but you risked more by making this journey with me.'

'I wanted to do it, Guy. I don't regret it for an instant.'

He moved closer and slipped his arm around her shoulders. 'Then what is it? Is there something you haven't told me?'

A reluctant smile curved Elsie's lips. 'You know Marianne. She's a little crazy sometimes, and when she falls for someone commonsense flies out of the window.'

'I know that very well. I saw it happen several

times when we were in London. Who is it this time? Not Hendrick?'

'No, silly,' she said, chuckling. 'Actually, it was much more serious than that, and very dangerous. I didn't tell you before because I didn't want to worry you, but Marianne was seeing a German officer.' She shot him a sideways glance. 'Don't look like that, Guy. It started out innocently enough, but she couldn't help herself. She loves him, or she thinks she does.'

'For the first time since we started on this trek I don't feel guilty about taking you away from what I imagined to be a fairly safe assignment, or at least as safe as anyone can be in war-torn Europe.'

'It was fate that threw us together again.'

He dropped his gaze. 'I should be out there fighting for my country, and protecting the people I love.'

'That's what got you injured in the first place.' She raised her hand to touch his cheek with her fingertips. 'You're a hero, Guy. You very nearly gave your life for your country, and I'm proud of you.'

'You are?'

'Don't look so surprised. Of course I am.' She leaned forward and kissed him on the lips. It was a passionless gesture, such as she might have bestowed on a much loved child, but the colour flooded his cheeks and she realised her mistake too late.

'Thank you,' he murmured, turning away. 'I think it's time we got some shut-eye.'

'Guy, I'm sorry. I didn't mean to embarrass you.'

He returned to his bed. 'You didn't. I just need to get some sleep.'

'Yes, of course.' She felt suddenly alone and abandoned as he settled down with his back to her. The last thing she had wanted was to upset him. She had acted on impulse and she could still feel the imprint of his lips on hers. A sudden onrush of emotion threatened to swamp her. Whether it was pity for Guy, or her own sudden and desperate need for affection, she could not tell, but she needed to hold him and be held in return. She needed to feel that she was not alone in an alien world. She moved to his side and curled up against his body, slipping her arms around him and resting her cheek against his shoulder. He did not move, and for a moment she thought he must have fallen asleep, but then his fingers curled around her hand.

'I'm here because I want to be, Guy,' she whispered. 'We'll get through this together, or not as the case may be, and I'm glad I came with you.'

His grip on her hand tightened. 'Are you still in love with the Frenchman?'

The question came as a surprise and she stiffened. 'I – I don't know.'

'But you still think about him. You told me so.'

'Yes. No, I mean I don't know,' she said softly. 'The war has changed everything. It's changed all of us.'

He eased himself round so that he lay on his back,

308

staring up into the rafters. 'I've been fighting off the desire to take you in my arms and kiss you, but when we're back at home I'm going to do my best to make you forget you ever knew that French fellow.'

There was no answer to this, nor did he seem to expect one, and she closed her eyes, comforted by the nearness of him. This was a different man from the shy, unassuming person she had known in London. He was still kind and courteous but his experiences in the battlefield had added a touch of steel to his character that had either been hidden or she had simply overlooked in the past. She fell asleep clutching his hand as if it were a lifeline.

She was awakened by someone shaking her by the shoulder, and she opened her eyes to darkness. 'Come.' The miller's wife shook her again. 'Come.'

Elsie sat up, disturbing Guy who groaned and raised himself on his elbow. 'What's going on?'

'I don't know, but I think she wants us to go with her.' Elsie struggled to her feet. She was still fully dressed and she searched for her shoes. 'I wish I spoke Flemish.'

The miller's wife moved to the doorway, beckoning furiously. 'Come.'

'We're coming,' Guy said, getting to his feet. 'Can you see my boots anywhere, Elsie?'

'I just tripped over one.' She found them and

helped him to put them on. 'It looks as if we're on the move at last. Can you manage the stairs?'

'I'm fine. You go first and I'll follow.'

The kitchen was lit by a soft glow from the range and a cool breeze whipped in through the open door, bringing with it the scent of damp earth. The miller ushered them outside into almost complete darkness.

'What's going on?' Guy demanded warily. 'Where are we going?'

A man stepped out from behind the stationary sail. 'I'm taking you to Holland. Come with me now. We must hurry. It will be light in a few hours.'

'You speak English,' Elsie said eagerly. 'That's wonderful.'

'My mother was English, but that's not important. I have a boat which will take you part of the way.' He strode off towards the river that Elsie had seen in the distance on their arrival at the windmill.

She turned to the miller and his wife, who were standing in the doorway. 'Thank you,' she said in Flemish. 'Thank you.' She linked her hand through the crook of Guy's arm. 'Are you all right?'

'We'll hold each other up,' he said cheerfully. 'Let's go before we lose sight of him.'

The river was about half a mile away, or so Elsie estimated, and she could feel Guy beginning to tire as they reached the place where their guide's boat was tied up alongside a mooring stage. Traces of flour on the wooden planks bore witness to the transport of produce from the mill, but there were no other craft in evidence. Their guide helped them to board the rowing boat and with a deft flick he released the mooring rope, climbed in and picked up the oars. The craft slid across the oily black surface of the river with barely a splash of the blades as they sliced through the water.

'Are you taking us over the border?' Elsie asked in a low voice.

'When we join the River Scheldt you will be transferred to another vessel which will take you to Flushing. I would think that arrangements have been made to find you a passage to England, but I can't be certain.'

'It can't be that easy.' Elsie reached for Guy's hand and held it in a tight grip.

'We have to reach the Scheldt before sunrise,' their guide said cheerfully. 'But I am a champion rower, so you can just sit back and enjoy the scenery.'

Guy slipped his good arm around Elsie's shoulders. 'We can't thank you enough.'

Elsie nodded in agreement. 'So many heroes,' she said sleepily. 'So many brave people we have to thank.'

She opened her eyes to a cold grey dawn. The silver surface of the river was pockmarked by falling rain. Guy had covered her with his jacket, but she was damp and shivering as the small boat drew alongside a huge barge. Their guide tossed a rope to a crewman and they were helped on board. There was just time to repeat their thanks before the rower pulled away and was lost in the mist. Elsie's teeth were chattering, but she was more concerned for Guy, who was soaked to the skin. His face was ashen and he was shaking with cold and fatigue. To Elsie's surprise it was a woman who emerged from the accommodation. She bustled towards them with a welcoming smile. 'I am the captain's wife,' she said in English. 'Come with me. You must get out of those wet things.' She led them to a comfortably furnished saloon that could have been the parlour of any house ashore. 'My husband has some garments which might do for you,' she said, eyeing Guy critically, 'and I have just the thing for you, miss.' She led Elsie to a cabin at the rear of the saloon and opened a drawer beneath the bunk. She sorted through the neatly packed clothes and selected a dark blue woollen skirt and a cream calico blouse. 'These belong to my daughter, Anneke.' She chuckled and patted her ample belly. 'We are much the same shape at the moment, but she will be slim again after the birth of her baby.'

'You will be a grandmother soon,' Elsie said, smiling. 'That's lovely.'

'Anneke is staying with her husband's people in Amsterdam until the baby comes.' The captain's wife was suddenly serious. 'We will have to go through a German checkpoint when we cross the border into Holland. It is usually straightforward, but in case we are searched you must pretend to be Anneke, and your friend will be her husband Wouter. Will you explain that to him?'

Elsie grasped the woman's hand. 'We will be forever in your debt.'

'Nonsense, girl. We are just doing our duty – no questions asked.' She made for the doorway. 'Give me your wet clothes and I will dry them for you.'

'How long will it take us to get to the border?'

'A couple of hours, that's all, and we will reach Flushing before dark.'

'Do you know what will happen to us then?'

'Only that you will be met by someone, and they will organise the rest of your journey.' She slipped out of the cabin, leaving Elsie to struggle out of her wet things and take on her new persona as Anneke, the barge captain's pregnant daughter. Elsie brushed her hair and plaited the damp tresses, winding them around her head. Surveying the result in a mirror pinned to the bulkhead, she smiled at her reflection. 'So now you're Anneke,' she whispered. 'I've had so many incarnations in the past two years that I've almost forgotten the real me.'

She picked up her soiled clothing and went into the saloon to find Guy struggling into a pair of baggy trousers. He secured them with a leather belt and shrugged on the jacket provided. He sat down suddenly. 'Damnation,' he said breathlessly. 'My leg is still weak. Lying around all day hasn't helped to strengthen my muscles.'

She dumped her bundle on the table and hurried over to help him. 'Let me take off your boots.'

'No. I've got to manage on my own.'

Ignoring his gruff refusal she knelt down and unlaced his boots.

'I'm sorry, Elsie,' he said apologetically. 'I didn't mean to snap, but I'm sick to death of being dependent on others. Sometimes I wish they'd killed me outright.'

'Don't say things like that.' She peeled off his wet socks and replaced them with dry ones. 'Feeling sorry for yourself isn't going to help and it's not like you. You've been so strong all the time we were hiding out.'

'You're only sorry for me. You don't really care.'

She leapt to her feet, grabbed him by the shoulders and shook him as hard as she could. 'Stop it. Of course I care.' She tightened her grip, giving him another shake. 'If this is a ploy to get sympathy you're not getting any from me. We're almost there. You can't give up now – Wouter.'

He stared up at her with a baffled frown. 'Wouter?'

'That's your new name,' she said, giggling. 'You're Wouter and I'm your wife, Anneke. She's the captain's daughter and she's about to give birth any day now.' She snatched up a cushion and tucked it under her blouse in an attempt to make him laugh. 'We're going to be parents, Wouter.' She danced about the saloon, clutching her bump. The ridiculousness of quarrelling over nothing hit her forcibly.

She was laughing and somehow she could not stop. Guy stood up and caught her in his arms as she was about to pass him for the second time. He held her with surprising strength and his mouth found hers in a kiss that caught her by surprise, and even more astonishing she found herself kissing him back. The cushion slid to the deck and she realised dimly that her body fitted exactly to his, as if they had been created as one. At last, dazed and breathless, she tried to pull away. 'Let me go, Guy. This is crazy.'

'I don't agree.' His eyes were dark with desire as he held her gaze. 'I wish it were true. I wish I was Wouter or whatever his name is, and that you were my wife.'

Her knees threatened to give way beneath her and her heart seemed to be doing somersaults inside her breast. His kisses had taken her to another dimension, far away from the dangers they still faced, but now it was time to face reality. She stared down at the cushion where it lay between them. 'We dropped the baby. It's lucky it wasn't a real one.'

He released her and sat down abruptly. 'I suppose you think this is all a joke.'

She picked up the cushion and wrapped her arms around it, holding it close. 'No, Guy. I'm not laughing.'

'I'm sorry,' he said, bowing his head. 'I took advantage of you. It won't happen again. I've resisted the temptation all these months – I shouldn't have kissed you.'

She opened her mouth to argue but the captain's wife chose that moment to enter the saloon, putting a stop to the argument. She carried a tray laden with bread, cheese and rosy red apples which she set down on the table. 'I'm sure you're hungry,' she said cheerfully. She took in their changed appearances with a pleased smile. 'You could pass for Anneke and Wouter, but let's hope we get across the border without incurring a search. The German soldiers turn everything upside down. Heaven alone knows what they think they might find.' She scooped up their wet garments. 'I'd better get on if I'm to have these ready for you when you leave us.'

'Thank you,' Elsie said wholeheartedly. 'You're very kind and we're truly grateful.'

She beamed at them. 'It's always a pleasure to help young lovers. It does my sentimental heart good to see you two together – just like my Anneke and her Wouter.'

Elsie smiled and nodded. She dared not look at Guy in case she burst into hysterical laughter. 'Thank you for the food,' she said hastily. 'I'm starving.'

'Of course. Young people always are.' The captain's wife smiled and left the saloon, closing the door softly behind her.

Elsie busied herself slicing the bread. She hoped that Guy could not see that her hand shook as she pared slivers from the cheese. Her pulses continued to race and she could still feel the pressure of his body against hers. The taste and scent of him lingered, and she was finding it difficult to concentrate even on the simplest task. She told herself that being thrown together had created a false set of emotions. It was not love. It was not. She turned to Guy. 'Would you like some bread and cheese? The apples look good too.'

After breakfast, there was nothing to do but sit and wait for the moment when the barge sailed into neutral Holland. Elsie knew they should have been celebrating the fact that they had come this far, but the atmosphere in the saloon was strained. She could not look Guy in the face without blushing, and he seemed equally ill at ease. He lay back on the bench and feigned sleep. She could tell by the way he was breathing that he was simply lying there with his eyes shut, but at least it saved her the bother of trying to make polite conversation. She was edgy and frightened, and in an emotional maelstrom. She had never thought of Guy in a romantic way; even when he had proposed to her in the teashop she had managed to remain objective. She had always liked him, but things had changed dramatically since Hendrick had carried the injured soldier into the kitchen of the Merchant's House. She stole a glance at Guy's prostrate figure. She had dressed his wounds and bathed his naked flesh, so that she knew his body almost as intimately as she knew her own. She had slept at his side and taken comfort from his nearness. She had shared his fears and they had laughed at the same silly things. She snatched up the cushion and held it close. It had been the baby they had momentarily shared and then lost. It had not been real, but for a few seconds it had seemed real. She wanted him to open his eyes and smile at her. She wanted him to love her again, but she knew that she had missed her chance. They had simply shared a moment of madness, and now it was over.

She sat back on the hard seat, still clutching the cushion, as she tried to conjure up a vision of Henri. She closed her eyes; she had held on to the dream for so long that she had imagined it to be real. She tried hard to resurrect the feeling she had for him, but it was like walking through a peasouper. Each time she felt that she was drawing closer to Henri she found that he had moved on. His shadow was fast disappearing into the mists of a forgotten memory.

She opened her eyes with a start and sat bolt upright. She was still drugged with sleep, but the noises on deck were real enough. She was more than familiar with the sound of orders being barked out in German. Guy was already on his feet and he had opened the saloon door. The voices were growing louder, and even though she could not understand a word, it was obvious that they were not going to cross the border without an inspection. 'What will we do?' she gasped. 'Guy, you must hide. I might get away with it, but you won't.'

He looked round the saloon, but all the furnishings were built in and bolted to the deck. 'You couldn't conceal a mouse in here.' He closed the door. 'Get up and go into the cabin.'

'There's nowhere to hide in there.'

He moved towards her and took the cushion from her hands. 'Our baby,' he said with a grim smile. 'You must pretend to be in labour, and I'll act like the anxious father to be. If you scream loud enough it might just work. It's our only chance.'

Elsie hurried into the cabin and kicked off her shoes. She leapt onto the bunk and grabbed the cushion, securing it under her clothes. Guy knelt at her side and as the door burst open she let out an ear-splitting scream. His look of alarm was as genuine as that of the young German soldier who stood in the doorway, his jaw slackened in surprise as he took in the scene.

Acting for all she was worth, Elsie writhed and yelled, clutching Guy's hand until she heard his knuckles crack. She gasped for breath and screamed again. Tears coursed unchecked down her cheeks and her sobs were genuine. She held on to Guy, forgetting everything other than the need to keep him safe. She gave no thought to her own danger, or the fact that she could be arrested as a spy and might face a firing squad. She let out yet another loud howl and the captain's wife pushed past the soldier, shouting at him in rapid Flemish. He backed into the saloon and she slammed the door in his face. She leaned against it, closing her eyes and her lips moved as if in silent prayer.

Elsie groaned and was working herself up for another spate of screaming when Guy laid his finger to his lips. 'I think they're leaving.'

The captain's wife opened the door and stood there, her head cocked on one side. She uttered a sigh of relief. 'They've gone ashore. Thank God for that.' She turned to Elsie with a smile. 'That was quite a performance. I almost believed that you were in labour.'

Guy withdrew his hand and flexed his fingers. 'Are you all right, Elsie?'

She lay there exhausted but triumphant. 'I've just given birth to a lovely plump cushion,' she said, and found she was crying.

'We're moving again.' The captain's wife made to leave the cabin. 'This calls for a cup of real coffee. I have a small supply that I keep for special occasions.'

Elsie sat up and swung her legs over the side of the bunk. 'I'd give anything for a cup of tea,' she whispered.

Guy smiled. 'I know a charming teashop in Piccadilly.'

Chapter Eighteen

Felicia looked up from reading the newspaper without a flicker of surprise. 'So you're back, Elsie. How was it in Paris?'

'Interesting,' Elsie said, taking off the woollen beret that the Red Cross worker had given her when she and Guy had landed at Harwich.

Felicia peered at her over the top of her reading glasses. 'You look frightful, darling. Where did you get that rig-out?'

'It's a long story.' Elsie hesitated, gazing anxiously at Felicia. 'I know there's no reason for me to be here now, and I promise I'll look for accommodation elsewhere, but I wonder if I could stay with you for a while?'

Felicia took off her reading glasses and stared at her in overt astonishment. 'It never occurred to me that you'd go anywhere else. I've missed having you and Marianne around the place, and Anthea is hardly ever at home these days.'

'Are you sure, Felicia? I don't want to outstay my welcome, and I'm not even sure I have a job to go back to.'

'Darling, it's wartime. London has been bombed

and there's talk of food rationing, apart from the fact that millions of young men have lost their lives. We're all in this together and you can stay here as long as you like.'

Elsie breathed a sigh of relief. 'I don't know what to say other than thank you.'

Felicia reached across the back of the sofa and tugged at the bell pull. 'I'll get Gerda to run a bath for you.' She sniffed and wrinkled her nose. 'There's a distinct smell of fish about you.'

'That would be really wonderful.' Elsie was too tired to go into details of their journey from Flushing to Harwich in a small fishing boat. They had narrowly escaped being sunk by a German submarine, and Guy had been seasick from the moment they left the relatively calm waters of the Scheldt estuary. They had arrived with the false papers given them in Belgium to identify them as well as their British passports, and had been taken straight to the nearest police station. Eventually, after a long night spent in a prison cell, they had been released. Guy had been taken to an army hospital and she had received a rail pass authorising her to travel to London. She might have spent longer in jail had it not been for a telephone call from Military Intelligence confirming her story. 'Who's Gerda?' she asked wearily.

'She's a Belgian refugee. I got her from your people – they're always on the lookout for someone to offer employment and accommodation even now. She's a good girl, but she doesn't speak very good English. Anyway, I'm off again in a couple of weeks. I'll spend the rest of the year entertaining the troops. What about you, Elsie?'

'I've got to report to Room 40 tomorrow. I hope they'll give me my old job back with Blinker's Beauty Chorus.'

Felicia frowned. 'Where's Marianne? Why didn't she come with you?'

'We got separated, Felicia. I'm not sure where she is at the moment.'

'Well, one thing is certain – Marianne will be all right. She's a survivor if ever there was one.' Felicia turned her head as the maid burst into the room. 'What have I told you about knocking first, Gerda?'

'I'm sorry, madame. I forget.'

'I want you to run a bath for Miss Mead, and then you can make up her bed. It's the room at the end of the corridor. She'll show you which one.' Felicia dismissed her with a wave of her hand. 'You'd better go with her, Elsie. She hasn't quite learned the layout of the flat yet, although heaven knows it's small enough. I'll see you at dinner.' She went back to reading her newspaper.

Elsie rose to her feet. She looked round the room – nothing had changed. Felicia had not changed either. She had greeted her as if she had just returned after a weekend in the country. She followed Gerda from the room feeling once again as though she had stepped into a parallel universe. Tomorrow she would get to grips with her old life, but for the present all she needed was a hot bath, clean clothes and sleep – lots and lots of it in a nice clean bed.

Next morning Elsie reported to Room 40 for a debriefing, and by the end of the day she was exhausted. She had almost lost her voice after repeating her story over and over again, but even now her main concern was for Marianne. She had given detailed descriptions of their work in the Merchant's House, but she did not mention Marianne's involvement with a German officer, and it was difficult to show concern for her friend without giving a specific reason. The heads of departments were only interested in receiving relevant information, and the moment she tried to ask a question she found herself sidetracked. Her last meeting that day was with a high-ranking official, who congratulated her on her efforts and offered to take her on again, this time as a translator. It was a step up from routine clerical work and Elsie was in no position to refuse, but she was still none the wiser as to Marianne's fate.

She was in the canteen, queuing for a cup of tea and a rather stale-looking Chelsea bun, when one of the secretaries she had worked with in the past came up to her with a beaming smile. 'So you're back then, Elsie. How did it go in Paris? Was it exciting and glamorous?'

Elsie managed a feeble smile. She had always liked Sheila Barratt, but they had never been particularly close, and now she was asking her about her time abroad as if she had just come back from a fortnight's holiday. 'How did you know where I'd been? It's supposed to be top secret.'

Sheila's cheeks flushed a dull pink. 'Sorry. I know I shouldn't talk about it, but there's no one within earshot, and you and Marianne are so lucky to have been sent on special duties. I've been stuck here typing reports and doing the boring stuff.'

'It was interesting,' Elsie said vaguely.

'Marianne obviously likes the rue Saint-Roch, since you came back on your own,' Sheila said, selecting the largest bun on the tray. 'Didn't you want to stay there with her?'

'Why do you think she's in Paris?'

'Because I typed a report saying so.' Sheila eyed her curiously. 'Didn't you know? I thought you two were practically inseparable.'

'There's a war on, Sheila. We weren't there for our health.'

'I didn't mean to put my foot in it.' Sheila paid for her tea and was about to walk away when Elsie caught her by the sleeve.

'I'm sorry, I didn't mean to snap. I'm still a bit tired after my travels. Do you know where she's staying?'

'As a matter of fact, I do. Of course, I can't tell you as it's all hush-hush.'

'But she's working at the rue Saint-Roch. You can tell me that much.'

'Yes. I don't suppose I'm giving too much away by telling you that.' She leaned nearer, lowering her voice. 'You won't tell anyone that I told you.'

'And where is she staying? Come on, Sheila, you've gone this far so a little more information can't hurt.'

Sheila was obviously desperate to impart the news. She looked round nervously and took a deep breath. 'She's staying with a family called Bellaire in the rue de l'Echelle. That's all I can remember, but for God's sake don't let on that I told you.'

'Of course not. Thanks.' Elsie took her tray and carried it to a table near the window. She sat down and sipped her tea.

Her initial feeling of relief that Marianne was safe was tempered by a sudden and irrational feeling of anger. She had been worrying unnecessarily all these months. Marianne had come through unscathed, and was probably enjoying the relative freedom of working in the rue Saint-Roch as well as a comfortable billet with Henri's family. She had somehow managed to extricate herself from a situation that could have been her downfall. How typical of Marianne, Elsie thought with a reluctant smile. She had played a dangerous game and had won.

Elsie nibbled the Chelsea bun, but it was as stale as it looked and she left it on her plate. It was time to return home to Cromwell Road. She would use Felicia's telephone and ring the military hospital to find out how Guy was progressing. Perhaps they would discharge him and allow him to return to his rented rooms in London. She longed to hear his voice again. It was only now that she realised how close they had become during their escape from occupied Belgium. She could tell Guy everything, knowing that he would understand. She left a threepenny bit under the plate for the overworked waitress and stood up. Sheila waved to her as she left the canteen and Elsie acknowledged her with a vague smile. Soon things would be back to normal, whatever normality was these days.

She did not get much information from the hospital near Harwich. All they would say was that Guy was being kept in for a few days. She replaced the receiver and went to join Felicia in the drawing room.

Felicia looked up from writing copious notes in an exercise book. 'Any news?'

'They won't say when he's being discharged. I can't understand it, because his wounds had healed and he was able to walk quite well, although he'll probably always have a limp.'

'I'm sure they know what they're doing, darling.' Felicia frowned and chewed the end of her pencil. 'Planning these touring shows takes longer every year. I hope to God this will be the last Christmas we have to do one. Each time we've done a tour the poor blighters look thinner, filthier and more worn down by the damned war. Most of them are just boys. It's heartbreaking.'

Elsie stifled a sigh and sank down on a chair by the window, gazing out into the rain. Getting back to a semblance of normality was not going to be easy. She was wishing that she could have spoken to Guy when she realised that the telephone was ringing.

'Answer that, will you, darling?' Felicia said with a vague wave of her hand. 'If it's for me, tell them I'll ring back later. I really have to finish this before I go to bed.'

Elsie stood up and made her way to the side table. She picked up the receiver. 'Hello.'

'Elsie, is that you?'

Her breath hitched in her throat. 'They told me you couldn't come to the phone. Guy. They said you were being kept in hospital.'

'I'm not supposed to be speaking to you now, but I had to tell you that I'm being transferred to an army camp up north. I don't know exactly where.'

'But that's not fair,' she protested angrily. 'You should be convalescent.'

'I'm perfectly fit for a desk job. I should think myself lucky that I'm not being sent back to France, but all I can think about is you, darling.'

The term of endearment made her heart do a funny little flip, and she was suddenly breathless. 'I miss you too, Guy.'

'I'd give anything to be with you now, but it's not going to happen.'

'You will take care of yourself, won't you?'

'I'm more concerned about you, Elsie. How are things?'

'Awfully strange. I feel as if I'm in limbo, but I'm fine. You mustn't worry about me.' She clutched the receiver even more tightly as the pips shrieked in her ear.

'I have to go, darling. I'm leaving right away.'

'Oh, Guy . . .'

'The teashop,' he said urgently. 'When all this is over we'll meet . . .' The line went dead.

Elsie stood for a moment, gazing at the telephone as if trying to will it to reconnect, but the dialling tone buzzed irritably until she replaced the receiver. Tears ran unchecked down her cheeks.

'Was that your friend from the War Office?'

'It was Guy.'

Felicia turned her head to give Elsie a searching look. 'If he's jilted you I'll have something to say to that young man.'

A reluctant gurgle of laughter rose to Elsie's lip and she dashed her hand across her eyes. 'Nothing like that, Felicia. He's been posted a long way from here. Heaven alone knows when I'll see him again.'

'Wartime romances seldom last, darling. Be thankful that you haven't committed yourself.'

'It's not like that.'

'If you say so, Elsie.' Felicia stared at her, frowning. 'You look exhausted, darling. You really ought to rest. Why not take a few days' compassionate leave and go down to Dorset? I'm sure it can be arranged.'

'But I'm to start back in Room 40 tomorrow.'

'A phone call to my friend Edith Lomax will fix that. I'll say that you need time to rest and recuperate, and as I'm in loco parentis my word is law. I'll tell Edith so in no uncertain terms. A few days in the country and you'll be a new woman.'

'I didn't know you knew her, Felicia.'

'You'd be surprised at the number of friends I have in high places, darling.'

Felicia's confidence in her own abilities was severely dented when Edith Lomax told her not to interfere in government business. In a way Elsie was relieved to be back at work. There was no real reason for her to return to Sutton Darcy. Tan Cottage was no longer her home and the manor house had merely been her place of employment. If Marianne had returned to England things would be different, but she was in the relative safety of the rue Saint-Roch and no doubt enjoying the luxury of the Bellaires' apartment. Perhaps Henri was there too? The idea did not thrill her as it would have done not so long ago. It came as a shock to realise that she no longer cared for him. Perhaps it had always been an illusion, but whatever the explanation she was no longer under his spell, although she still cared for him as a friend. She went back to work safe in the knowledge that as a translator she was still doing something for the war effort. It might not be as challenging as being a secret agent, but she felt she had had enough excitement to last a lifetime.

Elsie prepared to spend Christmas alone in the flat except for Gerda, who had nowhere else to go. Felicia was in Flanders and Anthea, who had been posted to East Anglia, had decided to return home to Yorkshire to spend time with her family. At first this decision puzzled Elsie. Anthea always said she had come to London in order to escape from her troublesome relations, but Gerda explained that Tubby McAvoy had been killed in action and that Anthea had taken it badly. Elsie sat down immediately and attempted to write a letter of condolence to Anthea, but her vision was blurred by tears as memories of good-natured, fun-loving Tubby came flooding back, and it took several attempts to compose just a few lines.

Her dressing table, which also served as a desk, was piled high with letters from Guy. They arrived once a week with unfailing regularity, and were filled with amusing anecdotes of life in camp somewhere in England. They always ended with the hope that he would see her soon. She missed him more than she would have thought possible, but there was little chance of his being granted leave and she knew she must be patient, but it was far from easy.

On Christmas Eve Gerda persuaded Elsie to accompany her to the church hall in Hackney where the annual party for the Belgian refugees was being held. They travelled by bus and arrived to find the proceedings in full swing. Mrs Johnson rushed up to Elsie, kissed her on the cheek and thrust a glass of warm beer into her hand. 'We thought you'd abandoned us, love. Where have you been all this time?'

Yet again, Elsie smiled and said it was a long story, and with that Mrs Johnson had to be satisfied. She bustled off to get her husband, leaving Elsie to chat with some of the refugees she had worked with in the past, while Gerda went to join the friends she had made since coming to England. It was only later, when Elsie was talking to the vicar, that she remembered her promise to Valentine. 'I know this is a long shot, but have you ever had anything to do with two brothers, Jens and Yannick Peeters?'

He sipped his beer, frowning thoughtfully. 'As a matter of fact I do remember them because they arrived unaccompanied. The youngest must have been twelve or thirteen and the older boy about sixteen. They came over in the first wave of refugees, and I can't remember exactly where we placed them, but I have a feeling it was on a farm in Hampshire. I'll have a record of it somewhere.'

'That's fantastic,' Elsie said eagerly. 'I can't tell you the details but their mother is a very brave woman. I promised her that I would try to contact them and give them her love.'

He shook his head. 'It's been a terrible time, but

at least we've been able to help a few of the poor souls to keep going until they can return home.' He glanced at Gerda who was dancing energetically with another girl. 'There's a success story, thanks to your friend Miss Wilby. She's found places for many of our Belgian guests with her friends and colleagues.'

'She's been very good to me.' Elsie avoided meeting his gaze, staring into the amber liquid in her glass. The talk of love and loss had reminded her sharply of her own bereavement. The pain of losing her mother was a constant ache that never completely went away.

'You look sad, Elsie.'

She looked up into Joe's kindly face and she was suddenly close to tears. 'I was thinking of my mother. She died at the beginning of the war.'

'I'm sorry, my dear.'

She forced her lips into a smile. 'So many people have lost loved ones. I'd like to do this small thing for Valentine, if it's at all possible.'

He put his glass down and took her by the arm. 'Come to my office. I'll look up the records for the Peeters brothers.'

In the quiet of the small, cluttered office, Joe rifled through the chaotic filing system contained in several cardboard boxes. He pulled files and leafed through them. 'I'm sure the details are here somewhere.' He shot her a sideways glance. 'I'd love to know what you were doing in Belgium, or is it classified information?'

'I'm afraid so, but when all this is over perhaps I can tell you then.'

'I can only imagine what you must have gone through.'

'What I did was nothing compared to the sacrifice of others.'

'In my book you're a heroine, Elsie Mead. I'm proud to know you.'

She clapped her hands to her hot cheeks. 'Now you've embarrassed me, Joe. I did what I was told, most of the time anyway.'

'You're too modest, my dear.' He selected a sheet of paper with a grunt of satisfaction. 'The good news is that I've found the farm where the Peeters brothers were sent.' He scribbled the address on the back of an envelope and handed it to her. 'Merry Christmas, Elsie. I hope and pray that 1918 will see the end of this terrible war and Europe will start to heal its wounds.'

Gerda had been invited to spend Christmas Day with a Belgian family who had rooms in Hackney, which left Elsie to spend the day alone in the flat. With her corned beef sandwich in one hand, she leafed through the train timetable that Felicia kept by the telephone. It was a humble Christmas lunch, but she knew that it was probably much better fare than the troops were having in the trenches. The truce that had happened in the first Christmas of the war had never been repeated, and the use of poison gas had hardened attitudes on both sides. Elsie had wept when she read accounts of the suffering caused by the evil new weapon, which killed indiscriminately or left the survivors with terrible after-effects. She wondered how many of the boys she had grown up with had survived the carnage. She could still remember them on that hot summer's day, marching off to war, singing at the tops of their voices. How many of them were singing now? It was a sobering thought and she realised that she had lost her appetite. She put her sandwich down, half eaten, and made a note of the train times to Southampton. Tomorrow she would set off for the farm where Valentine's sons had been billeted. It was the least she could do for a brave woman who risked her life daily to relieve the suffering of others. But for Valentine Guy would not have survived, and she must have been instrumental in getting Marianne back to the comparative safety of Paris. Valentine was the real heroine of the war as far as Elsie was concerned.

She set off early next morning and caught the first train to Southampton. After an hour or so she managed to get a bus to the village, and having asked directions from the bus conductor she walked to the farm, arriving tired and muddy but determined to find Valentine's boys. She entered the yard and was greeted by one of the farm dogs. It jumped up at her yelping excitedly and she was making a fuss of it when a young man stepped out of one of the outbuildings. He came towards her with a smile that reminded her forcibly of Valentine, and she knew she had come to the right place.

She spent a couple of hours in the warmth of the farmhouse kitchen, regaling Jens and Yannick with stories of her time in the Merchant's House, and they listened avidly. 'I can't wait to go home and see my mother and Hendrick,' Yannick said, blinking back tears. 'I was little more than a boy when we were forced to flee from our country.'

'We were lucky,' Jens said firmly. 'We have been treated like family and I always wanted to be a farmer.'

Yannick nudged his brother in the ribs. 'And he's engaged to the farmer's daughter, so his future is assured.'

'That is true,' Jens said, grinning. 'I will be taking my bride home to meet Mother when the war is over.'

'She is a wonderful woman,' Elsie said earnestly. 'It was a privilege to work with her, and I wish I could tell you more, but all I can say is that you should be very proud of her. She's a true heroine.' She stood up, reaching for her handbag. 'Now I have to leave or I'll miss my train home.'

Jens leapt to his feet. 'I'll drive you to the station, miss.'

'Thank you.' Elsie leaned over to kiss Yannick on the cheek. 'Give your mother my love when you return home. Tell her I'll always remember the Merchant's House and the time we spent with her.'

She followed Jens out of the farmhouse into the freezing cold of a winter's day. He helped her up onto the driver's seat of the farm cart and climbed up beside her. 'Looks like snow,' he said cheerfully. 'Let's hope the trains keep running.'

'Thank you for that cheerful thought,' Elsie said, chuckling. 'I can tell that you spent a lot of time with Hendrick when you were young. You have a similar gallows humour.'

Jens shot her a puzzled look. 'I don't understand.'

'Ask your fiancée, she'll explain.' Elsie pulled her collar up around her face in an attempt to keep out the cold. 'I'm so glad we met, and that I could tell you a little of the work your mother is doing, and Hendrick too. I hope to see them again one day, if only to thank them both. You will tell her that when you next see her, won't you?'

He flicked the reins to encourage the old carthorse to go faster. 'Of course I will, and I hope it will be soon.'

Elsie said goodbye to him when he dropped her off outside the station. It was bitterly cold and there was no fire in the waiting room. Coal, like everything else, was in short supply and had been rationed by the number of rooms a family had in its house, or so Bailey had told her grimly when she had asked for some to be sent up to the flat. But the trains were still running and eventually one arrived at the station, and although it was crowded she managed to find a seat. At least it was warm in the compartment and she had the satisfaction of knowing that she had kept her word to Valentine.

It was early evening when she arrived home. She let herself into the flat and was met by an excited Gerda. 'I'm so glad you're here. There's a gentleman waiting for you in the drawing room.'

Chapter Nineteen

For a wild moment Elsie thought it must be Guy who had been granted unexpected leave. She rushed into the drawing room unbuttoning her coat, and came to a sudden halt. 'Colonel Winter.' She could barely remember the last time she had seen Marianne's father, but on the few occasions she had spotted him in the grounds of Darcy Hall, or striding through the village, he had always been an impressive figure with his upright military bearing and authoritative manner. His fair hair was streaked with silver as was his moustache, and his chiselled, suntanned features might have graced an ancient coin bearing the head of a Roman emperor. Elsie had always been in awe of Colonel James Winter and that feeling remained.

'Elsie Mead.' He gave her a tired smile. 'You've grown up.'

She noted the lines at the corners of his startlingly blue eyes and the downturn of his lips, which had thinned with age. 'I have, sir.' She shrugged off her coat. 'If you've come to see Marianne, I'm afraid she's not here.'

He inclined his head. 'I only arrived back in

England a few days ago. I went straight to Darcy Hall and my brother told me that Marianne was working in London and this was the address he gave me, although they had lost touch. My sister-in-law, who loves to gossip, told me that you'd accompanied her to London.'

'That's not exactly true, sir.' Elsie took off her hat and gloves and laid them on a side table. 'I couldn't find work locally so I came to London of my own accord. It was by chance that I met Marianne again.'

'I see. Well, Josephine is inclined to get things wrong. Anyway, I haven't heard from Marianne for a very long time and I'm worried.'

'Won't you sit down, sir? Perhaps you'd like some tea?'

'No, thank you.' He hesitated, clearing his throat noisily. 'Marianne was never a good correspondent, but I really do need to contact her.'

'That might be difficult, sir.'

'I have some sad news that I need to tell her in person.'

'It's not up to me to divulge her whereabouts, sir. I'm sorry.'

He sank down on a chair by the empty grate. 'I wouldn't ask, but this is something that can't wait. Please tell me where I might contact my daughter.'

His obvious distress went straight to her heart and she relented. 'I don't suppose I should be telling you this, but Marianne is in Paris, and she's doing top secret work. That's all I can say.'

He recoiled as if she had struck him across the face, and making a quick recovery he threw back his head and laughed. 'Marianne is working for Military Intelligence?'

She laid her finger on her lips, glancing at the open door, but there was no sign of Gerda. 'Not so loud, sir. It really is hush-hush.'

'You seem to know a lot about it.'

'I was with Marianne in Paris. We worked together, but we became separated and I returned home. Now I work at the War Office as a translator.'

'I'm sorry. I didn't mean to sound patronising, Elsie. It's rather a shock to return to England after all these years abroad to find that my only child is employed by the secret service.'

Elsie crossed the floor to the cocktail cabinet and took out the bottle of Calvados that Felicia had brought back from her last trip to France. There was not much left but she poured a generous measure into a brandy glass and handed it to the colonel. 'Marianne is hardly a child now, sir. She's a woman with a mind of her own, but as far as I know she's safe and well.'

'Thank you.' He took the glass from her and sipped the fiery apple brandy. 'Won't you join me, Elsie?'

She shook her head. 'I've been travelling all day and I haven't eaten for hours. It would go straight to my head. Will you be staying for supper? I'm sure that Gerda could rustle something up, although it won't be much.'

'Thank you, but I should be getting back to my hotel.' He took another sip of his drink. 'I must see Marianne . . .' He hesitated, staring into the glass. 'It's a personal matter.'

'I'm afraid I can't help you any further, sir.'

He raised his head. 'A few weeks ago my wife contracted a particularly virulent form of malaria. I need to see Marianne to tell her of her mother's death.'

'I'm so sorry.'

'It was very sudden, and a terrible shock. I didn't want to send a telegram, and anyway the only address I had for my daughter was Darcy Hall.' He drained his glass. 'You of all people will understand how much this will affect Marianne.'

'I know how I felt when Ma died.'

'My sister-in-law was eager to fill me in on everything that had happened since I was last in Sutton Darcy. I'm sorry for your loss, my dear. Your mother was a lovely woman. I knew her well, as I did your father, of course.'

Elsie nodded wordlessly.

'I need to break the news to Marianne in person, if only to make up for the years when I wasn't there to be a father to her.' He bowed his head. 'Maybe it's too late, but I must try.'

'I think she's staying in the Bellaires' apartment in the rue de l'Echelle,' Elsie said softly.

He breathed a sigh of relief. 'Thank you, that's all I need to know. Now all I have to do is persuade the powers that be to give me a command in France. I put in for a transfer while I was still in Delhi and I intend to follow it up vigorously. I still have a few friends in high places.'

'So you'll go to Paris and see Marianne?'

'I will.' He rose to his feet. 'I'll keep your name out of this, so don't worry.' He held out his hand. 'Your mother would be proud of you if she could see you now.'

'And my father too, I hope.' She placed her hand in his and he held it in a warm grasp.

'Corporal Mead was a good man and a good soldier.'

Elsie had just seen the colonel off when the telephone shrilled, making her jump. She glanced at the elegant grandmother clock in the entrance hall and frowned. It was half past nine at night, rather late for a social call, and she was tired. She hurried into the drawing room and picked up the receiver. 'Hello.'

'Elsie darling, I'm sorry to ring so late, but I've only just come off duty.'

The sound of his voice made her spirits rise and she was suddenly wide awake. 'Don't apologise, Guy. You could telephone at midnight and I'd be thrilled to hear your voice.'

'Darling, I'll have to be brief. There's no easy way to tell you this, but I'm being posted abroad.'

'What?' The line was crackly and she thought she must have misheard. 'Say that again, Guy.'

'I know it's short notice and I can't tell you

anything more over the phone, but I'll be aide de camp to the colonel of my old regiment.'

'But you promised you wouldn't risk your life again. You've done enough, Guy.'

'I can't sit the war out in relative safety while my friends are risking their necks to bring about the end to this God-awful conflict.'

'But you're not fit enough,' she murmured dazedly.

'They need trained men, Elsie. I might not be able to fight in the front line but I can still do my bit and prove to myself that I'm not just a pen-pusher. You do understand, don't you?'

She was about to argue but the pips blared in her ear. 'Guy, can you hear me?'

'I'm sorry, darling. I haven't got any more change . . .' The line went dead.

Elsie replaced the receiver, struggling to cope with the idea that Guy would be mad enough to want to return to the battlefield. No matter what he said she knew that he would face the same dangers as the rest of his brigade. She sat down in the chair so recently vacated by Colonel Winter, staring into the empty grate. She shivered, but it was too late to light a fire and anyway it would be a shocking waste of coal. Suddenly she was angry. Men had it all their own way, leaving women to pick up the pieces. Guy had almost given his life for his country once and now he seemed to be prepared to do it all over again.

She jumped to her feet, pacing the room with her hands clasped tightly behind her back. Felicia was

344

doing her bit in France or Flanders and Anthea was whizzing around the country on her motorcycle, doing something active and worthwhile. Their efforts made sitting in a comfortable office translating documents into English seem quite feeble. She looked up as Gerda put her head round the door. 'Is there anything I can get for you, miss?'

Elsie shook her head. 'No, thank you, Gerda. I'm fine.'

'Goodnight, miss.'

'Goodnight, Gerda.'

The door closed again, leaving Elsie sitting in a pool of lamplight. The shadows in the room deepened but her thoughts were miles away. Perhaps she might be allowed to return to Paris and the rue Saint-Roch? It might be worth putting out some feelers when she returned to work next day. There must be something she could do that would satisfy her need to be proactive and useful. The Mead women, she thought wryly, were not used to sitting back and doing nothing. Ma was a soldier's wife and she would have urged her on. Elsie rose slowly to her feet and went to her room.

She went to work next day determined to make changes. There had been a woman driving the bus that took her from Cromwell Road to Whitehall, and a woman conductress had taken her fare and issued her with a ticket. The Red Cross and St John Ambulance had posted advertisements everywhere, calling for young women to join the Voluntary Aid Detachment as nurses, cooks, clerks, laundresses and motor drivers, but Elsie knew that this involved months of training or qualifications that she did not possess. She had not had the opportunity to learn to drive like Marianne, and she was not a trained nurse, nor was she a typist and she would not know where to begin in a laundry room.

She sat at her desk, toying with the idea of applying for a job in the munitions factory at Woolwich, but she did not want to make weapons that would destroy lives, even if the bombs and shells were aimed at the enemy. She chewed the end of her pencil, frowning at the print on the document in front of her, until eventually she received a sharp reprimand from her supervisor for daydreaming. It was not much of a dream, she thought, focusing her eyes on the page. She just wanted to do something useful, and above all she wanted to return to France. The meeting with Jens and Yannick had made her think even more of Valentine and Hendrick and their heroic efforts to save lives. She wanted to be worthy of them, but she was at a loss as to how to set about it.

At lunchtime she was in the crowded canteen, toying with a bread roll and staring into a bowl of brown Windsor soup, when she saw Edith Lomax approaching her table. 'It's Miss Mead, isn't it?'

Elsie half rose from her seat. 'Yes, Miss Lomax.'

'Do you mind if I join you? The canteen seems rather busy today.'

'Please do.' Elsie shifted her chair a little to the right, and Edith took the seat next to her.

'How are you getting on now that you're back in London?'

Elsie stared at her in surprise. 'It's all right, Miss Lomax.'

'You're surprised that I have such information at my fingertips,' Edith said, smiling. 'I've had good reports about you, and it's my job to know everything. I understand how you feel now.'

'You do?'

'I was young once, and like you I thought I could change the world, or at least do something to make a difference. I imagine that being deskbound is no substitute for the involvement you experienced previously.'

'I was grateful to be given my old job,' Elsie said tactfully.

'But it's not enough.' Edith tasted her soup and pulled a face. 'Dishwater. I know food is scarce but this is a travesty.' She pushed her plate away and broke her roll into small pieces which she buttered carefully. 'You'd like your old job back in Paris?'

'Oh, I would,' Elsie said earnestly.

'But I'm afraid that's not possible. It would be too dangerous for you and for Marianne to send you to Paris.'

'She's not in trouble, is she?'

'Far from it, but I can't allow you to return there. However, I might be able to arrange for you to have an interview with a friend of mine. You've heard of the FANYs, no doubt.'

'The First Aid Nursing Yeomanry? Yes, of course, but I'm not a nurse.'

'Can you drive a motor car or ride a horse?'

'I'm afraid not.'

Edith eyed her thoughtfully. 'But you're bilingual, that might help, and no doubt you could learn to handle a motor vehicle, given the right training.'

'Are you suggesting that I learn to drive so that I can join the FANYs?'

'Exactly.' Edith pushed her plate away. 'I think I might try the cottage pie, although it will be more potato than anything.'

'Do you think there's a chance I might be able to get this qualification?'

'It could be arranged. I hate to see a promising young woman held back by something that could so easily be remedied.' Edith Lomax rose gracefully to her feet. 'Leave it with me, Elsie. I have contacts and I might be able to help. You're no use to me if your heart isn't in your work.' She strolled off to join the queue at the counter, leaving Elsie staring after her.

It all happened so quickly. After a brief interview, which she thought she had failed miserably, Elsie received a letter telling her that she had been accepted as a probationer in the First Aid Nursing Yeomanry, and given instructions to attend a Royal Army Medical Corps camp in Surrey for her initial training. But first she had to purchase her uniform from Gamage's store in Holborn. This took all the money she had managed to save from her wages, but she did not begrudge a penny of it.

She arrived at the camp in Surrey on a blustery morning in late January. The sentry studied her papers and directed her to an office where she found three other new recruits, all looking as apprehensive as she was feeling. To her astonishment one of the girls leapt to her feet and embraced her. 'Elsie! I can't believe it's you.'

'Rosemary?' Elsie stared at her in disbelief. 'Have you joined up too?'

'I'll say I have. Isn't that a scream? You and I – back together again after all this time.' She turned to the other two girls. 'This is my old friend, Elsie Mead, can you believe it? We shared a room at the beginning of the war.'

'Who would have thought it?' The elder of the two girls stood up, proffering her hand to Elsie. 'How do you do? I'm Angela Braithwaite.'

Elsie shook her hand. 'Elsie Mead. I'm pleased to meet you, Angela.'

Angela dragged the other girl to her feet. 'And this shrinking violet is Daisy Coleman. Say hello, Daisy.'

Daisy shook her off with a mild protest. 'Really, Angela, I can speak for myself.' She shook Elsie's hand. 'How do you do, Elsie? I think we must all be a bit crazy to be here in the first place, but welcome anyway.'

Slightly dazed, Elsie allowed them to usher her to a seat. 'I can't believe you've signed up too, Rosemary.'

'I was tired of working in the Baker Street office, and I wanted to do something a bit more exciting. I'd heard of the FANYs, of course, but I thought they were all stuck-up toffs.' She shot an apologetic smile in Angela's direction. 'Sorry, no offence meant.'

'None taken, darling,' Angela said carelessly. 'I'd have joined up sooner but for the stupid rule that one had to be twenty-three. Twenty-one I could understand, but I don't think that being two years older makes any of us wiser or more competent.'

'Don't get on your high horse,' Daisy said, laughing. 'You'll get used to Angie, girls. She flies off the handle and gets very militant, but she's a jolly good sort really.'

'We were at school together,' Angela added, as if this explained everything. 'Cheltenham Ladies' College.'

'Really?' Elsie looked from one to the other, not wanting to admit that she had no idea whether that was a good or a bad thing.

Rosemary slipped her arm around Elsie's shoulders. 'So what have you been doing since I last saw you?'

'I've had an office job,' Elsie said vaguely. 'Nothing very exciting.'

'I can't wait to start training,' Angela said enthusiastically. 'And then hopefully we'll be sent on active duty.'

'It's four months' probation, don't forget.' Daisy sat down with a sigh. 'I'm afraid the war will be over before we can do anything really useful.'

Angela opened her mouth as if to argue but she closed it again when a military man burst into the room. He snapped to attention, glaring at each of them in turn. 'Good morning, ladies. I'm Sergeant Pepper and I'm going to be your chief instructor for the next two weeks. Just think of me as God and you won't go wrong. Don't think this is going to be a picnic on the Downs. You are going to work harder than you've ever worked before. Now who among you can drive a motor vehicle?'

Elsie and Rosemary shook their heads but Angela leapt to her feet. 'I can, sergeant, and so can my friend Daisy. I've raced at Brooklands.'

Sergeant Pepper gave her a steady look. 'I don't think that's going to be much help when you're driving a field ambulance in the Flanders mud, miss.' He clapped his hands together. 'Leave your luggage here, ladies, and come with me. We'll start right away.'

That evening, seated round a camp fire outside their tent, Elsie's hands were shaking with fatigue as she sipped her tea. Every bone in her body ached and her head was spinning from the information that she had tried to absorb during the day. Rosemary was groaning softly as she tried to make herself comfortable on the frozen turf, but Angela seemed oblivious to the cold and the torments of the flesh as she recounted stories of her exploits at mountain-eering in the Scottish highlands, and captaining the hockey team at Cheltenham. Daisy sat back with her eyes closed and allowed it all to wash over her.

'I can't see why we have to have riding lessons,' Rosemary complained, rubbing the small of her back. 'We're not going to be riding horses at the front.'

'I suppose we might have to,' Elsie said reason-ably. 'I mean, there might still be horse-drawn ambulances and carts over there. We don't know what we're going to face.'

'Everyone should know how to ride.' Angela took a packet of cigarettes from her jacket pocket and offered them round. 'What? None of you smoke? I bet you will after you've been at the sharp end for a month or two.' She struck a match and lit her cigarette. 'I can't wait to see action, although I'm not keen on the blood and guts business. I'm not a nurse, as I told Sergeant Pepper, and I'm not a cook. I doubt if we'll use half the things they're trying to teach us.'

'It's bandaging tomorrow,' Daisy said with an impish smile. 'You'll probably make your patient look like an Egyptian mummy.'

'I never pretended to be good with my hands.' Angela tossed her head and pins flew in all direc-tions as her long red hair escaped from the confines of a chignon. 'Blasted hair,' she said angrily. 'I wish now I'd had it bobbed like yours, Elsie.'

Rosemary ran her fingers through her soft brown hair and smiled. 'Elsie's a whizz with a pair of scissors. She cut my hair ages ago and I've kept it short ever since. It's so much easier.'

Daisy leaned forward, opening her eyes wide. 'Will you cut mine for me, Elsie? I love Irene Castle's bob, but Mummy made such a fuss when I suggested that I might copy it. She can't see me now, so there's nothing she can do about it.'

Elsie shrugged her shoulders. 'If you two have some sharp scissors and a comb, then I'm willing to give it a go, although I'm a bit out of practice.'

'You do yours though.' Rosemary reached out to tweak a lock of Elsie's hair. 'It always looks as though you've been to a professional coiffeuse.'

Daisy delved into her handbag and pulled out a pair of scissors and a comb. 'Do it, please, Elsie.'

'Me next,' Angela said eagerly.

Elsie had just finished cutting both heads of hair when Sergeant Pepper strode over to them. 'Lights out in ten minutes, ladies. You're in the army for the next two weeks so you have to obey the rules. Douse the fire and leave everything as you would wish to find it in the morning. You'll be up at six and there'll be a drill before breakfast. You'll need to be fit before you can go on active duty and it's my job to see that you are, and that means each one of you, Miss Coleman. No excuses.'

'Blooming cheek,' Daisy muttered as he walked away. 'Why does he always pick on me?'

'Because he can see what a lazy little thing you

really are,' Angela said, chuckling. 'Not much escapes Sergeant Pepper's beady eye.'

'Heaven help us.' Elsie scrambled to her feet. She passed the comb and scissors to Daisy. 'I'm not sure about the drilling, but I'm looking forward to learning to drive. It can't be that difficult.'

'No, no, no.' Sergeant Pepper slapped his hands on the dashboard of the military truck. 'Take your foot off the clutch slowly, Miss Mead. This is a motor vehicle not a bunny rabbit. It's meant to glide into action, not jump like a kangaroo.'

'Sorry, Sarge.' Elsie tried again, this time with more success. She had mastered the art of bandaging and passed the tests in first aid with flying colours. Her cooking skills were exemplary, once she had got used to cooking on a paraffin stove or over a camp fire, which pleased her greatly as this was one thing she did better than Angela, who seemed to excel in everything. Rosemary and Daisy struggled when it came to using a firearm, but Elsie discovered she had a good eye and when she conquered her initial nervousness about handling a gun she managed to hit the target most of the time. Angela, of course, was a crack shot, having grown up on a country estate that hosted shooting parties. Daisy never quite understood that she had to keep both eyes open when aiming, while Rosemary was so nervous that her hand shook uncontrollably and she rarely hit the target. Elsie loved horses and took to riding easily, and Daisy excelled when it came to horsemanship. Rosemary was afraid of horses, but she showed promise when it came to changing a tyre and the general maintenance of a motor vehicle. Somehow all four of them managed to complete their two weeks' initial training, and on the last day they waited eagerly to learn if they had achieved Sergeant Pepper's exacting standard.

Dressed in their civilian clothes, they assembled in the office where they had first met. 'I'm even more nervous now than I was on that first day,' Elsie said breathlessly. 'What will we do if we've failed?'

'Say goodbye to each other and san fairy ann,' Angela said airily, but Elsie was not fooled by her apparent unconcern: the taut lines at the corners of Angela's generous mouth and the wary look in her brown eyes gave her away.

'I don't want to go home a failure.' Rosemary glanced nervously at the door. 'He'll come breezing in here as if he hasn't a care in the world.'

'I don't suppose he has,' Daisy said with a wry smile. 'He'll have to put up with the next batch of recruits and he'll be rid of us.'

'He's coming.' Elsie took a deep breath. 'Now for it, girls. Will we be members of the First Aid Nursing Yeomanry when we walk out of here, or will we be looking for jobs outside?'

Chapter Twenty

The crossing from Dover to Calais was rough, and the sea was a tumult of grey water whipped into white-crested waves. Troops packed the deck of the cross-Channel steamer and the girls were not given any special treatment. Huddled in their great-coats, Elsie, Rosemary, Angela and Daisy sat on hard wooden benches along with several other women, some of whom were new recruits to the Nursing Yeomanry and others were returning from home leave. The noise of the engines was drowned out by the roaring of the wind and the pounding on the iron hull as it rode the waves and crashed down into the deep troughs.

It was dark and Elsie was well aware of the danger from German U-boats lurking beneath the water, but no one dared to voice their fears. These predators of the deep had already claimed many lives, adding to the threat from German warships and bombing from the air during daylight hours. Elsie could only hope and pray that they arrived safely. The start of their journey had been delayed by fog, but now as they neared the coast of France they were hit by the extreme cold, and as they entered Calais harbour snow was falling. Elsie was excited and scared at the same time but at least she was no longer sitting at home waiting for news, which was almost always bad. Every time the telephone rang she had feared the worst and the sight of the telegram messengers filled her with dread, but as far as she was aware Guy had as yet come to no harm.

The ship slid alongside the quay wall and they were disembarked with surprising speed. Snow was thick on the ground as she put her foot on French soil for the first time in over a year. The air was so cold that with each breath Elsie felt as though she was inhaling icicles. The women waited patiently on the dock, standing back while the men were marshalled into groups and marched off into the night, their booted feet trampling the snow until it was hard-packed and shone like glass. In the distance Elsie could hear what sounded like the rumble of thunder, but she realised with a shock that it was gunfire. Then, out of the darkness, a woman muffled to the eyes in a fur coat and hat strode towards them.

'Welcome to France, ladies. My name is Muriel Higson and I'm driving you to our camp outside St Omer. It's about twenty-two miles from here and the roads are in a terrible state, so it'll take some time to get there.' She turned on her heel and motioned them to follow her. 'We'll introduce ourselves properly when we get there – unless of course we get stuck in a snowdrift en route.' She chortled with laughter as she walked off, leaving them no alternative but to hurry after her.

'What have we come to?' Rosemary murmured as she grasped Elsie's arm for support.

'I don't know,' Elsie whispered. 'But I think we're going to find out.'

Their transport was a truck which looked as though it had seen better days. Muriel climbed into the driver's seat and one of the more senior women sat up front with her, leaving the others to make themselves as comfortable as possible on the hard wooden benches beneath the canvas roof. Muriel drove off and the truck lurched over ruts and skidded on the frozen surface of the road, but she handled its erratic progress with considerable expertise.

During their training Elsie had become familiar with this type of vehicle which served the dual purpose of transporting personnel and supplies as well as being used as a field ambulance. The trucks they had practised on had been relatively new and they were maintained regularly. They were cleaned and polished by the recruits as part of their job, but this vehicle was old and battered, and the smell of blood, urine and gangrene had not been completely erased by the generous application of Lysol. Rosemary shivered and moved closer to Elsie. 'I'm beginning to wish that I'd stayed at home.'

Angela nudged her in the ribs. 'Shut up, Rosie. We're here to do a job and this is just the beginning.'

Rosemary began to cry silently, huge tears coursing

down her pale cheeks. 'Leave her alone,' Elsie said softly. 'I daresay we're all feeling a bit like that, only we don't want to admit it.'

'I confess I do.' Daisy cupped her gloved hands and blew on them. 'I wish I'd worn my sheepskin mittens. I'd no idea it would be so damn cold.'

Angela produced a packet of cigarettes and offered them round, but there were no takers. 'Suit yourselves.' She lit up and smoked in silence as the truck careered on into the night.

Although she was stiff with cold and could no longer feel her feet or her fingertips, Elsie was drifting off into an uncomfortable doze when the vehicle skidded wildly, lurched and came to a sudden halt. She opened her eyes with a start and found Rosemary in a heap on the floor. 'Are you all right?'

'She's fine.' Angela bent down and heaved Rosemary back onto the bench. 'We seem to be stuck.'

Muriel leapt out of the cab and came round to the back of the vehicle, lifting the flaps and peering inside. 'I need volunteers,' she said briskly. 'Three of you take shovels and dig us out and the rest of you can give us a push when I get the engine started.' She walked back to the cab and climbed in. 'The quicker you dig us out, ladies, the quicker we'll get to the priory and a cup of hot cocoa.'

Everyone clambered out into the freezing darkness and Elsie grabbed a shovel together with Angela and Daisy, leaving Rosemary to help the others push when given the go-ahead. Elsie had not had a proper look at the vehicle in Calais and she was shocked to see that there was no glass in the windscreen. She worked hard digging the front wheels free of the snowdrift, but she was still curious. 'What happened to the windscreen? Did you have an accident before you got to us?' She turned to Muriel, who was leaning against the bonnet smoking one of Angela's cigarettes.

'We take the glass out,' Muriel said with a casual shrug of her shoulders. 'It's safer that way in case of shelling. A faceful of broken glass is the last thing we want.'

'But how can you drive without headlights and with the snow blowing in your face?'

'With great difficulty,' Muriel said, chuckling. 'Which is why I swerved too late to miss that particular drift.' She tossed the dog-end over the hedge. 'How are we doing girls? The next push should get us home.'

When they eventually reached their destination Elsie stepped out of the vehicle, stiff and sore and on the edge of complete exhaustion. She gazed in awe at the Gothic building, which had been built many centuries ago and was situated on a hill surrounded by woodland. With the moonlight reflecting off the snow, the Priory looked like a setting for Bram Stoker's *Dracula*. Muriel had explained, during one of their brief comfort stops, that the priory had once been a Cistercian monastery, but was now a military hospital. Its towers, spires and pinnacles were constructed in grey stone, and the flying buttresses gave the building the appearance of something that had been constructed not only for the glorification of god, but was a creation by man that would last until the end of time, and this was the place that Muriel called home. Elsie suppressed a shiver, thinking of the comparative cosiness of Tan Cottage and the luxury of Felicia's apartment. If the interior of the priory was anything like the forbidding exterior, they were in for an uncomfortable stay.

Muriel strode up the steps and rang the bell. Its clear peal echoed off the surrounding countryside like a call to prayer, and moments later a tousle-haired orderly opened the heavy oak door. The rusty groan of its iron hinges sounded like a soul in torment, and the sound of their footsteps echoed off the high vaulted ceiling as Elsie followed the others into the gloomy interior. Lit by candles in storm lanterns, the inside of the priory was even creepier than its Gothic façade, and equally cold. The orderly disappeared through a doorway leaving Muriel to escort them to their dormitory in what had once been the wine cellars. 'We call it the cave,' she said cheerfully. 'There's acres of room, but not much privacy. You'll get used to that in time.' She lit a candle and handed it to Angela, who happened to be the nearest. 'We have to be economical with these. Like everything else they're in short supply.' She turned to the group in general. 'Try to get some sleep.' She waved her hand in the direction of a pile of palliasses and thick grey blankets. 'Make yourselves comfortable and I'll send someone down with a jug of cocoa. You'll be shown round properly in the morning. Breakfast is at six, so you've got about four hours' kip. Night night, ladies.' She walked off and disappeared into the darkness.

Elsie looked round at her colleagues, all of whom, even Angela, appeared to be stunned into silence. She took some bedding and laid it on the stone floor. 'I'm worn out, I don't know about the rest of you.'

A murmur of assent was followed by a scramble for the palliasses, which they placed close together, and within minutes they were huddled in their blankets. Despite her attempts to get comfortable Elsie still could feel the cold striking up through the flagstones and she wondered if she would ever feel warm again. Then a young French ward maid appeared carrying a tray of mugs filled with hot cocoa, and was welcomed with cries of delight.

'This is the best thing that's happened today,' Rosemary said, sipping the hot drink laced with condensed milk. 'I never liked cocoa until now, but this is ambrosia.'

'Nectar of the gods,' Angela agreed, wrapping both hands round her mug.

Elsie drank hers, feeling the warmth seeping through her chilled bones. 'Cheers,' she said sleepily. 'Let's hope the monks don't haunt this place.'

Rosemary moved a little closer. 'Don't say things like that, even in jest.' She glanced around at the deep shadows and the shapeless forms of their new colleagues who had slept through their arrival, no doubt exhausted by the demands of their work. 'I think I prefer sleeping in one of Sergeant Pepper's ghastly tents.'

'I'm just glad to stretch out at last.' Daisy abandoned her tin mug and lay down, pulling the coarse blanket up to her chin. 'I've never slept in my clothes and my overcoat before, and I'm still bloody freezing.'

Elsie snuggled up as best she could. 'G'night, girls. I wonder what tomorrow will bring.'

'It's already tomorrow,' Rosemary said sleepily.

Elsie was awakened from a deep sleep by the sound of voices and the pitter-patter of scurrying feet. She opened her eyes and it was still dark, but there were fragmented patches of candlelight as the old hands rose from their beds and made themselves ready for the day.

'Best get up,' one of them said cheerfully as she hurried past. 'Breakfast is at six sharp and if you're late you'll go without. It's first come first served here.' She raced off together with several others, leaving their bedding neatly stacked. Elsie scrambled to her feet and woke the others. Angela groaned and told her to buzz off, but Elsie dragged the blanket away from her and did the same to Daisy and

Rosemary. By this time the rest of the new girls had awakened and were gazing round dazedly.

They found the dining room by following a young nurse who had risen late and was hurrying along the cloister with the tails of her white cap flying out behind her like agitated seagulls. The welcome sight of a blazing log fire greeted them as they entered the refectory, but the heat it might have given out was lost as it wafted up into the high ceiling. Elsie's breath steamed in clouds around her head, and as she took her place at one of the long oak tables she wondered how anyone managed to survive in such conditions. A mug of hot tea helped to bring her back to life, and she took a bread roll from one of the baskets set on the table, but there was neither butter nor jam to make it more palatable. Copying one of the nurses who obviously knew how things were done in the priory, she broke the coarse rye bread into small pieces and dipped them in her tea.

'Don't worry, love,' the older woman said, rising to her feet. 'You'll soon get used to it. I've been in several camps since the start of the whole thing, and this one isn't too bad. You'll get the hang of things.' She strolled off, exchanging pleasantries with a couple of nurses from the next table.

Elsie swallowed a mouthful of food. 'Thanks,' she murmured, but her new friend was already out of earshot. One thing Elsie had noticed straight away was that everyone here moved swiftly, as if they were in a tearing hurry. Perhaps it was simply to keep warm, or maybe it was so that they could cram all the work expected of them into their waking hours. She was about to find out.

Muriel rose from the table on the far side of the room and came over to them. 'I hope you managed to get some sleep,' she said, looking round at their expectant faces. 'You're all here as drivers, not nurses, so when you've finished your meal I want you to come out into the courtyard where we keep the trucks and ambulances. You'll work in pairs, teaming up with the experienced drivers, and you'll be expected to keep your vehicles clean, disinfected and well maintained. You've all undergone your initial training, but this is the real thing. We're dealing with life and death here. It may seem like a cushy billet not too close to the firing line, but there's always the danger from the air. Being in a former monastery doesn't mean that we're safe from incendiary bombs or shelling.' She smiled cheerfully. 'But we're here to do a job, ladies, so follow me.' She walked off purposefully and Elsie jumped to her feet along with the others.

'It's like being back at school,' Angela complained, stuffing the last of her bread roll into her mouth.

'You'd better get used to it,' Elsie said, grinning. 'We've signed up for this, and we're here to do our bit. I'm ready for anything – I think.'

But the reality of their work was beyond anything Elsie or any of the other new girls could have imagined. They had travelled through the countryside in the dark with snow to soften the outlines of the devastation caused by almost four years of war. Daylight revealed a different world of villages razed to the ground and a wasteland of frozen mud where once crops had flourished. The roads were rutted and pitted with shell holes, making driving in such wintry conditions even more hazardous, but as Muriel had said, they had a job to do. Elsie and Rosemary were assigned ambulance duty that day, and from morning until well after dark they ferried the injured from the ambulance trains to the casualty clearing stations, and then on to the permanent hospitals where they would undergo treatment. The less badly injured or those suffering from gas poisoning or the dreaded Spanish flu were taken to the priory, and all this was done under more or less constant bombardment.

The first day was a living nightmare and both Elsie and Rosemary returned late that evening too tired to eat the frugal meal of soup and bread, and too exhausted to do anything other than wash their hands and faces in cold water and slide into bed.

The next day Elsie was so stiff she could hardly move, but somehow she managed to raise herself, and judging by the groans and moans from the others she could tell that they too were suffering. There was no escaping the duties that they had taken on with such enthusiasm. Their days in training seemed like a picnic compared to the reality they had to face now, and she realised how little people at home knew of the real suffering and carnage brought about by war.

Gradually as the weeks went by she grew used to the physical demands placed upon her, and the camaraderie amongst the women and a sense of humour kept her sane. In the beginning they had all, without exception, been distressed by the condition of the men they sought to help, and Elsie found it impossible to hold back tears when she cradled a dying soldier in her arms, or comforted a young boy who should never have been allowed to enlist in the first place and now, even if he survived his terrible wounds, faced a life as a cripple. On occasions when she could bear it no longer it was the thought of Guy that kept her motivated. She had helped to save his life once, and if he were lying injured on a battlefield she could only hope that a woman like herself would come to his aid. The injured men were all someone's son, husband or father, and all of them were in desperate need. The hardships she faced were many, but she was not about to give up. Poor food, unsanitary living conditions, bed bugs and chilblains were a small price to pay when compared to the sacrifice of young men's lives.

It was a harsh winter, some said it was the coldest for many years, but gradually the temperature began to rise and the thaw set in. This in itself caused problems as the melted snow left a sea of mud and roads that were even more difficult to negotiate. Elsie had become proficient at changing tyres even at the roadside, kneeling in thick mud, and it became a joke between herself and Rosemary that when the war was over they might open a garage on the outskirts of London and work as mechanics as well as manning the petrol pumps.

Despite the constant barrage of bombs and flying shrapnel, and the scourge of the flu epidemic that had taken the lives of several of the nurses as well as many of the patients, there were lighter moments when someone arrived back from home leave and brought food parcels and letters from loved ones. There was always someone's birthday to celebrate with cheap wine purchased in the town, which lightened the mood and left them with terrible hangovers next morning. But after taking a couple of aspirin and a cup of black coffee, the indomitable girls of Priory Camp were back on the road. Headaches were forgotten, and they set off not knowing whether they would ever return.

Although the town of St Omer was shelled regularly, by some miracle the priory escaped, and as winter gave way to spring the gardens of the old monastery burst into bloom. Vast sheets of golden daffodils waved in the breeze and clumps of primroses spread like pools of sunlight at the edge of the woods. The days lengthened and temperatures improved, but night raids increased, and the town was heaving with troops who were allowed a couple of days' rest before returning to the front.

At the end of April Elsie was due for home leave, but she did not relish the thought of returning to

London. She would be pleased to see Felicia but it was Marianne who came second in her thoughts only to Guy. She had no idea where he was but he had not appeared on any of the casualty lists she had been privileged to see, although that was small comfort. There had been a rumour that the Germans were pushing forward and getting close to St Omer, but it had proved to be false, and Elsie put in a request to be allowed to travel to Paris. Muriel had questioned her closely but had seemed satisfied by her explanation that she had once worked there and wanted to visit a friend. She was granted a week's leave and given a travel permit.

Rosemary drove her to the railway station and gave her a hug. 'I'm off to England tomorrow,' she said cheerfully. 'I'm going to stay with my Aunt Bessie in Dover.'

'I thought you were going home to your mother's house in Essex?'

Rosemary shook her head. 'I had a letter from Mum. She's married Alf, the plumber who used to live next door but one. He's had his eye on her for years, and then when my stepdad died in the flu epidemic he made his move.'

'Don't you like him either?'

'I can't stand him, but it's Mum's life. She's got to do what's best for her.'

Elsie returned the hug. 'Never mind, Rosie. If we don't get blown to bits by a German bomb we'll start that garage together.'

Rosemary gave her a shove towards the platform. 'Your train's coming. Have a lovely time in Paris.'

'I will. Be a good girl in Dover. I'll see you in a week's time.' Elsie boarded the train and found herself in a compartment filled with American soldiers. They were a lively bunch and were delighted to find someone who spoke English. She was glad that she had been able to take a bath and put on clean clothes before setting out, as these affable young men would not have found her so interesting had she been in her usual muddied state, with overpowering body odour and unwashed hair. She could not help comparing these healthy, bright-eyed boys with the sick and dying British soldiers she had tried so hard to help, and she wondered if they were aware of the horrors of trench warfare, gas poisoning and shell shock.

She arrived in Paris and said goodbye to her new friends with some regret. Their cheerful conversation had lifted her spirits and their confidence that they would help to win the war had been touching. There was always hope, she thought, as she climbed into a waiting fiacre outside the station and gave the driver instructions to take her to the rue Saint-Roch. She had decided to start there as there was a good chance that she might catch Marianne at work; if not, she planned to walk to the rue de l'Echelle and call at the Bellaires' apartment. It was all a bit of a risk as she did not know if Marianne was still in Paris, but it was worth a try.

The cab dropped her outside number 41 rue Saint-Roch, bringing back poignant memories of her time there. She had been little more than a girl when she first came to Paris, cherishing romantic dreams about her handsome Frenchman. It seemed like a lifetime ago and not a mere three years, but the world had changed and so had she, or perhaps she had merely grown up.

She straightened her forage cap, adjusted her uniform jacket and opened the door. Once inside she had to explain her mission to the desk clerk, who looked her up and down with a sceptical eye, as if suspecting her of being in fancy dress. But her persistence paid off and she was shown into the small interview room, where she was left to wait for what seemed like hours. Eventually the door opened and Marianne stood there, staring at her in disbelief, and then her face lit up with a smile. 'It is you, Elsie. I thought at first that they were pulling my leg.' She rushed forward and flung her arms around her. 'It's wonderful to see you.'

Half smothered by Marianne's embrace, Elsie managed to extricate herself. 'I missed you too, you dreadful girl. Why didn't you write and tell me where you were? I had to find out through official channels.'

Marianne held her at arm's length. 'What in heaven's name are you wearing? That uniform is absolutely ghastly and it does nothing for you.'

'I'm in the FANYs,' Elsie said, laughing.

'That sounds vaguely rude. What sort of outfit is it?'

'The First Aid Nursing Yeomanry, you idiot. You must have heard of them. We're at the front, driving ambulances and setting up hospitals. It's vital work, saving lives.'

'You always were a bit of a heroine, but that wouldn't suit me. I'm absolutely useless at that sort of thing.' Marianne slipped her arm around Elsie's shoulders. 'It's good to see you. I was devastated when Valentine sent you away.'

'We've such a lot to catch up on, Marianne. I've got a week's leave but I have to find somewhere to stay.'

'Nonsense, darling. You'll stay with me at the rue de l'Echelle. Selene has gone to le Lavandou for the summer, but Philippe won't mind. Anyway, he's out all day at the bank and doesn't come home until late.' She released Elsie and moved swiftly to the door. 'Wait here a moment while I fetch my bag. We'll go to the Café Goulet for lunch and we can talk without being interrupted, that is if you don't count Raimond who is as garrulous as ever. I'll be back in two shakes of a lamb's tail.'

She was gone, leaving a waft of L'Heure Bleu in her wake.

The Café Goulet had not changed since Elsie's last visit, neither had Raimond. He greeted her as if she were a long lost friend, and gave them the table in the window. The glass was still furred with city dirt on the outside and the sill on the inside was speckled with the bodies of dead flies. The check tablecloth was spotted with red wine and the clientele did not seem to have changed much either. Elsie was certain that she recognised the workmen who sat at the next table and the old man who was perched on a bar stool with a glass of absinthe and water on the counter in front of him. He turned his head and winked at her.

Raimond went behind the bar and returned moments later with two large glasses of red wine. 'Our menu is rather short today,' he said, folding his hands over his grubby apron. 'It's onion soup. I am afraid that beefsteak is almost impossible to come by, unless one deals with the black market, which of course I do not.'

'Thank you, Raimond, but onion soup would be delightful, as always,' Marianne said with a smile. 'How is Madame Honorine today?'

'She is well, but working very hard at the hospital. There are many casualties still. I'll fetch your order.' He hurried off in the direction of the kitchen.

'It's good to be back in Paris,' Elsie said, sighing. 'I didn't realise how comparatively easy things were when we came here, or how bad they would get.' She met Marianne's concerned look with a smile. 'But let's not talk about depressing things. What happened in Belgium? What about Dieter?'

'It was thrilling while it lasted, but to tell the truth, Elsie, I was getting a bit scared.'

Elsie stared at her in surprise. 'You? Scared? Never!'

'Not physically scared, darling. But I knew that he was serious and, to be honest, I was cooling off.' Marianne shrugged her shoulders. 'You know me; I'm inclined to be shallow when it comes to relationships.'

'I don't think that's true at all, but how did you end it?'

'He was transferred to the front. It was all very sudden and I was quite upset at the time, but then Valentine arranged for me to return to Paris, and I've been here ever since.'

'And you started back at your old job?'

'Again, I had little to do with it. I think it was all fixed before I left the Merchant's House, but I had to find somewhere to live. I couldn't face going back to that ghastly room and that awful Madame Chausse.'

'Did you go straight to the Bellaires' apartment?'

'No. I was too proud to admit that I'd made a mess of things and I booked into a horrid little *pension*. Anyway, I had to go to the bank to withdraw some money, and I happened to bump into Selene. She insisted that I should move in with them and who was I to refuse?' Marianne laid her finger on her lips as Raimond bustled towards them carrying two steaming bowls of soup. 'Best talk about mundane things. We'll chat later. There's something I must tell you, but this isn't the time or place.'

Chapter Twenty-One

Marianne would say no more and Elsie was left to wonder what surprises her friend had in store for her. They finished their lunch and walked back to the rue Saint-Roch. 'I'll collect my case and go for a walk by the river,' Elsie said as Marianne was about to open the door. 'Do you still finish at five?'

'On a normal day, yes, but today is special. I'll use all my considerable powers of persuasion to get the afternoon off. I'm owed it for all the overtime I put in.' She pulled a face. 'Don't look so surprised. I'm very conscientious these days. I do my bit for the war effort, in my own special way.' She opened the door and headed for the stairs, leaving Elsie standing in the vestibule. She smiled to herself. Marianne would never change. She was as mercurial as ever and still determined to get her own way. Elsie checked with the receptionist and went into the waiting room to collect her battered cardboard suitcase. She did not have long to wait before Marianne put her head round the door.

'Come on. We'll go to the flat and drop off your case and then we can do as we please for the whole afternoon. Isn't that a simply heavenly idea?'

They walked arm in arm through the dusty streets. Paris had changed little as far as Elsie could see, although Marianne said there had been air raids earlier in the year. It might be a city virtually under siege but Paris wore its scars with pride and the people who thronged the streets exuded an air of stubborn resilience. It was all in stark contrast to the devastation and destruction that Elsie had seen in the villages surrounding the battlefields.

Marianne produced a key from her handbag and let them into the Bellaires' apartment on the first floor. Elsie had thought that Felicia's flat was the height of luxury, but entering the Bellaires' Paris home was like stepping into another world. The entrance hall must, she thought, have been inspired by the architecture of the Palace of Versailles, and no expense could have been spared. Ormolu sconces were placed at intervals on walls covered in pale green silk damask, and a huge crystal chandelier sent prisms of light dancing on the ceiling. Her feet sank into the thick pile of the Aubusson carpet, which was patterned with delicate pink and cream flowers, and the air was redolent with the scent of white lilies spilling out of a Sèvres vase. Elsie tried to look casual as she followed Marianne into the drawing room, which was equally magnificent, with its Louis Quinze furniture and tall windows draped in rose velvet with opulent swags and tasselled tie-backs.

Marianne tossed her straw hat onto a chair and

dropped her handbag onto a side table. 'Make yourself at home, Elsie.'

Elsie glanced down at her khaki uniform and serviceable lace-up boots. 'I feel a bit out of place here, Marianne. Maybe I should find a cheap hotel nearby.'

'Nonsense, old thing. Don't talk such rot.' Marianne picked up a silver cigarette box and lifted the lid. 'Do you smoke? I know you didn't before the war, but everything changes.'

Elsie shook her head. 'No. I tried it once, but I didn't think much of it to be honest.'

Marianne perched on the edge of a spindly-legged sofa and reached for a match holder. She lit her cigarette and sat back, inhaling deeply. 'Do sit down, Elsie. You look as though you're waiting for a bus.'

Elsie took off her forage cap and sat down gingerly on one of the dainty chairs. 'It's like being in a museum. I'm afraid to touch anything.'

'You'll get used to it. The Bellaires have oodles of money even allowing for the war and everything.' Marianne blew smoke rings at one of the three chandeliers in the room. 'Smoking calms the nerves, or at least that's what I was told.'

Elsie gave her a searching look. 'You said there was something you had to tell me. What is it?'

Marianne hesitated for a moment, frowning. 'You were rather keen on Henri, as I remember.'

'I never said so. What gave you that idea?'

'I know you so well, darling. Anyway, you're

absolutely transparent, like a sheet of glass. You used to blush every time he spoke to you . . .'

'All right,' Elsie said hastily. 'So I liked him rather a lot. What's that got to do with anything? I'm with Guy now, and I love him.'

'Really? You're in love with dear old Guy, the sweetest, kindest, most boring man in the War Office?'

'That's not fair. He's not boring when you get to know him. He's shy and sensitive but he's got a wonderful sense of humour and he's terribly brave.'

Marianne held up her hand. 'Sorry I spoke, but you must admit you weren't smitten on your first date.'

'It wasn't a date exactly. He took me to Hackney to a Christmas Eve party for the Belgian refugees.'

'My point, darling. That wasn't the most exciting way to begin a relationship.'

'You're impossible,' Elsie said with a reluctant smile. 'I was a bit smitten by Henri in those days. Who wouldn't be?'

'I agree, but what made you fall for dear old Guy? Or were you just sorry for him? You must have spent a long time in his company while you were making your way home and having all those adventures you told me about over lunch today.'

'I got to know him, Marianne. That's the difference. I stopped pining for someone I knew I could never have, and I began to see what a truly wonderful person Guy is.'

'Well, I'm happy for you, and it makes what I

have to say next so much easier.' Marianne stubbed her cigarette out in an onyx ashtray. 'Because Henri is here, only thankfully he's spending the day at the bank, which has given me time to prepare you.'

'Prepare me for what? What are you talking about, Marianne?'

'I suppose it doesn't matter now, but when you turned up unexpectedly the first thing that came to my mind was how you would react when you found out that Henri and I have an understanding, as Aunt Josephine would put it.'

'You're engaged to Henri?'

'Not officially.' Marianne's eyes twinkled mischievously. 'Actually we're getting married tomorrow. Nobody knows anything about it, not even his father.'

'Getting married?' Elsie stared at her, dazed with shock. 'But you don't go in for long relationships. You told me so at lunch. That's so unfair on Henri.'

'This is different, darling. Henri and I practically grew up together.'

'Yes. You always said you were like brother and sister.'

Marianne trilled with laughter. 'That's all changed, and I realised that I've always loved him. He feels the same.' She leaned forward, her expression suddenly serious. 'You aren't upset, are you, Elsie? I know you said you've fallen for Guy, but you don't still have feelings for Henri, do you?'

Elsie stood up and went to sit beside Marianne, taking her hand and giving it a squeeze. 'What I felt for Henri was something like a schoolgirl crush. It was always a dream and I got over him ages ago. If this is what you really want then I'm happy for you.'

Marianne gave her a quick hug and then pulled away. 'I don't usually embrace females but I make an exception in your case. You really are like a sister to me, Elsie, and I'm glad you've taken it like this.'

'And you're getting married tomorrow? Why the sudden rush? You're not . . .'

'How could you think such a thing?'

'Sorry, but why deprive his parents of their only son's wedding? They approve of you, don't they?'

'Of course they do. It's just that Henri has a few days' leave and this awful war is dragging on. Who knows when it will end, and we've got used to living for the moment. It just seems that the time is right for us now, so we're having a civil ceremony in the town hall.'

'I thought you'd want a white wedding and a huge reception.'

Marianne smiled ruefully. 'I might have done before the war, but it doesn't matter to me now. Anyway, Henri is a Catholic and I'm supposed to be Church of England, so that rather rules out a religious ceremony.'

'Has this got something to do with your father and his visit? He told me that your mother had died and I'm so sorry, Marianne.'

Marianne rose to her feet and went to the window to gaze down at the street. 'I didn't see much of my parents while I was growing up, but that didn't make me love them any the less. I suppose I thought they were a permanent fixture and one day they'd take over Darcy Hall and we'd be a family again.' She turned her head to look at Elsie. 'Is it wrong to want to belong to someone and have a family of my own?'

'Of course not, and I'm sure that Monsieur and Madame Bellaire will forgive you and that your father will understand.'

'Thanks, Elsie. I'm so glad you're here.'

'Me too.'

'We must find you something else to wear. I won't have my chief bridesmaid looking like a sack of coal, even if it is wartime.'

'But Marianne . . .'

'No buts, darling. I've got a wardrobe filled with haute couture clothes. Some of them I bought in Red Cross sales and Selene has been terribly generous. It's lucky we're the same size and what suits me also looks good on you.' She marched over to the sofa and dragged Elsie to her feet. 'I haven't had so much fun since we changed clothes while we were at the Merchant's House.'

'I'm not swapping places with you this time, Marianne Winter. You're the one who's going to marry Henri, not me.'

Marianne's wardrobe was impressive. In fact it was a whole room dedicated to clothes, shoes and accessories, and her bedroom was as opulent as the rest of the apartment. They spent the afternoon going through the racks of gowns with Marianne selecting the ones she thought suitable and insisting that Elsie should try them on, ignoring her protests and a request for something simpler.

Standing in front of the cheval mirror with her shoulders drooping, Elsie studied her reflection. 'I look a complete fright in this, Marianne.' She plucked at the eau de Nil silk.

'That's one of my favourites,' Marianne protested. 'Stand up straight and don't slouch.' She circled round Elsie. 'Perhaps you're right, but I can't understand why this one doesn't suit you. I look wonderful in it, or so I've been told.'

Elsie stepped out of the gown and replaced it on the hanger. 'I'm too skinny for a dress like that, and I'm as weather-beaten as a navvy.'

'You are a bit too slim,' Marianne said reluctantly. 'It's quite fashionable these days, but you need feeding up, my girl.'

Elsie stared at the pile of discarded gowns that Marianne had tossed onto a chair. 'Do I have to dress up? It is wartime, and my uniform is quite clean. It just needs ironing.'

Marianne uttered a shriek of dismay. 'I'm not turning up at the church with you looking like a prison wardress.' She seized a cream tussore dress. 'This is one that Selene gave me. I've never worn it because it's a bit tight over the bosom, but it should fit you.'

'This is the last one,' Elsie said, holding up her arms so that Marianne could slip it over her head. 'If this one doesn't look right . . .' She stared at the young woman who gazed back at her from the mirror. 'Oh, my goodness. I look so different.'

'That's the one.' Marianne stood back, arms akimbo. 'I have perfect taste, and you look absolutely splendid. Now let's find a hat that goes with it and some gloves, and shoes. You can't tramp down the aisle behind me wearing those ghastly boots.'

An hour later, wearing one of Marianne's less formal outfits consisting of a navy-blue skirt and a white blouse with a sailor collar, Elsie was able to relax a little even though the chair in the drawing room had a slippery seat and she was afraid she might make the wrong move and slide to the floor. She sipped tea from a bone china cup.

'I thought the French only drank coffee,' she murmured as the maid left the room.

'I had to teach Cook how to make tea,' Marianne said airily. 'I have some sent from Fortnum's every month, although it's become ridiculously expensive. It's my one extravagance, so don't look at me like that, Elsie.'

'The western world is falling apart and you have a maid and a cook at your disposal. I can't believe it.'

'I don't employ them, darling. My future father-in-law lives up to his old standard and who am I to quibble?' Marianne reached for the silver teapot and refilled her cup. She was suddenly alert as she put the pot back on the tray. 'That sounds like Henri. He must have come home early.' She glanced anxiously at Elsie. 'Are you ready for this?'

Elsie's hand shook as she put her cup and saucer down on the table. 'Of course I am.' She braced herself to meet the man who had captured her heart in what seemed like another lifetime.

Henri strolled into the drawing room. 'I came home early, Marianne . . .' He broke off, staring at Elsie. 'I don't believe it. Elsie?'

She rose to her feet, holding out her hand. 'Hello, Henri.'

'I didn't know you were coming.' He raised her hand to his lips. 'Did Marianne tell you about us?'

'I know that I have to congratulate you,' Elsie said, smiling. He was even more handsome than she remembered, but there were furrows between his brows and lines of worry on his forehead. The war had changed him in a subtle way that she could not quite define, but she realised now that she had been in love with a phantom. This was the real Henri Bellaire and he might be as handsome as Adonis, but she was in love with an ordinary mortal. No one could compare to Guy.

He glanced over his shoulder. 'Did you have a hand in this, Marianne?'

'Absolutely not. I was as surprised as you when Elsie turned up at the rue Saint-Roch, and delighted, of course.' She patted the empty space beside her on the sofa. 'Come and sit down, darling. Would you like tea, or something stronger?'

Henri walked over to the bell pull and tugged at it. 'I think this calls for a celebration. I obtained a crate of champagne, don't ask how, but this seems an appropriate moment to sample a bottle.' He went to sit beside Marianne. 'I've heard all about your time with La Dame Blanche, Elsie. You girls did a wonderful job helping injured soldiers to safety.'

Elsie shot a quizzical glance at Marianne, who was smiling innocently. 'We were glad to do our bit.'

'But I was more than happy to return to Paris after Elsie and Guy had left,' Marianne said, linking her hand through Henri's arm. 'If I'd remained in Belgium we might not have met again and realised that we were destined to be together, my darling.'

Henri gazed into her eyes with a tender smile. 'It was fate, Marianne.' He kissed her on the tip of her nose. 'It was written in the stars.' He turned his attention to Elsie. 'So how do you come to be in Paris? Are you going to work at the rue Saint-Roch?'

Marianne tucked her hand through the crook of his arm. 'She's doing something much more heroic. Tell him about it, Elsie.'

Next morning, after a blissfully peaceful and comfortable night's sleep in a bed that would have been grand enough for a princess, Elsie was awakened by the maid bringing in a pot of hot chocolate. Such luxury was unimaginable, even in peacetime. Elsie sat up in bed sipping the drink, which had probably come from a similar and highly illegal source like the champagne, but was none the less tasty for that. She appeased her conscience by making a silent promise to work even harder when she returned to the priory, and vowed never to complain about the skimpiness of their meals or the lack of variety in their diet. It was, she supposed, the way of the world. The rich would always be rich and the poor just had to get on with life as best they could. It was pointless to rail against matters she could do nothing to change.

She finished her chocolate and rose reluctantly from the comfort of her bed, but the lure of her own bathroom and the prospect of a hot bath made it worth the effort. The bathroom was tiled in pink marble and the claw-footed bath looked inviting. She turned on the gold-plated hot tap but the water gushing out was cold, bringing back memories of their time in the lodging house ruled over by Madame Chausse. Elsie perched on the edge of the bath, doubled up with laughter. It seemed that the wealthy were no more immune from the power cuts than anyone else. Perhaps there was some justice after all. She had a strip wash in cold water but even that was a luxury compared to the facilities rigged up in an outhouse in the priory grounds, where last winter they had had to break the ice in the stone sink with a hammer.

Refreshed and dressed ready for the wedding, Elsie made her way to the room where they had dined the previous evening in the company of Monsieur Bellaire. Marianne had kept the conversation flowing and Philippe Bellaire had retired early, saying that he had papers to study before he went to bed. He had been kind and courteous to Elsie, but rather vague, as if his mind was on other things, and she was dismayed to walk into the dining room and find him there on his own. He looked up and frowned as if he had forgotten her existence, but then he smiled and half rose from his seat. 'Good morning, Mademoiselle Mead.'

She pulled out a chair and sat down. 'Good morning, monsieur.'

'I trust that you had a good night's sleep?'

'Yes, thank you. It was sheer luxury after sleeping on a palliasse for months.'

'The croissants are still warm,' he said, passing the plate to her. 'Or if you prefer I can ring for the maid and she will bring toast. I know that you English love your toast and marmalade. I have a supply sent especially for Marianne.'

Elsie took a croissant. 'I haven't tasted one of these since before the war.' She reached for the butter. 'I prefer the apricot confiture anyway.'

He smiled and sipped his coffee. 'I remember now. Your mother was French, wasn't she?'

'Yes, she was.' She bit into the flaky pastry, hoping that he did not see the tears that sprang to her eyes when she thought of her mother.

Monsieur Bellaire leaned back in his chair, dabbing

his lips with a starched white napkin. 'They think I don't know,' he said, chuckling. 'But a wedding, even one arranged in a hurry, is hard to conceal from a parent.'

Elsie gulped and swallowed a mouthful of croissant. 'You know about it?'

'This is my home. I might spend most of my time at the bank, but when a crate of champagne arrives under cover of darkness it makes one suspicious. And my son, who normally spends his leave asleep, has been rushing about like a madman. He made the mistake of confiding in my head clerk because he needed to have the banns posted ten days before the event and he knew he would not get home in time.'

'I don't know what to say. I suppose they wanted a quiet wedding without any fuss.'

'They will get their wish, but I will be there, as will Henri's mother. I sent a telegram to the villa in le Lavandou the moment I heard of his plan. Selene will be arriving at the Gare de Lyon in less than an hour, and I will be there to meet her.' He pushed back his chair and stood up. 'This will be our secret. My wife and I will attend the civil ceremony to witness our only son marrying the young woman we had always hoped he would take to be his wife.' He patted her on the shoulder. 'Don't look so worried. Nothing will spoil their day and tomorrow Henri returns to his unit. Who can blame him for marrying in haste?'

Elsie sat for some time after he had gone, wondering whether she ought to warn Marianne and Henri, but that would mean betraying a confidence. She spread apricot jam on the last piece of croissant and popped it into her mouth. Why was life always so complicated?

In the end she said nothing. Henri left early and Marianne was in high spirits as Elsie helped her into her ivory silk gown. 'It was made for a society woman at the start of the war,' Marianne explained, smoothing the material over her slender hips. 'But her fiancé was killed and she never claimed it. I hope it isn't an ill omen.'

'You don't believe in nonsense like that,' Elsie said firmly. 'It's just pre-wedding nerves making you jittery.'

'I suppose so. I must admit I didn't think of it when I bought the dress.'

Elsie reached for the circlet of orange blossom and the veil. 'Stop worrying, Marianne. Sit down and let's see if I can get this right first go.'

They arrived fashionably late at the town hall to find Henri pacing the floor. He looked splendid in his dress uniform, but agitated. He came to a sudden halt when he saw his bride and for a moment he looked stunned at the sight of her, but then his expression gave way to one of pure delight. He came slowly towards Marianne, holding out both hands.

'You look even more beautiful than usual, my darling.'

Marianne's face was misty beneath the white veil, but Elsie could tell that she was smiling, and the bouquet of lilies, white roses, stephanotis and trailing fern trembled in her hands. 'I think we should go in,' she whispered. 'That official looks rather impatient.'

Henri took her by the arm. 'It's our day, my love. I won't allow anyone to spoil it.' He turned his head to give Elsie a beaming smile. 'You look lovely too. I'm glad you're here with us today.'

'Thank you, Henri.' She glanced at the official, who was staring pointedly at his pocket watch. 'I think there are other couples waiting to get married.'

Henri led Marianne up the red-carpeted staircase and the mustachioed official snapped to attention as he opened the door to the chamber where weddings were solemnised. Elsie followed them into a room furnished with rows of gilt chairs, but only three of the seats were occupied. Marianne uttered a gasp of surprise at the sight of Henri's parents, and then the other wedding guest rose to his feet. Colonel Winter strode down the aisle to embrace his daughter.

'Papa,' Marianne murmured, her voice catching on a sob. 'How did you know?' Elsie snatched her bouquet before the blooms were crushed by the colonel's tender embrace.

'Philippe sent a telegram to HQ. I've been in France for months but this is the first time I've been able to get even a few hours' leave.' He released Marianne, turning to shake Henri's hand. 'I couldn't be more pleased, my boy.'

Philippe Bellaire cleared his throat noisily. 'I think the registrar is eager to begin, James.'

'Of course.' Colonel Winter stepped aside. 'I apologise for the delay.'

Selene smiled graciously and resumed her seat. 'Sit down, Philippe. There will be time for congratulations later. We've booked a table at the Ritz for luncheon.'

Marianne flicked back her veil. 'I knew this would happen,' she whispered as she took the bouquet from Elsie, but she smiled as she took her father's arm. 'I'm glad you're here, Papa.'

'I've missed so much of your life, Marianne. The very least I can do is see you happily married.' They approached the table where the mayor waited to perform the civil ceremony.

Elsie awoke next morning with a headache. The luncheon at the Ritz had been a great success, despite Marianne and Henri's previous wish for a quiet celebration. Philippe had booked a room for the happy couple so that they could spend their one-night honeymoon in luxurious surroundings far different from the conditions in camp, and Elsie had returned to the rue de l'Echelle with Marianne's parents. Selene had opted to stay the night with the intention of returning to le Lavandou in the morning, and both she and her husband had taken care to make Elsie feel that she was part of the family. They had dined at home and drunk even more champagne, which Elsie regretted the moment she opened her eyes.

She sat up in bed, sipping her hot chocolate and

wondering whether she ought to cut her leave short and return to the priory. Marianne would no doubt be going back to work as soon as Henri's leave was up, and now that she was a married woman she might want to spend her spare time looking for a flat where she could set up home.

Elsie replaced the cup on its saucer and slid her legs over the side of the bed. She felt as though there were demons with pickaxes inside her skull, and she staggered into the bathroom to raid the well-stocked cabinet for seltzer and a couple of aspirin tablets. She bathed in lukewarm water and, feeling much better, she slipped on the wrap that Marianne had loaned her. She was about to sit down at the dressing table and brush her hair when the bedroom door opened and Marianne flew in. She rushed past Elsie, heading for the bathroom. The door slammed shut but Elsie could hear her retching.

She waited until the sounds stopped. 'Are you all right, Marianne?'

'No. I'm sick.'

'Was it too much champagne? I've been suffering a bit myself.'

'I only had one glass.'

The spectre of Spanish flu sent a shiver down Elsie's spine. The pandemic had swept Europe and it was not over yet. 'I'm coming in,' she said, opening the door.

Chapter Twenty-Two

Elsie burst into the bathroom to find Marianne seated on a chair by the washbasin, holding a wet flannel to her forehead. 'Why have you come home so early?'

'Henri had to re-join his regiment.' Marianne groaned, resting her head in her hands.

'Should I send for a doctor? Are you feverish?'

'I'm not ill.' Marianne raised her head, smiling weakly. 'I'm in pod. In the family way – pregnant.'

'You can't be. Not after one night.'

'Don't be such an innocent, Elsie. Henri and I have been lovers for over a year. Not very often, of course, because he's not had much leave, but it must have happened when he had a 24-hour pass a couple of months ago.'

'But you denied it, Marianne.'

'All right – I lied.'

'Does he know?'

'Of course he does. That's why we got married in such a hurry.'

'You haven't told his parents?'

'They're very sweet but they're also very old-fashioned, and I wouldn't dare tell Papa. I'll have to make out that it's a seven-month baby or something of the sort.' She turned to face Elsie with a persuasive smile. 'You're the only one who knows, and I want to keep it that way.'

Elsie sat down on the edge of the bath. 'And I thought you were sickening for the flu.'

'Don't mention that word. I'm going to keep well and have this baby. By my calculations it will be born in October, and hopefully the war will be over long before then.'

'Is Henri pleased?'

'He's delighted. We weren't planning to start a family so soon, but we both want it desperately.'

Elsie stood up and wrapped her arms around Marianne. 'I'm very happy for you. It will be a beautiful baby, of that I'm certain.'

'I think I'll go to my room and lie down,' Marianne said, struggling to her feet. 'If anyone asks just tell them I'm exhausted after the excitement yesterday. They'll understand.'

'What about work? Will you go back to the rue Saint-Roch?'

'For a while, I suppose, but not for long. I intend to look after myself and the little one. Henri will have a son and heir he can be proud of, as well as a wife who adores him. I can't think how I was so blind for so long.'

Elsie opened the door for her. 'I know what you mean. I was the same with Guy. I just hope and pray that he's all right, because I haven't heard from him for months. At least you know that Henri is alive and well.'

'Bad news travels fast,' Marianne said, patting her on the shoulder. 'You'd hear soon enough if the worst had happened. I'm going to report in sick tomorrow so you and I can go flat-hunting together. It will be fun.'

Despite all their efforts, accommodation of the type Marianne wanted was hard to find, but she was in a buoyant mood. 'It will take time,' she said cheerfully as they left the last apartment they viewed, which looked as though a bomb had dropped on it, the former tenant having been an artist with a drink problem. She pushed an empty absinthe bottle out of the way with the toe of her black patent leather shoe. 'Never mind. I'm not in a hurry and something will turn up.'

'I wish I could stay longer,' Elsie said wistfully. 'But my leave is up tomorrow and I have to return to the priory.'

'You're not too far away. You must come again as soon as possible. I need you, Elsie.' Marianne grinned mischievously. 'You can tell your superior that Madame Bellaire is in desperate need of a brilliant coiffeuse, and the future of the whole Bellaire dynasty depends on keeping the mother-to-be happy and content.'

'You always were a little crazy, Marianne,' Elsie said, laughing. 'I can imagine how that would go down.'

'I know, but you must try to visit more often. Henri seems to think that the war will be over before the winter takes hold, and I trust his judgement.'

Elsie returned to the priory, receiving a rapturous welcome from Rosemary. 'I didn't go to Dover in the end. Cancelled. Anyway, it's been ghastly without you,' she said earnestly. 'I had to pair up with Audrey Summers and you know what a pain in the neck she can be. She grumbled non-stop about anything and everything until I could cheerfully have strangled her.'

'How has it been apart from dear Audrey?' Elsie picked up a tin mug and sipped the strong tea sweetened with condensed milk. Only a few hours earlier she had been drinking from a delicate bone china cup in the palatial surroundings of the Bellaires' Paris apartment. She glanced round the cell-like room with its stone sink and the paraffin stove which the girls used to make hot drinks when they were on duty. A damp musty smell mingled with the odour of the paraffin and a waft from the latrines outside. The contrast between the life of the wealthy in the relative safety of Paris and the stark conditions under which the FANYs worked hit Elsie more forcibly than ever, but she was glad to be back. This was where she had chosen to be and the hardships they endured were as nothing compared to those of the men in the trenches.

'We've had air raids almost every night,' Rosemary continued, seemingly oblivious to Elsie's lapse in attention. 'The hospital in town was badly damaged and one of our girls and a VAD had a lucky escape when the floor collapsed close to their beds, making a great chasm three storeys deep.'

'It sounds dreadful, but I'm back now to keep you company. At least I don't prattle on like poor Audrey. She's her own worst enemy.'

Rosemary finished her tea, and held out her hand for Elsie's mug. 'I'll wash these and then I'm afraid it's back to work for you, my girl. The ambulance I was driving yesterday needs to be hosed down and disinfected. I was on all night so this is supposed to be my rest period.' She uttered a hollow laugh. 'That's a joke in itself. We've hardly gone off duty and some of us slept on stretchers in the ambulances because we knew we were going to be called out in the night.'

Elsie drained her mug and gave it to Rosemary. 'I'll get my overalls on and be with you in two ticks.'

'It's so good to have you back.'

Elsie grinned and waved as she left the room. She changed into her overalls and was walking through the cloisters heading in the direction of the courtyard when she heard the klaxon sound. She broke into a run and found that Rosemary had beaten her to it and was standing by the ambulance taking instructions from Boss, the nickname they had given their supervisor. 'What's happened?' Elsie demanded breathlessly. 'It's very quiet for an air raid. All I can hear is the distant crump of the big guns.'

Boss turned to her with a grim smile. 'A lorry was caught in the crossfire a few miles from here. There might be casualties or it could be a breakdown: they're in urgent need of help and all the other girls are out so you'll have to go.'

'The old truck is in a bit of a state, Boss,' Rosemary said, screwing up her face in disgust. 'I wouldn't put a dead goat in there.'

'They'll be in a worse state where they are now. Best get going.'

Elsie climbed into the driver's seat. 'Hop in, Rosie. You can doze while I drive.'

'When I get back to London I'm going to sleep for a week.' Rosemary leapt in beside her with surprising agility for someone who claimed to be exhausted. Elsie grinned and signalled to Boss, who cranked the engine: the motor coughed and spluttered and groaned into action. 'That's how I feel,' Rosemary said, closing her eyes. 'Wake me up when we get there.'

Elsie drove off with a smile on her lips. Much as she loved Marianne and had enjoyed her brief sojourn in what seemed like paradise, she was glad to be back with the women she had come to look upon as her family. The Bellaires' beautiful apartment seemed like a world away, and now she must face the reality of war.

The vehicle lurched over the rutted roads and she had to swerve in order to avoid the deepest potholes. It was a glorious day but the sun shone down on a scorched landscape. Trees were denuded of their leaves and bare branches pointed up at the cerulean sky like broken fingers, and piles of rubble marked sites that had once been thriving communities. The ominous thunder of heavy artillery was growing louder. Boss had given her directions scribbled on a piece of paper torn from a notebook, but landmarks were difficult to spot and signposts had been torn down long ago.

It was pure chance that led Elsie to take the right turning and as she rounded a bend in the lane she had to brake hard to avoid running into the back of the truck. Rosemary awoke with a start. 'Blooming hell,' she muttered. 'You're driving hasn't improved.'

'You've been spending too much time with Audrey,' Elsie said, chuckling. 'We're here, and it's obvious what the trouble is.'

Rosemary squinted into the sunlight. 'It looks like they had an argument with a tree and the tree won.'

Elsie opened the door and stepped down onto the sun-baked mud. A group of women were huddled at the roadside; they all looked pale and shocked, and some of them appeared to have minor injuries. Elsie hurried over to them. 'We're here to help,' she said, pointing to the Red Cross on the side of the ambulance. 'Is anyone badly hurt?'

A tall thin woman dressed in khaki flicked a cigarette over the hedge and came slowly towards her. She was limping and there was a jagged cut on her forehead but Elsie would have known her anywhere. 'My God,' she murmured. 'Felicia?'

'Elsie? It can't be.'

'It's me all right. I can't believe it's you. What happened?' Elsie slipped her arm around Felicia's shoulders. 'You'd better let me take a look at that cut. It looks nasty.'

Felicia's pale lips curved into a grin. 'You were always the practical one, darling. Marianne was the madcap, as I remember.' She held her hand to her head. 'I must have cracked it on the windscreen.' She lowered her voice. 'I'm afraid our driver bought it. A shell exploded in front of us and he was hit by shrapnel and flying glass. He's still in the cab.' She glanced over her shoulder at the silent women. 'I think Sally might have broken her arm, and Edna has hurt her neck.'

'We'll soon have you fixed up,' Elsie said confidently. 'Sit down for a moment, while we take a look at your driver.'

Felicia went to sit beside one of the women, who was sobbing quietly, and she put her arm around her. 'We'll be all right now, Edna. We're in safe hands.'

Elsie beckoned to Rosemary and they walked slowly round to the front of the badly damaged vehicle. 'This truck isn't going anywhere in a hurry,' she said, shaking her head.

Rosemary wrenched the door open. 'Your friend was right. This one is past helping, but I'm not sure that the rest of the party will want to travel with a corpse. They're pretty shaken up as it is.'

'We can't leave him here,' Elsie said firmly. 'I'll fetch a stretcher and we'll put him in the ambulance before we see to the walking wounded.'

'Will we take them to the priory?' Rosemary asked in a low voice. 'I mean, they're civilians. Maybe they ought to go to the hospital in St Omer.'

'You told me that it had been bombed. Anyway, they've been risking their lives entertaining the troops. I think it's the least we can do for them.'

'Maybe they'll give us a song or two,' Rosemary said, giggling.

A loud crump made the ground shake beneath their feet. 'It's not safe here,' Elsie said hastily. 'We'd better get moving or we'll end up as casualties ourselves.'

She drove back to the priory taking a circuitous route in order to avoid the heavy bombardment that continued all day. They were not in the direct firing line but stray shells exploded to the left and right of them, sending up columns of dust and soil and raining them with shrapnel. Elsie ignored the cries of distress and muffled sobs coming from the body of the ambulance, keeping her eyes focused on the road ahead and hoping that they would have enough petrol to get them to safety. Rosemary had volunteered to travel with the injured women and Felicia opted for the passenger seat. She sat chain-smoking until she had run out of cigarettes. She crunched the empty packet between her fingers. 'It's a filthy habit,' she said, sighing. 'I'll cut down when I get home.'

'How are you feeling?' Elsie shot her a sideways glance. 'That was a nasty bang on the head.'

'It aches a bit, but nothing worse than having drunk too much champagne.' She tossed her cigarette end out of the open window. 'Those days are long gone, but we were actually on our way home when the shell exploded in front of us.'

'You were heading for Calais?'

'That was the plan. We've been touring the battlefields since before Christmas and we're all ready for a spot of leave, but then fate took a hand.' Felicia peered out of the window. 'Where are you taking us?'

'We're stationed at an old priory not far from St Omer. We should get there within the hour,' Elsie said, swerving to avoid a gaping hole in the road.

Felicia grabbed hold of the seat, bracing herself for the next jolt as the surface of the road appeared to have been torn up by tank tracks. 'I thought the bump on the head had addled my brains when I saw you walking towards me. You're supposed to be safely ensconced behind a desk in the War Office.'

'I joined the FANYs,' Elsie said simply. 'It seemed the right thing to do and although it's been tough I don't regret a day of it.'

'You were such a quiet little thing when I first met you. But then look at me.' Felicia plucked at her khaki trousers. 'What would my audience in London say if they could see me now?'

'They'd give you a big cheer and a standing ovation.'

'Thank you, darling. That makes me feel so much better about myself. When I look in the mirror it gives me quite a fright.'

'Nonsense, Felicia. You've got amazing bone structure and you don't need greasepaint to make you look beautiful.'

Felicia wiped her eyes on her sleeve. 'Stop it, Elsie. You're making me cry.' She shoved her hands into her jacket pockets. 'I'd give anything for a cigarette.'

'Hold on, there's another huge pothole straight ahead.' Elsie swerved and the ambulance tipped dangerously, but she managed regain control to a chorus of screams from the women in the back. She ducked instinctively as a plane flew overhead. 'It's all right,' she whispered breathlessly. 'It's one of ours.' She gunned the engine. 'Not far now.'

Safely back at the priory Elsie and Rosemary helped their passengers to alight and gave them into the hands of the nurses who hurried out to meet them. Wheelchairs were brought, although all but one of the women could walk unaided, and the driver's body was taken to the makeshift mortuary. Rosemary said she was too tired to think of food and went straight to the dormitory, but Elsie went to the ablutions and stepped into a tin bath half filled with tepid water. She sponged herself down, closing her eyes and imagining herself back in her bathroom at the Bellaires' apartment, but the smell of carbolic soap and blocked drains shattered the image and she climbed out, drying herself on a threadbare towel.

Felicia and her troupe of entertainers were in the refectory when Elsie went to get her meal. She joined them at their table and was greeted by applause. She glanced round at the amused faces of her colleagues and felt herself blushing as they thanked her one by one. 'It was nothing really,' she murmured. 'It's all in a day's work. You wouldn't believe what some of the women here have to go through.'

'Today's experience was enough for us, darling,' Felicia said, waving her spoon like a conductor's baton. 'We're simple entertainers, aren't we, girls?' She received a muttered chorus of assent as the women tucked into the vegetable soup.

'You've kept up morale,' Elsie protested. 'You're all heroines, and we just do what is required of us.'

'When do you think they'll take us to Calais?' Felicia asked in an undertone. 'Some of the girls are pretty shaken and desperately in need of home leave.'

'It's not up to me. You'd better ask Boss.' Elsie jerked her head in the direction of her supervisor, who had just walked into the room. 'She might have some idea.'

Felicia turned and waved her hand. 'Excuse me, madam. Might I have a word?'

Elsie exchanged amused glances with Muriel, who was sitting further down the table. It took a brave woman to summon Boss as if she were a maitre d' at a posh hotel, but Felicia was unrepentant. She stood up and proffered her hand. 'How do you do? I'm told that you are the person in charge of this amazing group of women. Felicia Wilby, maybe you've heard of me.'

'I'm afraid not.' Boss shook hands briefly and then folded her arms across her chest. 'What can I do for you, Miss Wilby?'

'We need transport to Calais. Can this be arranged?'

'I'm afraid all our limousines are booked out at the moment and the chauffeurs are fully occupied, but we'll try to make you as comfortable as possible during your stay here.' Boss inclined her head and walked over to the top table.

'Well!' Felicia exclaimed, resuming her seat with a sigh. 'That was a put-down if ever there was one.' She gave Elsie a quizzical look. 'What did I say to put her back up?'

'Nothing, Felicia. We're all tired and overworked, and she has a lot of responsibility. I'm sure she'll find a way to get you to Calais as soon as she can.'

'We'll earn our keep,' Felicia said earnestly. 'We've lost our pianist but I'm sure that someone here can play the piano, if you have one. We'll give a show

405

tomorrow night, those of us who can still stand up, that is.'

Edna, with a makeshift collar supporting her injured neck, banged her spoon on the table. 'All of you who feel up to the challenge say aye.'

A chorus of assent rippled round the table.

'I'll accompany you,' Muriel volunteered. 'I'm a bit out of practice, but I'm sure I can manage.'

Felicia acknowledged her with a gracious tilt of her head. 'Thank you, darling. We'll get some sleep and have our first rehearsal in the morning. Tomorrow evening there'll be fun and jollity in the camp. We've even entertained the King when he visited the troops, so you can be sure of a good evening.'

The next morning Elsie and Rosemary were up early as usual to take their ambulance to St Omer. They were to ferry the most severely wounded from the last bombing raid to the station, where the men and some of the injured nurses would be put on hospital trains bound for Calais.

Elsie had awakened with a severe headache, but she took a couple of aspirin and climbed into the ambulance beside Rosemary, who had volunteered to do the driving that day. Elsie felt unwell but ignored the symptoms, thinking it was probably just a summer cold. She had worked through worse as had all her colleagues, and there was too much to do to allow a minor illness to get in the way.

They returned late in the evening to find the concert party in full swing. Elsie had not eaten all day but she had suffered from thirst and had drunk several flasks of water. Rosemary had been anxious but Elsie had made light of her affliction. 'I'm just tired,' she said crossly. 'I'll be fine after a good night's sleep. Don't fuss, Rosie.'

They left the ambulance spanking clean and ready for next day and made their way to the walled garden, following the sound of music and singing that echoed round the grounds of the old priory, followed by enthusiastic applause.

They found seats amongst the nurses, doctors and auxiliaries who sat with their patients, some of the men lying on their beds that had been wheeled out into the grounds for the evening's entertainment.

Felicia was in the middle of 'I'm always Chasing Rainbows', which she followed quickly with 'Oh! How I hate to Get Up in the Morning', 'I'm sorry I made you Cry', and when she ended with 'Home Sweet Home' there was hardly a dry eye in the audience. The dancers limped through 'Tiger Rag' but it was received rapturously, and then Felicia as a finale dedicated 'The Rose of No Man's Land' not only to the nurses but to all the women who risked their lives at the front.

Thunderous applause drowned the rumble of the heavy artillery and Felicia, together with her troupe, took so many bows that in the end they begged to be allowed to leave the stage and rest. Boss strode up to Felicia and slapped her on the back. 'That was inspiring and wonderful. Thank you.'

Felicia stared at her in surprise. 'It's heartfelt, but it's what we do and have been doing since the war began.'

'You deserve to go home,' Boss said in a choked voice. 'I've had a word with my superiors and you and your ladies will be taken to St Omer tomorrow or the next day, depending on how many casualties need to be moved, and you'll leave on the troop train for Calais.'

Elsie had been sitting beside Rosemary and she leapt to her feet to congratulate Felicia, but quite suddenly the world seemed to spin around her in concentric circles. Voices grew louder and then faded away, and she felt herself falling into a deep, dark abyss.

Chapter Twenty-Three

She could hear muffled voices that seemed to fade away into whirring silence only to return again with more insistence. Sometimes it was her mother's voice, faint and very far away, and then Guy was speaking to her in such hushed tones that she could not make out the words. She wanted to tell him to speak up and come closer but her efforts were in vain and he faded into nothingness. She was vaguely aware of faces leaning close to hers but she did not recognise any of them, and when she tried to communicate they did not seem to understand. She was swimming in an inky sea with the waters closing over her head. If she opened her eyes she could see the sunlight sparkling above her but her limbs were leaden and she could not give the push needed to take her to the surface. Down she went, sinking deeper and deeper until she hit the bottom with a bump.

'Elsie, can you hear me?' The voice was familiar but still far away. 'I think she opened her eyes, for a moment, doctor.'

Someone was holding her hand. Elsie forced her eyelids to open, trying hard to focus.

'Elsie, my dear, you've come back to us.'

'Felicia?'

'Yes, darling, it's me.' Felicia's features were becoming clearer and to her surprise Elsie realised that she was crying. She had never seen Felicia moved to tears.

'Why are you crying?' she murmured, mystified.

'Me? Crying? What nonsense.' Felicia dashed her hand across her eyes. 'You've been very ill, and I thought we'd lose you, but you're on the mend now, darling.'

A man Elsie did not recognise peered over Felicia's shoulder. 'I think she'd better rest now, Miss Wilby. Elsie has a long way to go before she's fully recovered.'

Felicia released Elsie's hand and stood up. 'Yes, doctor, of course. I do understand.'

The doctor took Elsie's temperature and placed his stethoscope on her chest. He listened and then unplugged it from his ears with a satisfied nod. 'A remarkable recovery, but now it's rest, rest and more rest for you, young lady.'

'Thank you, doctor,' Felicia said humbly. 'I'm very grateful for all you've done, especially under the circumstances.'

'There's little enough I can do against this terrible disease. Spanish flu has killed millions.' He picked up his bag. 'I'll see myself out. Just make sure Miss Mead has plenty of fluids and try to build up her strength with small meals. My late mother used to swear by calves' foot jelly.'

'I'll send Gerda to Fortnum's right away. They're sure to have stock ready for such emergencies.'

'Good day, Miss Wilby. I'll call again tomorrow.' He lowered his voice. 'But should her condition deteriorate don't hesitate to send for me.'

Felicia moved to the door and opened it. 'I will, and thank you again, doctor.' She closed it after him and went to stand by the bed, looking down at Elsie with a smile of sheer relief. 'I thought we'd lost you.'

'Where am I?' Elsie asked dazedly. 'The last thing I remember was being at your concert in the priory grounds, and then nothing.'

'Don't overtax yourself, darling. You're back in your old room in my flat, and you're on the mend, that's all that matters. I'm going to tell Gerda to make you a nice cup of tea. How about that?'

'A cup of tea would be lovely, but how did I get here?'

Felicia leaned over to plump up the pillows behind Elsie's head. 'I insisted on bringing you home. Your formidable boss lady found us places on one of the trains taking the injured to Calais, and we returned to England on a troop ship. Now no more questions. You heard what the doctor said: you must rest.'

'Just one thing,' Elsie said weakly. 'How long have I been like this?'

'Two weeks – two long and exhausting weeks when we didn't know whether you'd pull through.

Gerda and I have taken it in turn to sit up all night with you, but now we can relax and help you regain your strength.'

Elsie lay quietly after Felicia had left the room. She had lost two whole weeks of her life but she knew that she was extremely lucky to have survived the vicious onslaught of the killer disease. She dozed off, and awakened for long enough to sip a cup of sweet, milky tea before sinking into a deeper and more natural sleep.

For several days Elsie drifted between waking and sleeping. On a diet of calves' foot jelly laced with sherry, chicken broth made especially for her by Gerda, and milk puddings that normally she would have refused, she gradually regained her strength to the extent that after a week the doctor allowed her to sit out of bed in the afternoons. Felicia read excerpts from the newspapers, keeping Elsie up to date with the progress of the war, and a letter arrived from Rosemary making light of their trials and stressing the fact that Elsie was missed by everyone.

'Is that from your friend Rosie?' Felicity asked casually. 'She was very distressed when you were taken ill, but I've been sending reports of your progress. I just hope they reached her.'

Elsie looked up from the crumpled letter with a misty smile. 'I don't know, because this one has taken nearly two weeks to get here. She says she hopes I won't be away too long.'

'Don't even think of returning yet,' Felicia said severely. 'The doctor told me that you'll take weeks, even months, to recover your strength fully. You wouldn't be much use to them in that state.'

'Yes, of course you're right.' Elsie felt the ready tears stinging the back of her eyes. She knew it was just weakness that made her cry at the slightest thing, but she missed her friends and she felt like a fraud lying about all day while they risked their lives on the front line.

Felicia delved in her pocket and pulled out another grubby envelope. 'Cheer up, darling. I've kept the best 'til last. I suspect that this is from Guy. You kept calling for him when you were delirious.'

Elsie's hand shook as she opened the envelope, taking care not to tear it. 'I haven't heard from him for months.' She scanned the brief letter with tears running freely down her cheeks. 'He's safe, or he was when he wrote this. It's taken nearly three months to find me.'

'It's hardly surprising, Elsie,' Felicia said in a bracing tone. 'It's a wonder that post gets through at all. As long as you don't receive an official telegram you know that he's survived.'

'Yes, of course. I know that, but I can't help worrying, especially with all this time on my hands.'

'The doctor said you can get up for longer but you mustn't overdo it, and as soon as you feel stronger we'll go out for a carriage ride in Hyde Park. We'll wait for a nice day, and the fresh air will

413

work wonders. Anthea is coming home at the weekend so you'll have young company for a change.'

Elsie reached out to touch Felicia's hand. 'I'll be delighted to see her, but you've been wonderful. I don't know why you've been so good to me when we're not related in any way, but I am grateful.'

'Don't be silly,' Felicia said, her thin cheeks flushing with colour. 'Of course I've looked after you: you're practically one of the family. If I'd had a daughter I would have been proud to have had one just like you.'

'You'll make me cry again,' Elsie said, sniffing. 'You must have better things to do than sit with me. What about your stage work and the concert parties?'

'The girls and I have earned a brief respite, darling. As to the stage, I've been offered a part in *Chu Chin Chow* at His Majesty's because one of the female leads is leaving. The show has been a terrific success and will probably run and run.'

'But you're undecided?'

'We've done so much for the boys on the front that it feels as if I'd be letting them down by staying in London.'

'I'm sure the theatre gives pleasure to many of the men who've come home on leave, and you've done more than your fair share in Flanders.'

Felicia gave her a searching look. 'What would you do in my place?'

'I don't know, but the war can't last forever,

although I feel much as you do in that I ought to hurry up and get better so that I can return to France to see this thing through.'

'We'll see,' Felicia said vaguely. 'Anyway, what does Guy say? Just spare me the romantic bits.'

'He begs me to keep out of harm's way, which is rich coming from a man who didn't have to put himself forward and could have stayed safe in a desk job.'

'We do what we feel we must do,' Felicia said, sighing. 'Marianne has put herself out of action by getting pregnant. Life goes on, I suppose.'

Suddenly Felicia looked her age and her former glamour seemed to have deserted her, leaving her looking thin and frail. 'I think you should take the stage part,' Elsie said slowly. 'You've been a heroine, Felicia. Let someone else take over now.'

'You mean I'm looking old and past it,' Felicia said with a wry smile. 'Don't deny it, darling. My mirror tells me the same thing every morning, and to be perfectly frank I could do with the money. Voluntary work is all very well but it doesn't pay the bills.'

'And I should be thinking about going back to work.' Elsie rose unsteadily to her feet. 'I can't sponge off you forever.'

'I'm not on the breadline yet, so you mustn't worry. It's just that I'm used to a certain standard of living when I'm at home, and I have to think of my future.'

Elsie leaned over to brush Felicia's cheek with a kiss. 'You're a wonderful woman and I love you.' She straightened up, steadying herself with one hand on the back of the sofa. 'I'm going to try to make it to the bathroom on my own, even though my legs feel like jelly. If I can't return to duty in France, maybe I can go back to my job in Room 40. I'm lucky to be alive and I know it.'

Felicia stood up. 'I'm right behind you. Sing out if you need a helping hand, darling.'

'Thanks, but I'm determined to make it this time.' Elsie reached the door and clutched the lintel, taking deep breaths. 'I can do it, Felicia. It might just take a bit of time, but I'll get there in the end.'

It was Friday afternoon when Anthea arrived at the flat in Cromwell Road. She breezed into the drawing room, taking off her leather helmet and gauntlets and tossing them onto a chair by the door. Elsie had her feet up on the sofa but she swivelled round with a cry of delight. 'Welcome home.'

Felicia looked up from the script she was studying and smiled. 'Yes, welcome home, darling.'

'Thanks, Auntie. It's good to be home.' Anthea hurried over to the sofa and sat down beside Elsie, giving her a hug. 'It's a relief to see you looking well. You gave us all a terrible fright.'

'I owe it all to Felicia. I don't know what would have happened if she hadn't brought me back to London.'

Felicia rose from her chair and tugged at the old-fashioned bell pull. 'This calls for a cup of tea, or would you prefer something stronger? I managed to secrete several bottles of Chambertin in my luggage when we returned from France.'

'A glass of wine would be lovely.' Anthea bent down to unlace her boots. 'I've ridden all the way from Norfolk and I'm absolutely whacked.'

Felicia tugged again at the bell pull. 'Damn. I forgot that I gave Gerda the afternoon off. I won't be long, girls. You can catch up but save the best bits for when I return with the wine.' She strolled out of the room leaving the door open as if afraid she might be missing something.

'Dear Felicia,' Anthea said with an affectionate smile. 'She never changes.'

'You should have seen her in France. She was a different person there, Anthea. But for her I might have died.'

'I know. She kept me posted and I'm jolly glad she did. I was worried about you and so was she.'

'Well, as you can see now, I'm very much better.' Elsie leaned back against the silk cushions. 'That's enough about me – what about you? You certainly look a picture of health. The outdoor life seems to suit you.'

Anthea leaned closer, waving her left hand under Elsie's nose. 'I want you to be the first to know.'

'You're engaged?' Elsie stared at the diamond solitaire winking in a ray of sunlight that filtered through the open window. 'That's wonderful. Who's the lucky chap?'

'He's a pilot in the Royal Flying Corps, or I should say the Royal Air Force, which it is now. He's stationed at Marham in Norfolk, which is where we met. I almost ran him down one foggy morning last winter.'

'What's this? You're engaged?' Felicia had come into the room carrying a bottle of wine which she placed on the coffee table. 'You sly little minx. Why am I the last to know?'

Anthea blushed to the roots of her hair. 'Sorry, Auntie. I just couldn't wait to tell someone.' She eyed her aunt warily. 'You don't think it's too soon after poor Tubby, do you?'

'My dear girl, Tubby was a wonderful man but it's nearly two years since he died. I'm glad you've found someone who makes you happy.' Felicia moved swiftly to the cocktail cabinet and took out three glasses and a corkscrew.

'What's his name?' Elsie asked eagerly. 'Tell all, Anthea.'

Felicia opened the bottle with a satisfactory pop of the cork and filled three glasses. 'Sip yours, Elsie,' she said sternly. 'We don't want to give you a relapse.'

'Thank you, but the doctor said a little red wine or port would help to build me up.' Elsie took a sip to prove the point. She turned to Anthea. 'Here's to you and what's his name?'

Anthea raised her glass. 'It's David. David Foster and he's gorgeous. I'm crazy about him.'

'I can't wait to meet this paragon,' Felicia said, chuckling. 'No, seriously, darling. I'm very happy for you.'

'And so am I.' Elsie put her glass down on the table. 'I think I'd better stick to tea for a while.'

Anthea leapt to her feet. 'I'll make it. I've grown quite domesticated since I've been living in camp with a group of girls. We have to look after ourselves or starve so we take it in turns in the kitchen. I can make cheese on toast and fry an egg with the best of them.'

'Wonders will never cease,' Felicia said, reaching for the silver cigarette box. She selected one, lit it and inhaled deeply, exhaling a stream of smoke with a satisfied sigh. She went to sit in the armchair nearest the window. 'I accepted the part in *Chu Chin Chow*,' she added casually. 'I thought it through and came to the conclusion that I'd better leave the concert parties to the young ones. I'm getting too old to live under canvas and traipse around Flanders in a truck.'

'You're not old,' Elsie protested. 'You'll still be doing your bit to entertain the chaps on leave. I just wish I wasn't so useless.'

'You're lucky to be alive, darling. You just need more time to recuperate and once you get back on your feet there'll be no stopping you.'

Anthea returned carrying a tray of tea which she

placed carefully on the table in front of Elsie. 'There. What do you think of that? I even remembered to put the milk in a jug instead of leaving it in the bottle.'

'Thank you,' Elsie said, chuckling. 'You'll be housewife of the year. Have you set the date yet?'

Anthea picked up the teapot and strained the tea into a cup, adding a dash of milk and passing it to Elsie before she answered. 'Actually, that's why I came home this weekend. We're getting married in the village church next Saturday and I wanted you both to be there.'

Elsie and Felicia exchanged surprised glances. 'I'd love to, but I don't think I could make it all the way to Norfolk,' Elsie murmured.

'And I start rehearsals for my new part on Monday,' Felicia added with a rueful smile. 'Honestly, darling, there's nothing I'd like better, but with transport as it is nowadays I'd find it difficult to do in a day, and I go on stage the following Monday.'

'Of course,' Anthea said hastily. 'I do understand. It's difficult for Mummy to get away too and Daddy doesn't approve of wartime marriages so he's refused to give me away.' She sipped her wine, eyeing them over the rim of her glass. 'Actually, they don't approve of David and they've both refused to come.'

'Why?' Felicia demanded. 'That doesn't sound like my brother. It's Pamela who's the snob. I'm sorry, darling, but you know it's true.'

'I thought they'd be different because David is a pilot, but his father is a butcher and his mother is a piano teacher. Apparently they don't match up to my parents' expectations.'

'I'll have a few words to say to Arnold,' Felicia said crossly. 'I thought better of him.'

'I'm so sorry.' Elsie put her cup down with a clatter. 'I'd give anything to be there, but I can only just make it as far as the bathroom without my legs giving way.'

'I understand.' Anthea made an attempt at a smile. 'It would have been lovely to have you both there, but I can see it's out of the question.'

'I could happily strangle my brother for being so pig-headed.' Felicia exhaled smoke like an angry dragon. 'You're his only daughter, for heaven's sake.'

'Don't get upset, Auntie. That's just the way he is.'

Felicia downed the rest of her wine in one gulp. 'I'm afraid it's out of the question for us to make it to Norfolk, but could you and David get to London? I know a church wedding is probably what you want, but there's always the register office.'

'I suppose we could, since no one in my family seems interested,' Anthea said thoughtfully. 'David has three days' leave and so have I.'

'That's settled then.' Felicia seized the wine bottle and refilled their glasses. 'We'll drink to that. Leave the arrangements to me, darling. You'll have a wedding to remember and I'll give Arnold a piece of my mind when I next see him, the pompous idiot.' She raised her glass. 'Here's to you and David.'

Anthea drank the toast and settled back on the sofa with a contented smile. 'I knew I could rely on you, Auntie.'

'Do you think his parents will come?' Felicia asked with a mischievous smile. 'A butcher in the family would be such an asset in these days of rationing. I can't remember the last time I had a fillet steak.'

The weekend was spent making arrangements for Anthea's wedding. Elsie was caught up in the whirl of excitement that Felicia managed to generate. The newspapers were filled with accounts of the Germans' attempts at crossing the River Marne and the counter-attacks by the French, followed by those of the British and American armies. But the war was not yet over, and the temporary halt of the German army was overshadowed by the huge losses that had been suffered and were yet to come. The best they could do was to put a brave face on things and pray that the end would be soon.

Anthea returned to duty on Monday, having promised to invite David's parents to the wedding, and to pass on Felicia's offer to put them up for the weekend. Felicia herself left for the theatre, leaving Elsie a list of instructions which she must carry out that day. She had to telephone the register office to confirm the booking for one o'clock on the following Saturday, then there were flowers to order and a booking to be made for the wedding breakfast at a hotel where the newly weds would spend their one-night honeymoon. The menu would be severely restricted due to food rationing which had been introduced while Elsie was in France, but she did not think that would bother anyone, least of all Anthea and David. Elsie was happy for them, but her heart ached for Guy and in her low moments she wondered if she would ever see him again.

She had just put the telephone receiver down when Gerda entered the room bringing her a cup of tea. 'I thought you could do with this since you've been left with all the work, but it is exciting, isn't it? I love weddings.'

Elsie took the cup from her with a grateful smile. 'Thank you, Gerda. You're a treasure. I don't know how we'd manage without you.'

Gerda hesitated, staring down at her clasped hands. 'I was going to tell Miss Wilby first, but she was so busy I didn't get a chance.'

'What is it, Gerda? You're not ill, are you?'

'No. I'm very well.' Gerda unclasped her hands to reveal an engagement ring. 'It's not like Miss Anthea's but it's all that Niels could afford.'

'Niels? You have a boyfriend, Gerda? You kept that quiet.'

Gerda's cheeks flushed bright pink. 'We're both in the social club organised by Mr Johnson. I mean, Joe. The vicar insists that we call him by his Christian name.'

'You are a dark horse, Gerda.' Elsie could see by her puzzled expression that Gerda was not familiar with the saying. 'I mean, you kept that a secret. Is Niels from Belgium? '

'Yes, he came to England at the beginning of the war with his mother and sister. They're from a village close to where I was born.'

'I'm very happy for you, Gerda. Have you known him long?'

'We met last summer at a picnic that Joe organised for the children in Victoria Park,' Gerda said eagerly. 'After that we saw each other on my afternoons off and sometimes we went to the music hall. Niels likes the theatre and I was hoping Miss Wilby might give us tickets to see her on stage.'

'I'm sure she will.' Elsie stood up to give Gerda a hug. 'Congratulations. I'd love to meet your fiancé.'

'Would you really? I mean he's not a pilot like Miss Anthea's gentleman. Niels is a plumber and he lives in Hackney.'

'Of course I'd like to meet him. As soon as I'm fit enough to use public transport I'll come to one of the social gatherings in Hackney, and you can introduce us.'

Gerda beamed with pleasure. 'I'd like that.' She bustled out of the room with a spring in her step.

Elsie went back to her list but she found herself wondering what would have happened had she accepted Guy's ring that sunny afternoon in Lyons teashop. She sighed and reached for the telephone directory: there were important matters to arrange, and it was no use thinking of what might have been.

Anthea's wedding was a quiet affair with just Felicia, Elsie and Gerda attending the register office. David's parents were unable to find anyone to look after the shop at such short notice, but they promised to organise a get-together of all the Foster relatives as soon as the young couple had leave, and were obviously delighted to welcome Anthea into the family. Anthea's parents remained aloof, although Arnold Wilby sent his daughter a cheque, which she opened along with greetings telegrams after the meal in the hotel. 'That much!' She passed it to David.

Felicia glanced over his shoulder. 'Guilty conscience,' she said tersely. 'My brother deserves a smacked derriere, and Pamela is a silly snob. I'm sorry, Anthea, but it's only the truth.' She drained her champagne glass and placed it on the table, waiting for a refill.

'I'm sure they'll come round in time,' Elsie said hastily. 'Everything is upside down in wartime.'

David put his arm around his bride's shoulders. 'Don't worry, darling. They won't be able to resist the Foster charm when I eventually get to meet them.'

Elsie raised her glass. 'I'll drink to that.' She had taken to David the moment they met. He was not exactly a dashing hero and no one could describe him as handsome, but he had a nice smile and he was obviously head over heels in love with Anthea. They were at ease with each other and shared a similar sense of humour, and Elsie could see them living happily ever after. But even on such a happy occasion it was impossible to forget that they were still at war. There was hardly a table where one of the guests was not in uniform, and some of the younger men bore scars that would be with them for the rest of their lives.

Anthea leaned her head against David's shoulder. 'I don't care what anyone says or thinks. This is the happiest day of my life, and no one is going to take that away from me.'

'Mine too.' David raised his glass. 'To my beautiful bride, and to Felicia and Elsie, not forgetting Gerda, who all worked so hard to make this day perfect.'

Felicia drained her glass in one swallow. 'And now, I think we should leave you to enjoy what little time you have together.' She glanced at Elsie. 'Besides which, this is Elsie's first outing and we don't want her to have a relapse.'

'I'm perfectly fine, Felicia.' Elsie rose from her seat, feeling pleasantly light-headed from the effects of the champagne. 'You will invite us to your party in Yarmouth, won't you?'

David stood up. 'Of course we will. A few days on the bracing Norfolk coast will do you the world of good.' He turned to Felicia. 'I can't thank you enough, Aunt Felicia.'

She recoiled with a shudder. 'Don't you dare call

me aunt, it makes me feel a hundred and one. I've told Anthea about it often enough. It's Felicia from now on. Just Felicia.'

'Felicia,' he repeated, brushing her cheek with his lips.

Anthea embraced everyone, including Gerda, but Felicia cut her short when she started to thank them all over again. 'We're off, darling. It was lovely but I know when to make an exit, stage left.'

Outside the hotel the doorman hailed a taxi and they piled into it, giggling like schoolgirls. The merry mood lasted until they reached Cromwell Road, but the laughter died on their lips as they entered the building and were met by a serious-faced Bailey. He handed Elsie a telegram.

Chapter Twenty-Four

Elsie's knees buckled beneath her and she collapsed onto the chair in Bailey's cubbyhole. Felicia took the telegram from her nerveless hand. 'Shall I open it?'

Elsie nodded wordlessly. Her heart was hammering inside her chest and the blood pounded in her ears. Telegrams meant one thing in wartime. She held her breath.

'I'll go upstairs and put the kettle on,' Gerda said, making for the stairs.

'Shall I fetch a glass of water?' Bailey asked anxiously.

Felicia ripped the envelope and took out the telegram with a shaking hand. 'It's not Guy. Can you hear me, Elsie? It's not Guy.'

'Thank God,' Elsie gasped. Relief gave way to curiosity. 'What does it say? Who sent it?'

'It's from Marianne. It's Henri, I'm afraid. He was killed in action. I'm so sorry, Elsie.'

'Henri's dead?' Elsie struggled to grasp the fact. In her mind's eye she could see Marianne and Henri on their wedding day. It had been such a happy occasion, similar to the one they had just witnessed.

'Let me help you upstairs, Elsie. You need a good

strong cup of tea and I could do with a tot of brandy for the shock. Bailey, be a good chap and take her other arm. You look as though you need a drink too.'

'Poor Marianne,' Elsie murmured as they helped her to her feet. 'I can only imagine how she must be feeling.'

'Marianne will be well looked after,' Felicia said firmly. 'Come along, Elsie. Best foot forward. You won't help Marianne by falling apart. She'll need family and friends more than ever with the baby on the way.'

'I know she gets on well with Henri's parents, but they'll be more concerned about their own feelings than Marianne's.'

'Give them credit for a bit of human kindness,' Felicia said sternly. 'Marianne is carrying their son's child. Of course they'll take care of her. Come along now. Let's get you upstairs.'

With Elsie safely ensconced in an armchair Felicia opened the cocktail cabinet and took out the last of the Calvados. Bailey was lingering in the doorway and he cleared his throat, staring at Felicia until she remembered that she had offered him a drink. She poured a tot for herself and handed him a glass, which he downed in one go. 'Ta, Miss Wilby. That's warmed the cockles of me heart.' He tipped his cap and left them, passing Gerda as she hurried into the room with a tray of tea.

Elsie sat back in her chair and let them fuss round

her, but all she could think of was Marianne and how she must be suffering. She wished with all her heart that she could be there to comfort her, but independent travel was virtually impossible. Had she been fit she would have re-joined her unit, but that too was out of the question.

The best she could do was to concentrate on regaining her health and strength, and she set out to do just that. She forced herself to eat the plain but nourishing meals prepared by Gerda, and she exercised daily. At first she went for short walks but she pushed herself to the limit, gradually increasing the pace and distance.

In the weeks that followed, Felicia was absorbed in her work at the theatre, coming home late every evening and sleeping until late next day. As a result Elsie saw very little of her and Gerda was there in body, but her mind was clearly on other things. She went about in a dreamy state, and spent all her free time making plans for her wedding to Niels. Elsie was bored and she was lonely, and she wanted desperately to return to work, but when she attended an interview at the headquarters of the nursing yeomanry she was given a medical and advised to wait for another three months before re-applying. She returned to the flat feeling let down and despondent. The summer was coming to an end and she needed to do something other than sit around the flat all day.

She had accompanied Gerda to Hackney on

several occasions and met Niels, who she decided was a thoroughly decent young man and obviously devoted to Gerda. She visited Joe Johnson and his wife, who were both delighted to see her, but the Belgian refugees were now settled and most of them spoke perfect English so her services were no longer needed.

She could have volunteered to drive a bus or work in the Post Office or on the railways, but she was determined to re-join the services in one way or another, and her main objective was to be sent back to France so that she could be there for Marianne when her baby arrived. There was one avenue left to her and on a warm morning in early September, dressed in a businesslike navy-blue shantung blouse and skirt with a matching straw hat perched on top of her bobbed hair, Elsie set off for Whitehall and Room 40.

She had to wait for over an hour, seated on a hard wooden chair in a corridor with people bustling past her as if she were invisible. Finally, when she thought she had been forgotten, she was shown into the hallowed office of Edith Lomax.

'Take a seat, Miss Mead.' Edith steepled her hands, and gazed at Elsie with raised eyebrows. 'What can I do for you?'

'I contracted Spanish flu,' Elsie said simply. 'I was one of the lucky ones who survived and I was sent home to recuperate. I'm well now but when I applied to re-join my unit in France I was told it would be another three months before they considered me fit enough to return to duty.'

Edith angled her head. 'Are you're asking me to take you on again as a translator?'

'I'll do anything. I'll serve in the canteen or scrub floors if you'll let me.' Elsie eyed her warily. 'Or I could go back to the rue Saint-Roch. I know my way round Paris and . . .'

'And you want to be near your good friend Marianne Bellaire, whose husband was killed at the Marne.'

'You know about that?'

'It's my business to know everything about the people who work for the department. As a matter of fact I was about to get in touch with you, and you've saved me a telephone call.'

'You wanted to speak to me?' Elsie stared at her in surprise. 'May I ask why?'

'Marianne might have left the service because she is expecting a child, but she is still in Paris, and is now a potential security risk.'

'I don't understand. Why is she a risk? Marianne would die rather than betray her country.'

'She is in a vulnerable position because of the knowledge she possesses. The Germans were caught on the back foot at the Marne, but they're not beaten yet and they're not going to give up easily. Marianne knows the names and details of many of our agents, which we don't want to fall into enemy hands, but now she is a French citizen and as such is beyond the jurisdiction of the British government. Do you understand what I'm saying?'

'You want her brought home?'

'Exactly, and who better to perform such a task than her good friend Elsie Mead?'

'You'll send me to Paris?'

'Give me a couple of days in which to have the necessary papers prepared and you may consider yourself back in the employ of the British secret service, but it will be for this one task only. Bring Marianne safely back to England whether she wants to come or not.'

'I think she will. In fact I'm sure she will, especially if her baby is in danger.'

'Report here in two days' time. Everything will be arranged.' Edith stood up and extended her hand. 'Marianne is lucky to have a friend like you.'

Wearing the uniform of a nurse in the Voluntary Aid Detachment Elsie travelled to France on a hospital ship and then by hospital train from Calais to Paris. It was surprisingly straightforward, especially when compared to the journey she and Marianne had undertaken when they left Paris for an unknown destination and ended up in Brussels.

Paris seemed busier than Elsie remembered, and the uniforms of the French, British, American, Canadian and New Zealand military were seen on every street. Soldiers, sailors and airmen were snatching a few days' well-earned respite from the horrors they faced daily, and amongst them were the refugees from countries invaded by the enemy. As she alighted from the fiacre in the rue de l'Echelle, Elsie glanced up at the building, which looked a little dustier in the late summer heat, but was otherwise unchanged. She paid the cabby and rang the doorbell for the concierge, who recognised her instantly, despite her nurse's uniform.

Taking the stairs to the first floor Elsie was excited at the prospect of seeing Marianne, but she was also apprehensive. She had not heard from Marianne since the telegram giving the news of Henri's death and she did not know what to expect. She knocked on the door and waited. Moments later it was opened by the Bellaires' maid, who greeted her with a shy smile and ushered her inside.

'I've come to see Madame Henri.' Elsie made an effort to sound casual but the apartment seemed eerily quiet. 'Is she at home?'

'Madame Henri is in her room, but Madame Bellaire is in the drawing room. Shall I announce you, mademoiselle?'

Elsie nodded. 'Yes, please do.' Her worst fears seemed to have been realised. It was unlike Marianne to lock herself away. She put her small valise down and waited for the maid to reappear, and moments later she was ushered into Madame Bellaire's presence. Selene rose to her feet, extending a beautifully manicured hand.

'Welcome, Elsie. This is a pleasant surprise.' She looked her up and down. 'You are a nurse now?'

'Not exactly, madame.'

'You have come to see Marianne?'

'I am so sorry for your loss.'

Selene sank down onto the brocaded sofa. 'It is very painful still.' She stared down at her tightly clasped hands. 'Marianne is very distressed.'

'May I sit down?' Elsie edged towards a chair. She was not looking forward to breaking the news that she would be taking Marianne back to England, depriving a grieving mother of her first and only grandchild.

'Please do. May I offer you some coffee? It is ersatz I am afraid.'

'No, thank you.' Elsie perched on the edge of a gilded chair. 'I've come to take Marianne back to England, madame. There's no easy way to say this, but she and her baby are in danger if they remain in Paris.'

Selene looked up, her dark eyes wide with surprise. 'We are all in danger.'

'This is different,' Elsie said gently. 'Marianne and I worked for the British secret service at the rue Saint-Roch. They sent me to bring her home.'

'This is her home. She is a Frenchwoman now, and her child belongs here with its family.'

'Both their lives are at risk if they stay here, madame. Marianne has knowledge that could put many intelligence agents in mortal danger.'

'But she is safe with us. We won't allow anything to happen to her or the child.'

'You may not be able to protect them. Marianne must return to England with me. I'm sorry, but there is no alternative. As soon as the war is over she can choose where she wants to live.'

'This is outrageous. My husband won't allow it.'

'It's up to Marianne. She has to make the decision.' Elsie could see that Selene was unconvinced. She stood up. 'I need to speak to her.'

Selene nodded her head. 'Do what you must, but we will see what my husband has to say.'

Elsie realised that the conversation had run its course. Now she must face Marianne and break the news to her. She was not looking forward to it.

Marianne was reclining on a chaise longue, listening to gramophone music, when Elsie entered her room. She looked up and her frown dissolved into a tremulous smile. She raised herself to a sitting position, patting the empty space beside her. Despite the obvious signs of advanced pregnancy Marianne was painfully thin, and her pretty face was ravaged by grief.

'What are you doing here?' she demanded, her eyes filling with tears. 'You might have let me know you were coming.'

Elsie gave her a quick hug. 'My carrier pigeon couldn't make it today,' she said with an attempt at a smile, although she felt like crying at the sight of her friend's distress. 'How are you, Marianne? You look a bit peaky, as Mrs Tranter would have said.'

'You try heaving this great lump around day in, day out,' Marianne said, patting her swollen belly. 'I swear this little chap is going to be a rugby player. He kicked a cup of milk off my stomach the other day.'

'You're sure it's going to be a boy, then?'

'Absolutely. I'm going to call him Henri in memory of his father.' Marianne's voice broke on a sob. She leaned her head against Elsie's shoulder. 'Why did it have to be him? We were so happy, and now this.'

'I'm so sorry, Marianne.' Elsie stroked Marianne's tumbled curls, allowing her to sob until she had spent her grief.

'I'm sorry to cry all over you, but it was such a surprise to see you walk through the door. I've really needed you, Elsie.'

'I know. I've missed you too.'

Marianne reached for a clean handkerchief from a neatly ironed pile close at hand, and wiped her eyes. 'Why are you dressed like a nurse? Have you left the FANYs?'

Giving Marianne a chance to recover her composure, Elsie launched into an account of her illness and how Felicia had come to the rescue.

'I'm glad I didn't know you'd caught that dreadful disease,' Marianne said when Elsie stopped to catch her breath. 'I would have been so worried, but you look well now.'

'I am, although they won't take me back in the unit for a while.'

Marianne put her head on one side. 'I know you so well, Elsie Mead. There's something you're not telling me.'

Elsie took Marianne's hands in hers. 'I've been sent by the powers that be to take you home. You have to trust me on this.'

'But this is my home. This is where Henri's son should be born.'

'You're in danger and so is your unborn child. I've tried to explain things to Selene but I don't think she believes me any more than you do. You're a marked woman, Marianne. You were working for Military Intelligence for a long time and you know too much. They've sent me here to bring you back to England where you'll be safe.'

'You're joking. I'm no one in particular. Why would anyone want to harm me?'

'For the reason I just gave you. You know names that would be more than useful to the Germans. Think of Raoul, for instance, and the Tandel sisters. Then there are Valentine and Hendrick and all the other people you must have come across while you were at the rue Saint-Roch.'

Marianne was silent for a moment, her face pale with shock. 'I hadn't thought about it like that.'

'Think of your baby, Marianne. You must come with me and we have to leave first thing in the morning.'

'But my baby,' Marianne whispered. 'It's due in less than a month. I shouldn't be travelling at this time.'

'I'll be with you all the way, and we'll be on a hospital train with doctors and nurses and a hospital ship from Calais to Dover. You'll be in good hands.'

Marianne's jaw hardened into the stubborn line that Elsie knew so well. 'I don't see why it has to be so urgent. Surely another month or so isn't going to make much difference?'

'They have their sources. Are you willing to risk your life and the baby's by staying in Paris?'

'I-I don't know.' Marianne raised her hand to her brow. 'This has all come so suddenly. One moment I was safe and secure and now I just don't know.'

'You know I wouldn't ask you to do anything that I didn't think was in your best interests. After all, the war can't go on much longer, and when it's over you can return to Paris with your child, if that's what you want.'

Marianne nodded slowly. 'You're right, of course. You always are.' She smiled wearily. 'When this is all over I'll take you to le Lavandou. The Villa Mimosa is wonderful in the spring and the summer. We'll take little Henri and we'll swim in the sea and picnic on the beach.'

'It all sounds wonderful, Marianne.'

'You'll adore the south of France. We can go there every summer.'

'I'm sure we will, but what about now? Will you come with me?'

Marianne was about to answer but was distracted by someone knocking on the door. 'Come in.'

Elsie turned to see Monsieur Bellaire standing in the doorway.

'May I come in, Marianne?'

'Yes, Papa, of course.'

He approached them slowly, fixing Marianne with a serious look in his dark eyes. Elsie was struck by his likeness to Henri and she could understand why Marianne was so fond of her father-in-law. He pulled up a chair and sat down. 'Selene telephoned me at the bank, and I came straight away.'

'You don't want me to leave, do you?' Marianne asked urgently. 'I'll be safe here with you, won't I?'

He reached out to take her hand in his. 'I received a telegram from your father. His battalion is in the thick of it, but he's in possession of intelligence from London. He says you must do as they say and return there immediately.'

'Why me? I don't understand.'

'You are one of many that they are recalling. I can't tell you any more than that.'

'And you think I should go.'

'I have to agree with your father.'

'Then I will,' Marianne said, sighing. 'If you both say so then I must take notice.'

'That will be the first time ever,' Elsie said, smiling

with relief. 'You need to get your things together and we'll leave at first light.'

They arrived at the Gare du Nord early next morning to see the troop train pulling out of the station. They had left the rue de l'Echelle in good time but had been held up by an accident which had blocked the road, causing chaos even that early in the morning. A donkey cart had been in collision with a farm wagon loaded with sacks of potatoes, and the donkey had broken loose and cantered off down the street, leaving the wagon overturned and sacks that had burst at the seams as they hit the road surface. Potatoes rolled around like marbles with hungry people scrambling to salvage them and the farmer shouting expletives as they hurried away with his crop.

'What do we do now?' Marianne asked in dismay.

'There'll be another one along in a minute,' Elsie said with more conviction than she was feeling. 'We'll get the local train and hope to be in time to catch the hospital ship before it leaves.'

Marianne pulled a face. 'I keep getting pains. I hope it hasn't started.'

'I think you'd know all about it if it had. I'm no expert, but I've helped at a couple of births when we went to the aid of people whose homes had been bombed.'

'I'll tell him to stay put,' Marianne said with a glimmer of her old spirit.

'Wait here. I'll go and find out when the next train is due and which platform.' Elsie hurried off, praying silently that Marianne was not in labour. It was true that she'd assisted at two births, but the women were already mothers several times over and knew more about it than she did. It had been comparatively easy, at least for her. She made enquiries and returned to Marianne, who was looking reasonably calm. 'The train has just come in and it's the same platform. There's no need to hurry because it will be in for ten minutes, so the porter told me.' She proffered her arm and Marianne accepted her help without an argument, which again was a first. This new Marianne was a lot easier to deal with than her former self, but Elsie suspected that it would not last. Somewhere beneath the meek and mild surface lurked the old Marianne waiting to get out and set the world on fire.

Marianne came to a sudden halt.

'What's the matter?' Elsie asked anxiously. 'You're not having pains again, are you?'

Marianne clutched her arm. 'We're being watched. I may be pregnant, but I haven't forgotten my training, and I don't like the look of those men.' She jerked her head in the direction of three men dressed in working clothes who were loitering close to the barrier.

Shocked out of her complacent state, Elsie glanced over her shoulder. 'You're right. I'm a fool to have let my guard down.'

'What do we do now? They're between us and the platform. We'll never make it.'

'Keep going. Don't let them see that we've noticed them.'

'I'm not in a fit state to make a run for it,' Marianne said with a touch of her old humour. 'What do we do if they try to stop us?'

'We have to catch that train.'

'And so you shall.' A deep voice behind them made them spin round to see a familiar figure standing behind them.

'Raoul.' At any other time Elsie would have thrown her arms around him, but she stifled the impulse. 'How did you know we were here?'

He tapped the side of his nose. 'Never mind that now. I'm here to see that you board the train.' He beckoned to a group of porters, and they approached slowly, following them at a discreet distance. With Raoul at their side, Elise and Marianne went through the barrier unmolested. Elsie heard the sounds of a scuffle but she did not look back. Marianne stood on tiptoe to kiss Raoul's whiskery cheek. 'Thank you,' she murmured. 'I'll never forget what you've done for us.'

Elsie was certain that he was blushing as he muttered a response. She shook his hand. 'That goes for me too. Thank you. You're a brave man.'

'I'm a railwayman. Glad to be of service, ladies.' He bowed and opened a carriage door. 'Move over, soldier. Make room for the ladies.' He helped

443

Marianne up the steps into the carriage and two young soldiers hastily vacated their seats. Raoul saluted and slammed the door as the train moved off with a hiss of steam.

Marianne lay back in her seat and breathed a sigh of relief. 'I didn't think we'd make it.'

'We did and that's all that matters.' Elsie settled down beside her. She would not consider them to be out of danger until they were on the hospital ship bound for Dover. Marianne had her eyes closed and was soon fast asleep, as were most of their fellow travellers, and Elsie began to relax.

Marianne woke up just as the train pulled into the station at Calais. She clapped her hand to her mouth to stifle a cry of pain. 'It's real this time,' she whispered. 'It's started.'

'Keep calm,' Elsie said in a low voice. 'We're in Calais. You'll be fine.' She grabbed the arm of a young French officer. 'This lady's baby is coming. We need transport to take us to the docks.'

He stared at Marianne in horror. 'We have our orders, mademoiselle.'

'Then find your commander and tell him it's a matter of life and death. This woman must get on board the hospital ship bound for Dover. Do you understand?'

He nodded. 'I'll do what I can.' He leapt out of the open carriage door and disappeared into the crowd.

Elsie stopped a man in a business suit who was

about to leave the carriage and together they helped Marianne alight from the train. 'I refuse to give birth on a station platform,' Marianne muttered, gritting her teeth.

Elsie took Marianne by the arm. 'Walk slowly and let's hope the lieutenant has found us some transport.' She tried to sound positive but she had visions of having to deliver Marianne's baby in a station waiting room, and when she saw the young lieutenant pushing through the crowds towards them she could have cried with relief. 'Come with me,' he said, taking Marianne's other arm. 'The commandant has put his motor vehicle at your disposal.'

'Wonderful,' Elsie said, crossing her fingers and hoping that the ship would not have sailed.

The commandant's staff car was waiting for them outside the station and as soon as they were settled on the back seat the driver sped off, honking the horn, and weaving in and out of the trucks and horse-drawn vehicles as if it were his life that depended upon reaching the docks. Marianne clutched the side of the car, wincing and biting her lip as pains racked her body. Elsie could only sympathise and pray silently that they would not miss the boat.

They arrived on the jetty just as the gangway was about to be raised, but Elsie was out of the motor car almost before it came to a halt, running towards the ship, waving her arms and calling for them to wait. 'Stop, please. We need urgent medical help.'

Chapter Twenty-Five

Marianne's baby was born at sea with a military doctor and nurse in attendance and Elsie there to hold her hand, murmuring words of encouragement.

'It's a beautiful baby girl,' the nurse said, handing the swaddled baby to Marianne.

'She's gorgeous,' Elsie said, reaching out to touch the baby's fuzz of blonde hair. 'I suppose you'll have to call her Henrietta.'

Marianne kissed her baby's cheek and smiled dreamily. 'I thought I wanted a boy, but I've changed my mind. She's all I want.'

The nurse stood in the doorway clutching a bundle of soiled sheets and towels. 'As she was born at sea, maybe you ought to call her Marina.'

'Marina Henrietta,' Marianne said softly. 'That's a lovely name.' She closed her eyes and Elsie took the baby gently from her arms as she drifted off to sleep.

'Hello, Marina Henrietta Bellaire,' Elsie whispered. 'You are going to be much loved.'

'And no doubt she'll be spoiled rotten,' the nurse said, chuckling. 'We'll make her up a bed in a drawer. That's what my gran used to do in the old days.'

Elsie rocked the baby in her arms. 'She has fair hair and beautiful blue eyes, just like her mother.'

'Just like her auntie, too.' The nurse opened the door. 'I'll be back in a minute.'

'I'm not your auntie,' Elsie whispered. 'But maybe I could be your godmother. How would you like that, Marina?'

The baby gazed up at her and Elsie was certain that she had understood.

Felicia had said she disliked babies, but was clearly besotted with Marina from the first moment she saw her. Anthea was equally enchanted when she came to spend a weekend. David was on duty and she did not want to stay alone in the cottage they rented close to the airfield. It was like old times in the flat, especially on Friday when there was no matinee and Felicia was able to join them for lunch of meatloaf, boiled potatoes and cabbage. She produced the last bottle of wine from the supply she had brought back from France, and Marianne kept them entertained with highly exaggerated accounts of their escape from Paris. 'You'd think I was Mata Hari,' she said, laughing. 'I didn't realise I was so important that the Germans would want to kidnap me.'

'You wouldn't be laughing if they had,' Elsie said drily. 'You might have suffered the same fate as Nurse Cavell and many others.'

'I wasn't a spy,' Marianne protested. 'I was just doing my duty for king and country, as were you.

447

To be honest I thought that the troops on the front line were the only ones in danger, not insignificant little me.'

Felicia raised her glass. 'Darling, you were never insignificant, and neither could you be described as little before Marina was born.'

'I know, and I don't begrudge her an ounce of the weight I put on. Marina is the best thing that's ever happened to me, apart from Henri, of course, but then she's a part of him as well as me. He would have been so proud of her.'

Anthea turned to Elsie with a sympathetic smile. 'You're the last one of us to be a single girl. Have you heard from Guy lately?'

'I had a letter about a month ago and it had taken weeks to get to me, so I try not to worry. I'd hear soon enough if it was bad news.'

'Of course you would,' Marianne said, raising her glass. 'Here's to Guy and all the other brave men and women who're risking their lives to save us from the Hun.'

'The war can't go on much longer.' Felicia clinked glasses with each one in turn. 'Here's to us, the backroom girls. Let's hope we aren't the forgotten ones when historians chronicle the war.'

They drank the toast and there was a moment of silence, broken by the sound of the baby crying. Marianne put her glass down and leapt to her feet. 'She's hungry again, bless her. My charlies will be down to my knees by the time she's weaned.'

448

Felicia shuddered visibly. 'Don't. I feel quite ill at the thought, never having gone through the process myself.'

Marianne blew her a kiss as she left the room and Felicia reached for the bottle, refilling her glass with wine. 'Who would have thought that Marianne had a maternal side to her nature?'

'Well, I can't wait to be a mother,' Anthea said with a beatific smile. 'What about you, Elsie?'

'I expect so, but I haven't thought that far ahead. I need to find a job and earn some money. I can't expect Felicia to keep me.'

Felicia eyed her over the rim of her wine glass. 'You mustn't worry about that, darling, but if you really want to do something for me you could do my hair for me. I'm thinking about having a bob.'

'Of course,' Elsie said eagerly. 'It would suit you down to the ground.'

'I could put you in touch with some of the female cast who'd kill for the Irene Castle look, but the days of having a personal maid are long gone, except for the very rich, and long hair is such a bind.'

Elsie pushed her plate away, leaning her elbows on the table. 'You've given me an idea, Felicia. I could open up a salon for ladies to come and have their hair styled. Like a barber's shop only for women.'

'And they wouldn't need a shave,' Anthea said, giggling. 'Oh, dear, I'm afraid this wine has gone straight to my head.'

449

'Do you know, that's not as wild as it sounds,' Felicia said, frowning thoughtfully. 'You could rent premises in Mayfair and make a fortune out of fashionable women who want the latest look.'

Elsie shook her head. 'It's a lovely idea but it would take money, which I haven't got. But I'll be happy to come to the theatre and do the actresses' hair. It would be fun.'

'Me first, darling,' Felicia said, draining her glass. 'There's no time like the present. Get your scissors out and start cutting.'

Felicia's bob was an instant success and Elsie found herself inundated with requests from the female cast who wanted the latest hairstyle, and what was even better they were prepared to pay handsomely for the privilege. She was kept busy, which helped her to get through the days without news of Guy. The mere sight of a telegram boy was enough to make her break out in a cold sweat, but somehow she kept going. Having Marina in the flat had wrought a huge change in their lives. The airing rack in the kitchen was a forest of damp nappies, and the drawing room was littered with rattles and books on parenthood. But there were disadvantages to living on the third floor of a building without a lift, and manhandling a pram up three flights of stairs was out of the question.

September flew by and October brought rain and fog. Marianne worried that she could not take her baby for walks in the park, and the inclement weather only added to her growing desperation. One afternoon she pounced on Elsie the moment she walked through the door. 'It's no use; I can't bring up my daughter in London. I suppose I'm a country girl at heart and I hate being cooped up like this. It's bad for Marina too.' Marianne glanced at the window, the view obscured by a thick veil of fog. 'It's not good for her little lungs. I've decided to go home.'

'To Darcy Hall?' Elsie stared at her in surprise. 'But I thought you hated living there with your aunt and uncle.'

Marianne put her hand in her skirt pocket and pulled out a folded sheet of paper. 'It's a letter from my father. He's been invalided out of the army and he's coming home.'

'Is he ill?'

Marianne pulled a face. 'Gout,' she said tersely. 'He's had one attack too many and because of his age, I suppose, the army has decided he should retire on a full pension. He seems to think that it's all coming to an end and he's more than happy to come home. My aunt and uncle have been persuaded to return to their flat in London, so it will just be Papa, me and Marina.'

'What about your in-laws? Won't they expect you to live in France?'

'I'll take Marina to see them every summer. She'll love Provence just as I did, but I can't abandon Papa, and you'd be more than welcome if you wanted to come and live with us, Elsie.'

Elsie sank down on the nearest chair. 'Thanks, but I think I'll stay in London.'

'Of course, you want to wait for Guy. I understand that, but I'm sure we could find you a cottage on the estate if you and he didn't want to live in the city.'

Elsie smiled and shook her head. 'Thanks, again, but I'm building up a clientele, and if I could afford to rent premises I'm certain I could make a go of hairdressing.'

'But if you marry Guy you won't need to go out to work.'

'I don't see myself as just a housewife. Not after all we've been through.'

Marianne sat down on the sofa, curling her legs under her. 'Perhaps that's why I'm finding it so hard to settle down, but at least I'll have plenty to do at home and Papa will need someone to run the house for him.'

'We're a new breed, Marianne. We've had to be independent and it's not going to be easy to give it up. Women have been earning money doing men's jobs, and although that might change when the war's over I don't think we'll ever go back to the old ways. Who knows, we might even get the vote.'

'I never had you down as a suffragette, Elsie.'

'I was too busy surviving to think about such things, but now I can see what they were getting at.

Who would have thought that Elsie Mead would learn to drive an ambulance and shoot a gun, not that I ever fired one except at a target. I've learned all sorts of things about myself and I'm sure I can run a successful business, given half a chance.'

'I'm sure you can too,' Marianne said wholeheartedly. 'I'll miss you and Felicia, but when Marina's a little bigger we can pop up to town for a few days and go shopping, and of course I'll have to have my hair done in your new salon.'

'That's a pipe dream at the moment.'

Marianne leaned forward, her eyes sparkling with excitement. 'Not necessarily. I'm a wealthy woman, Elsie. Would you like a business partner?'

'A business partner? You?'

'A sleeping partner, darling. I could put up the money for you to rent a shop in Mayfair and install whatever you need. I suppose you'd have to have a couple of wash basins and chairs, all that sort of thing, and you can pay me back when you're in profit.'

'I don't know about that,' Elsie said thoughtfully. 'What happens if I lose it all?'

'You won't. I know you too well, Elsie. Once you've set your heart and mind on something nothing will stop you.'

Elsie found premises in Hay Hill close to Berkeley Square. It was a prestigious address and it was Felicia who had heard from a friend of a friend that the shop was up for rent. With Marianne's financial backing Elsie found herself in business. Marianne and the baby left with Colonel Winter for Sutton Darcy two weeks before the hairdressing salon was due to open. Elsie missed them terribly, but was kept fully occupied supervising the plumbers and workmen who were installing cubicles so that the clients could have privacy while their hair was styled. Felicia put the word around and Elsie started to receive bookings. At first it was the faithful from the theatre, but word spread quickly and at the end of her second week she had a full appointment book.

At the eleventh hour of the eleventh day of the eleventh month the armistice was signed and the war was over. Elsie and Gerda joined in the celebrations with Joe and his wife at the church hall in Hackney, and Gerda and Niels announced the date of their wedding. It was a joyful occasion for all but there was still someone missing and Elsie left early, taking a hansom cab back to Cromwell Road despite the expense. She knew that Guy was safe, but she had no idea when he would arrive back in England. It was going to be an agonising wait, and the man who returned might be different from the person he had been when they parted. She had seen men suffering from shell shock and the effects of poison gas, and had read accounts in magazines of couples who met as strangers after several years apart.

Elsie went about her day to day work with determination but she was anxious, and she missed Marianne. She would have been able to confide in her, but Felicia would not understand. Felicia's past love life was the stuff of legend, but she had never stayed constant in her affections and had discarded lovers for no better reason than that they bored her, or were too demanding. Felicia would tell her to move on if Guy failed to come up to expectations, but Elsie knew that was not in her nature. She was excited at the prospect of seeing him again but she could not help being nervous, and still there was no news.

Rosemary, Angela and Daisy returned at the end of November and Elsie joined them for a celebratory lunch at Lyons Corner House, Coventry Street. It was a lively party and they promised to keep in touch and meet at least once a month. Rosemary announced that she had given up the idea of being a mechanic as it ruined her hands, and she thought she might train as a nurse instead. Daisy had decided to return home to her family in Oxfordshire, and thought she might start a riding school. Angela winked and took bets on how long it would take for Daisy's farmer boyfriend to pop the question, which made Daisy blush scarlet and tell them not to be mean. It was altogether a happy occasion and everyone vowed to support Elsie's new venture, even if they only had a hairdo once a year. They parted with genuine regret, but Elsie knew in her heart that they would always remain friends.

Christmas was just over a week away and Elsie's appointment book was so full that she had taken on a young girl to wash the customers' hair, leaving Elsie herself to do the styling. It was Saturday and Elsie closed the shop at two thirty, even though she could have taken appointments to fill the whole afternoon. She gave Olive her wages plus a share of the tips, and locked up. The first two weeks in December had been reasonably mild but rather wet, but the sun was shining for a change and Elsie walked to Green Park station and caught the tube to Gloucester Road. It was a short distance to Felicia's flat and she greeted Bailey with a cheerful smile. 'Not long now until Christmas. Are you spending it with family?'

He grunted and his mouth turned down at the corners. 'Don't remind me, miss. Thank God it's only once a year. I can't wait to get back to my cubbyhole.'

She hurried up the stairs, not wanting to delve further into Bailey's complicated family affairs. She had promised Marianne that she would travel to Sutton Darcy for Christmas but that would leave Felicia on her own in the flat as there were performances on Christmas Eve and Boxing Day. She let herself in and having hung her hat and coat on the hallstand she went to the kitchen to make herself a cup of tea. Gerda had the afternoon off and was no doubt on her way to Hackney to see Niels, and Felicia would be at the theatre until late that evening. The flat echoed with silence and Elsie would have given anything to hear Marina yelling for her feed or Marianne singing a lullaby as she rocked her baby off to sleep.

She went to the sink and filled the kettle and was about to light the gas when she saw a note on the table written in Felicia's elegant copperplate.

Guy telephoned to say that he'll be at Lyons teashop, Piccadilly, at three o'clock. Up guards and at 'em, darling!

Elsie stood on tiptoe, staring at her reflection in the mirror above the fireplace. 'I look a positive fright.' She abandoned the kettle and hurried to her bedroom, where she put on a dab of lipstick, powdered her nose and brushed her hair until it shone. A quick glance at the clock on her bedside table made her groan with dismay. 'You'll have to do,' she said to her reflection in the mirror. She left the flat still struggling into her coat and tore downstairs, her high heels clattering on the marble treads.

'Going out again, miss?' Bailey emerged from his cubby hole. 'Do you want a taxi?'

'Yes, please, Bailey. Preferably a motor car and not a hackney cab – I'm in a terrible hurry.'

In the end it was a horse-drawn cab, but she had little choice other than to climb in and endure the much slower progress through the crowded streets. It was almost half past three when she arrived at the teashop. She burst in through the door and edged through the packed tables to the one she and Guy had always chosen in the window, but there was another couple there. She was too late.

She was about to leave when someone tapped her on the arm. She turned and found herself wrapped in a passionate embrace. 'Guy,' she murmured when he released her long enough to draw a breath. 'I thought I'd missed you. I thought it was all over.'

'Never,' he said firmly. 'This is just the beginning, my darling.'

She looked into his eyes and realised that nothing had changed. 'I really do love you, Guy. You know that, don't you?'

He smiled, and kissed her again.